D0971682

Testing the Current

a novel by

William McPherson

SIMON AND SCHUSTER · NEW YORK

Copyright © 1984 by William McPherson
All rights reserved
including the right of reproduction
in whole or in part in any form
Published by Simon and Schuster
A Division of Simon & Schuster, Inc.
Simon & Schuster Building
Rockefeller Center
1230 Avenue of the Americas
New York, New York 10020
SIMON AND SCHUSTER and colophon are
registered trademarks of Simon & Schuster, Inc.
Designed by Edith Fowler
Manufactured in the United States of America

10 9 8 7 6 5 4 3 2

Library of Congress Cataloging in Publication Data

McPherson, William.
   Testing the current.

   I. Title.
PS3563.C395T4   1984   813'.54   83-20252
ISBN 0-671-25251-8

The author wishes to acknowledge
the use of some lines from Wilfrid
S. Bronson's Fingerfins, The Tale
of a Sargasso Fish, published by
Macmillan in 1930.

This book is for
Jane Elizabeth McPherson

Plus de détails, plus de détails . . . il n'y a d'originalité et de vérité que dans les détails.

—STENDHAL

Kinderszenen

THAT summer morning, in the distance, Daisy Meyer bent her blond head over her club, a short iron for the short sixth hole, in effortless concentration on her practice swing. Still engrossed in her projected shot, and seemingly oblivious to the murmurings of the women on the porch, she walked over to the ball, addressed it, and crisply shot it off. For a moment the vision was fixed, motionless, beyond time—left leg straight, right knee bent, arms, shoulders, hips following through, ball suspended in flight—before the breeze stirred the leaves of the elms, her body unfolded, and the ball descended in its slow arc to the green, where it rolled to within a few feet of the cup, as, far across the fairways, the river began to flow again in the sunlight, catching it, and sending it back in sharp, dazzling beams of light.

Daisy wore a white sharkskin dress, and, from the steps, Daisy, her yellow hair, her white dress, seemed to shine as brightly in the morning sun as the ball that rested on the green. At least Tommy supposed the dress was sharkskin. It was what ladies usually wore on the golf course. It was what Emily Sedgwick, his future sister-in-law, had worn the morning of her first golf date with his mother. Tommy knew that because on that other morning Emily's enormous St. Bernard had swum across the channel from the Island where Emily and Daisy and the rest of them all summered, bounded across the fairway, and leapt, his forepaws to her shoulders, dropping water and mud on her crisp new dress, destroying the impression of freshness she had hoped to create. Tommy had not seen it but had heard the story many times. It made sharkskin seem the fabric of choice, as the Island was the summer place of choice—it was never known as anything but the Island, the words embroidered in green on the towels, in green on the bed linen, stamped in green on the letter paper—as, one summer, rum and grapefruit juice had been the drink of choice; as golf was the sport of choice. Golf had never been Tommy's choice, of course, but the choice imposed on him that summer when, as soon as school was out and his foot had healed, he was sent two mornings a week to the club for his lesson with Emil, the pro. It was not that Emil was hard, simply that the game was impossible: mashies, niblicks, spoons, brassies, drivers, midirons, putters, wedges, God knew what, never referred to by the number stamped on each club, only by the name that one was simply supposed to know, the way one knew, for example, never to bring a cat near Mrs. Appleton, who didn't play golf but summered on the porch, rocking, gossiping.

Mrs. Appleton, and a lot of other people, too, were surprised when Daisy Addington, Governor Wentworth's granddaughter, married Phil Meyer, who was Jewish, or part Jewish, even though his parents could be seen every Sunday in the same pew at St. James', singing as lustily as Episcopalians then permitted themselves to. Blood is thicker than baptismal water, and some remembered when Phil Meyer's grandfather had come around with a cart, a Yiddish-speaking peddler buying and selling junk, who made his children and grandchildren rich from other people's trash. When Daisy married Phil, his parents gave them a house—on the hill, the location of choice —and her parents stocked it with china and silver and linens. Between them they filled it with furniture, and whatever may have been lacking in what the Addingtons and the Meyers supplied, other wedding gifts filled in. Daisy and Phil had everything, it was said later, too much—that was the trouble. Tommy did not remember when Daisy and Phil were married, but he'd heard a lot of talk about it. Nor had he ever been in their house, but he had heard a lot about that, too, and he imagined it as being all white and yellow, like Daisy, golden with the sun streaming in, and very comfortable, with plump chairs and blue and white and yellow flowers in crystal vases; fragile and beautiful, like Daisy; comfortable, like Phil, who was more ruddy than fair, with thick wavy hair the color of red sand. He was a good golfer, too, like the rest of them, but kind.

They had no children. Tommy did not know much about children, being only eight himself, but he had a theory about where they came from. On the wedding night or shortly thereafter, he supposed, something terrible happened, something literally unspeakable, that magically determined the possibility and the number of children that issued forth over the years. It happened only once, and it was immediately erased from memory, else it would have shown on the face, the shame or the terrible memory. And certainly on Daisy's face there was nothing but pleasure and, this day, sunlight as she walked toward the green, her clubs slung over her shoulder, to sink her putt. Daisy never used a caddy, and she almost always sank her putts. Phil's face had a different look, quiet, thoughtful.

AT the end of that summer, just before school started again, Tommy's parents celebrated their twenty-fifth wedding anniversary, and the house where he had spent his life began to fill with silver: two candelabra from his Aunt Elizabeth in Grosse Pointe, who in the glamorous photograph in his parents' bedroom reclined forever in dappled sunlight on a wicker chaise; pairs of candlesticks, Sheffield vegetable dishes, a punch bowl, three platters, stuffing spoons, serving spoons, four curious salt dishes with blue glass liners, tiny salt and pepper shakers, candy dishes, cocktail plates, a cocktail shaker, even a silver statue of an antlered elk. There was so much silver Tommy wondered where his mother would put it all, but she liked silver and found a place for most of it. A gift his mother admired very much came from her sister Clara and his Uncle Andrew, who had an apartment in Chicago but lived in a small town near Duluth so his uncle could be near the mines and the timber that kept their establishments going and that provided the dozen silver goblets in the special case lined with blue velvet from Peacock's in Chicago. It was the best jewelry store in the city. To Tommy, the most interesting thing about the goblets was the way each one fit into its own velvet niche in the case. Even so, his father didn't like them. They made everything taste like tin, he said, and he refused to use them. Tommy secretly agreed. The goblets sparkled, but when he drank some water out of one of them the water did have a peculiar metallic taste.

It had always seemed to Tommy that his Aunt Clara's gifts were meant to be admired rather than enjoyed, which was also the way Tommy felt about her. The Christmas he was in kindergarten they had stayed with his aunt and uncle at their apartment in Chicago. Before the tree could be approached and the gifts opened, he had had to sit through soft-boiled eggs, which made him gag, broiled bacon because it must never be fried, orange juice, and coffee, in that order, because even adults should not drink orange juice and coffee on an empty stomach. His aunt that morning had worn an ice-blue satin dressing gown that matched her eyes and fell in heavy folds to her slippers, and she ate very slowly, pausing often to discuss President Roosevelt's criminal behavior. His Uncle Andrew was nice to him, though. He let him dial the telephone for him, and Tommy had never seen a dial telephone before. He didn't remember much else about that time in Chicago except that the train trip was fun. He had his own berth.

His parents' anniversary party was going to be a great event, a dinner and dance at the country club. There was going to be a real orchestra, and Tommy was going to be allowed to go for a little while because he was family. No other children would be there; it was a grown-up party. It was going to be at least as nice as the Sedgwicks' famous house party and dance, which Tommy did not remember at all but had heard about, mostly from Mrs. Steer, who was there despite the fact that the Steers had lost all their money in the Depression so Mrs. Steer had to make her own evening dress. His mother didn't talk about things like that. Tommy's father had actually made money in the Depression—somehow taken it out of the hole everyone else's was going into, Tommy supposed—and they were very fortunate.

•   •

14

EARLY that summer, when his foot had healed and the golf lessons had begun, Tommy was sitting on the broad steps leading toward the tee, watching the elms in the summer twilight and, beyond, the river. It was after dinner—he ate at the country club a lot on summer nights, with his parents and once in a while, as this night, with one or the other of his brothers, who were usually somewhere else, with their girls, probably—when Phil Meyer came through the swinging doors, sat down and put his arm over Tommy's shoulder, as if they shared a common sadness. "Mac," he said—he was the only person in the world who ever called him Mac, which was his father's name—"what's on your mind?"

Tommy was flattered and touched because it was generally assumed that, being eight, he had nothing on his mind, certainly nothing that would engage a grown-up's attention— nothing more than a skinned knee, eating hazelnuts from the bush or shaking green apples from the Slades' tree next door to his house, playing in the woods up the street or on the Island, catching bees in jars or toads in the hand, and chasing snakes through the endless days of summer. And at that moment, as he stared off into the dusk, beneath the paper lanterns hanging from the eaves of the long porch and the moss baskets of ivy and begonias, there was nothing on his mind that he could put into words, more a state of mind than anything on it—solitude, the mystery of life, that sort of thing, which, at eight, he had a sense of but lacked the structure in which to put it.

Tommy liked Phil. He was never sure if he should call him Phil or Mr. Meyer, because although Phil was a few years older than his brothers he was near of an age to them. He liked Phil's voice, softer than Phil's father's, which was warm but gruff and quite loud. Emily's mother called Mr. Meyer a diamond in the rough, and everyone agreed. Tommy liked Phil's hand on his shoulder, implying as it did a certain comradeship under the sky, an equality of man and boy. It was a heady feeling, there on the porch, that there might be something on his mind that would be of interest to an adult male in white flannels, handsome, an athlete, a married man but not like the other, much older married men who were his parents' friends. Tommy wondered where Daisy was. She was elsewhere, that was clear, and Phil was sitting here beside him, in white flannels—he always imagined Phil in white flannels— asking how his golf game was coming, what was on his mind. Golf game, imagine! An eight-year-old with a golf game! He might as well have asked him about the WPA. So they sat there in silence for a few moments, watching the purple and amber glow of the lanterns and the fireflies' rising from the lawn to signal in the stillness, while Tommy wondered what might be on his mind that would interest Phil Meyer. Not his skinned knee, not the abysmal shame that was too embarrassing to speak of, of not being able to swing the club, the mashie —it was supposed to be the easiest to handle—so as to hit the ball somewhere, anywhere. No, he could not say that, or any of the other things that flickered through his mind, such as what the women were saying as they watched Daisy tee off. They were talking about her, he knew that, because when he came along Mrs. Appleton said, "Little pitchers have big ears," and they all stopped talking. He supposed Mrs. Appleton thought he didn't know what she meant, but he wasn't that stupid. He knew they weren't admiring Daisy's shot, or her grace. Maybe they were envying the way she looked. None of them looked so cool, so elegant, so in control approaching the ball. None of them could play as well, either. Only Mrs. Steer was better at the game, and she hadn't been there that day. Except for Mrs. Appleton, though, some of them were pretty good at it. His mother was very good at it, but not so good as Daisy or Mrs. Steer, and so was Emily Sedgwick, his brother John's girlfriend. Sometimes his mother played with Daisy in a foursome, but not often. His mother was older, for one thing, and they moved in a different set, although everyone who came to the country club or summered in the old shingled cottages on the Island really belonged to the same set.

Because Tommy could not say any of these things, which did run through his mind, he asked a question, turning the subject away from himself. He was, as his father said, always full of questions, and this was something he was curious about. Paul Malotte had learned about it when he made his First Communion, but he couldn't explain it either. It was the commandment they talked least about in Sunday school, one of the mysteries of the adult world, else why the name?

"What's adultery?" he asked. There was a long pause. The fireflies played, the lanterns burned soft and steady, music and laughter and the sounds of dancing floated out from the clubhouse.

"Adultery?" Phil Meyer gave him a quick look. "Well, I guess you'd say it's something that married people do. Maybe they used to like each other, maybe they still do," he replied, "but something happens and they end up hurting each other a lot."

"But they're not supposed to do it," Tommy said. Paul had said so. It was one of the things you couldn't do, like stealing or murder.

"No," Phil said, "they're not supposed to do it. You don't need to worry about that yet, Tommy. Worry about keeping your eye on the ball. You keep your eye on the ball and the rest of the game just comes naturally." Phil took his hand away from Tommy's shoulder, gave him a playful tap on the arm, man to man, and went back into the clubhouse, the wide screened doors swinging after him. A few minutes later Tommy's brother was calling his name, impatient to take him back to the Island while his parents stayed on to play bridge.

IN those days the country club was the center of Tommy's life. It wasn't much of a country club, as he discovered later when his brother John, married then, took him to Tam O'Shanter and Westward Ho, two really fancy clubs outside Chicago, with swimming pools and tennis courts and vast fairways and crystal chandeliers and many, many rooms. But its members believed it to be the oldest in the state, among the oldest in the country, and they were very proud of it. Certainly it looked old, and it had its own charms. The dining room was made of split birch saplings and birchbark panels, lighted by wooden chandeliers and sconces with birchbark shades. The same people took their dinners there every night, or so it seemed—every night he was there, at least: the older Meyers, who drove a maroon Buick; the Sedgwicks and Mrs. Addington, Daisy's mother, who came over from the Island, sometimes with her own mother, Mrs. Wentworth, sometimes with Mr. Wolfe if he was in town, or old Mr. Treverton; Dr. and Mrs. Rodgers, who often ate by themselves, usually in silence, interrupted occasionally by perfunctory words about one thing or another—the salt that wouldn't shake, the weather, the monotony of the chicken, the freshness of the whitefish. Dr. Rodgers smoked Camels and had a voice like falling gravel. He would always say, "Hello, boy"—Tommy thought he couldn't remember his name—and Mrs. Rodgers, who had the most amazing thick white hair knotted around her head and whose nails were short but brightly polished, would smile and say, "Good evening, Tommy," in her cultivated, throaty voice. Dr. Rodgers was thin, but Mrs. Rodgers was fat. And some nights Daisy and Phil ate there too, often with the Griswolds, or at least they used to, and sometimes with Mr. Wolfe. Mr. Wolfe used to eat there with Mrs. Slade, too, but she didn't come to the country club anymore. It had been a long, long time since Tommy had seen Mrs. Slade at the country club. And every night, when Tommy and his parents and whomever else they were with would pass by the groups of diners, they would pause and exchange greetings, and his mother would nudge him if he forgot to say "Good evening" in return.

After dinner they would go to the lounge, where usually Mrs. Appleton was already playing the slot machines. The lounge was on the other side of the big ballroom, and the older Meyers almost always got there first. Mr. Meyer would roar, "Hello there, boy," and extend his enormous hand, but Tommy knew that Mr. Meyer knew his name. Mrs. Meyer, who often looked a little wobbly and whose hair was so thin her scalp gleamed through the wisps, would nod. When Mr. Wolfe was there, he would sometimes ask Tommy to play cribbage. He was trying to teach him the game.

The lounge was paneled in old yellow pine. Behind the bar were rows of bottles, and some of the colors and some of the names were beautiful and strange: Triple Sec, Chartreuse, Forbidden Fruit. Tommy liked to look at them, and he wondered if they tasted as good as they looked. The Chartreuse was green, green as an emerald. Forbidden Fruit was purple, and its bottle was round and fat and bound with thin metal wires the color of gold. Tommy checked the bottle every time he came in. No one ever seemed to drink it; the level of the purple never changed. Bob Griswold, when he was noisy, liked to say that Forbidden Fruit was the tastiest fruit of all, but he never drank it either. The slot machines stood on a shelf built into one wall, behind a panel that could be raised and lowered. When it was closed, you couldn't tell the machines were there. They had one nickel machine, two dimes and two quarters, and people liked to play them after dinner. The state inspector always dropped by the pro shop before he came into the clubhouse. Emil would lend him a new driver and give him a box of Acushnet Titleist balls, the best, to drive from the practice tee while he went into the clubhouse to make sure the panel was closed. If the state inspector saw them, he would have to take them because they were against the law, but they made up the club's annual deficit and more, or Mrs. Appleton did, with her endless supply of quarters.

The club was run by a Negro steward. Her name was Ophelia. The word "Negro" was never used in her presence, because the condition it described was thought to be embarrassing at best and irreversible in any case, and polite people did not call attention to the ill fortune of others, particularly when the others couldn't help it. Their feelings might be hurt. Similarly, it wasn't nice to stare at cripples on the street, at the stump where the plumber's thumb used to be, or at Mrs. Hutchins in the bar. His mother always said Mrs. Hutchins was a lovely person, but she couldn't be talking about the way she looked, which, to an eight-year-old, was as alarming as it was riveting. Tommy couldn't keep his eyes off her, or off her hands, bright with diamonds, which were usually clasped around a small glass of bourbon the color of strong tea. She had migraines, and the migraines gave her a facial tic that went off whenever she lifted the glass to her lips, causing hand and face to twitch violently and drops of bourbon to splatter on her bosom. Mrs. Hutchins knew he watched her, waiting for the glass to move, the spasm to begin. She would glance at him as she dabbed at the bourbon on her dress, laugh a little as if to say, "Oh, foolish me," and smile. Mr. Hutchins made money from bread. He had a chain of bakeries spread over several hundred miles, so he had to travel a lot. Tommy liked Mrs. Hutchins, and he liked Mrs. Barlow, too. He wasn't supposed to stare at her, either. Mrs. Barlow was the fattest person Tommy had ever seen. She was so fat that now, even on a calm summer day, she couldn't make it to the Island, where she used to have a small cottage. As she was leaving the Island late one evening the summer before, the rowboat sank beneath her, fortunately immediately upon her settling into it from the dock where the water was shallow so the consequences were not serious. Still, it took five men to get her out. Of course, the boat was small and, as his father said, already loaded with departing guests. "Or was it departing with loaded guests?" he would ask when he told the story—"I can never remember." His father liked to tell stories like that. They all needed a hot toddy afterwards, and then they spent the night. Mrs. Barlow crossed over the next morning alone, except for the Indian rower, and she never came back. There used to be a Mr. Barlow, but he was gone, either into the ground or off on the train, Tommy could never remember which, and he didn't remember Mr. Barlow, either.

But it was Ophelia whom he loved. He was also afraid, afraid that he would say the word "Negro" in front of her, making her angry or sad. Yet the color of her skin was as indisputable, and as exotic, as the bottle of Forbidden Fruit on the shelf behind the bar, or as some of the pictures in his *Lands and Peoples* set. Tommy always wanted to ask her about it, but he didn't want her to think that he'd noticed. After his golf lesson that summer, Ophelia would make him a toasted cheese sandwich, with a lot of sweet pickles on the plate, and a milkshake or a root beer or ginger ale float. For dinner she made biscuits and fruit conserves and Southern-fried chicken, which she knew how to make the right way because she was from Kentucky. More than once, when he had been sick, she had sent a chicken sandwich home for him, and she was careful to use only the white meat. Ophelia brought her relations up from the South every summer, when the club was busiest, and there were many of them: nephews, cousins,

20

children, in-laws. His mother called them Ophelia's shirttail relations because no one knew exactly how they were connected. That's what his mother said, anyway, but Ophelia knew. Ophelia was beautiful and soft, and so was her daughter, Katherine, who had long, slim hands. In the winter Katherine and her husband taught at a college for Negroes in the South. In the summer they waited table, and George helped tend the greens. Ophelia and Katherine were very refined people, the finest type of colored, everyone said. She was a good steward; the club was lucky to have her.

It was Ophelia's nephew—his name was Buck and he was almost fourteen—who told Tommy one summer day when they were playing by the small creek that divided the seventh from the eighth fairway, exactly what things did happen between men and women, that they did these things all the time, that some people—Bebe, for instance, and her girls from the west end of town—got money for doing them, that sometimes but certainly not always these things resulted in babies, and that he himself had seen these very things happen several times already. "Junior and Bebe, they always at it," Buck said. "They be doing it all the time. But Junior, he don't have to pay. He gets it for free. He say Bebe should pay *him*, he's so good at it."

Buck used words Tommy had never heard before. He listened awestruck, incredulous, and he made Buck repeat the story. Amazing, Tommy thought, absolutely amazing, and he tried to store the information away in the back of his mind. He didn't want to think about it. He didn't want it to disturb the surface, but he couldn't forget it, either. He didn't know if he believed it or not. Maybe only Negroes did it, surely not the people he knew, not the people who played golf and went to dinner dances and served tea to his father's two Canadian cousins who looked like the Queen Mother Mary with their enormous hats and walking sticks and had even been presented to the King and Queen on their Canadian tour; not the people who gave cocktail parties and dinners and, on New Year's Eve, wore tuxedos and long dresses and popped champagne corks into the big Indian canoes suspended from the ceiling in the club's foyer. The canoes were called Montrealers and were very old. There were two of them, and a third in the dining room. A similar but smaller one had been made around the turn of the century by an Indian a long way up in Canada, beyond the end of the Algoma Central Railroad, and brought down by water and portage to the Island, where for many years now it had rested upside down on two wooden sawhorses at the Sedgwicks'. Tommy had never seen it in the water; he didn't think it was ever used.

TOMMY believed a lot of things, although belief was confused in his mind with hope. He believed, for instance, that the next time he coaxed his brother David into playing cards with him that David would not insist on playing Fifty-two Pickup, which meant that David spun the cards from the deck across the entire living-room floor and then Tommy had to scramble to pick them up; and when David did insist on it, as he almost always did, that Fifty-two Pickup would somehow become a real card game, like rummy, in which he might sometime get the deal. It never did. And once, when Tommy was in kindergarten and just before he turned six, he still believed that his mother's age was twenty-two, his father's twenty-three. His mother had told him.

He learned otherwise quite by accident, and after he learned it, it seemed so obvious that he was ashamed he could have been such a fool. He was, after all, supposed to be a smart little boy and very observant—so his mother always said—and since John was then twenty and David going on nineteen, in college both of them, simple arithmetic might have revealed the truth. But as his father often told him, he wasn't very good at simple arithmetic. His father could never make him understand why two and two *had* to make four. "It's a given," his father would say. "Why couldn't we say it made nine?" Tommy would ask, making his father very angry. Arithmetic seemed to Tommy a convention, like many others. Nonetheless, he firmly believed his mother's story, and so, when Mrs. Steer asked him how old his mother was one Saturday morning in her kitchen where he was playing with her daughter Amy, Tommy replied, "Twenty-two."

Mrs. Steer whooped with laughter. She always whooped when she laughed, and it was often loud.

"Yes, she's twenty-two," Tommy insisted.

"What makes you think that, Tommy?"

"My mother told me," he replied, but already he had stopped believing it. He could feel his face beginning to flush.

"Of course she's not twenty-two, Tommy," Mrs. Steer said, her voice softening. "Let me see, you'll be six very soon," and she put her hands on the counter, tilted her head toward the window, and began to calculate. "I'm just forty-two. Dick is forty-seven." Dick was Mr. Steer. "David is the same age as Vint." Vint was her son. And she counted various years and dates and remembered anniversaries and concluded, "Why, your mother must be forty-three or forty-four. I think she'll be forty-four in July."

The shame filled his face. His mother had lied to him. Mrs. Steer was right. He had even insisted on its absurd truth. But at least he would not cry, although he wanted to, not cry and compound his ridiculous shame. Instead, he asked if he might have a slice of her bread, which she made herself every week as an economy because the Steers had lost a lot on margin calls in the Crash. She talked about things like that, the Crash and the Depression. Tommy always imagined the Depression as a large, gaping black crater below a skyscraper, filled with clothes and furniture, dollar bills, gold jewelery, and a few dead bodies fallen from the building.

That evening, when his mother was sitting at her dressing table getting ready to go out, Tommy stood behind her and asked, with all the innocence and guile he could muster, which was quite a lot, "How old are you and Daddy, Mother?"

"Twenty-two, darling, and Daddy's twenty-three," she replied, glancing at his face in her mirror as she brushed her hair.

"When did you vote?" he asked.

"Your father's right, you do ask a lot of questions." She was slightly exasperated. "Let me see, when was the last election . . . ?"

"I know you're not twenty-two," Tommy said, his voice level.

"Now how do you know that?" his mother asked gaily, teasing him, rummaging in the drawer for her lipstick, which she always sucked into a little point like a pencil.

"Because Mrs. Steer told me you're forty-three or forty-four, and I *know* she's right. You lied." The tears he could not shed in front of Mrs. Steer, lest she think him a still greater fool and a sissy besides, welled up in his eyes and trickled slowly down his cheeks. His sense of betrayal was dismaying and acute. It was almost as if he had learned that his mother was not really his mother, or his father his father, but that he was a foundling, taken before his memory awakened from the Evelyn MacCracken Children's Home, a graceless brick structure with a fire chute that sat by itself in the midst of a large and treeless lot on top of MacCracken Hill.

"Oh, my baby," his mother said, when she looked up from her lipstick and saw his face in the mirror. "You mustn't be so sensitive. Don't cry. It was just a joke, a little white lie, not a real lie." She turned toward him. "It didn't mean anything —just a silly little teasing joke.

"Wipe your eyes," she commanded, handing him a scrap of tissue, dismissing his tears, "and stop being silly about it. You mustn't be a baby." His mother was very matter-of-fact, but at the same time she hugged him, and gave him her amethyst to play with, and helped him pick the jewelery she would wear that night. When she was dressed they went downstairs and she sat at the piano while his father finished his shower. Tommy sat in his favorite brown silk chair while his mother began to play the music they both loved, *Kinderszenen*, "Scenes from Childhood." She only got through the second song, which was called "A Curious Story" but in German, before his father was dressed and they had to leave. Tommy was comforted, but he didn't forget who had lied, and how she had been caught.

BUT that was all a long time ago: before Mrs. Appleton died and Mr. Appleton married Daisy's mother, before Daisy and Phil were divorced, before Emily Sedgwick wore his grandmother's diamond and both his brothers were married; long before Mr. Sedgwick resigned from the Edison, sold all his father's bank stock and the big house, and the Sedgwicks moved to Arizona, before the war began and Tommy's brothers went off to fight it, before Mrs. Steer gave up her garden and the Steers moved away—before many things had changed. The war disrupted the easy rhythms of life in Grande Rivière, turning the sleepy old fort with its red brick officers' quarters laid out in a decorous oval around the grassy parade ground into a bustling army base with thousands of soldiers living in Quonset huts, even tents, that sprang up overnight, it seemed, and everywhere—on his very street, in the fields and the woods he played in, in the place where his favorite hamburger stand used to be. Whole areas of town were taken over and closed down to civilians, which he and his parents and his friends had suddenly become. Chain-link fences and barbed wire were thrown up around the park by the river at the same time that the graceful old wrought-iron fences were dismantled and shipped away to be melted down for the war effort. The fountains with their play of colored lights were removed for the duration. The Japanese stone lanterns and the temple gate that stood in the park disappeared, along with the statue of the two naked boys sucking at the teats of a wolf that stood in front of the Courthouse and that used to puzzle and embarrass Tommy every time he saw it. One day a barrage balloon appeared across the street, and soldiers to guard it. For a while the sky was thick with the silver balloons, protection against the air raids that might come at any moment but never did. Tommy's father kept buckets of sand in the attic in case an incendiary bomb should hit. The maid's room became an air-raid shelter with blackout curtains at the windows, a portable radio, a deck of cards, a cribbage board, and a supply of canned food and water. An officer lived for a time in the big guest room, and sometimes another officer in the little guest room, too. Then someone they knew was killed, and then another and another. Little flags went up in windows all over town, some of them with gold stars if a son or a brother or a father had been killed. Tommy's father kept a map of the world on the wall in the upstairs hall, and they put pins in it to mark the progress of the war. Suddenly, with the war, everyone he knew seemed always to be moving, always traveling despite the difficulty: taking trains to Fort Lauderdale for the sun, or to Newport News or Long Beach or Boston or New York, the women to see their husbands, sons, naval officers, the men for the war effort; or to Washington, where

Daisy ended up with another husband, and, occasionally, Bob Griswold appeared on business for the Edison, where he'd become a director and the company attorney as well. They would never meet, although they once were very close. Strange things happen in life—a ticket here, a ticket there, and twenty, thirty, forty years later the destination.

One

Tommy loved his brother John. John was dark and handsome, though not so tall as his brother David, who was six feet and had played center on the basketball team when he was in high school, and the summer Tommy was seven played tennis with Madge McGhee and Daisy Meyer, and sometimes golf with Daisy, too. John just played golf, sometimes with David or his parents but usually with Emily Sedgwick. Tommy's mother said that John was "almost as handsome as your father. I have three handsome sons, but none of you is as good-looking as your father." Tommy didn't understand that. He thought that he himself looked weird, a skinny little frame topped with a cowlick and huge, flapping ears, but that John was much more handsome than his father and certainly easier to get along with.

When John and Emily were home from college, they talked all the time on the telephone, his brother lounging in the chair in the corner of his parents' bedroom, talking in a low voice so no one could hear. When Tommy asked Emily what they talked about so long and so often, she told him, "Sweet nothings, just sweet nothings." Once, just for fun, he even called her himself—"Four-oh-six," he said to the operator, remembering her number because he had heard his brother give it so many times—and Emily answered, but when she said "Hello," Tommy had nothing to say so he hung up, giggling. He would tease his brother by singing out "Four-oh-six" at

29

unexpected moments. John might blush, but he didn't get angry the way David did when Tommy teased him. John would even play rummy with him on occasions that became special for that reason, and for his eighth birthday he gave him forty-eight crayons, Binney & Smith Crayolas in the green-and-yellow box that opened to reveal the colors pointing up in rows, each row a little higher than the one before it. Tommy's mother could never see the need for forty-eight crayons; eight or twelve seemed plenty. He had lots of gifts for his birthday that he knew were more expensive, but few that pleased and thrilled him so much as this. John could please everybody except, on occasion, usually at dinner, his father, although John could not know that; he was at college, and at the table his mother would read his letters home. Each new letter seemed indistinguishable from the last, and the reaction it provoked was as predictable as the carrots on his plate.

"Dear Mother and Dad," the letters would begin, and John would launch into a discussion of life in the Beta house. His father would look pleased; he liked fraternities and he was proud that John was president of his, with a special room of his own on the first floor. He didn't even mind the house bills. Then the subject would turn to his classes. "Astronomy seems fine," his mother would read as Tommy and his father ate and listened, "it's a pipe," which would bring a trace of a frown to his father's face. He didn't mind the house bills, but he didn't believe in paying for pipes. For a long time, Tommy thought John was learning in astronomy class how to make telescopes from the kind of pipes they had in the cellar, and he wanted his brother to show him how until John explained that a pipe course was something different. It was easy. "But I'm really worried about economics." John always worried about economics, which made his father mad. He thought economics was important, a lot more important than astronomy, and if he had learned to run a business, he didn't see any reason why David and John couldn't. "I guess we'll just have to wait and see," John would say. "Time will tell." John invariably ended his discussion of economics with "Time will tell," and his father just as invariably exploded.

"What the hell does he mean, 'Time will tell'?" his father

would ask. "Why doesn't he know?" Once he even exclaimed, "What kind of a dumbbell is he?" Tommy would try not to giggle, his usual reaction to his father's passing rages, except when they were directed toward him, and if he had giggled then, this one surely would have been. He wondered why John bothered to tell his parents what he worried about; even he knew better than that, and he was fourteen years younger than John. He thought he'd tell him sometime to forget that sentence because it made his father so angry, especially when the next paragraph—a short one and the last—usually began, "By the way, I'm a little short of the old cash"—he always called it "the old cash"—"and I sure could use a little extra to see me through this month." His father would scowl. "This month? It was the same story last month! He might not spend so much money if he'd learn some economics. Has he been up to Appleton lately?" he would ask Tommy's mother, and she would reply, attempting to soothe him, "Why, I don't know, dear. I don't suppose so. At least, he didn't mention it." John went to Northwestern, which was near Chicago, and Emily Sedgwick went to Lawrence, which was in Appleton, Wisconsin. They weren't very far apart, and it seemed likely to Tommy that John might have been to Appleton, but at least he knew better than to say so. Tommy knew John and Emily went back and forth a lot, visiting each other's colleges. That seemed very grown-up to him: train trips and corsages and housemothers and chaperones and homecoming weekends and spring dances; sorority sisters and fraternity brothers, college songs and secret codes and handshakes and nighttime rituals— a lot more exciting than playing marbles with Paul Malotte, the boy who lived at the end of the street and went to the Catholic school, whose nose ran all the time and whose father had been bitten by a rabbit and died. Emily was a Pi Phi— like her mother and grandmother, she liked to explain—but she would not explain the meaning of the mysterious characters on the gold and jeweled pin she wore on her sweater. "It's Greek," she said, "and it's a secret." Chained to that pin was his brother's Beta Theta Pi pin, and everybody expected that eventually, when they were both graduated and John was working, Emily would get his grandmother's diamond.

That pleased Tommy's mother and father, even if John did take too many trips to Appleton, and it pleased the Sedgwicks, too.

It was different with David. Whenever David tried to please his parents, especially his father, he produced the opposite effect, or so it seemed to Tommy. He started college the year after John—the same year Tommy started kindergarten—to study business, and he joined John's fraternity. His father liked that, but David didn't. He didn't like business, and he stayed in college only two years. The next year, when Tommy was seven and in second grade, David stayed home and worked for his father. His father didn't like that, although David was out so often and so late that it seemed to Tommy as if he were hardly there at all. His father didn't like that, either.

In the fall of the year David was home, Tommy and his parents took the train to Chicago. David couldn't go; he had to work. It was the second time Tommy had been there, and the second time was a lot better than the first. He thought the train was exciting, sitting on the blue plush seats in their compartment that turned into a bedroom at night, sleeping in berths as the train pulled west and south, eating in the dining car, where Tommy spilled his peas and they rolled all over the floor, to his embarrassment but real relief, since he hated peas almost as much as he hated beets and asparagus, and only a little less than he hated carrots. The porter shined his shoes that night, just as if he were a grown-up, and in Chicago he saw a lot of skyscrapers, a lot of stores with escalators, and more people than he had ever seen in any one place. They stayed at the Palmer House, not in his Aunt Clara's apartment, and Tommy had his own room that connected to his parents'. They kept the door open, though. On Saturday they took another train, to Evanston, to go to a football game and to visit his brother John at his fraternity house, one of the biggest houses Tommy had ever seen and he'd thought that he lived in a big house. John's fraternity house seemed full of light and huge leather couches and chairs. It had a double staircase that divided above the front entrance, wrapping around the doorway as it descended grandly to the foyer. Tommy liked to run up one side of the sunlit double stairway and down the other. There was a bar in the basement with a drawing of a naked woman above it and a Wurlitzer nickelodeon. Tommy was embarrassed by the picture, but he stared at it when he thought no one was looking, memorizing its detail, which was sort of shadowy. There was a big dog named Whisky, who did tricks. People were always coming in and going out, and the place was filled with shouts and laughter and pretty girls in fur coats. Tommy and his parents had dinner there, in the big dining room. There were a lot of other parents too. Everyone treated Tommy's very politely, and they all asked about David. After dinner his parents went back to the Palmer House and Tommy was allowed to spend the night in his brother's room on the first floor. He spent the entire next day exploring, playing on the staircase, looking at the trophies, the fraternity paddles, the figure in the bar, playing with the dog, listening to John's fraternity brothers joke about cramming for exams, about beer busts, about who was losing at bridge and how much, about girls and especially about the girl they called the punching bag. She was a Tri Delt. They joked with Tommy, just as if he were one of them, and they told him that when he grew up, he'd probably be a Beta too. Like Phil Meyer, Tommy thought, but it turned out that Phil Meyer wasn't a Beta. Tommy wasn't sure he'd ever grow up that much, to be as easy, as assured, as handsome as John and his friends. It seemed a fearsome and not altogether likely prospect.

The train, the skyscrapers, the escalators, John's fraternity house, his friends, the Palmer House, the porters on the train, the bellhops in the hotel—it was all one grand adventure to his wide eyes, almost as exciting as Richard Halliburton's *Book of Marvels* that his mother had read to him, the Chicago River as exotic as the Bosporus, and Lake Michigan, the China Sea. Tommy could hardly wait to tell David all about it; but David wasn't home when they arrived late that autumn afternoon.

The house was gleaming but cold. Tommy could still smell the floor wax and the furniture polish, a little like lemons. Mrs. Munter, the Finnish lady whose husband worked for Tommy's father, must have cleaned it that day and had probably turned down the furnace, as she was very frugal, his mother said, and wouldn't have wanted to waste heat on an empty house. Tommy always called the Finnish lady Mrs. Munter, as did his mother, but he called the Indian girl Rose, and he called her husband, who only helped on the Island, Bill. His mother said that Rose liked children, although she and Bill never had any of their own, and she was good to her mother, who spoke only Indian and traded baskets for old clothes. Rose was always urging him to eat cookies and doughnuts, which she herself devoured, and his mother had to speak to her about that; he wasn't supposed to eat so many sweets. Rose was good to Tommy, but he didn't think his mother thought Rose was always good to her; sometimes Rose was unreliable.

A fire had been laid, fresh-cut kindling placed carefully like lattice over the andirons and beneath the logs, and every trace of ash had been scoured from the hearth. It looked immaculate, almost too clean to use, but it was gloomy that afternoon, and dark. Tommy longed to have a fire and asked his father if he wouldn't light it. "Who did this?" his father asked, looking at the fireplace. "You can't have a fire without ashes. Who took all the ashes out of the fireplace?" His father seemed angry. Why had he asked, Tommy wondered, and why couldn't there be a fire without ashes? Somehow, sometime, perhaps when his grandparents had lived there and the big old house was almost new, perhaps when he was a tiny baby and they had just moved in, a fire must have been started without ashes. Of course David must have done it; Tommy knew immediately. It was David's job to empty the ashes. Usually he just took a few scoops and threw them into a bucket, leaving Mrs. Munter or Rose to clean up after him, but when he put his mind to it David could be extremely neat. Sometimes he cleaned and ordered his room until it looked like a doctor's office, everything spotless and everything in its place. It was like David to do this, if he took the notion, and yes, he had swept and washed every speck of ash from the fireplace and laid the new fire, neatly crossing stick over stick to make a bed for the logs, the big one at the back, a smaller one on top resting against the bricks and two of the same size in front, just so.

Tommy learned that night that a fireplace should never

be emptied of all its ashes, and David, when he came home, learned it too. His father seemed very angry, for reasons Tommy did not understand. He could not understand why there should be a lot of arguing over a little pile of wood ash in the fireplace. He was not sure his father understood, either.

After a supper of milk toast, which his mother served him on his own small table in a corner of the dining room, Tommy went to bed, feeling very sad for his brother, who was only trying to please.

TOMMY loved his brother David that night without reservation; there was no vengeance in him, which was unusual in the ordinary course of his life with David. David cheated at Steal-the-Pack and made him play Fifty-two Pickup. He teased him without mercy, but David himself could not be teased. David tattled. He told his mother that Tommy had asked Mr. Lamontagne to give him an ice cream cone, though he naturally expected that David would charge it with the other groceries, and his mother spanked him with the Ping-Pong paddle. "Mr. Lamontagne's not in business to give you ice cream cones," she told him. "He's got better things to do with his money." She was mad at David, too; he'd bought the wrong vanilla. It was imitation. "It looks the same but it's not," she had said, and made David take it back when she had finished with Tommy. Once David told his mother that Tommy had stolen a nickel from his dresser, which he had, and again he was punished but that time he didn't get spanked. David tantalized Tommy with quick glimpses into his special box, the one he kept locked on his dresser, and then, before Tommy could catalogue its contents or seize an object, David would snap it shut, lock it, and slip the key into his pocket. All Tommy ever saw, amid the profusion of treasures, was a deck of playing cards secured with a rubber band, a pair of cuff links, and three sets of dice, one red, one black, and one very small ivory pair, his favorite. Tommy wanted more than anything a box of his own that he could lock. David told Tommy that he was a nuisance, and he knew he could be. David hardly ever wanted to play with him. He really wanted to be somewhere else with someone else.

David's main interest was his girl. It certainly wasn't his

work, Tommy knew that, and his father had said that David didn't understand that college was work, too. One day in David's room, when Tommy was delving into his brother's mysteries, he discovered a slim packet of letters, tied with a blue silk ribbon and addressed to his brother at college. It was strictly forbidden to read other people's mail—"Yes, even postcards," his mother had said—but these envelopes had already been opened. Tommy knew it would be wrong to read them, but impossible not to. He resisted only for a moment. Tommy was certain they would be much more interesting than the family letters that came to the house addressed to his parents and were read to everyone, and he was right. They were delicious. They were hilarious, and the handwriting was easy to read, too. "Dearest darling, I love you so much and miss you. . . . Dearest angel, I am sending you kisses and wish you were here so I could deliver them in person, on your eyes, your ears, your funny nose, your lips. . . ." It was true, Tommy thought, his brother did have a funny nose, and the thought of his being kissed, of *her* kissing *him*—on his eyes, ears, nose, and lips—astounded him. He was amazed, but he was gleeful. His brother would be *furious*, but what revenge! His mother was furious, too, when she found Tommy lying on David's bed, reading David's private letters. She didn't care if the envelopes had been opened, and he was spanked. But she did not tell David—one punishment was enough, she said—and Tommy's revenge was indeed sweet.

He took his time about it, wanting to be positive his mother had not told David, waiting for his mother to forget about the incident. But one night at dinner, Tommy began crooning to himself, "Dearest darling, dearest angel, I am sending you kisses and wish you were here so I could deliver them in person"—his father looked at him as if he were crazy—"on your eyes, your ears"—suddenly louder—"your *funny nose!*" His brother by then had looked up from his preoccupations, and *knew*. He turned red. He turned white, and red again. He jumped up from the table and started around to the other side to grab Tommy, who had moved quicker and was already on his way up the stairs, shouting now, "your eyes, your ears, your funny nose, your lips, I love you so much," and into the bathroom where he locked the door. He waited for a long time to come out, until his mother said they would remove the door from its hinges unless he unlocked it that minute. For some days, whenever David was around, Tommy stuck pretty close to his mother.

IN the spring, right after Easter, when everyone but David, who had to work, was on vacation from school and the thornapple thicket had begun to show a little green, David's girl friend came to dinner with John and Emily. It was the first time Margie Slade had been to the house for a meal, although his brother had known her for a long time. Margie was twice an orphan. Her real mother, who Tommy's mother said was a poor but a good woman—he imagined her walking down the street in a threadbare coat, smiling sadly—had died shortly after her birth and her father had gone to Detroit. Margie had another name then, until the Slades adopted her and changed it to Margaret, which she hated, but everyone called her Margie. Margie's father and his brothers owned the coal company and a big dock. Tommy had never known Margie's parents, and both of them had died, two years apart, her father just last winter. She was still in high school, and now she lived in their house with guardians instead of parents and a maid who brought her orange juice and black coffee every morning. Bob Griswold gave her an allowance and paid all her bills. It didn't seem like an altogether bad deal to Tommy, and he sometimes wondered who would be his guardian if his parents were killed, and if a lawyer would bring him an allowance every week, and if he would be rich.

Margie's aunt, whose name was Maxine, lived next door to Tommy in the house that had once belonged to the former governor of the state. Tommy thought it was one of the nicest houses in town. It had a library with a fireplace and a complete set of Jenny Slade's Nancy Drew mysteries, which Tommy always wanted to read but didn't because he was a boy. It had another room that Mrs. Slade called the drawing room, which also had a fireplace and several pieces of spindly furniture covered in light blue silk that no one ever sat on. The Slades' living room was cavernous and dark—Governor Wentworth

37

had kept his books there but Mrs. Slade had torn out the shelves—and directly above it was Mrs. Slade's bedroom, equally large, with a small refrigerator and a wall that was all mirrors. Above that was a game room paneled in wood containing the governor's billiard table covered in green felt and so big Tommy couldn't imagine how it got up there. However it got up there, Tommy guessed the governor couldn't get it out because it was still there. Tommy was very curious about the Slades and their house. His own house was comfortable enough but lacked mystery, except for his secret places in the attic, the cellar with its fruit room, and the back stairway, and his family sat down to breakfast every morning and dinner every night, not always together but always in the dining room. He never saw the Slades eat a meal together, and he never saw any of them use the dining room. Mrs. Slade liked soft-boiled eggs, which she ate with butter from a little cup, sometimes in the kitchen but usually in her bedroom. The Slades didn't belong to the country club anymore, and they never seemed to go out for dinner; they hardly went out at all. In the morning Mr. Slade did drive to the dock in the Dodge, and return at the same slow pace in midafternoon. Once in a while, in the afternoon, Mrs. Slade went out in her Packard, sitting alone in the back seat while Reilly, the furnace and yard man, drove. "Take me for a ride, Reilly," she would call down from the sun porch off her bedroom as Reilly worked around the garden, "I want to see the river," and a few minutes later she would appear downstairs, dressed. Mrs. Slade often yelled at Reilly for one thing or another, yet she seemed to like him and sometimes she would call him up to her bedroom to talk to her. Mrs. Slade's yelling didn't mean much. Mrs. Slade could be very grand, but at one time or another she yelled at almost everyone: Etta, the maid, Mr. Slade if he was around—he spent most of his time in his own room—once in a while at her daughters who were three and five years older than Tommy and kept away from their mother as much as they could. Lily and Jenny were Tommy's excuse for going to the Slades' house in the first place, but his real reason was Mrs. Slade, the only woman he knew who could really swear, who stayed in bed a lot, who wore negligées or even used the word, and who would fling a fur coat over her shoulders and say, "Well now, Tommy, how does Mrs. Rich Bitch look today?"

Tommy thought Mrs. Rich Bitch looked like a movie star, with her blond head, her red lips, her negligées, furs, and jewels. He was sorry when she got mad one day and threw the fur coat in the furnace, but she had others, and she looked terrific in all of them. Mrs. Slade liked to show Tommy her clothes—she had a lot of them—and her jewelry, which glittered like no jewelry he had ever seen. She would reach into a drawer and pull out a necklace with stones the size of hazelnuts, hold it up to her throat for him to admire, and drop it on the floor, reaching for a bracelet, another necklace, a brooch.

"Are those really rubies?" Tommy asked her, staring wide-eyed at the baubles littering the floor, the dressing table, piling up on her wrists.

"Hell, yes, they're rubies," Mrs. Slade said. "Well, some of them are. They're all red, anyway. And see, emeralds are green." She pawed around in the drawer and produced a green ring, flashing it before his eyes. "That was my mother's. She liked emeralds a lot more than she liked old Daddy."

Tommy had never seen jewelry like that. His mother had a small pair of diamond earrings with a sapphire in the middle, a diamond arrow, and a sapphire ring that if you held it right you could see a star in it, but nothing like this. Not even Mrs. Hutchins had jewelry like this. Nobody did. Tommy thought it must be worth a fortune, and he was dazzled, not so much by the stones as by Mrs. Slade, who seemed as glamorous, as beautiful, and as rich as any movie star.

Tommy had been with Mrs. Slade the afternoon of the day David's girl friend came to dinner, which gave him plenty of things to talk about should anyone ask him anything, which Margie finally did.

"What have you been up to today, Tommy?" Margie asked, giving him his chance.

"Mrs. Slade showed me the needle she sticks into herself," Tommy said, full of excitement, "and she did it right while—"

"You're not eating your carrots, Tommy," his mother interrupted.

"Yes," Tommy said, "she did, right in her leg, and—"

39

"Tommy," his father said, "that will be all." It was a command. His mother reached over to his plate, picked up his fork, and stuffed carrots in his mouth. "You're not eating your carrots *or* your mashed potatoes. Finish your plate at once. That child," she said to no one in particular, "is a terrible eater."

Well, Tommy thought, it *was* interesting that Mrs. Slade stuck needles in herself, just like a doctor. Anyone would think so. Mrs. Slade was the most interesting person he knew, and he didn't care what his parents thought. No one else threw a fur coat in the furnace, or fired her maid and ordered a whole staff of men in white jackets from Marshall Field's in Chicago, but they stayed only a week or two and then Etta came back, or kept a safe on her sun porch that once he put a peanut butter sandwich in, or showed him her operation. He knew better than to mention the operation. When Tommy was in kindergarten, Mrs. Slade had gone away for a long time, to the Mayo Clinic, and when she came back her breasts were gone, or part of them anyway. Tommy didn't know that then, but later she told him. "You never know how you feel about your tits, Tommy, until they cut 'em off," and she opened her negligée and showed him the tubes of flesh flapping from her chest like laundry on a line. To the best of his knowledge they looked like ordinary breasts except they were a little short and had no nipples. That was when she started taking her shots. And then, when he had just started first grade, her bed caught fire and burned her. The fire department came, Mrs. Slade went to the hospital, and her bedroom had to be painted. After she came home she had to have more shots and she lay for some weeks swathed in bandages like a mummy, only her eyes peering out. She liked to have Tommy visit her then. She didn't like the nurses, and Dr. Randolph couldn't be there all the time. "You'll keep me cheered up, won't you, Tommy? A few bandages won't bother you," she said. The bandages didn't bother Tommy, and he was glad that he could cheer her up. He used to see her a lot, and finally she got rid of the bandages and the nurses, and Dr. Randolph taught her how to give herself the shots. When she got better, she went to New Orleans with Dr. Randolph. Mr. Slade didn't like to travel. As far as Tommy knew, that was the only time Mrs. Slade ever went on a trip, except to the Mayo Clinic. Right after that, Dr. Randolph went on a trip by himself, and he was gone a long time. He wasn't even home for Christmas.

So what, Tommy wondered, had he done? It was sure he had done something, because his parents and his brother David looked very disturbed, and Margie distinctly uncomfortable. Emily started talking about college—she wondered if Margie was considering Northwestern—and his mother began to talk about what she'd read in the paper that day. She seemed to have read the whole thing. No one else said a word, and Tommy stared at his carrots, lying in a sea of sticky gravy on his plate. It made him sick when his mother mashed his food around, mixing everything up. He was always very careful to make sure the carrots never touched the potatoes, or the potatoes the meat, even though he knew they all ran together in his stomach. He didn't like to think about that. He wanted to leave, and he asked to be excused, which he was, and he went outside to play. No one looked at his plate.

That night, when Tommy was getting ready for bed, his brother John told him some things he didn't know about the Slades. "Mrs. Slade's a dope fiend," he said.

"A dope fiend," Tommy asked—"what's that?"

"It's someone who takes morphine," John said. "That's what Mrs. Slade gives herself in the shots."

"How do you know that?"

"Everybody knows that. Everybody knows it but nobody talks about it, except you, blabbing away in front of Margie."

"If nobody talks about it, how does everybody know about it?" Tommy asked. "She doesn't wear a sign." But he knew what his brother meant. He meant it was one of those things they weren't supposed to talk about, like Mrs. Hutchins' twitching in the bar, as if not mentioning it meant it didn't happen.

"Why does Mrs. Slade take morphine?" Tommy asked. It sounded delicious.

"Because she's a dope fiend," John said. "Sometimes you're sure a dope. Watch out, or you'll be a dope fiend too, or an alcoholic like Mr. Slade. They're both drunks, just like

Margie's parents were, and Mrs. Slade's a dope addict besides. The whole family's crazy. Look, stop asking questions," his brother said, "and don't tell where you heard it."

Tommy didn't tell, but it certainly was interesting. It made Mrs. Slade seem even more exciting. A real dope fiend, and living right next door! Tommy could hardly wait to see her again. But at least he understood now what he'd said at dinner, and why everyone looked so stunned. He wasn't supposed to know about Mrs. Slade's shots; he wasn't old enough.

The next morning his mother told him he was spending too much time at the Slades', and he was not to play over there for a while. "It's not a suitable place for a child your age," she said.

THAT same spring, before John's graduation but after Margie came to dinner the first time and while the house was still being redecorated, Tommy's parents went away for a while and Mrs. Moran came to run the house and cook the meals for him and his brother David. Mrs. Moran was an old lady whose husband had been an engineer on the railroad but was now dead, and she liked to tell stories about roundhouses and cowcatchers and blizzards so thick the great headlight on the locomotive shone straight into a swirling wall of whiteness but the engine steamed through, sparks flying, pistons churning, boiler hissing. She would tell him about Pembine Junction, where the sleeping cars were switched in the middle of the night to the Chicago train, and if you weren't in a sleeping car you had to get off that train and wait for another or else you'd end up in Minneapolis. She would tell him about riding to Trout Lake in the cab of the locomotive, and of country people flagging down the train at Engadine or Paradise Crossing; of waiting at the railroad yard for her husband's train to pull in, and how its coming would be signaled by the clanging of its bell, and then the engine would round the bend; and she would tell him of the sound of whistles in the night, and of their meaning. Every whistle had a meaning.

Tommy liked Mrs. Moran very much, and he was always happy when she came to stay. She smelled of face powder and talcum the way he remembered his grandmother smelling, and she never seemed to tire of playing cards with him or of telling him stories, nor did he ever tire of listening. Sometimes she would take him to see her friends, people with names like Carrie and Pearl whose husbands had also worked on the railroad but who were now widows like Mrs. Moran and Mrs. Addington, and who would give him a cookie or two to fatten him up. "Doesn't his mother ever feed him?" one of the women asked Mrs. Moran, as if he weren't in the room. "He's all skin and bones. That boy must eat like a bird!" Then Tommy would remember that he didn't like visiting, that he didn't like dark houses with doilies on the backs and arms of chairs and under the lamps, that he liked cookies but he didn't like being talked about as if he weren't there, although he had grown used to it, and that it was the journey he liked, not the destination. But he didn't let it show.

While his parents were away and Mrs. Moran was taking care of him, David got engaged to Margie. It happened in May on the big couch in their living room that his mother was getting a new slipcover for, and Tommy was all but a witness to it. Certainly he was the first to know. School had been dismissed early that day, and Mrs. Moran was going to be out until evening. Rose was supposed to fix dinner for them, but Rose was a terrible cook and Tommy hoped that David would take him out for a hamburger, which was something Tommy never got to do when his parents were home because they ate ground round and at a hamburger stand you never knew what kind of meat you might get.

Tommy ambled slowly home. It was a beautiful day. He stopped on the bridge for a while and looked over the railing at the canal swirling by below him. The canal was very dangerous; sometimes people drowned in it because the current was so swift. The canal drove the turbines that made the electricity for his father's plant—an odd name, Tommy thought, for a place in whose dust and shadow no green thing could possibly have grown. He walked on, looking at the tulips in Mrs. Steer's garden, shuffling along his street toward his house, happy in his own thoughts. When he came up to the porch he noticed that the mail was still in the mailbox. That was fun.

Tommy loved being the first to get the mail, and he opened the box and stood on the porch sorting through the letters. Nothing for him. There never was, unless his parents sent him a postcard, which they hadn't. Nothing for David, either—ha, ha—not even a letter from Miss Pink, the Mercurochrome lady. Of course, she hadn't written in a long time, as far as Tommy knew. There was just the ordinary mail for his parents, which was never very interesting, and something that wasn't ordinary. It was a letter with the strangest and most beautiful stamps on it, and more than one, too. They were not at all like ordinary stamps. Mr. Sedgwick might like these, Tommy thought. Perhaps he should show him the envelope. Mr. Sedgwick had a big stamp collection that his father had started and he had continued, adding to it as he found new stamps that he liked. Mr. Sedgwick said that it was very valuable, and he kept it locked up. Stamps were valuable, but not all stamps, just unusual stamps. Tommy wondered if these might be valuable. He thought he'd better handle the letter carefully. It was addressed to his mother, in a handwriting that Tommy didn't recognize—it wasn't any of his aunts', or his brother John's. He didn't recognize the pictures on the stamps, either. The statue of the animal didn't look like anything you'd find in the woods around Grande Rivière, and he had never seen a volcano. Tommy could hardly wait until they studied geography in school. That wasn't for two more years, fourth grade, when they got to go to the second floor. Until you were in the fourth grade, you weren't allowed on the second floor. It would be a long wait. Tommy liked geography. He had a set of books his parents had gotten, the same time they'd given him *The Book of Knowledge* which had a lot about astronomy. The set was called *Lands and Peoples,* and they were beautiful books, full of pictures of jungles and ruins, European cathedrals and villages in England, polar bears in the Arctic and penguins in Antarctica. There were pictures of Mexico, too, and these stamps said Mexico on them. He'd have to see what it said about Mexico in his books, and look at the pictures again. He had another book about Mexico, too, and a boy named Pedro.

Tommy opened the door and threw the letters on the table in the hall with the rest of the mail they were saving for his

parents. He looked into the living room and found David and
Margie on the couch. "No mail for you, ha, ha," he said. It
was strange that they hadn't even picked up the mail. He must
have startled them because Margie had jumped up and was
standing by the couch pulling at her sweater, and David just
sat there looking irritated. Tommy forgot all about the mail.
He went into the living room. There was an air of anticipation about David and Margie, and they acted as if they wanted
to be rid of him, which made Tommy eager to stay. His mother
would say he was being contrary. Tommy sat down on his
chair, the brown silk one that his mother was going to move
upstairs because it didn't go with her new color scheme. There
was nothing particular he wanted to do anyway, so he just
swung his legs over the arm of the chair and leaned against the
other side—he liked to sit that way when no one was there to
tell him to straighten up—and he tried to get David and
Margie interested in something, but there was no talking to
them.

"Don't you have some homework to do?" his brother finally
asked him.

"There's no homework in second grade," Tommy said.
"Let's play cards." He was giggling with excitement.

"We don't want to play cards," David said, sounding more
annoyed. Margie was looking bored, as if at any moment she
might begin to drum her polished fingernails on the table.

"Not even Fifty-two Pickup?" Tommy asked.

"No," David said. "Hey, I almost forgot. Mrs. Randolph
has something for you."

"What?"

"A plant."

"A plant?" Why would Mrs. Randolph have a plant for him?
But it was nice of her if she did.

"It's for Mrs. Moran," David said. "She wants you to go
over and pick up a plant for Mrs. Moran."

"That's funny," said Tommy. Sometimes he thought he
believed anything anyone ever told him, and at other times
he didn't believe anything. This was one of his doubtful times.
It was clear, though, that there was to be no playing with
David and Margie, so he finally left.

The Randolphs lived across the street. Mrs. Randolph was

45

one of Tommy's good friends, more predictable than Mrs. Slade, funnier than Mrs. Steer. Mrs. Randolph laughed a lot, enjoying her own jokes and encouraging his, and Tommy liked that. She and Dr. Randolph had a beautiful rose garden that they'd put in the spring before, which Tommy also liked. Their youngest son, Jimmy, was two years older than Tommy but still, if Tommy had a best friend, he supposed that Jimmy Randolph was it, despite the difference in their ages. He'd let Tommy try his bike. Like Tommy, Jimmy was a lot younger than his brothers, although he did have a sister eight years older, but she was big, too.

The Randolphs bought Cokes by the case, and even Jimmy was allowed to drink as many of them as he wanted. Dr. Randolph drank it all the time. "Two years ago I used to drink whisky by the bottle," he would shout—he always seemed to shout—"and now I drink Coke by the case!" And straight from the bottle, too. "No," said Tommy's mother, who would sometimes buy Vernor's ginger ale but not Coke, "you mustn't drink it from the bottle. You never know whose mouth it's been in." She was right, of course, you never did know whose mouth it had been in, but Dr. Randolph did it and he *was* a doctor. Tommy didn't care much about Vernor's anyway, and he got all the Coke he wanted, straight from the bottle, at Dr. Randolph's, who no longer allowed whisky or cigarettes in his house.

Dr. Randolph told his father that he should drink Coke instead of whisky, too, and stop smoking cigarettes as well, but his father wouldn't listen to him. Dr. Randolph wasn't his doctor, anyway; he went to Dr. Rodgers, if he ever had to go to the doctor, and once in a while Dr. Scanlon, who was the doctor at the plant. But Tommy didn't. He wouldn't go to anyone but Dr. Randolph now. Once his father had taken Tommy to the plant to see Dr. Scanlon because he had a boil on his neck, and Dr. Scanlon had put him under the lamp. Dr. Scanlon was famous for his lamp, but Dr. Randolph didn't approve of Dr. Scanlon or his lamp. Dr. Randolph didn't approve of any other doctor. He called them all quacks, or frauds, or sons-of-bitches, or dumbbells, or tit-pinchers. "He ought to know," Tommy had heard his father say to his mother. "There's nobody like a reformed drinker. Any day now he'll

46

get religion." But Dr. Randolph had noticed the boil on his neck, and he asked Tommy what he was doing about it. Tommy told him that Dr. Scanlon had put his lamp on it.

"Jesus X. Christ," Dr. Randolph shouted. "You've seen Mrs. Henderson, haven't you? You know what happened to her, don't you? That fiddle-headed old fart put his lamp on her, too!"

"P.T.," Mrs. Randolph exclaimed—she always called him by his initials—"P.T.! Stop that talk!"

"That man's an asshole and the boy ought to know it," Dr. Randolph said. "Besides, the boy's heard worse. Tell the old lady you've heard worse, Tommy. Tell her you love it."

Tommy laughed. Of course he loved it. He also loved Mrs. Randolph. There was no right answer. No matter what he said, one of them would be mad. So he didn't say anything. He laughed instead. He always tried to laugh his way out of embarrassing dilemmas, and this was one of them. He might not be much of a fighter, but he was good at laughing, and he had learned that it was possible to win in a tough situation if you pretended there was nothing to lose. Among the grown-ups he knew, only Dr. Randolph and Mrs. Slade talked like that, and not even Mrs. Slade said the things Dr. Randolph did. When Tommy's father was angry he would swear, but he never said things like "fart" or "tit" or, as Dr. Randolph once hollered out, banging the dining-room table with his fist, "Piss on a plate!" One time when he was mad at David, Tommy's father shouted, "Christ on a crutch," also banging his fist on the table, but when Tommy laughed his father told him to be quiet.

"Yeah," Dr. Randolph said, "Mrs. Henderson went under Dr. Scanlon's lamp and they had to cut off her legs. What do you think they'll have to do to your neck?" he asked, peering at it and bending it a little to examine the boil.

Well, Tommy didn't suppose they'd have to cut it off, but it did make him think, and he decided to put his faith in Dr. Randolph rather than in Dr. Scanlon's lamp. He was never sorry.

Neither Dr. Randolph nor Jimmy was home when Tommy ran up to the Randolphs' door that afternoon for Mrs. Moran's plant. That was good. Tommy didn't have time to play. He had to get the plant and run back home to find out what was going on. Tommy knew that *something* was going on, and he knew it was something he'd be interested in. So when Mrs. Randolph opened the door he told her in one long breath, "My brother's at home with Margie and he told me I had to come over here and get a plant but I know he's up to something and I've got to get back there to find out what and—"

"Tommy," Mrs. Randolph said. "Upon my word! Sit down, my little friend, before you burst. Catch your breath. Have a Coke." She got one for him and one for herself, and made him sit down across from her at the dining-room table. "Now tell me," she said, "what's all this about?"

"I'm so excited," Tommy exclaimed. "I'm so excited!" He couldn't sit still in his chair but bounced up and down. He was afraid that if he stood up he'd spin like a top. "Davey is up to somethng, I know he is. Oh boy, oh boy! And I have to get back to find out."

"Wait just a minute, Tommy," Mrs. Randolph said. "The plant's not ready yet. David just this minute called to say you'd be coming by to get it. Why don't you help me pot it up? And while you're doing that, you can tell me what makes you think David's up to something."

"He just *looks* as if he's up to something," Tommy said. "He just looks it. And he was trying to get rid of me, so he must be up to something." Of course he was up to something. Something strange was in the air. David had called Mrs. Randolph? Tommy thought Mrs. Randolph had called him. He'd better hurry. He finished his Coke as soon as he could and waited for Mrs. Randolph to finish potting the plant. She called it a Christmas cactus because that's when it bloomed. Mrs. Randolph gave away a lot of plants, but there was something funny about this. He wondered if this was some trick on his brother's part. David was very good at tricks; there was no question about that. Mrs. Randolph took a lot of care with the plant, patting it in place, watering it, letting it drain, making sure that it was firmly set in its pot. Tommy didn't know there was so much you could do to put a plant in a pot. Finally she finished.

As soon as she handed it to him, Tommy thanked her and ran across the street, throwing open the door and racing into

48

the living room where he found David and Margie, still on the couch. But this time his brother didn't look annoyed and Margie didn't look bored. They seemed flushed with pleasure, excited, happy. Tommy knew he'd been right; they had been up to something.

"Look, Tommy," Margie said, extending her hand. "Look what your brother gave me. Isn't it beautiful?"

"Wow," Tommy said, looking at the ring on her finger, "some headlight!" He liked to use sophisticated slang like that. He picked it up from *Life* magazine, or from listening to his brothers and their friends—words like "headlight" for diamond ring, and "gams" for legs, and "hell's bells," which he'd picked up from his father. That always made his brothers' friends laugh.

"You're engaged? You're going to be married, then?" Tommy asked. "Oh, boy! I knew it! I knew it! I have to tell Mrs. Randolph." And he raced back across the street to tell Mrs. Randolph that Margie was sitting on their couch with an engagement ring on her finger, and that he was the first to know it, and that she was the second, even before his parents. His parents. He hoped they would be happy, too. Tommy had heard his father say that Margie was going through her money like a house afire, eating right into her capital, and that wasn't good but it wasn't all her fault. It was encouraged by Bob Griswold and President Roosevelt's New Deal, too. His brother was spending a lot of money, too, Tommy thought; diamonds were expensive. And then he ran back home so as not to miss anything. He forgave David for everything—for the teasing, for the cheating at Steal-the-Pack, for telling on him and getting him in trouble with his mother, for everything. All he wanted was to sit close to Davey and Margie, to feel their warmth and their happiness, and his own happiness and excitement, which was, he thought, the most he had ever felt in his entire life.

"Come on, Davey," he begged, "take us out for hamburgers. We don't have to eat here, do we? Rose is cooking. Ugh."

With Tommy sitting in the middle, holding their hands, the three of them drove down the River Road to his favorite hamburger stand near the country club, and they had hamburgers with raw onions, and French-fries and Cokes, which were Margie's favorite foods as well as his. Tommy knew he would like Margie a lot. She hugged him and said he'd be her brother now. "Do you think you can stand having an older sister?" she asked him.

Stand it? Tommy couldn't imagine anything better. And then he wondered if he would now be related to Mrs. Slade, and he was sure he would be, in some way, so of course he could go over there to play. You can always play with your relations.

No matter how Tommy looked at it, David's engagement was wonderful news, and he and Margie treated him that afternoon not as if he were a child but as if he were their friend. Tommy was very glad his parents were away, because if they'd been home it would have been exciting, of course, but different. It would never have happened on their living-room couch on a Wednesday afternoon, with him practically a witness. He wouldn't have known about it until later, because David and Margie would have had to tell his parents first, and there would have been a lot of grown-up talk, and he would have been called downstairs and they would have told him, and then they all would have sat around talking but he wouldn't have had a chance to say anything except congratulations. As it was, Tommy could hardly stop talking, and he didn't once use the word "congratulations." He didn't even mind it when his brother and Margie dropped him off and went up to her house in the evening, leaving Tommy at home with Mrs. Moran. He was anxious to tell Mrs. Moran the news, and he had his own things he wanted to do. He could hardly wait for his parents to come home too, so he could surprise them with the news.

And were they ever surprised. David had asked Tommy not to tell but to let him break the news, which Tommy did, but barely. When his parents pulled into the driveway in the late afternoon not long before dinner, Tommy began to dance with glee, unable to contain his excitement. "They're home! They're home," he shouted to David, who had gone upstairs to shower and change after work. His parents came in the house in a flurry of coats and bags and stamping of feet. "You're home at last!" Tommy cried. "You're home at last."

"There, there, darling," his mother said, sweeping him into her arms. "It's all right. Mommy's finally home, and she won't go away again for a long time." She turned to David, who had come down the stairs, to Mrs. Moran, and to Tommy's father, and said, "I've never seen him so excited to see us."

Tommy was glad to see his parents. Of course he was. He knew that buried somewhere within their bags would be a present for him, which he always hoped would be something he really wanted but was usually a sweater or a shirt or once a blue jacket and pants that his mother really liked—nothing like the Crayolas John had given him, the fountain pen from his father, the grown-up windbreaker from David, or the beautiful Monopoly set that Margie had given him for Christmas. But Tommy's excitement had not so much to do with his parents' returning home—after all, they came and went a lot; there wasn't anything particularly unusual about that—or with the surprise that might be in store for him, as it did with the surprise that awaited them.

"Tell them, Davey, come on! Tell them, tell them," Tommy said. "Tell them the news!"

"What's the news?" his father asked.

"Yes, what's the news?" his mother repeated. She was still pleased by her welcome. "What is it?"

"Wait a minute," said his father. "Hold it until I call the plant." Tommy thought his father *always* had to call the plant. Everything came to a halt while his father went to his telephone in the library. Tommy could hear his father's voice. "MacAllister talking." He never said "Hello" or "How are you?" when he called the plant; always "MacAllister talking" or "MacAllister here," as if they might not recognize his voice, and he would get right down to business, asking questions, giving orders: about the stacks or the furnaces whose glowing fires Tommy could see from his bedroom window, reflecting against the sky at night; about the shipping room, the lime kilns or the drum factory, where David worked and hated it. At work his father spoke another language, Tommy thought, secret, a language whose combinations were hard to understand, as if it were a kind of code.

While his father was on the telephone, Tommy's mother looked through the mail on the table in the hall. "Is this all, David?" she asked him.

"Yes," David said, "that's all. As far as I know."

"You know we saw Madge McGhee in Philadelphia," his mother said. "She was home for the weekend. She asked about you. She said you never answer her letters." Tommy always recognized Madge's letters. She wrote in ink the color of Mercurochrome and called it hot pink, which Tommy and his brother John thought very funny.

"That's right," David said. "I never do answer her letters." Madge's handwriting was round and fat and slanted backwards. David would open her letters and drop each page as he read it into the wastebasket, one by one, as if he couldn't care less, which was, in fact, how he said he felt about them. "I couldn't care less about her letters," he told his mother. That was one of Madge's expressions; she said it all the time.

"I don't think that sounds very nice," his mother said. "Madge is an attractive girl. You ought at least to reply to her letters. It's only polite."

"Hey, Tommy," David said, "help me carry this stuff upstairs, will you?" Tommy reached for the biggest bag. He had to use both hands and still he could barely lift it. "That's too big," his brother said. "Take a smaller one." So Tommy took the biggest one he could lift, which was the second-biggest bag and also took two hands, and struggled up the stairs with it as his mother went through the mail again and asked Mrs. Moran if that was all of it, and his father continued talking to the plant. Tommy had to take the bag up one step at a time, but he got it there. "Okay, muscle boy, you did it," his brother said. "Now go get the smallest. And keep your mouth shut, please?"

"I will," Tommy said, and he went back for the smallest bag, which his mother kept her jewelry and makeup in. When they got all the bags upstairs, and David had hung up his parents' coats, and his father had finally gotten off the telephone and fixed a drink for himself and Tommy's mother, David stood in the living room and told them the news.

"Well," he said, as Tommy sat on his hands on the piano bench to keep them still, "Margie and I are going to get married."

"Whoopee!" Tommy shouted. "Can you believe it? Isn't that wonderful? Isn't that"—he reached for the word—

52

"*splendid*? They're going to get married! I'm going to have a sister! And they've already told me I could stay with them in their house sometimes." Tommy got up and gave his father a little hug, which surprised both of them. Then he gave his mother one. His parents were smiling at him.

"Well, Tommy," his father said, "better get a grip on yourself. They're not married yet." He turned to David. "Had you thought of talking this over with your mother and me?" Now his father was neither smiling nor frowning, and his voice had flattened. Tommy settled down and looked again at his father. "When did this happen?"

"I'll tell you when it happened," Tommy interrupted. "It happened last Wednesday afternoon, right on that couch"—he pointed to the big soft couch in the living room—"and I knew about it before anyone. I was the first to know." His voice became softer. "I found them." He felt awed by the enormity of it. "I found them." His mother had sat down on the other couch and was looking toward the window. His father started to speak again. "Wow," Tommy exclaimed, repeating the line he hoped would make them laugh, "some headlight!"

No one laughed very hard, however, except Mrs. Moran, who had come in at that moment to say that dinner was ready. They went into the dining room and sat down. They talked only a little bit about David's engagement; they'd discuss it later, his father said. The trouble with being an adult, Tommy often thought, was that you had to spend so much time discussing everything, going backwards and forwards over the same thing but never actually getting anywhere. John L. Lewis was as bad at the end of the discussion as he was at the beginning, and so were the Reuthers, who were ruining Detroit. Tommy did not look forward to that part of being grown up. He wondered what his parents would find to discuss about David's engagement. He thought you were supposed to celebrate engagements, like weddings and anniversaries and christenings.

Tommy's mother talked about their trip East. She loved Lord & Taylor; it was probably her favorite store—not so large as Field's, but awfully good. They'd gone to a Broadway show and dancing in the Rainbow Room with the McGhees, who'd joined them in New York for a couple of days, before they'd all gone to Philadelphia together. The McGhees lived outside Philadelphia, and they'd had a party for Tommy's parents. That's where they'd seen Madge. She went to Bryn Mawr, and most summers she came to the Island with her brother Phelps and with Mr. and Mrs. McGhee, who weren't her parents but her aunt and uncle. Her real parents had been killed in an auto accident when she and Phelps were little—they didn't even remember them—and the McGhees had brought them up because Mr. McGhee and their father were brothers. Mrs. McGhee and Mr. Aldrich were cousins—practically everybody seemed related somehow—and that's how the McGhees started coming to the Island in the first place. Mrs. McGhee had spent her summers there ever since she could remember. They always stayed at the Aldrich cottage now, but Madge didn't like it much.

"God," she used to say, "I wish I could get out of this dump like that bastard Phelps." Phelps was older and went to Yale. Madge always called him "that bastard" if he wasn't there, or if he was she would say, "Phelps you bastard," all in one slow breath, and he would reply very coolly, "Yes, bitch?" Phelps never stayed very long on the Island. He always had to visit friends in Maine or Massachusetts or Long Island.

Madge and Phelps were well suited to their names, Tommy thought. They sounded like rich people's names, not like the names he heard every day. Madge seemed like a glamour girl, the kind they showed pictures of in *Life* magazine. Tommy's mother said she was a strawberry blonde. She wore white shorts, played tennis but thought golf was boring, painted her toenails and her fingernails, took sunbaths all the time, smoked cigarettes, and spoke in a rich deep voice like syrup pouring. She talked about nightclubs, college, boarding school, her girl friends who were all debs like herself, boys, weekends at Princeton, and catching trains for New York where she met dates under a clock in a hotel. She spent a lot of time in New York. Philadelphia, she said, was dreary. Dreary. The Island was beyond dreary. It was hopeless. Nonetheless, she seemed to brighten up in the evening, even for one of the ordinary parties that took place, it seemed, every night before dinner at one cottage or another, or at the country club on the shore. She brightened up around Vint Steer, who was David's friend and Amy's brother, and around David, too, when he had stopped seeing Margie. It was funny. When David came back from college the summer before and started to work, he and Margie didn't see each other, despite all her letters. Those letters made Tommy smile.

Toward the end of that summer, Madge had been David's girl friend. She'd been Vint's at the beginning, but everybody was friendly about it. Once when David took her to a dance at the country club, she had worn a strapless dress. Tommy wondered how it stayed up, but his brother John told him not to worry about that, that it didn't stay up for long. Tommy giggled, and thought how funny it would be when her dress fell down and how embarrassed she would be. When John teased David about her, as he often did that summer, he would call her Hot Pink. "Hot Pink showing pink tonight?" John would ask, laughing wildly. "Hot Pink is *hot stuff!*" David wouldn't say a word. But Tommy was glad his brother was going to marry Margie, not Madge. Maybe Vint could marry Madge.

In the excitement of his parents' homecoming, and the relating of David's news, Tommy forgot all about his parents' surprise for him. And so did they. His mother discovered it the next day when she was unpacking, and gave it to him. It was a blue beret, and she liked it quite a lot.

EARLIER that year, Tommy's father had brought him a present from New York. Tommy was very surprised, because his father never bought gifts, not even for his mother. He said she had everything she wanted, but he would always give her a check for Christmas anyway. He didn't like to shop, his mother had explained, and he didn't have the time, either. But he did bring Tommy a black fountain pen with a gold clip. It was a birthday present that arrived two days late because his father couldn't get home in time for his birthday. Tommy had had it only a couple of months; he'd never even used it. He kept it with the Crayolas John had given him and with his other treasures in his safest place. Tommy thought

55

it might become his most prized possession; it was hard to tell. The pen had a gold point, a gold band around the cap, and a gold clip and filling lever, and it came in a white case with a strip of gold around the edge. If you opened the lid to a certain point and let it go in the right way, it snapped shut with a solid thwack. Tommy liked to do that, though it irritated his mother if he did it over and over. The pen was held tightly in its box by two tiny elastics, and it looked very much like those pens Tommy saw advertised in the magazines, the pens with a white dot on the cap that were supposed to last a lifetime.

"Really a *lifetime*?" Tommy asked his mother. A lifetime seemed like a very long time indeed.

"Well, probably not really, Tommy," she replied. "Hardly anything lasts a lifetime."

Tommy thought of the antique desk and chair in the downstairs hall that had belonged to his grandfather and his grandfather's grandfather and had lasted longer than all of them; and of his grandfather's gold watch, which was not a wristwatch but a pocket watch and was attached to a gold chain with a gold nugget hanging from it and another gold ornament that held a reddish stone with his grandfather's monogram carved into it. The stone was called a carnelian, a word Tommy thought very elegant and strange. He liked to turn it over on his tongue. The watch was found on his grandfather's body when it washed ashore one spring five months after he had drowned. His brother John told him that was how they'd identified him. They couldn't tell to look at him; his face had been mostly washed away. But all that happened long before Tommy was born.

Tommy never knew either of his grandfathers, or his mother's mother either, who had died of pneumonia on New Year's Day a year or two before Tommy was born. He had known only his father's mother, who had lived with them for a while. The house had once been hers, and Tommy's father and his brother and sister had grown up in it. Tommy's grandmother smelled of talcum and dried flowers, like the old lusterware jar she kept in her bedroom. The jar was filled with dried rose petals saved from the roses on his grandfather's coffin. They were older than Tommy. She almost always wore lavender or purple and a long string of pearls with a clasp blue as ink—"For the opera, Tommy," she would say with a laugh, for of course she never went to the opera; there was no opera to go to. But she would hum a lot and sing "Let me call you sweetheart, I'm in love with you," or her favorite hymn, "O God, our help in ages past," as she walked through the house, alone in her thoughts. A warm and pleasant smell wafted around her, and tortoise and bone hairpins drifted from her as she passed, leaving a trail so that you always knew where she'd been. Long after she went to the hospital and died, those pins would turn up in odd corners of the house. She kept them in an ivory box on her dressing table. Her dressing table was cluttered with ivory and tortoise boxes, including a strange one with a hole in the middle of its lid. Tommy could never figure out what that was for; it was always empty. There were little containers of rouge—"pots," she called them—which his father said she used too much of, and boxes of pinkish powder and great fluffy puffs and puffs that were not fluffy. It was curious to him that women were always powdering their faces; when he tried it himself once he didn't like the way it felt at all, or the way it looked, either. There were also a hand mirror made of tortoiseshell and a buffer for her fingernails and little scissors with tortoise handles and a thing like a knife and orange sticks for her cuticles. His grandmother was proud of her fingernails and of their moons. She would examine Tommy's hands and tell him that he'd have fine nails too, if only he'd stop biting them.

Everyone said his grandmother was a beautiful woman and a wonderful cook, like Mrs. Barlow who made angel-food cake like no one else and a punch from green tea that was served before the champagne at weddings and christenings. The punch took several days to make, and while it was curing it turned the color of butterscotch, though it didn't taste like butterscotch. He had tasted some once, at the country club. It was in a cup somebody had left in the card room. Tommy's grandmother did three things in the kitchen: she made red currant jelly late in the summer when the currants turned ripe, black currant biscuits for Christmas breakfast, and the stuffing for the Thanksgiving turkey, tearing bread into small pieces the day before and dropping them into the heavy glazed bowl with the dark brown bands while his mother prepared the pumpkin and the mincemeat pies and plucked the turkey and poured hot paraffin over it which congealed and was peeled off with the pinfeathers. Pinfeathers, Tommy thought, was another queer word.

His grandmother was tall and stood straight, and on the street she walked with a cane. One day, when his grandmother had taken him shopping, a friend of hers told Tommy, "Young man, I'd know you anywhere. You look just like your mother." Tommy did not want to look like his mother, who would sometimes put one of her hats on his head and say that he looked better in them than she did. A few minutes later, on the same street, another friend said, "Why, Barbara"—that was his grandmother's name—"anyone would know he's a MacAllister. He's the image of his father." Tommy sometimes examined his face closely in the mirror at home, his dark brown eyes peering back at his unruly hair, his cleft chin, ugly nose, and big ears, but he didn't see his father in it or his mother. He didn't think he looked like his brothers, either, but pretty much like himself. He certainly didn't think he looked, as his mother once told him, so pretty that he should have been a girl. That made Tommy's skin turn hot and prickly. "Look at his little legs," she told his grandmother, "they're pretty as a girl's."

"No, Emma, they're not," his grandmother said. "They're the legs of a fine, strong young man. He's a handsome boy." Tommy was grateful to his grandmother for that, and he allowed her—without complaining, though he hated it—to comb his hair with water, slicking it down flat, and send him off to school.

His grandmother had died just a few days after their trip to Chicago in the fall. She'd been in the hospital for a long time, and then she just died. Everyone said it was a blessing, although Tommy didn't understand why it was a blessing to be dead. She was very old, though, exactly seventy years older than Tommy, seven and seventy-seven, a lifetime apart. She and his father used to argue a lot about her pills; his father was always trying to make her take them and she was always refusing to swallow them.

"No, John," she used to say—John was not his father's name but his grandfather's—"I won't take your damned pills." His father didn't like that. When he spoke, he expected people to mind.

TOMMY's father didn't like women to swear, to wear pants or shorts, to dye their hair, or to contradict him. He especially didn't like to be contradicted, but people did once in a while. Mrs. Steer told him at a party on the Island, when his father was talking about John L. Lewis's union trying to organize the plant, that he had the politics of Louis Quatorze, and his brother David shouted, "Off with their heads," and Mrs. Steer whooped with laughter and clapped his father hard on the back, causing his drink to slop.

Mrs. Steer was the only Democrat Tommy knew except for Mr. Steer, who was a Democrat because Mrs. Steer was. She argued politics and told everyone that she'd voted for Roosevelt. His father said it wasn't anyone's damned business how a person voted and he would never tell, but everyone knew anyway. Mrs. Steer used to wear her son's overalls when she worked in her garden, and his father said she might as well be a farmer, she looked more like a man than a woman and as much like a horse as a man. And it was true, there was something horselike about Mrs. Steer, and Tommy laughed when he said that. But when Tommy said that Mrs. Appleton had a pink snout and looked like a pig, which she really did, his father didn't think it was funny. Tommy didn't see the difference, especially when Mrs. Appleton looked a lot more like a pig than Mrs. Steer did like a horse or a man. Mrs. Steer was as tall as his father and had a long nose. She was lanky, people said, and she loped. Tommy liked the way she walked; it was fast but it looked easy. "Saw Varla Steer cantering down the River Road today," his father said one evening. "If we put her in harness she'd be my odds-on choice."

Varla was an odd name, Tommy thought, but interesting, like something out of a book. It was Danish, like Mrs. Steer, who'd been named for an aunt who moved from Copenhagen to Oslo and died and left her a heavy gold bracelet with her name engraved in flowing script on the clasp. Mrs. Steer had a lot of things that came from Denmark where she'd been born: furniture, silver and china, little ornaments, old jewelry that fit in leather cases, and photographs of her mother and her aunts in silver and wooden frames. There was a photograph of her father, too, in a small leather case lined with faded brown velvet that opened and shut like a book. He was a smiling, handsome man, Tommy thought, with curly hair that was dark and thick. He looked as if he laughed a lot, and he looked very young, much younger than Mrs. Steer, more the age of Phil Meyer. Mrs. Steer's hair was white, and she didn't smile much. When she did, though, it was nice. The photographs of her mother and her father and her aunts in their wooden and silver frames were kept on Mrs. Steer's dressing table, along with a photograph of herself in an evening dress taken the Christmas before she was married. "To remind me," she told Tommy, although Tommy didn't know what it was supposed to remind her of. Except for her hair, which had turned white after Vint was born, when she was still in her twenties, she looked the same to Tommy as she looked in the photograph taken all those years before.

Mrs. Steer had moved from Copenhagen to Detroit when she was thirteen, but she could already speak English, and French and German, too. In Denmark they started learning languages when they were Tommy's age, and they went to school even on Saturday mornings. She had come with her mother. Tommy thought they were following her father, but he went back to Denmark or maybe to England where he had business, and Mrs. Steer's mother moved to New York when Mrs. Steer went to the university. New York was more like Copenhagen, Mrs. Steer said. It had an opera, and her mother could smoke the little cigars she liked. Women in Denmark smoked cigars; no one thought anything about it. When her mother died they didn't bury her but cremated her in a special furnace and Mrs. Steer kept the ashes somewhere in her house. He'd never heard of anything like that. It was spooky. Somewhere in the Steers' house was a box of ashes from a dead person. Tommy wondered where the box was kept, what it looked like, and what the ashes looked like, too, but of course he couldn't ask. Mrs. Steer hardly ever talked about her mother, and she never talked about her father. Tommy supposed he was something like his mother's father, who had gone out West when his mother was a girl and eventually died there. He had built the library in Grande Rivière, and on the wall above the card catalogue there was a plaque with his name on it. When Tommy discovered that, he felt quite proud, and his mother said that yes, his grandfather had built the library and a number of other buildings as well, and that he had gone West to build more. But like Mrs. Steer, Tommy's mother never talked about her father; Tommy always had to quiz her about him, and even then he didn't learn much.

Mrs. Steer kept a stack of books and magazines, some of them in French and German, on the table next to her chair. Tommy's mother could read German too, at least a little, but Mrs. Steer said it wasn't the same. Mrs. Steer was like that, and nobody did what Mrs. Steer did as well as she did it. She was very smart. His mother said she was a perfectionist. Tommy always thought that ought to be good but his mother said that was why Mrs. Steer had migraines. Mrs. Steer read a lot of the time and liked to solve problems in calculus. She had gone to college when she was only sixteen and gotten a Phi Beta Kappa key which she kept in a jewelry box. The only other person Tommy knew with a Phi Beta Kappa key was his Uncle Christian. He was his mother's brother, and he was different, too. Mrs. Steer did a lot of things that other women didn't do. She read a lot, of course, and sometimes talked to Tommy about what she was reading. No other grown-up talked to him about that. She argued with men and slapped them on the back. She had a deep voice that boomed at parties, though she didn't like parties. She smoked a lot of cigarettes, which she kept on the table next to her chair along with a silver porringer full of matches. They were kitchen matches and she struck them on the underside of the table, which was not an ordinary table but a large oval lithograph of George Washington under glass, in a polished walnut frame set on a luggage rack. Sometimes she scratched the match tip with her fingernail and it would burst into flame.

61

When she smoked, she would hold the cigarette between her second and third fingers or, when she was working, between her lips. The cigarettes stained her teeth as well as her fingers, and after she had had her teeth cleaned at the dentist's she would stop smoking for a few days. She said she never inhaled but just held the smoke in her mouth until she released it, sometimes in a sudden great puff, sometimes in a slow blue stream that she would suck in through her nose. Tommy loved to watch Mrs. Steer smoke, to see if the ash that grew slowly longer and longer would drop on her lap, on the book she was reading, on the floor, or in the ashtray, which was a thin silver leaf of a kind of tree that grew in Denmark. It was perfect in every detail, even to the veins and stem and toothy edge, and it looked as if it had been molded from a real leaf. Mrs. Steer had six of them, and they fit so snugly together you had to use your fingernail to separate them.

Mrs. Steer played golf better than his mother, better than Daisy Meyer even, better than any woman not only in town but in that part of the state, and she had silver trophies with her name on them to prove it. She played better than most of the men, in fact, and when she had beaten all the ladies at the country club she hardly ever played again. When she decided her house needed redecorating, she didn't call Mr. St. John but did almost all of it by herself, not with wallpaper, like most of the houses Tommy knew, but with paint that she herself mixed. The living room was covered with canvas drop cloths one whole winter, but when she finished it looked beautiful, and she never did it again. When she took up rughooking, she ordered special dyes from Boston and Philadelphia and dyed her own wool and drew her own patterns on the burlap and put her initials and the year in the corner. She baked bread every week, but in November and December it seemed as if she baked day and night, filling up coffee cans with an endless variety of cookies and cakes that could not be touched until Christmas Eve, when she would put on a long dress and give a big dinner, like Christmas Eve in Denmark. His parents didn't go; his mother had her own tree to decorate that night, which she did, sometimes with his brothers after Tommy had been put to bed, arranging the lights and hanging the balls and finally draping the tinsel from the branches. Tommy's mother saved the tinsel from year to year, and each year it became more wrinkled. Tommy hated tinsel and couldn't understand why his mother, who had forty pairs of shoes in her closet, refused to buy a new box of tinsel now and then. "It's good enough," she would say. "It's perfectly good." No one else thought so, though, and after the holidays had passed everyone helped with the lights and other ornaments, but she took the tinsel from the tree by herself.

Tommy thought the Steers' tree the most beautiful he'd ever seen. Many of the ornaments had come from Denmark with Mrs. Steer's furniture. There were brilliantly colored birds with tail feathers, little mushrooms with red caps and white dots, shells of nuts made into sailboats, and a tiny carousel that played music like the old burled box on a lamp table that he and Amy were never allowed to touch but that Mrs. Steer would sometimes play if asked. But what really thrilled him about Mrs. Steer's tree were the candles that she would light especially for him late on Christmas afternoon, making the whole room glow against the descending dark and snowy outdoors. She would play the music box then, and make hot chocolate for him and Amy and pour a glass of sherry for herself while Mr. Steer sat with his drink and told stories about his childhood or the war. He'd been wounded in France and come home with a metal plate in his skull and a leg that didn't work right, but he was a hero. He told how he and Mrs. Steer spent their honeymoon in his college fraternity house. Mrs. Steer said he had told her he was going into the foreign service, like his brother-in-law Mr. Aldrich, which was why she married him, but he didn't; he took over his father's insurance business instead. Once he had an office in the Shaw Building downtown but he gave it up because of the Depression and worked from a small room he made in a corner of the cellar. Mostly, though, he worked with wood. That was what he liked to do. He could whittle all sorts of things out of it. On the Island he made Tommy a heavy slingshot with thick elastic bands, a leather pad for the stone, and a handle you could really grip, almost like a tennis racquet's. Tommy was very proud of it. It was a real weapon. He could have killed

63

a squirrel with it, if his aim had been good enough. Mr. Steer also made him a whistle. He slipped the bark cleanly off a twig, handing Tommy the hollow tube. Then he poked the core out of the glistening white stick, cut a notch in it, sliced one end at an angle and plugged the other, and there was the whistle. Mr. Steer himself could whistle louder than anybody, just with his lips, and when he whistled for Amy—three quick notes followed by a swooping long one and another short—you could hear him from almost any place on the Island or on their street in town. Mr. Steer may not have walked very well, but he could do a lot of other things. Once he made Amy a playhouse that was big enough to stand in and had windows and a tiny but real stove. He had a lathe in his cellar, and Tommy liked it when Mr. Steer let him watch as he turned blocks of wood into the spools and spindles that piled up beneath his workbench. Tommy liked the smell and feel of fresh wood, and he liked to watch the chips flying from Mr. Steer's lathe. Tommy wanted to try the lathe himself but Mr. Steer said he was too young, and he kept his workroom locked when he wasn't there. Tommy liked Mr. Steer, but he was unpredictable and usually wanted to work alone.

One day Mrs. Steer told Tommy that Americans made a serious mistake, marrying for love. "In Denmark," she said, "marriages are arranged, and they work out better." Mrs. Steer hadn't gotten married in Denmark, though. She'd gotten married right in Grande Rivière.

"But Mother," Amy said, "how could you marry somebody you didn't love?"

"You learn," Mrs. Steer replied. "Or you don't. There are more important things in the world." Tommy and Amy looked at each other and rolled their eyes. Amy read movie magazines at her friend Ann Rodgers', had a movie-star coloring book, and thought a lot about love. Mrs. Steer was already embroidering linens for Amy's wedding. Tommy wondered if she would arrange it, the way they did in Denmark. Mrs. Steer was like that, strange but interesting. Tommy knew that Amy was sometimes embarrassed by her mother, and he supposed that if she were his mother, he'd be embarrassed too, at least sometimes. But she wasn't his mother, and he liked her a lot.

Mrs. Steer talked to Tommy very seriously about politics, about science, about the genius Albert Einstein whose theories you could only try to understand if you knew a lot of calculus, about her school days in Denmark and at the university, where she got in trouble for smoking, about many things, some of which he didn't really understand. She talked to him not as if she were instructing him but as if he were interested, which he was. And she listened to him, too, as if what he had to say interested her. Tommy very much liked his conversations with Mrs. Steer. She said what she thought, with less politeness than conviction, and what she thought was often startling. She thought Mr. Sedgwick was an idiot, for instance, and she said so, which was surprising in a grown-up. A rule in Tommy's house was that you never spoke critically, especially of an adult. It was a rule that applied mostly to Tommy, though certainly he never heard his parents call Mr. Sedgwick an idiot but he was sure they sometimes thought he was boring. Mrs. Steer thought Bob Griswold was a playboy, "and not a very bright one at that." She liked people who were bright, even if she didn't agree with them. She thought Dr. Rodgers was bright, but she often disagreed with him. Tommy didn't know if she thought Daisy Meyer was bright or not, but she thought Daisy was a good golfer. She was the only woman Mrs. Steer wanted to play golf with.

Tommy's mother remembered when Mr. and Mrs. Steer were engaged. Mrs. Steer was teaching math and French in the high school and she would force Mr. Steer to walk with her through the snow, and when he fell, because of his bad leg, Mrs. Steer would pull him up and then push him back in the snowbank, laughing. Then she would make him get up by himself and Tommy's mother said that was the only reason Mr. Steer was walking today. Tommy didn't see why being pushed in the snow made a person walk. Amy told him that her mother had done the same thing just recently, not in the snow but in her bedroom. She shoved Mr. Steer hard against the wall and he fell down, and she stormed out for a walk. Amy had to help him up. That worried her. It worried her a lot. But to Tommy everything seemed normal enough at the Steers' house, or as normal as it ever had been, since Mr. Steer worked at home and, except for Christmas and Easter, fixed all the meals and did the grocery shopping as well. He had to do the grocery shopping because he didn't let Mrs. Steer drive his car, although she knew how, and it was too expensive, he said, to call Mr. Lamontagne's market and have the groceries delivered.

Sometimes Mr. Steer called his wife the Great Dane. "Woof, woof," he would say, "anybody seen the Great Dane this morning?" when he could easily have looked out the window and seen her working in the garden, which was another thing Mrs. Steer did for a while and better than anybody else. Only Dr. and Mrs. Randolph came close, and they spent a lot of money on theirs and just grew roses. Mr. Steer said that to make Tommy laugh, and Tommy always did. He liked predictable events, just as he liked walking by Mrs. Steer's garden on his way to school. In the spring it was full of tulips and hyacinth and narcissus and daffodils, and later huge heavy peonies the color of cream, and blue delphinium and pale pink poppies that she raised from special seeds ordered from England. When she started the garden she had truckloads of manure brought in from the country, and the Steers' whole place, which was fairly large, smelled like a barnyard, and looked like one too, his father said. But the manure was dug into the earth—Mrs. Steer made Vint help her but she really did most of it herself, starting every morning at dawn and working until dark—and when the seeds were planted and the garden began to grow and blossom and the strong colors were weeded out, sweet fragrances drove the barnyard smell away, the honeybees and the hummingbirds came, and the garden began to glow like one of her own rugs, but on a huge scale. In the meantime, Tommy's mother's garden continued to grow in its desultory way with the occasional assistance of Jim the Indian and a comment now and then from his mother or, before she got sick, his grandmother, who of course never wore pants or shorts and didn't dye her hair, either, although she would say "damn" now and then.

"WHAT do you think of that?" Tommy's grandmother would ask herself, and reply, "I think damn!" Tommy would

66

laugh. He didn't know what she was talking about, but he certainly liked her answer. A while before she died she began calling his father "John," and she would call Tommy "James," which was his father's real name although most people called him "Mac." "James," she would cry, rushing onto the porch, thinking the boy she'd spotted on the street was Tommy, "get off that bicycle this minute. You'll be killed. Damn those bicycles," she would mutter under her breath. Tommy was, in fact, standing right behind her, giggling. "I'm right here, Grandma, and my name isn't James, it's Tommy." His grandmother's hands would flutter vaguely in the empty air, touching at her hair and dress, and she would return to the cool of the house, shaking her head, looking distracted, and dropping a hairpin here and there, which Tommy would pick up and hand to her. He liked his grandmother, but she had become a puzzle to him.

The house was filled with people when she died. His Aunt Martha—she was Tommy's father's sister—had come from Minneapolis with his Uncle Charles, their three children, and a girl who took care of them. That was when Tommy fell in love with his cousin Charlotte who was five years older and very beautiful. Everyone said she looked like his grandmother. Tommy told his mother that when he grew up he wanted to marry Charlotte, but his mother had said that would be impossible. "Cousins don't marry each other," she explained, although Tommy knew that Mr. and Mrs. Sedgwick were cousins and they were married, too. But he wasn't supposed to talk about that, and besides, they weren't close cousins. Oh, there were so many things he couldn't do! He couldn't marry his cousin, he couldn't eat with his elbows on the table, he couldn't stay up after eight o'clock on school nights or eight-thirty in the summer—it was still light then, when he was sent to bed—he couldn't eat standing up, he couldn't drink milk from the bottle even if his brother David did, and he couldn't go to his grandmother's funeral because children didn't belong at funerals, although his cousins—Steve was even younger than Tommy—all went. Tommy wasn't to be allowed to go to the funeral home either, but he coaxed so— he wanted very much to be like his cousins, with the same grown-up privileges—that his father finally relented and took him up the morning of the funeral when no one would be there. The room was long and filled with banks and banks of flowers which gave the unnaturally cool air a thick, sweet scent. Tommy's grandmother lay in a long coffin covered with so many roses that they all but concealed its polished wood. The top half of the lid was raised to reveal his grandmother, lying on pale silk, in a lavender dress and the pearls she always wore, the pearls his grandfather had given her when Tommy's father was born, her hands clasped stiffly around a blood-red rose. Tommy stared at her, shocked by her utter stillness, and wondered what he was supposed to feel. What he did feel, for a brief moment, was a lump in his throat, and then curiosity. So this was what a dead person looked like, almost like a live person but very still and very silent. Tommy looked up toward her face, at the faint fixed smile on her pink lips, the rouged cheekbones—would his father think there was too much?— and the nostrils like two black cavities leading to the brain. Her hair was neatly done, but there were no bone or tortoise hairpins in it. Somewhere below the waist, beneath the bottom half of the lid, she vanished into the silk of the coffin, and Tommy wondered if she was wearing the black shoes that laced, the kind she always wore. He wanted to touch her hand or her face. He wondered what a dead person felt like. For a second tears came to Tommy's eyes, but only for a second. He knew it would be right to cry—he had heard how his cousins had sobbed and had to be taken home by the girl; they had told him—and he wondered what was the matter with him that he couldn't cry and didn't even feel like it. He composed his face into a somber, serious look that he thought would be appropriate to the occasion, but he was, really, curious. He had never seen a dead person and he wanted it to register on him. It was part of growing up, visiting the funeral home, looking at bodies, and he did want to be grown up and free of the burden of childhood. So he stood there looking respectful, his hands clasped behind him, head slightly bowed, until his father touched his shoulder and said they must leave now.

On their way out, the undertaker told his father that he hoped he was pleased, it was such a beautiful casket and he hadn't seen so many flowers since Dr. Edwards died. His father asked the undertaker to remove the pearls before the funeral, and in the car he told Tommy that he'd behaved very well. Tommy didn't know what to say so he didn't say anything, and they drove home in silence. Later Tommy's father told his mother that he'd been very brave and had behaved in a much more grown-up way than his cousins. When Tommy heard this he was uncomfortable because he felt that his cousins had cried because they had to whereas he had not because he could not, though he wished he could. He could never force his tears; either they came or they didn't, and sometimes they came for reasons Tommy did not grasp. He was rarely disturbed by the presence of his feelings, no matter how bad, but he was sometimes bothered by their absence. And sometimes he didn't know what his feelings were supposed to be, or what they actually were.

Two

For a long time traces of his grandmother's powdery smell lingered in her bedroom, in her closet even after the clothes had been sorted out and given away, in the dresser scarves, in the lampshade of pale rose silk—the color of her underwear, Tommy always thought, and the thought made him giggle—in those jars and pots and boxes of ivory and tortoise on her dressing table. The warm and yeasty scent seemed locked into the very wallpaper and the plaster and lath behind it. It had a life of its own, independent of his grandmother's whose life was over. Tommy thought about that, about what it meant, "over." Her life was over. It was a blessing. He thought of her lying now in her lavender dress on the pale silk of her coffin, alone in the darkness of the earth, the rose grasped in her hand. He thought of the soft skin stretched over her cheekbones, and he imagined her eyes behind their closed lids, fixed and straining toward the surface, her face expressionless, her body still, waiting for what he did not know. He thought of the whole vast population of the dead, of all those bodies lying amidst the roots of the trees in the cemetery by the river, composed, quiet, facing the earth above them and the earth the sky, separated from one another by the limitless, embracing soil and from the crushing weight of the world itself by their solitary wooden cases lined with silk. How lonely it seemed, what flimsy protection. He wondered if his grandmother's good smell was warming the winter earth, and if she knew when the sun was shining, when the snow falling, and when the grass would grow again.

If no one was upstairs, Tommy would sometimes slip into his grandmother's room—his mother didn't like it if she found him there—to look at her orange sticks and nail buffers and hairpins, to graze with his fingers the dishes on her dressing table. Sometimes he would climb onto her bed and lie on the quilt that covered it, pressing the pillow to his nose, gazing at the figure of the old-fashioned lady in a long dress languidly posed on a bench in an imaginary garden, the scene framed in a garland of golden roses on the deep red porcelain lamp the color of his grandmother's china, which his mother was even then rearranging in the cupboards below. He looked at the rose-colored lampshade and thought of her underwear still neatly folded in one of the drawers of her chiffonier and of the little ribboned sacks of fragrance that she tucked among her garments.

His mother, when she found him in his grandmother's room one afternoon, told him that it was morbid to lie there day-dreaming and he must not be morbid. "We bury the dead," his mother said, giving him a brisk pat and hurrying him out of the room, "and then we get on with it. We don't hang the crape in this house," she said, moving him downstairs and toward the closet. "Grief is something we carry inside us—here, get into your snowsuit—it's not polite to inflict it on others. Now go play outdoors. You don't see your father walking around with a long face, do you? He has to work. And you have to go outside for a while. You spend too much time in the house. That's why you're looking peaked." She gave him a hug, kissed him at the door, and closed it behind him.

True, Tommy's father did not go around with a long face—though sometimes, Tommy thought, his mother looked sad, but only for a moment. Then she got on with it. Tommy's father rarely even mentioned his grandmother, nor did anyone else. She was gone, and life went on. Sometimes they talked about her lawyer and who was getting what of the things she'd had. Tommy knew that he and his brothers were getting something but, except that John was getting her diamond ring because he was the oldest of all her grandchildren, he didn't know what and he wasn't supposed to know, either. He didn't believe that was grief, nor did he think that what he was doing in his grandmother's bedroom had anything to do with grief. He was just lying there on her bed, smelling her pillow, looking at the figure on her lamp, and thinking about her in the cemetery, although he was supposed to think of her among the angels in heaven. Protestants went to heaven. Grief was something else. Grief was when Paul Malotte's father was bitten by a rabbit and died, and the undertaker hung black ribbons on their door. The Malottes cried all the time and prayed for Mr. Malotte who was suffering in purgatory, and Paul couldn't come out to play marbles and all his crying made his continually leaking nose flow all the more copiously. That was grief, and Tommy didn't know anything about it. Tommy was more fortunate than Paul Malotte. Maybe the Malottes were crying because they'd been poor before but now they were really poor. They didn't even have a refrigerator, but an old-fashioned icebox that held cakes of ice delivered in a horse-drawn wagon, like the milk and cream and butter and eggs that were delivered to Tommy's door by Mr. Matson, who also delivered milk to Mrs. Farnsworth and, very early one morning not long before Tommy's grandmother died, found her dead in her bed. Frances always heard the bottles rattling and came to the door, Mr. Matson explained, but she didn't come that morning so he went in and found her. "It was still dark, Mrs. MacAllister," he said as he was collecting for the milk at Tommy's house. "It gave me a terrible shock, seeing her like that. It'll be a long time before I get over that one. She was quite a lady." "Yes," his mother replied, "it's a shame."

"Well, everyone knows her door was never locked," Tommy's father told his mother later in that noncommittal way he sometimes had of speaking, as if he might be making a joke but you were never certain that it was a joke so you didn't know if you ought to smile or simply nod in agreement. Everybody knew that nobody in town locked their doors when they were home anyway, so Tommy didn't see what was strange about Mrs. Farnsworth's being unlocked.

Once Tommy's father asked his mother, "Did you hear what happened to the woman who wore bloomers?" "No," his mother replied cautiously, "what?" "Nothing," his father said. Then, when his mother looked blank, his father said, "Oh, I forgot—you're English," as if that explained something, and he would shake his head and chuckle to himself. Tommy thought that was a pretty funny joke, although he couldn't say why except that bloomers were just funny, and he told the story to his brothers, who would get him to repeat it to their friends. "What happened to the woman who wore bloomers, Tommy?" they would ask, setting him up, and Tommy would try to imitate his father's flat tone: "Nothing." His brothers and their friends would laugh uproariously. Tommy didn't think the joke was *that* funny, but he liked the response it drew and he didn't have to be coaxed to tell it.

Nobody cried when Mrs. Farnsworth died. They just talked about her and the milkman, and how she certainly drank a lot of milk. "If Mrs. Matson drank that much milk she might not be in a wheelchair," Tommy's father said. Mrs. Matson was an invalid, and the Matsons had no children. She sometimes made curtains for Tommy's mother, which Mr. Matson would deliver and hang. Their farm out the River Road was near one that Tommy's father had wanted to buy earlier that year when he had an urge to leave the Island and his mother's house and live on a farm. He thought it would be healthier for them all, and that it would give Tommy's mother a new interest. Although Tommy liked the bleeding hearts that grew in rampant profusion in front of the empty, spooky-looking house, the bleeding hearts and the kerosene lamps were the only things he did like about it. He did not like the way the water tasted when it came out of the pump, although he liked to work the pump itself. Most especially he did not like the cold and smelly outhouse full of spiders. His mother told him, though, that if they ever moved there—and she doubted they ever would—they'd have running water and indoor bathrooms, and they wouldn't use kerosene lamps. Tommy was sorry about the kerosene lamps, but not the loss of the outhouse. He didn't know which he dreaded more, going to a one-room schoolhouse in the country with the farmers' children, or taking the school bus each morning into town. The farm boys who did come to school in town all smelled peculiar,

76

a combination of wet wool and spilled milk and horse manure, and they wore boots all winter long, indoors and out, and they were rough. His teacher, Miss Case, said they never changed their socks, and she would send them home with notes to their parents, telling them to please see that the boys had clean socks. The girls were dumb.

His mother told him not to worry. If they did get the farm, it would be a long time before they moved there, and even if they did he wouldn't have to take the school bus every morning, although he would have to carry his lunch. And he wouldn't have to wear boots, either, but could wear his regular shoes, and of course he'd have clean socks every day. Nonetheless, Tommy was relieved when his father got over that notion and they returned to the Island for the summer as usual and he started second grade from his house in town. So was his mother. She never wanted to be a farmer's wife, she said. "It keeps Mrs. Matson at home," his father said, and his mother replied, "Yes, in a wheelchair. Do you want me in a wheelchair, sewing curtains?" Well of course no one wanted his mother in a wheelchair. What a terrible thought, to be like Mrs. Matson, or Mrs. Henderson, who didn't even have any legs. He'd rather his mother were like Mrs. Farnsworth than like that. Tommy always liked Mrs. Farnsworth. She had a wonderful cottage on the Island, and in town she lived in a dark old house on Elm Street, full of heavy furniture and lamps with fringed shades. She burned the lights day and night, as if she instead of Mr. Sedgwick owned the Edison. She was always nice to Tommy when he came there with his brothers, who were friends with her son Nick. Nick was a year older than David and a year younger than John. Mrs. Farnsworth was sometimes Mrs. Kingsfield, and Nick now called himself Nick Kingsfield, although he had been Nick Farnsworth. Nick's father was Mr. Kingsfield, but Tommy had never seen him. He had moved away many years before. Mrs. Farnsworth's parents were Farnsworths too, and they had lived in the same big house until they died, also a very long time ago.

Sometimes it seemed to Tommy as if everything had happened a long time ago, and that his world was peopled with

77

as many shades of the dead or the missing as with the living. Mrs. Steer's lithograph of George Washington had come from the Farnsworth house when Mrs. Farnsworth was selling some of her things, as she did every once in a while because she needed extra money and couldn't touch Nick's. She couldn't break her father's will. She couldn't even get Nick's allowance raised. "Fortunately for Nick," Tommy's father said. Nick's money came from old Mr. Farnsworth, who had made a fortune in Calumet & Hecla before it collapsed. So did Mrs. Farnsworth's, but she'd spent hers, a lot of it on Mr. Kingsfield, who according to Mrs. Steer was a fortune hunter from Brooklyn, but charming. When Tommy asked his mother why Mrs. Farnsworth wasn't Mrs. Kingsfield, she told him that Frances liked her father's name. "It was a fine old name," she said. The name business was completely mystifying to Tommy but he liked Mrs. Farnsworth anyway. She reminded him of Mrs. Slade because she smoked, too, and also called the milkman by his first name, which was Andy. Mr. Matson called her Frances, and he called Mrs. Slade Max. In Tommy's family the milkman was always Mr. Matson, although Tommy, when he saw him at the Slades', called him Andy too. He wouldn't hear of Tommy's calling him Mr. Matson then.

Nick had gone to military school and Tommy's mother said he had beautiful manners. Tommy liked Nick, and so did his parents. Nick had a hard life, his father said, although until his mother died Tommy didn't see what was so hard about it. It wasn't as if they were poor like the Malottes, and he didn't think his parents felt sorry for them. They never said the Malottes had a hard life, though it seemed to Tommy that they did. They even had to raise their own vegetables, and until Mr. Malotte died they kept rabbits to eat. Probably they should have had the farm, Tommy thought; then they could have kept cows, too, and Paul could have milked them.

Nick always called Tommy's father "sir," and he would say "Yes, ma'am" to his mother. Tommy thought that calling his mother "ma'am" was fairly strange—the word made him squirm—but she liked it. Tommy himself couldn't get the word out of his mouth, and "sir" wasn't much easier.

•   •

78

NICK Farnsworth came to Tommy's house that Thanksgiving, and he said "No, sir" and "Yes, sir" to the older men, and "No, ma'am" and "Yes, ma'am" to the older women, and especially to his father's Canadian cousins, Maud and Gertrude, who were spinster daughters of his father's great-aunt. Tommy had to greet them as Cousin Maud and Cousin Gertrude, and dutifully kiss their papery cheeks, avoiding if possible Cousin Maud's mole that sprouted long hairs. He didn't like the kissing, and their brooches scratched. He wasn't sure they liked it either. His mother called the sisters Tommy's kissing cousins. He had difficulty thinking of them as cousins at all, because they were so old, older even than his grandmother whose cousins they had also been. The kissing was more difficult, because they couldn't bend very easily and Tommy couldn't stretch very far, and he was transfixed by Maud's mole that he had to concentrate to avoid. They didn't smell nearly so good as his grandmother, and kissing her had always made Tommy a little uncomfortable, too. Cousin Gertrude was practically deaf, and wore a big black hearing aid around her neck with wires connected to the plugs in her ears. The sisters looked formidable, like craggy fortresses with great unyielding fronts, as if they were all stony bosom from their shoulders to their thighs. They could have possessed neither breast nor bum; it was hard to imagine them with thighs. If Tommy squinted so that he couldn't see their feet or their heads, they looked the same front and back, solid and impregnable from either direction. Tommy never saw them without their hats or their canes, and their hats, like the sisters themselves, were striking and almost identical, like great predatory birds—feathered wings flapping at the air, claws embedded in their skulls—who in a demented moment had seized on these two old ladies in their long dresses and their canes and were hanging on for dear life. Except they were dead, like the ancient animals they wore around their necks, spineless furry creatures with tiny flapping feet, beaded eyes, and narrow muzzles that snapped shut on their own tails.

Sometimes, but especially in the fall, it seemed to Tommy that he came from a very bloody race: old ladies encased in dry skins and topped by stuffed birds, drawing their dusty, lifeless smell from ancient animal corpses; slaughtered creatures served at the table and glistening with pink juices; even their plates were garlanded with heaps of dead game, the tureen and serving dishes—relics of his mother's mother's family—with the heads of living animals whose mild eyes stared at him from beneath the glaze. Tommy imagined his father—he wasn't old enough to go hunting from the camp so he could only imagine it—tracking the deer through the dark forest, following the spoor, finger loosely clasping the trigger of the rifle he had carefully cleaned and oiled until it gleamed, waiting to fell and gut the animal that this Thanksgiving Day was hanging by its heels, belly slit and ribs wrenched open, from a rafter in the garage behind the house, awaiting the knives of the butcher. The rifle itself, with its steely blue barrel and burnished stock, was the same kind of lever-action Winchester the cowboys had used to shoot buffalo and Indians on the prairie. His father had told him that as he let him run his hands along its wooden stock and feel his own small finger on the cold trigger. Tommy thought of tramping silently with his father and mother through the dappled woods and sunlit hills that smelled of autumn, flushing the ruffed grouse from its cover which his father would then bring to earth with his 12-gauge shotgun, a much-admired piece with pump action that his own father had bought from V.L.&A. in Chicago and that had a kick, they said, as mean as a mule's. His father held the gun tight against his shoulder when he fired so that his body absorbed the recoil; otherwise it might have broken his shoulder, which was why Tommy couldn't fire it: he wasn't strong enough yet. Once he was allowed to fire his mother's .410, though. His ears rang and his shoulder hurt all day, and it was decided that he'd better grow another year or two before trying it again. His father could gut and strip the still warm bird without a knife, piercing its throat with his thumbnail and quickly peeling off the feathered skin all in a piece. It might have been a piece of fruit. When the job was done, the once magnificent bird looked very puny, as if all its flashing life were contained in its plumage. The birds, too—not the grouse but duck and geese—were hung in the garage to draw, and the remembered sweetness of blood and oily feathered

wetness at this moment filled Tommy's nostrils, driving out
the warm smell of the roasting turkey that suffused the room
and the entire big house.

EARLIER that fall, in the black morning before dawn,
Tommy had been taken from his bed to accompany his father
and three of his friends to the blind they had rented from a
farmer whose frozen, furrowed fields lay below the flyway of
the ducks and geese coming down from Canada. Tommy
stumbled across the fields in the semidarkness, trying to avoid
the frozen cowpies and still keep up to the men, to the blind
that looked on the outside like an ordinary haystack. He
crawled through the small entryway, after Mr. Sedgwick and
Mr. Hutchins and Mr. Steer and followed by his father, and
he huddled there in silence, wrapped in his mackinaw, envel-
oped in tobacco smoke and the cold damp smell of earth and
wool, watching the sky lighten to gray, the stars dim and
extinguish, waiting for the geese to resume their southern
flight—like the Sedgwicks who usually went to La Jolla early
in the New Year when winter had settled in with all its force.
Tommy peered through the opening at the opaque slate skies,
straining to catch sight of the birds which, if the hunters were
lucky, might drop down to feed and thus be blasted from
the sky. This was supposed to be fun, but Tommy didn't see
anything fun about it. It was cold and wet and gloomy. If he
moved, his father's hand would stay him; if he spoke, he was
hushed. Nobody could say a word or even move quickly for
fear it would alarm the birds, who knew the sound of human
voices meant trouble. The waiting was interminable. If this
was a man's world, Tommy thought he'd just as soon remain
a boy.

Suddenly the geese appeared. It was thrilling to see them
flying in their majestic V straight across the sky. There was
something grand about it, awesome, stately, and magnificent.
The sight gave Tommy goose bumps, which made him smile.
So this was what they meant by goose bumps. Then, honking
as if they had the croup—which his mother had said he'd
surely get if his father took him out at that hour, in this
weather—they circled above the grainfield and dropped down,

great wings flapping, to feed on the stubble. Tommy could sense a change in the men's breathing. It became shorter, quicker. He listened to the geese moving through the stubble, sporadically clucking, gabbling, now and then a muted honk as if they were talking to one another about the quality of the meal, the state of the weather, their plans for the day's flight, the length of the journey. It seemed an amiable domestic conversation, like one at his own dinner table when there was company. One of the geese stood apart, not eating but guarding the pack, his head bobbing back and forth, first in one direction, then another until all the points of the compass had been covered and covered again. When he faced the blind he seemed to peer into Tommy's very eyes and Tommy was sure that he'd been seen, but the goose gave no sign of it. For a moment the men relaxed a little—half smiling, half awed— as if they wished to capture and preserve this numinous domestic scene so ordinary and so ineffable. The moment was brief. A current ran through the blind—their very heartbeats seemed suspended—and suddenly, as if by some prearranged signal, the men stood as one, the guard gave a wild honk of alarm, the geese lumbered to the air, and the guns exploded in a shattering, thunderous roar. The birds seemed suspended for a moment in the liquid air before they dropped slowly from the sky, feathers floating after them. Smoke curled from the guns. The fumes of spent cartridges filled the air, and the men began to shout and clap one another on the back and laugh and talk at once.

"Great shot!"

"What a sight!"

"How many did we drop?"

"That deserves a little drink!" Mr. Hutchins pulled out a flask of whisky and passed it among the men. "How about you, Tommy?" he asked. "A little nip to warm you up? It'll put hair on your chest."

Everyone was very friendly, and Tommy's father, surprisingly, allowed him to drink from the flask. "Careful, now," he said, his arm on Tommy's shoulder as Tommy tipped the flask to his mouth, "this is strong stuff." The whisky burned like fire in Tommy's throat. He had never tasted whisky before. He gasped and choked and his eyes watered, but he swallowed it. The men all laughed and patted him on the back. "That'll make a man of you, Tommy," Mr. Hutchins said. Then they all went out to the field to pick up the dead and dying birds. There were a lot of them; only a few had escaped. The men drank a little more whisky, lit their cigars, and they were home by nightfall, the geese hanging limp in the garage.

That night Tommy thought it would be good to be rocked in the big old rocker in his mother's bedroom as his mother used to do when he was little, singing *"Bye baby bunting, Daddy's gone a-hunting, gone to get a rabbit skin to wrap my baby bunting in."* He could hear the sweet thin tune now. But he was going to put away the tattered blanket he loved, with its cool satin binding frayed beyond repair, and he was too old for lullabies and rocking. The next morning, as his mother had predicted, Tommy had the croup.

WELL, it was all a bloody business, right down to the rabbit skin that his father had never actually gone to get, and the golden pheasant feathers on his mother's new hat, and the shoes Mrs. Sedgwick was wearing now that matched her handbag and were made from the hide of an alligator. Tommy's family had a dog that his father had wanted to train to go after birds, but once on the Island she caught a duck on her own and tore it to pieces, chewing it up feathers and all in the hideaway she had hollowed out behind the woodshed. She even snarled at Tommy's father when he tried to snatch the bird from her jaws, but otherwise she was a gentle dog. Tommy's father was disgusted and said she was ruined for hunting. Once a dog had tasted blood she'd be certain to devour the bird instead of retrieving it. His father was disappointed in her and gave her over to his mother, who kept threatening to get rid of her but so far she hadn't. She insisted that it was his father's dog, though everyone knew the dog's true loyalty was to Tommy's mother. His father wanted everything to be perfect according to his plan, and when he was disappointed in something, he seemed to feel personally affronted and never even looked at it, as if it had ceased to exist in his mind, which was where it counted. Tommy had seen this happen many times.

When the Bargers' dog died, Mrs. Barger had had him

stuffed, like the antlered head of the magnificent bull moose that glared balefully down from the mantel above the stone fireplace on the Island. Of course, everyone said that Mrs. Barger was odd. Pets were supposed to be buried; prey was stuffed if you didn't eat it, and the walls of the house on the Island were studded with the dusty heads of buck, the slender hornless heads of doe. They even hung their coats on a rack of antlers beside the door, and at the Sedgwicks' the severed foot of a deer was nailed to the back of each bedroom door. You were supposed to hang your pajamas on it. The Sedgwicks had a bearskin rug, too, stretched out before the fireplace. If you stepped on the dusty bearskin—something Tommy always tried to avoid—its nails clattered dully on the wooden floor. Mr. Sedgwick liked to point out the bullet hole over the spot where its heart had been. He had shot the bear someplace, a long time ago, and it looked as if it had been a long time ago. The bear's head was like a rock, its nose dry and rubbery, and its mouth was opened in a perpetual fierce snarl. You could see its teeth and its hard pink tongue, the color of Mr. Sedgwick's plate—that's what he called his false teeth, which he often had to fumble with behind a napkin at dinner while everyone pretended not to notice.

Mr. Sedgwick's men at the Edison had laid the cable that brought electricity and telephones to the Island from the shore. It was always called the Island though it was not one island but a cluster of them, separated by narrow, swiftly flowing channels and connected by small rustic bridges that the winter's ice damaged almost every year. The Indians had to repair them each spring so that the islanders could get from one to another without using a boat. The bridges were strung with tiny colored lights that at night twinkled like jewels on the black flowing water, their colors playing and fusing in the current. Each of the islands had a name, too, Indian names, but nobody ever used them. One of them was called Fire Island because in the very old days, before they built the lighthouse, sailors used to burn fires on the beach at a spot still called the Sailors' Encampment to warn ships approaching in the darkness of the dangerous bend in the river; and another was unofficially named Boomer Island, for Amy Steer's pet rabbit that was its sole inhabitant until he was put away after Mr. Malotte died. Sometimes they had picnics there. The entire length of the big river was dotted with islands—Duck, Summer, Pleasure, Iroquois, Sugar, St. Joseph's, Ste. Anne's, Beaver, Lime, Drummond, Big Whitehead, Little Whitehead, Squirrel—and there were hundreds more in Georgian Bay. But regardless of what the river charts called them, to Tommy and his family and their friends their small wooded cluster across from the country club was known simply as the Island, and if you said you were going to the Island for the summer, everyone knew what you meant, even if the Island was really six or seven. The islanders lived on only three of them. Boomer Island, the smallest, was for picnics and berries and wild flowers, and Fire Island, which was the farthest and the biggest, was for picnics and swimming because it had a beach. Nobody ever went to the others; there were no bridges. The cottages were mostly rambling, shingled affairs, gabled, dormered, and turreted, with screened porches and wooden walls on the inside and big stone fireplaces. Each cottage was different, yet one seemed much like another. The Aldrich cottage, where the McGhees always stayed, was one of Tommy's two favorites; it was a big log cabin—the only log cabin on the Island—with a Dutch door. The Farnsworth cottage, his other favorite, was a shingled house weathered to a silver sheen with blue trim and a round room in a high turret that Mrs. Farnsworth sometimes used to take him up to. You could see way up the river from that room. Mr. Wolfe's cottage was interesting because it was full of strange objects he'd picked up in his travels. His work took him to many dangerous places, and he came and went a lot. Sometimes he wasn't there very much at all, but last summer, the summer after Tommy's parents decided not to buy the farm, he'd been there the whole time. Mr. Wolfe spoke Spanish, too, and he knew a little Indian, though not the Indian that Rose's mother spoke. The Wentworth cottage was the biggest, and years ago an Indian had finished the huge living room and the balcony that overlooked it with burlap panels and split birch saplings—like the country club but fancier. The burlap had once been painted red and decorated with rope scrollwork in Indian designs, but the paint was faded now and the rope fell apart if you touched it. It was supposed to be very grand, but it smelled musty and damp and always seemed cold, even on the warmest summer day. Tommy's own cottage was smaller than Mrs. Wentworth's. His mother called it the little shingled cottage by the sea, even though the water was fresh and the ocean was hundreds of miles downstream. Tommy's bedroom was downstairs and faced the woods. He liked listening to the sounds in the woods late at night when the Island was asleep. The Sedgwicks had an island to themselves. Except for Boomer, it was the smallest and contained only their three cottages—the big house with the bearskin rug and a lot of pottery from Guatemala, which Mrs. Sedgwick had visited when the Aldriches were there in the Foreign Service, a smaller house that Mrs. Sedgwick's mother lived in, and a two-room guesthouse with a Franklin stove that was built out over the water so that if you spent the night there you could hear the waves lapping beneath it and you felt as if you were sleeping on a boat. Tommy loved to spend the night in the Sedgwicks' guesthouse, listening to the sounds of the water and the transparent, silvery voices that floated so eerily over it, in patches, on calm summer nights.

Old Judge Aldrich, who had bought the islands from the government many, many years before and then arranged for his friends—most of them the parents of the present occupants —to build their summer houses on them, had written a book about the place. The book was mainly about the early Indians who camped there in the summer for the fishing. Each cottage had a copy of the leather-bound volume with engravings of tepees, of the Indians spearing fish in the shallow channels and drying them on sticks over their fires, of the signal fires burning at the Encampment, and photographs of some of the cottages under construction and of the first summer residents, and of the Logans' and the Fishers' yachts. The Logans were very rich and famous friends of Judge Aldrich, and the Fishers were friends of the Logans. They came from Cleveland. In the old days they used to stop their boats at the Island on their way to their camp far up Lake Superior. They had to drop anchor in the South Channel, between the Island and the shore, where one year the Logans' boat ran aground and they stayed for a week. That's how long it took to free it. The whole town went down to the shore to see the yachts, which were very big and white, like passenger ships. On the wall of Tommy's cottage there was a faded photograph of his father, Mr. Aldrich, and Mr. Steer as boys, swimming from the Logans' yacht before it sank one year in Lake Superior. Tommy's grandmother used to tell the story of how the Logans and the Fishers had sailed out from their camp on an excursion, and while they were ashore with their picnic, the boat went down. "You know the Logans," she would say, although no one did know them anymore, "they do hate to lose a yacht."

They were all dead now. Judge Aldrich himself was buried on the Island, which also contained an ancient Indian cemetery with little wooden shelters built over the graves, the houses of the dead. Indians still lived on the Island, too, in the summer, and sometimes they put bunches of wild flowers on the Indian graves and nailed the little shelters back together when they fell apart. The Indians lived in a couple of remote houses that had been set aside for them on the other side of the island the Steers and Mrs. Addington lived on. The children weren't supposed to go there. The Indians didn't spear fish anymore but dangled a hook and line from one of the bridges or docks. Sometimes, at night, they would go out in a rowboat with a flashlight, but that was called "shining," and it made Tommy's father and the other men very angry when they caught them. It was not sportsmanlike. The Indians spent most of their time keeping the houses in repair, the pumps working, the cottages cleaned, and the paths through the woods clear. One or two of them would work at the start of one of the parties on the Island, but they usually left early in the evening. Sometimes, though not always, they would show up the next day to put things back in order. That was the way the Indians were. Sometimes they showed up for work and sometimes they didn't, and everyone complained about that but there wasn't anything anyone could do about it, not even Mrs. Sedgwick, who would go over and rap on Ruth's door, insisting that she come to work. But Ruth wasn't there, the Indians said. Mrs. Sedgwick never believed them, and she would accuse Ruth, when she did show up, of hiding from her. "Are you afraid of me, Ruth?" They all laughed about that, about Mrs. Sedgwick's boldness—even Mrs. Sedgwick—but Tommy didn't think Ruth was afraid of Mrs. Sedgwick; she just had other things she wanted to do.

To the islanders, the islands were all one—just the Island —and they were really one big family, though not always a happy one. Mrs. Sedgwick and Mr. Steer would have terrible political arguments when everyone gathered at half past five, even the children until they were sent to bed, often at the house where they were. Mrs. Sedgwick and Mr. Steer argued about Spain, about President Roosevelt, about the colored people although they agreed about the Indians, the only thing, it seemed, they did agree about. They even argued about the Duke and Duchess of Windsor, whom Mrs. Sedgwick insisted on calling Mrs. Simpson. Mrs. Simpson was common, she said. Though Mrs. Sedgwick was an American, she believed the British monarchy was the best form of government, that it gave the people something enduring to respect, and that Edward had betrayed his duty to the Crown for a common tart. That's what she said. Tommy supposed that if the United States had a king and queen, Mrs. Sedgwick would probably be a duchess, and he thought she supposed so, too. The Duchess of Sedgwick. It had a nice authentic ring. Mr. Steer, though, hated the Royal Family and said they should have thrown the rest of them out with the Duke and given the jewels to the people. Mrs. Sedgwick said he was a Bolshevik. "I'm a Bolshevik and you're the Queen of Roumania," Mr. Steer shouted, lurching on his cane and trying to plant it in the ground for support. Mrs. Sedgwick flushed and threw her arms up in exasperation, rings flashing, the long silken fringe of her shawl rippling around her.

"Dick," she said in her high, musical voice, trying to appear calm, "why must you be so contentious? It's a lovely evening and all the ladies look so pretty." Mrs. Sedgwick always looked like raspberry or lemon sherbet, Tommy thought, or like peaches and blueberries, in one of the flowing, flowered dresses made of batiste by a seamstress in the Bahamas, which she'd visited one winter. And Mrs. Sedgwick would float off like the Queen of Roumania, her laughter tinkling in the cool night air, leaving Mr. Steer sputtering and leaning on his cane. But Tommy knew she was really mad. Royalty was a sore point with her. Amy Steer was embarrassed.

The repercussions from these arguments would sometimes last for days; they were always talked about the next morning, but in whispers so the children shouldn't hear. Mr. Steer had had too much to drink, of course. "Dick's not a radical," Tommy's father often said; "he's just irascible."

It seemed to Tommy that Mrs. Sedgwick liked her drinks, too. When his father asked if he could freshen hers up, she would laugh in her silvery way and say, "Oh, maybe half a one, Mac," but she had a lot of halves. In that way she was something like his mother, who always said she didn't really like the taste of whisky but drank it to be sociable, though she refused to drink Mr. Sedgwick's martinis anymore. He had a special technique for making them, swirling the vermouth with a great flourish from glass to glass, then filling each one with gin—he always brought his own and kept it on ice—and dropping in two olives at the end. The martinis made his mother sick, though that was supposed to be a secret, which was why she no longer drank them. Tommy knew they made her sick because once last summer when his father was away for a few days and everyone had gathered at Mr. Wolfe's, his mother was drinking Mr. Sedgwick's martinis and felt faint and left the room. Tommy found her sitting on Mr. Wolfe's back steps with Mrs. Sedgwick fanning her and Mr. Wolfe holding a washcloth to her forehead. "It's the vermouth," his mother told Mr. Wolfe, sounding very weak. Then Mrs. Sedgwick shooed them both away and they went to look at the Indian arrows on Mr. Wolfe's wall. They were very long, and Mr. Wolfe told him and Amy that the Indians up north in Canada shot bears with them. Later Mr. Sedgwick said that it couldn't have been the vermouth. "Maybe Emma's allergic to olives," he said. At least it wasn't kerosene, which was poison. Mr. Sedgwick mixed up the kerosene jug with the water jug once, and filled his mother's drink with it. She had to run to the kitchen and spit it in the sink. She was very careful of Mr. Sedgwick's drinks now.

When it was Tommy's parents' turn to give a party—and

of course they had to invite the Steers and the Sedgwicks and everyone else—his father and mother would figure out ways to keep Mrs. Sedgwick and Mr. Steer away from each other. They also had to keep him away from Mr. Aldrich, his brother-in-law. Mrs. Aldrich was his sister, but she wasn't at all like Mr. Steer. Tommy's parents' strategies usually worked for a while but tended to fall apart later in the evening. Sometimes Mr. Steer, who said he didn't like the parties anyway and rarely gave one himself, would stay home. That was a relief to everyone, though it seemed to Tommy the parties were more exciting when Mr. Steer was there. Mrs. Steer often stayed home. She said she'd rather read something interesting and also avoid a headache. Mrs. Sedgwick, she said, was impossible—"Oh! Ella Sedgwick," she would exclaim—and for that matter so was Mr. Aldrich; Mr. Steer, too, whose behavior often irritated her but whose sober judgments she generally agreed with: they were, after all, hers first. "Moreover, Tommy," she said, "your father's not the easiest man in the world to get along with." Tommy had to agree with that. Often, if Mrs. Steer didn't mind company, Tommy would stay with her on those evenings she spent at home. They would have some of their more interesting talks then, as the distant sounds of the party drifted across the water and the lights from the bridge twinkled in the night on the river. After a time the disagreements would blow over and the islanders would start afresh.

Once last summer Tommy's father had had the dredge come down to deepen the shallow sandy channels between the islands. Just as Mr. Sedgwick had laid the cable under the river, so Tommy's father arranged for the dredge because he knew the man who ran the dredging company. The company worked on the slip at the plant so the freighters could unload their coke and limestone for the furnaces. Tommy's father could arrange a lot of things, even for the land that part of the golf course was on to be given to the country club. His company owned it but didn't want to pay taxes on it. Tommy's father was a powerful man, which made Tommy proud at the same time that it embarrassed him. Sometimes he wished that his father were like the other fathers, the fathers of the children he went to school with, instead of working for him, as many of them did. Once at school Tommy said that his father was somebody else. But the children of the other fathers didn't have an island to go to, either, or a nice pleasant-smelling house with their own bedrooms. Bob Bonner, whom Tommy went to play with one day after school, lived three blocks away in an apartment that smelled of yesterday's dinners, contained a big chair that reminded Tommy of sitting on a hairbrush, and had a linoleum rug in the living room. Although it was good for playing cars, Tommy hated the looks and feel of that cold linoleum rug that slid on the wooden floor under his feet, that curled up at the edges and was so brittle if you stepped on a corner of it you were liable to break off a piece, which would make Mrs. Bonner angry. She was large and fat, almost as fat as Mrs. Barlow. She was impatient with Bob and awkward around Tommy, and she wore a big housedress that looked too flimsy to contain her. She blamed Bob when Tommy broke off a piece of the linoleum, although she could see that Tommy had done it. Bob was nice about it, though. He said he was used to getting blamed for things his younger brother did. Bob slept in the same room with his younger brother, and his baby sister slept with his parents. Bob Bonner's apartment faced Tommy's father's plant. It was on the second floor, and from the window you could see the men streaming out when the four-thirty whistle blew at the end of the day shift. That meant Tommy had to leave. Bob's father would be home in a minute and it was their dinnertime. Although Tommy liked Bob and Bob seemed to like him, Tommy went to Bob Bonner's only once. He didn't go back, and he was ashamed to invite Bob to his house, where the grass was green and the rooms were large.

When the dredge came to the Island, all the families stood on the shore and watched the tugboat shift it into the right position and the boatmen shout and wave their arms to one another signaling faster, slower, to the right, to the left, up, down. Tommy's father, Mr. Sedgwick, and Mr. Aldrich ran up and down the shore shouting more directions—"Watch the dock!" "Not too close to the shore, you'll hit the tree!"— as the big shovel scooped the mud from the bottom and dumped it in an ever-growing pile on the dredge itself. Before the dredge arrived, all the men with the help of Bill and Jim and a couple of other Indians had to dismantle three of the bridges, taking them off their pilings and laying out the boards on the land so they could be put back together as soon as the operation was over. They had to do that for the dredge. The dredging itself lasted only two days—just the channels between the Sedgwicks' island and the one the Steers lived on, and the main island where Tommy's family and most of the others lived were deepened—but for a week or so everyone had to use rowboats to go from one to another while the bridges were slowly replaced. The Indians didn't always show up when they were supposed to, and the men were better at directing the work than actually doing it, which Tommy could tell the Indians thought was pretty funny. They never laughed, but he could tell. Mr. Wolfe said the Indians were like that, and he knew a lot about Indians, more than anybody except for Governor Wentworth and Judge Aldrich, who was dead.

As the dredge clanked and steamed and churned the water in front of her house, Mrs. Steer stood on the shore with Tommy and Amy and Michael Aldrich, shaking her head. Deepening the channels was a serious mistake, she said. It disturbed the fish the Indians caught. It muddied the water for days. It made the currents flow faster and the swimming more dangerous for the young people and for herself as well. She was the only one of the older women who went swimming— the only one he had ever seen in a bathing suit, although he'd seen a picture of Mrs. Sedgwick in a bathing suit at La Jolla but everyone did it there, Mrs. Sedgwick explained. Daisy Meyer went swimming when she and Phil stayed at her mother's, but she was younger. Of course, Madge McGhee and Emily Sedgwick went swimming sometimes but they liked to sunbathe better, and the Aldriches' daughter did, too. All the boys went in—Phelps McGhee, Vint Steer, and Nick Farnsworth, Tommy's brothers and the Aldriches' grown sons —but except for Mr. Wolfe and Phil Meyer, hardly any of the men went in the water, either. But Mrs. Steer went swimming every morning, beginning early in the season and continuing until the water was very cold, stroking from her dock to the Boomer Island bridge and back against the current, four times altogether, in a steady Australian crawl. She was a good swimmer, better than his father, who hadn't gone swimming in years, and certainly better than his mother, who didn't even know how. It was interesting that Mrs. Steer did. She'd learned in Denmark and swum at the university. Tommy's mother hadn't gone to college, either. She went to work, instead, and helped pay for her sisters and her brother to go. Mrs. Steer and a man from the Coast Guard station on the next island up-river who used to come around sometimes—to sniff around Madge McGhee, Mrs. Steer said—taught Tommy and Amy and Michael Aldrich how to swim. Michael was Amy's cousin who was two years older. The three of them were the only children on the Island except, occasionally, for the visiting grandchildren of some of the islanders, but they were babies.

Worst of all, the dredging made the currents so swift they were eroding the islands. Erosion was always a problem. Every year the men would confer about it, and their elaborate solutions, which involved pilings and jetties and too much money, never worked very well. They always tried to do it as cheaply as possible, which Mrs. Steer said was also the problem. Regardless of their efforts, the big front lawn of the Sedgwicks was a little less big each year. Tommy could see that from pictures taken a long time ago, and also by the diminishing distance of Argo's doghouse from the riverbank. Argo was Emily Sedgwick's St. Bernard. And each year the ground around the weeping willow at the edge of Mrs. Sedgwick's side garden, the garden that faced the Steers' across the channel, was a little more soggy. Once you could walk around the tree without getting your feet wet. Now if you walked up to it the soil squished like a sponge, leaking water. It was dangerous to get too close to the willow, the children were warned, because the current swirled around the island at that point, into the channel, and it would carry them away if they fell in. Mrs. Steer said the Sedgwicks' island was in bad shape. In the middle of it, in the woods behind the big house, there was a marshy spot where the water bubbled up. Mrs. Steer told Mr. Sedgwick that sometime he'd have not one but two islands, that it would simply be cut in half by the rushing river. "One of these days, Tom," she said in her straightforward way, "you'll roar over in your launch and find another channel to dredge, the one running through the middle of your island."

"Nonsense, Varla," he fumed, and Mrs. Sedgwick said, "Well that wouldn't be anything to gloat about, would it?" The Sedgwicks didn't like to be told that at all, and Tommy couldn't imagine such a thing. It was a terrible thought. The men didn't believe the dredging was a serious problem, though, and as the channels were undeniably filling in and they needed to be deep enough to accommodate Mr. Sedgwick's motor launch, it had to be done.

MR. Sedgwick and Tommy's father took the launch on their shooting trip to Iroquois Island that fall. Governor Wentworth—he'd built the house in town where Mrs. Slade lived—had a summer camp there, several miles down the river. It was a big island and he owned all of it. He didn't live with Mrs. Wentworth anymore. Mrs. Wentworth, who had read the Bible twice through when she and the governor crossed the Gobi Desert a long time ago—it took a whole year —lived in Edgewater, the house the Indians had decorated with burlap and rope and birch saplings. Mrs. Wentworth wanted Tommy and Michael and Amy to call her Gaki, which was what her grandchildren had called her when they were still young and even after they grew up. Daisy Meyer still called her Gaki, but Mrs. Wentworth was Daisy's grandmother. Tommy found it hard to call her that. Once the governor had lived on the Island, too, until he adopted the college student who was at the university when Mrs. Steer was there. People said she was part Indian. Mrs. Steer said she advertised in the paper for a statesman to adopt her, which the governor did, but after his term was over, not while he was still governor. She was his daughter for many years, but last summer the governor had the adoption cancelled and he married her. Every single one of the islanders was speechless, aghast—it was so completely beyond the pale, they said, that they had no words to describe it—but they talked about it the rest of the summer, in tones of astonishment, amazement, and awe, and in front of the children, too, who tried to figure it out among themselves.

Michael Aldrich said the governor always liked Indians and had written a book about Indian history before the white men came up the river looking for beaver skins. "He wants the Indians to improve themselves, and says they shouldn't be allowed to buy whisky," Michael said. Maybe that was it—the governor was improving the Indians. He always wanted to improve things. In the days when people still visited him on Iroquois Island—the invitation was in the form of a command, Mrs. Steer said—the governor would run shouting through the camp at dawn, waving his arms and pulling people from their cots, and make them jump naked in the lake. They had to be naked. All those old people naked in the lake! Some of them with big stomachs, and their skinny white hairless legs and their bare bums—and bare everything else, too! It seemed both shocking and hilarious, and Tommy and Michael and Amy giggled about it. But the men and the women went to separate areas, Mrs. Steer said, and nobody had a choice. Governor Wentworth checked to make sure they all jumped in, and he did, too. The governor also insisted the men and women sleep in separate cabins, the women's lodge and the men's lodge. Mrs. Steer said he disapproved of cohabitation and thought that was the way the Indians did it, before the Frenchmen introduced them to whisky and disease. The cabins had no electricity—there was none on his island—no running water or indoor plumbing, just outhouses. It sounded terrible to Tommy. His parents had gone only once, when he was a baby, and command or no, his father refused to go back. "What does he think he is, a Finn? Jumping in the lake at five in the morning," his father exclaimed, as if that were all there was to be said about it. When Tommy told him that Mrs. Steer said the governor thought it was very improving, Tommy's father looked at him, grunted, and went back to his newspaper.

The governor, who had a column in the newspaper, wrote that his daughter now his wife was the New Beauty and he changed her name to Bellanova, which he explained meant New Beauty in Latin, and said that together they were going to work for a new world order and against the old oppressive religion—but not like the Bolsheviks; more like the Fabians. Tommy's father said the governor should have called her Belladonna, because she must have given him a lot of it. The islanders clearly thought the governor's new marriage wasn't improving anything, and they didn't know what to say to old Mrs. Wentworth, so they didn't say anything. They just patted her on the arm and smiled in a sympathetic way, and remarked when she was out of hearing about how amazing she was, what a wonderful woman. They didn't know what to say to Mrs. Addington, either. She was his daugher. It was a terrible situation, and everyone wondered what would happen to the governor's money. He was very old, and nobody expected him to live very long—"especially after a few doses of Belladonna," Tommy's father said. Mrs. Addington moved into Edgewater with her mother right after the governor got married, and gave her own cottage to Daisy and Phil. Daisy said the governor was an old fool, it was as simple as that, even if he was her grandfather, and all the islanders agreed, though they didn't say so to Daisy; they just laughed about it among themselves, after a while.

The governor's wife—to everyone Mrs. Wentworth was still his wife even though he'd divorced her many years before—gave the stained-glass Resurrection Window to the church the same summer. Everyone, even the Steers, went to the dedication service, which happened the very Sunday after the governor's sudden marriage. The bishop came and patted Mrs. Wentworth on the arm and said in his sermon that she was a generous woman, full of forbearance. Everyone liked and admired old Mrs. Wentworth. She was a very great lady, they said, noting that she sat straight as a ramrod in the front pew at the dedication, acknowledging nothing. She sat by herself, too; Mrs. Addington sat in the pew behind her, with Daisy and Phil. Mrs. Wentworth continued to go to the parties on the Island, smiling graciously as if nothing had happened, and she gave her own annual party in Edgewater at the end of the season. Tommy supposed that if they had a king and queen, Mrs. Wentworth would be a duchess too.

Despite the governor's marriage, which meant that nobody

would visit him anymore, in the duck season when the governor had already gone to Georgia for the winter with Bellanova, Tommy's father and Mr. Sedgwick put their decoys in Mr. Sedgwick's launch and took it to Iroquois Island while Mr. Hutchins followed by car with his dogs, which were well trained and good hunters. Mr. Hutchins didn't like boats, and there wasn't room in the launch for the dogs anyway. The men spent the weekend in one of the governor's small cabins that was always left open and returned with a bunch of ducks, which the grown-ups all went to the Hutchins' to eat. Tommy was glad he couldn't go. He didn't like to eat duck or goose or partridge or venison. He didn't like to eat anything his father had shot. It wasn't so much that his father had shot it—he would have felt the same if Mr. Hutchins or Mr. Sedgwick or Mr. Steer did—as that when it appeared on the platter, fresh from the oven, Tommy saw it hanging in its feathers or fur from a rafter in the garage, looking very dead but with its remembered life still intact, an animal greatness that maybe the creature could no longer know but Tommy could imagine. Besides, he didn't like the taste, so something else would be fixed for him. "After all, he has to eat *something*," his mother would say.

Tommy remembered last spring, when his parents were looking at the farm on the River Road, how they'd sometimes stopped at Mr. Matson's. While his father discussed properties and farming with Mr. Matson, and his mother talked to Mrs. Matson in her wheelchair about how much she liked the bedroom curtains Mrs. Matson had made for her, Tommy played around the Matson farm, exploring the edge of the pond, looking warily at the cows in the pasture, and venturing into the dim barn to jump in the haymow, watching the glowing motes of dust in the slanting rays of yellow light, the birds dart in and out. On the barn floor he stopped to pet the horses in their stalls and to look from the other side of his pen at Bill the bull. Bill was a mild creature and too old to be of use to anybody, Mr. Matson said, but he kept him on, the way he'd keep a pet. Tommy liked to stand outside Bill's pen and tease him a little. Bill would toss his head back and snort amiably, and Tommy wondered if he dared climb up the rails and try to pat his nose. He seemed a friendly animal, like Ferdinand in Tommy's storybook, but Mr. Matson cautioned him to be wary. An old bull can get ornery, he said. One time Bill wasn't there and Tommy asked Mr. Matson where he'd gone. They were just sitting down to the dinner Mr. Matson had cooked. The Matsons had their dinner at noon, and Mr. Matson insisted Tommy and his parents eat too. "Mr. Matson, what happened to Bill the bull?" Tommy asked. "He's the meat loaf," Mr. Matson replied. "You're eating him." Tommy was indeed eating him, chewing the meat at that very moment, but he stopped right then. If his father had shot the Thanksgiving turkey—and after all, he didn't even *know* the animals his father shot—Tommy wouldn't have eaten that either. But the turkey came from the store so it was all right.

TOMMY thought about these happenings this Thanksgiving Day as his parents' guests moved about the living room. He turned them over in his mind, like a movie playing in his head, he thought, and he wondered if Mr. Sedgwick and Mrs. Sedgwick and Mr. Hutchins and Mrs. Hutchins and Cousin Maud and Cousin Gertrude and his brothers and Emily Sedgwick and Nick Farnsworth and all the others, if they had movies playing in their heads, too, and if they were seeing the same movie or if they all had different movies playing simultaneously but separately. It was a funny thought, and Tommy tried to imagine the movie each of them might be playing, but he wasn't very successful at it. They were all talking so much, he supposed they couldn't have much of a movie running in their heads anyway.

While Tommy was pondering this question, sitting on the stool in the corner next to the radio and the bookshelves, his brother David poked him on the head and said, "What's on your tiny little mind, tadpole?" David sometimes called him "tadpole," or worse. "Come to the party. Mother wants you to pass the hors d'oeuvres." So Tommy got the tray of celery stuffed with cheese from the kitchen and began passing it from one guest to another, moving through the clusters of people, dodging elbows, offering celery, now to Mr. Hutchins,

98

who was telling his mother that Mrs. Appleton had heard that Mr. Wolfe, who'd been away all fall, would be coming for Christmas, which his mother said she'd also heard, and she told Tommy he should offer the celery first to Cousin Maud and Cousin Gertrude because they were the eldest. So Tommy carried the tray toward the cousins. They were sitting erect at either end of the stiff old sofa with the feet that looked like lions' paws, but they didn't care for any celery.

Tommy's father was teasing them. He could get away with teasing his cousins because Tommy's mother said they doted on him, just like his mother, and he could do no wrong in their eyes. When he was in a good mood, Tommy's father liked to tease, and he liked to tell stories, too, and he wanted the guests in his house to enjoy themselves and he made sure they did.

"My great-aunt Mary Farwell, the mother of these girls"—his father gestured toward the two old ladies on the sofa—"had a fur muff. Maud, you old sweetheart, I'll bet you've got it with you today—or is it your turn to carry it, Gertrude? When I was a boy," his father said, "I thought the muff was the brother of these little creatures here," and he shook one of the paws dangling from Cousin Maud's fur piece. "Aunt Mary used to wear both of them. It was colder in those days, though. And that was good for you girls—you don't have to take turns with them. Good Lord," he said, in a tone of mock astonishment, "these animals must be going on a hundred!"

"Now James, don't tell that foolish old story," Cousin Maud said. "I've never believed it." She knew what was coming, and so did Tommy, who giggled in anticipation.

"What? What's that you're saying?" Cousin Gertrude asked.

"When Aunt Mary was an old lady she didn't see too well," his father went on, but a little louder, "and she didn't go out much. But one day she and my grandmother took the train to Sudbury. Probably they wanted to make sure the mine was still running. It was their nickel, after all, and a girl has to watch her nickels—right, Maud?" Tommy was an appreciative audience for his father's funny stories, and he laughed out loud: not only was the mine a nickel mine, but the cousins were very close with their money. His mother said they bought day-old bread at half-price. Tommy had visited the mine once.

It was just a ramshackle wooden shed at the entrance to a black tunnel descending gradually into the earth, a railroad track coming out of it. He and his father and Mr. Hutchins followed the track for a little ways, into the mouth of the mine, past a broken wooden car that still stood on the rails, but then it began to get dark and they turned around. It could be dangerous, his father said. The timbers were old and rotten and the roof might fall in. The mine hadn't been worked in years, but his father remembered when it was full of men who wore little carbide lamps on their heads and carried picks and shovels, filling the cars with ore. The men lived in the tiny wooden houses that dotted the neighboring hillsides. Nobody lived in them now, and the whole place was silent and bleak.

His father continued telling the story. "So Aunt Mary wrapped her furs around her neck and pulled the muff from the closet and went to the station. But she didn't put her hands in the muff until she got on the train. And when she did, out of the muff jumped a family of mice. They'd been nesting there between outings. Now as I said, Aunt Mary didn't see too well. In fact, she hardly saw at all, so she didn't notice the terrified mice running wild through the car. But everybody else did, and there was a terrible hue and cry—women screaming, trying to jump on their seats, men chasing mice— a great hullabaloo. Aunt Mary leaned over to her sister—my grandmother was ten or fifteen years younger—rapped her cane on the floor and said, 'I say, Julia, I say. What's this fuss about?' 'It's about the mice that just jumped out of your muff, Mary,' my grandmother said. And Mary replied, 'Don't be ridiculous, Julia! Mice in my muff! Such foolishness!' That settled *that*," his father said, "but Aunt Mary must have thought about it for a minute, because then she leaned over to my grandmother and said, 'Anyway, haven't these people seen a little mouse before?' "

Everyone laughed at Tommy's father's story, even Cousin Maud and Cousin Gertrude, who knew it by heart so it didn't matter if she really heard it or not. Only he could get them to laugh. He could get anybody to laugh when he wanted to, and laughter and easy conversation rippled through the room that afternoon. They talked about the hunting season just passing, the Christmas season approaching too soon, the trouble in Europe and how Colonel McCormick said that Chamberlain had made everything all right and that it was Europe's business anyway and not America's, which Mrs. Steer thought was shortsighted and she quoted from an article in *The New Republic*. Tommy's father thought the real problem was Japan, and Mr. Sedgwick thought it was the new minimum wage, and they both agreed on that and told Nick Farnsworth that it was the rare man nowadays who gave a fair day's work for a fair day's pay. Nick Farnsworth said, "Yes, sir. I'm sure you're right, sir." But they didn't talk very much about politics. It was, after all, Thanksgiving, and nobody seemed intent on an argument. Mrs. Sedgwick talked to the cousins about the new king and queen, and the three of them pitied the duke who used to be the king and deplored the duchess who had taken him in, but the duke was weak where he should have been strong—"not like your old-fashioneds, Mac," Mrs. Sedgwick said. "They're strong where they might have been weak. But I believe I would have another, thank you. I'm a little chilly and they *are* delicious." Mrs. Sedgwick was often chilly. "Nobody makes an old-fashioned like yours, Mac." Tommy's brother David mumbled that it would be cheaper to turn up the furnace than to fuel Mrs. Sedgwick—he didn't like her very much—and his father began refilling glasses.

Tommy's father drank only Scotch whisky, himself, with plain water. Soda was for sissies, he said. But if anyone asked, and always on special occasions, he served his guests old-fashioneds. Tommy thought they looked delicious and he liked to watch his father make them, muddling the cube of sugar with a dash of bitters in the bottom of the heavy glasses with his monogram on the side, adding the whisky, the soda, and then the slices of orange and a red maraschino cherry with a little juice from the bottle for color. He made Tommy and Amy and his cousins old-fashioneds, too, with ginger ale and without the whisky, and gave them their own muddlers. The muddlers were clear glass with a thick round ball on the bottom and on top a tiny delicate bird with open wings. Each bird was different and a different color. Tommy's was the color of turquoise. When Tommy's father did things well, he did them very well, with a kind of happy, careless ease that was a pleasure for everyone to watch. It made Tommy proud to see him like this, and he helped his father serve the round of drinks.

TOMMY'S Aunt Elizabeth—his mother's youngest sister, the one with the huge brown eyes whose photograph hung in his parents' bedroom—was telling Mrs. Steer about the time she was desperately in love with Geoffrey Steer, Mr. Steer's brother. Tommy's aunt and uncle had come from Grosse Pointe for the holiday and also for the deer hunting, which his uncle liked to do with Tommy's father. *"Desperately,"* his aunt was saying as Tommy came by with her drink. "He was my first real beau. Maybe I was just grateful, but I thought I was desperately in love." She sounded wistful. "Unfortunately, he wasn't so desperate about it as I." His aunt laughed at the memory. "One of my sorority sisters found me sobbing in my room. Sobbing!" Her voice was full of wonder. "Just sobbing! Jeff had simply stopped calling, and I was devastated. I didn't dress well enough for his fraternity brothers or something. At least that's what I always thought. I'm sure I looked perfectly terrible." She laughed again, and sipped at her drink. Tommy had trouble picturing his pretty, stylish aunt ever looking terrible. She always appeared very elegant to him. "My clothes were all hand-me-downs, you know— what there were of them—and my best dress probably looked like something Louise would wear, though I think it was Clara's." Clara was her oldest sister, the one whose eyes matched her ice-blue dressing gown and who had an apartment in Chicago. Louise was another sister who'd married a farmer and lived in the country. She had a hand pump in the kitchen. Nobody talked much about Louise. She'd gotten very sick when she was nineteen and had never been the same after that.

"We were very poor then," his aunt said. Tommy's Aunt Elizabeth was the only person in his mother's family who ever mentioned their having been poor. "I remember asking my mother, when I was a very little girl, 'Mother, why did we used to be so rich'—it did seem as if we'd been rich once—

'and now we're so poor?' We hadn't seen our father since he arrived with fur coats for each of us—Mother, Clara, Tommy's mother Emma, Louise, myself—even my brother Christian. Can you imagine? I was five years old and had a fur coat! Father left a few days later with our brother Jonathan—he was the oldest of us all—back out West to make another fortune, and none of us ever saw him again. Mother never even mentioned his name. I didn't know until I was grown up that he'd gone bankrupt, and I certainly didn't learn that from Mother. We never saw Jonathan again, either. Mother got a telegram two or three years later saying he'd died of tuberculosis and been buried in Portland. That was the only time I ever saw a tear in her eye—sitting in the kitchen, holding that telegram. Right after they left, poor Mother took all the fur coats and sold them—how I loved that coat, and how I cried when it went!—and eventually she opened the flower shop. For a long time Christian and I kept waiting for Father to walk in the door in the evening, bearing extravagant gifts, and when he hadn't shown up by bedtime we would whisper together in the dark about whether he would be there in the morning when we woke up, and what the gifts might be. We knew they'd be splendid!" She laughed again. "Later, I sometimes told people my father was dead—and eventually he was. I think his going away affected me more than it did the others, except for Christian. Clara, Emma, it never seemed to affect them. They were a lot older, of course, and they were more like Mother. Strong. She never looked back. I never heard her utter a word of complaint, and she insisted on keeping the flower shop until she died. I don't know who Christian and I were like, but I don't think it was Mother. Of course, we were so young. Now I can't even remember what he looked like. . . ." Her voice trailed off. Her deep brown eyes seemed suddenly full. She grasped her drink with both hands and looked off into the distance, as if, Tommy thought, her father might suddenly appear there and come toward her, maybe carrying a fur coat over his open arms. Tommy stood rapt, immobilized, riveted to the spot, and flooded with a sense of her loss. Mrs. Steer seemed under the spell, too. Tommy imagined his aunt as a little girl—the poor little match girl

103

in the story—and his own eyes filled with tears. The enormous sadness of her story was like something out of a fairy tale but it lacked a fairy-tale ending. He waited for his aunt to supply one, and after a moment she resumed talking but she was back on the subject of Jeff Steer.

"Jeff simply dropped out of my life without so much as a word," his aunt said, "and when my friend found me crying my eyes out, she took me in hand and dictated this letter to Jeff. Oh, it really told him off! And I mailed it. I *mailed* it! Can you imagine? I was so embarrassed afterwards."

Mrs. Steer laughed. "Yes, Elizabeth, I can well imagine," she said, "and I know what the letter said, too." Tommy's aunt looked astonished. "I've never forgotten it. It said: 'You needn't think you're the only clothespin on the line just because you've got a wooden head.' Wonderful!" Mrs. Steer laughed again, but nicely.

"Varla, how did you ever—"

"Jeff showed it to me," Mrs. Steer said. "I was his great confidante in those days. He was the youngest. He told me all his troubles, and believe me, you were one of them."

"I'm so embarrassed," his aunt said.

"Don't be," Mrs. Steer replied. "Jeff was smitten with you. He was at least as desperately in love with you, but he thought you were too good for him."

"She thought so, too," said Tommy's Uncle Roger, who'd come up at the end of the story. Uncle Roger was Aunt Elizabeth's husband, and he liked to tease. "They all thought so, those Bigelow girls. Their mother told them, and their mother was a Hopkins, and you know what *that* meant. And of course they were right." He squeezed his wife's hand. "But they all found men who could support them in the style that was their due, even if we weren't quite good enough—didn't you, Elizabeth?" Tommy's uncle was laughing, but his aunt looked annoyed. "Smart girls, those Bigelows. Except for Louise. Now, if only Christian could have done the same. . . ." Christian was Tommy's bachelor uncle. He was witty and sophisticated and always treated Tommy as if Tommy knew what was going on. Uncle Christian lived with Tommy's rich Aunt Clara and Uncle Andrew—he worked for his Uncle Andrew—and, like

Clara, always carried a book with him—Proust, Gide, George Eliot, Virginia Woolf, Beerbohm—not quite like the books in Tommy's house, which came in the mail from the Literary Guild or else looked as if they'd been there forever: the *Messages and Papers of the Presidents*, sets of Dickens, H. G. Wells, Robert Louis Stevenson, Emerson, the *Harvard Classics*, that sort of thing.

"Roger! Stop that!" Tommy's aunt stamped her foot. "You've interrupted Varla's story. You could get us a drink, that would be something you could do. Varla," his aunt said, turning to Mrs. Steer, "what must you have thought of me?"

"I thought you must be very clever," Mrs. Steer said. "I'd never seen a letter like it. It seemed very funny, and very American. I told Jeff to stop moping around, that he'd probably deserved every word of it. He was a socialist then. As you know, he's changed a lot."

"Well," his aunt said, "I never went out with Geoffrey Steer again. If he ever knew how hurt I was! But I found someone else. I was *determined* to find someone else. He was a Sigma Nu from . . . oh, I don't know, Wisconsin, I guess . . . and when he visited me at Ann Arbor I would put on my very best outfit—not Clara's castoff; I made this one myself—and parade him by Jeff's Phi Delt house, pretending to ignore it, of course. I would have plucked out my eyes before I'd glanced in *that* direction. Oh, I was shameless," she said, sipping the drink Uncle Roger had brought her, "but it was such innocent fun, such silly, sweet, innocent fun."

Emily Sedgwick, who always seemed to move in a cloud of perfume and fur, face powder, cocktails, and cigarette smoke, had heard the end of his aunt's story. "Oh, Mrs. Chase," she said to her, "that must have been sweet revenge. All the Phi Delts think they're the cat's pajamas. I prefer the Betas, myself." She smiled quickly, blinked her eyes, and paused, waiting for the response. Tommy's brother John was a Beta, and Emily was wearing his fraternity pin linked with a fine gold chain to her own sorority pin, the one with the secret words in Greek. "All us Pi Phis—I guess I should say *we* Pi Phis—prefer the Betas. It was the same in my mother's day. She was a Pi Phi, too, you know, and so was my grandmother. I was a double legacy." Tommy's aunt and Mrs. Steer seemed to know that but they murmured appreciatively, although Tommy knew that Mrs. Steer thought fraternities and sororities were a lot of foolishness. Emily Sedgwick was lovely; everyone said that. She played a nice game of golf and a better game of bridge, and she and John made an attractive couple. Everyone expected they would have a charmed life ahead of them.

Tommy's aunt, though, had spoken as if it were different being a grown-up married woman, a member of the Junior League and the Boat Club, the wife of a physician in Grosse Pointe, Michigan, and not nearly so much fun as parading by the Phi Delt house in her fancy dress on a weekend afternoon. Tommy's Uncle Roger had been a Deke at Stanford—"that's the Harvard of the West, you know," his aunt often said, and said again that afternoon to Mrs. Steer—and she'd met him while he was going to medical school at Ann Arbor. She fell in love with his car, she said with a laugh. Uncle Roger played the banjo and the mandolin, and Tommy thought he was a lot of fun.

"Medicine runs in our family," his aunt told Emily and Mrs. Steer. "All those Hopkins on our mother's side with dreadful names like Jeremiah and Ezekiel and Asachal—whatever *that* is—were physicians back in New England. Or if they weren't physicians, they were clergymen. Always doing good, you know. And one of them was a commanding officer in the Revolutionary War. We could be Colonial Dames, but who'd want to be? They're so stuffy. Well, Emma and Clara might. Not because they're stuffy, of course. Emma is certainly not stuffy. She always said she threw her hip out of joint carrying me around when I was a baby, but I notice she's still able to dance. I *love* to dance, myself, but now it practically takes an Act of Congress to get Roger onto the floor, at least with me. And then he makes me feel like a barge with a tugboat." Tommy laughed. His aunt was so tiny and so pretty that nothing could make her feel like a barge, and his uncle didn't look much like a tugboat, either.

"Elizabeth," said Mrs. Steer, also laughing, "you're the first ninety-eight-pound barge I've ever seen. He should dance with me. He'd think he had the *Queen Mary* in tow."

"Well," Tommy's aunt said, "at least I get the damage treated free. That's one advantage of marrying a doctor. And after all, I was only trying to keep up the family tradition as best I could."

"Which tradition is that?" Tommy asked.

"Medicine," his aunt replied. "Medicine, of course. Emma or Clara has some of our great-great-grandfather Hopkins' letters. He had a beautiful hand—he was said to be famous for it—but the letters read like sermons. Long, boring sermons." His aunt talked rapidly on, seized by the subject of her family. Maybe she couldn't think of anything else to say. "He was writing to his grandson—that would be your great-grandfather, Tommy. He was a real pioneer. The first white settler in Saginaw or Coldwater—one of those places. He built a cabin and then a stockade and the town grew up around him. Clara says the cabin is still there. He took his medical books with him from the East—practicing medicine without a license, I suppose, though in those days and in those places I don't imagine any license was needed, just a healing hand. He went back to Connecticut for his bride, and then she delivered the babies."

Emily Sedgwick rummaged through her bag for a cigarette and asked if anyone would like one. She called them coffin nails. No one did, and Tommy's aunt scarcely paused. "Tommy, your great-aunt was a nurse in the Spanish-American War and then went to medical college in Philadelphia." She turned to Mrs. Steer. "She married a Harvard man, but he never amounted to much. They moved to San Francisco because of her lungs, and she wanted to help fallen women." His aunt flashed a weak smile. "I guess she thought there were a lot of them in San Francisco." She took another sip of her drink. The glass was almost empty. "She should have stayed home. My father's brother married a whore! Of course I didn't know that then. I only saw her once. She came to call to find out where my Uncle Tom had gone and my mother wouldn't receive her. Christian and I had to tell her that Mother was resting. Mother *never* rested! *We* didn't know where Uncle Tom had gone. We scarcely knew him, but I liked him. He was kind."

Tommy's mother had been standing near them, talking to Mrs. Hutchins and Tommy's Aunt Martha, but Tommy could tell she had one ear on their conversation, and she came over to them when Emily asked Mrs. Steer if she had a match. "It would be nice if you'd go entertain your cousins, Tommy," his mother said. "You're letting Amy do all your work." She turned to his aunt. "Elizabeth, where do you get these stories? Surely you've told enough."

"But they're *true*," his aunt said. "Don't you remember?"

"No," his mother said, "I don't. I've never heard those stories."

"And don't you remember that Father's other brother, Christian's namesake, committed suicide?"

"Elizabeth," his mother said, "he died in a boating accident. You do have the most active imagination. She always did," his mother said to Emily and Mrs. Steer.

"You were older—grown up, really," his aunt said. "It's always the youngest who remember. You remember how we called Aunt Polly 'Auntie Doctor' because she hated her name, don't you? She said it was only fit for a parrot." His aunt laughed. So did his mother.

"Yes," she said, "I do remember that."

"Maybe you'll grow up to be a doctor, Tommy," his aunt said. "That would be nice."

Tommy didn't think he'd want to be a doctor if he had to be like those people with names like Jeremiah, but if he could be like Dr. Randolph or his Uncle Roger, that might be fun. His brother David told him that Uncle Roger had bought him his first pair of long pants. David had to wear short pants and then knickers until he was thirteen. So did John. Tommy's mother had promised him that he wouldn't have to wear knickers, and that he could have long pants when he was ten. That was doing better than David and John, but it still seemed a long way off, almost three years. His mother said she liked him in short pants. She also liked him in the golden curls he'd had until he was two and a half, and she still kept a lock of that severed hair between tissues in the big Bible that his father's grandfather had carried from Scotland to Canada, and that Tommy's own grandfather had brought to America. "You used to be such a sweet child, with such a lovely, even disposition," his mother said with a puzzled shake of her head. "What happened to that sweet child?" she would ask when he misbehaved, or cried, or was angry. Tommy was glad he couldn't remember the curls; it was enough to have to hear about them.

Tommy's mother moved off to attend to her guests, and his aunt began telling Mrs. Steer about a lunch she'd had recently with his Uncle Roger's sister at the Boat Club. Janet was older than Roger, she hadn't married because she feared every man who asked her was after her money—"and it's not even *that* much money," his aunt said—and she was a problem, a difficult problem. Mrs. Steer interrupted her before she'd finished her story about the problem of Janet and the lunch at her club. "Is this the life you wanted, Elizabeth?"

"Why, of course it is, Varla," his aunt replied, surprised. "Isn't this the life *you* wanted?"

"It's the life I have," said Mrs. Steer.

Tommy's aunt looked nonplussed, the way Tommy's father used to describe Fred Barger. "He was the only man I ever knew who was stumped for an answer when you said 'Hello,'" his father said. Mr. Barger had also died that fall. A lot of people died that fall, and his parents seemed to visit the funeral home often.

"THANK God for the funeral home," Tommy's mother said to Mrs. Sedgwick and his father's sister Martha, who had come back for Thanksgiving to pick up some of his grandmother's things. "It's so much easier on everyone than it used to be. When Mother died we kept her at home, and it was hard on all of us but especially hard on the boys. It was even worse when they found Grandpa MacAllister—the closed coffin, so many months after his actual death—but at least we weren't living in the house then. I don't know why Evelyn kept Fred at home."

His mother was perched on the edge of the comfortable couch where Mrs. Sedgwick and his Aunt Martha were sitting. Tommy had been sitting there, too, but his mother told him his fidgeting was disturbing Mrs. Sedgwick, so he got up. They were talking about the Bargers and how, when Mrs. Barger's dog died a few years ago, she'd had him stuffed—just like the animal heads and the Aldriches' little fox on the Island, Tommy thought—and he now stood on rollers in a corner of Mrs. Barger's house.

"Rollers," exclaimed his aunt. "The first time I saw that I damn near fainted!" Although Tommy's father didn't like it, his sister Martha talked like that. She had married a divorced man, and his father didn't like that either, though he liked Charlie. "I thought of asking Evelyn if the dog had his walk today, but I was afraid of the answer."

Mrs. Barger once told Tommy and his mother that when her dog died, she thought she'd die, too. He was just like a child to her, and she liked to see him right there with her, and being able to move him from place to place made her feel as if he were still alive. It was a great comfort, she said. When Mr. Barger died, and Tommy's parents were leaving to go to the Bargers' house, his father said that he expected to find Mr. Barger stuffed and sitting at the dining table. "I hope we don't have to shake hands," he said, and he repeated the story as he passed drinks to the three ladies.

"It must have been a great relief, Jamie, to find him in the coffin," Tommy's Aunt Martha said. She called his father "Jamie." His grandmother had called him James, as did his Canadian cousins. Everyone else called him Mac.

Of course, Mrs. Barger was strange; everyone agreed on that. She was very High Church, and was constantly threatening to go to Rome but so far she hadn't. The Bargers owned the Barger Block and several other buildings on the main street of Grande Rivière, with shops on the ground floor and doctors' offices and apartments on the floors above. Mrs. Barger sometimes scrubbed the steps herself. She said it was penance but Tommy's father said she was just tight. Tommy had seen her himself with her scrub brush and pail in front of her buildings. Everyone in town had seen her; she was easy to spot. She wore nothing but red, ever: shoes, hat, gloves, handbag, coat, dress. When she scrubbed the steps of her buildings she wore red pants that a seamstress had made for her. Only her fingernails were plain. Mr. Barger refused to let her paint them, or to have her hair bobbed. Those two things she could not do. The day after Mr. Barger died, she covered herself in black from head to foot and went to the beauty parlor to have her hair cut and her nails polished a brilliant scarlet. Tommy's father said that at Mr. Barger's funeral her fingernails lit up the whole church. They were brighter than the stained-glass windows. Mrs. Barger also had a glass eye. Tommy was grateful that she wasn't there for Thanksgiving. Shortly after Mr. Barger died so she was still wearing black except for her nails, she had come to dinner. It was just Mrs. Barger and his parents, and Tommy had sat at the table with them. She talked a lot about Fred and how he had suffered.

"Just look at this, Mac," she said, reaching into her purse, pulling out an envelope of photographs and waving one in front of his father, who was putting crackers in his soup, one of his habits that his mother didn't like. "Here he is in the hospital, only three days before he died." She began to weep. Tommy's father looked aghast. His mother called for Rose to clear the soup. Nobody had even finished. "I took the pictures myself. I'm sorry that some of them are a little out of focus." His mother helped Rose pick up the soup plates, and they returned with the meat and potatoes and the limp carrots. Tommy leaned over to see the pictures that Mrs. Barger was stacking up beside his father's plate. His mother began talking about an article in the evening paper. His father carved the roast. He didn't say a word. "And here he is the day he died. And I took this one right after he died, minutes after his last breath." Tommy thought Mr. Barger looked as if he were snoring. His mouth was open. Mrs. Barger continued weeping and piling up the photographs next to his father. "May the souls of the faithful departed rest in peace, amen," she said, raising her eyes to heaven and crossing herself twice, before and after. Tommy's father served the plates, asking Mrs. Barger in a tight voice if she cared for gravy on both the meat and the potatoes. "Yes, both, please," she replied, "I'm starving. And here he is at the house, in his lovely casket. It was Mr. Hall's best." Mr. Hall was the Protestants' undertaker. "I got a picture from every angle," she said, displaying a series like a hand of cards. "I don't think he ever looked better."

Mr. Barger might never have looked better, but his father

certainly had. He was white, and his lips were very tight. Tommy's mother continued talking about the article in the paper, but nobody picked up on the subject. Mrs. Barger cut her meat and began to eat, chewing and dabbing at her eyes with her napkin. Tommy couldn't believe what happened next. Mrs. Barger reached up to her eye—her right eye, the one next to Tommy—grappled with it, and removed it. "It hurts," she said, setting it on the table right next to Tommy so that the unblinking, disembodied eye as big as an egg, bigger than any eye he could have imagined, stared at him while he tried to focus on his carrots.

Tommy's father excused him from the table without his even asking. He was very nice about it. His father looked as if he'd like to leave too, but he was always polite to guests and couldn't. They were having canned raspberries and cookies for dessert, but Tommy didn't come back for it. Mrs. Barger didn't come back for dinner again, either.

WITHOUT its leaves the big mahogany table in the dining room was round and easily sat six, but when all its leaves were in place there was room for sixteen. The day before Thanksgiving, Tommy's mother and Rose and Tommy's two aunts had set up the big table and also a smaller round table for the children—Tommy's three cousins and Amy Steer, who would be there for dinner with Mrs. Steer; Mr. Steer was still at hunting camp with Vint—and for Tommy's brother John and Emily Sedgwick because they'd like to be together and Emily was thought to be good with children. That night Tommy's parents had taken both his aunts and uncles to dinner at the country club while Tommy and his cousins ate in the room off the kitchen, which was sometimes the maid's room—there was a cot in it—and sometimes the breakfast room because it had a big square table and chairs, but most often it was just the den because that was where the Ping-Pong table was set up. It was also the room in which his grandmother had strained the currants through the empty sugar sacks for the red currant jelly she loved. Tommy's grandmother had died early in November so she didn't make the stuffing she always made the day before Thanksgiving, nor would she be making the currant biscuits for Christmas breakfast. It was a custom Tommy would miss. He missed seeing his grandmother in the kitchen with the brown glazed bowl by her side, humming as she pulled apart the bread for the stuffing, tearing it into tiny pieces. Just as he could recall at will his grandmother's voice and her warm, powdery smell that still lingered in her bedroom, so he could remember the pungent smell of her stuffing, and though the china and the silver and the fluted goblets with the green stems were the same, the stuffing was not. Even Tommy's mother agreed, and she had made it.

Tommy's cousins were his Aunt Martha's children. Neither his Aunt Clara and Uncle Andrew, nor his Aunt Elizabeth and Uncle Roger had any, although his mother said they wanted them, of course. Everybody wanted children. Tommy had heard his Aunt Elizabeth say that she was too small to bear them, which Tommy found odd, though she was scarcely larger than a child and not so tall as his cousin Charlotte, who was just twelve. Charlotte and Julia were two years apart, but Steve was nearly a year younger than Tommy. They were from Minneapolis, and they had a lot of fun together and with their parents. They seemed a happy family. Charlotte was his favorite. Julia was funny, but she wasn't as nice as Charlotte. Charlotte was very beautiful. People said she looked like Tommy's grandmother, a resemblance Tommy tried but failed to see. Charlotte was tall. She had long dark hair and deep brown eyes with thick lashes—the MacAllister eyes, people said, though Tommy remembered his grandmother's eyes as being watery and pale. Charlotte's were more like his father's but warmer, and Tommy himself was said to have his father's eyes. "Look at those lashes, Emma," his grandmother said once. "He'll be a killer when he grows up." Tommy examined his eyes in his grandmother's mirror but he didn't see anything special about them; they weren't like Charlotte's. His voice wasn't, either. Charlotte's was soft and low.

Tommy liked all three of his cousins, even though they seemed very different from him. Their presence allowed him to be his own age. It was fun to be his own age, to toss rolls across the table and to punch, to throw salt and to make faces over the vegetables and to make fun of the grown-ups, instead of being the polite little boy who Mrs. Appleton said one day at the country club, after she had dropped all her quarters in the slot machine, would never have dirty ears like her grandson. "You'd never have dirty ears, would you Tommy?" she asked. Mrs. Appleton said her grandson was a real boy; she spoke to Tommy as if he were an imitation, like the imitation vanilla that wasn't as good as the real thing, though it looked the same. Mrs. Appleton liked her grandson but Tommy didn't think she liked him. But that was all right; Tommy didn't like her either. Still, he could feel his ears burn when she said that, and he was forced to say that yes, he did too have dirty ears sometimes, just like any other boy. Of course his mother wouldn't take him to the country club with dirty ears, and he didn't have any choice about being polite. Tommy hated it when his mother washed his face, neck, and ears. She was especially rough on the ears, and she would never let him do it himself. The only reason she let him brush his own teeth was that one day he had simply clamped his mouth shut and she couldn't get the toothbrush into it.

Often Tommy ate alone, at his own small table in the corner of the dining room near the kitchen door. Tommy's father didn't come home for dinner until later, and, if his father and mother weren't going out, they would eat together then, but that was usually too late for Tommy. He liked his little table, though, with the chairs that fit him but were too small for his mother. So was the table; she had to sit sideways at it. And, because Tommy hated to be the only one eating, his mother would have a bite or two with him—Tommy insisted on it—but mostly she just pretended, moving her knife and fork around a little and drinking her coffee while she kept an eye on him to see that he ate his whole dinner. Sometimes, if his mother was busy or out, Rose would eat with him, and then they would sit at the big table in the room off the kitchen. Rose would never have fit at Tommy's table. Rose didn't pretend to eat, either. Rose ate; she ate a lot, and she wasn't too fussy if Tommy didn't finish his plate. She'd give him dessert anyway. Sometimes his mother would make them Indian pudding, which Tommy thought was funny in an embarrassing sort of way—eating Indian pudding with an Indian. Tommy asked Rose if the Indians ate a lot of Indian pudding, but Rose said no. "The only place I've ever had it is at your house," she said, picking up the cream pitcher and pouring a big dollop of the thick cream over it. And then she laughed. "It's good, though," she said. "Those Indians must have been good cooks." She laughed again, and Tommy wondered if Rose thought the whole idea of eating Indian pudding here, with him, was a little strange, too, but he didn't ask her. He just watched while she took another serving. He hoped she would talk about the Indians, now that they were on the subject, but all she said was "I still like ice cream better." Rose really did like dessert. She also liked mashed potatoes and corn, but not most other vegetables. She and Tommy agreed on that. Tommy's mother told Mrs. Sedgwick that Rose didn't eat to live; she lived to eat. Mrs. Sedgwick said, "I always thought she lived to drink."

Tommy liked having dinner with his cousins, without his mother there to mind his manners. That night Steve made rude belching noises and Charlotte told him he was behaving like a pig, and everyone laughed and shouted at once. They passed around one of his father's cigarettes. He smoked Lucky Strikes; Emily Sedgwick smoked Chesterfields. The cigarette made Tommy cough, but Charlotte smoked it as if she'd been smoking all her life. Afterwards they played tag in the long upstairs hall, running in and out of the bedrooms, hiding in closets and under beds, behind chests and chairs, in the back stairway that was always cold in winter. They made a tremendous racket until Rose told them that their parents would be home any minute and they had to go to bed or everyone, including Rose, would be in trouble. So they got into their pajamas and Charlotte told them a ghost story. She made her voice sound very spooky, and they all curled up together to hear about the man with the golden arm.

Steve slept in Tommy's room on the rollaway cot. It was strange having another person sleeping in his room. Steve slept with his mouth open, like a baby, and Tommy lay awake listening to his breathing. The only time Tommy had ever shared his room was in the summer, on the Island, when Michael Aldrich would sometimes spend the night with him.

Sometimes, on the Island, he stayed at Michael's, too. On the Island they had to share the bed. The Aldriches came to Grande Rivière only for the summer; the rest of the time they lived in foreign countries. Mrs. Aldrich and Michael and some of their older children—there were five of them all together, but Michael was a lot younger than the rest—usually came for the whole summer, but Mr. Aldrich couldn't spare more than a month. He had to stay abroad and work. Tommy was never allowed to spend the night at Jimmy Randolph's, though Jimmy had invited him and Tommy always wanted to. Tommy's mother said he had his own bed to sleep in, and that was where he belonged. Now the house was so full that David and John had to share John's room so that Charlotte and Julie could have David's. Tommy's Aunt Martha and Uncle Charles slept in his grandmother's room, which his mother now called the big guest room, and his Aunt Elizabeth and Uncle Roger slept in the little guest room. There were six bedrooms in Tommy's house, and they were all filled. It gave Tommy a good feeling to have so much life in his house this Thanksgiving holiday.

EIGHTEEN grown-ups and five children sat down for dinner on Thanksgiving Day: Tommy's two aunts and uncles, the two Canadian cousins, his brothers and Nick Farnsworth, Emily Sedgwick and her parents and Mrs. Sedgwick's mother, the Hutchins and Mrs. Steer and Amy. Cousin Gertrude shouted—she always shouted, because she thought no one else could hear, either—"A very festive occasion for a household in mourning," but everyone went right on talking. Nobody paid any attention. Tommy's Aunt Martha had really come to pick out what she wanted of his grandmother's furniture. A lot of the furniture in Tommy's house had belonged to his grandmother. His mother thought it was old-fashioned, like mourning, and if Martha didn't take some of it, she wasn't going to keep it all. She would get rid of what she didn't want—she didn't know how; give it to Archie, maybe—before their silver wedding anniversary next August. They were planning a big party then, she told Martha, and she wanted the house to have a fresh look. She wanted it to be hers. "The only things I want—and I don't really want them myself, Mac does—are your grandfather's desk and chair in the hall—or were they your great-grandfather's?" Tommy's mother said. "And I'd like the china that matches the lamp in Grandmother's bedroom, if that's all right with you. I've been using it for years, and there's another set that's just as good." Tommy's father and his Aunt Martha and their brother Archie had grown up in the house, and his grandmother had lived there for many years, almost since the house was built, until Tommy's father bought it from her, she took a smaller apartment downtown, and Tommy's family moved in. Tommy didn't remember that; it had happened when he was a tiny baby. He did remember when his grandmother came back, though, for a visit that gradually extended until finally she moved her bedroom furniture into the big guest room and her ivory and tortoise boxes and her lamp and the china that she knew Tommy's mother liked, and she just stayed. "We're going to redecorate in the spring," his mother said.

"Oh, Emma," Aunt Elizabeth interjected. "You always want to throw everything out." To Mrs. Steer she said with a kind of helpless laugh, "Isn't she the limit? Martha, I'll take what you don't want."

"What would you do with it, Elizabeth?" Tommy's mother asked. "You've got lots of furniture. Better to be rid of it."

"Oh, I'd like to have something from the family," Elizabeth replied, "even if it's Mac's family. You have that stiff old sofa of Mother's, and most of what's left of the china. Poor Auntie Doc," she said to Martha, "she had most of the Hopkins family furniture—they had beautiful furniture; some of it came by wagon from New England—and the family silver, too. She sold it all off, piece by piece, before she died. For a pittance, I'm sure. None of us knew she was doing it. She was too proud to admit she needed money. Pride! Those people knew about pride! Oh, how can you get rid of all this, Emma? It's *family*!"

"Perhaps that's why," said Mrs. Steer.

"Now it's time for the hymns," said Tommy's mother, walking toward the piano. "Does anyone's drink need freshening?" Singing the hymns was a Thanksgiving tradition in Tommy's house, and it was one that his mother liked to observe, al-

117

though she said one day to Tommy that the hymns were just a habit, which made their custom seem like biting your nails, which Tommy sometimes did, or sucking your thumb, which he could not remember doing. He had been broken of that habit years ago. His mother had already told Tommy that she was not making currant biscuits for Christmas breakfast. "That was Grandmother's custom, not mine," she said, "and besides, I don't have the right touch with biscuits."

To Tommy it wasn't the taste or the texture that mattered; he liked the custom, and he liked to think that even though his grandmother was dead, something of her presence lived on, if it were only biscuits rising in the oven. He liked the custom the thornapples had of turning green early in the spring, of the Indians' appearing at the door in early May with bunches of trailing arbutus they had gathered from the matted leaves and melting snow of the woods. The thick, heavy fragrance rolled forth in waves of sweetness from their delicate pale flowers, rising to fill whatever room they were placed in. Tommy liked it when his mother made popcorn for him on Sunday evening and served it in a bowl of milk. They would eat it together, as if it were cereal. Her own mother used to do the same thing when his mother was a child, popping the corn on a wood range like the one Tommy's family had at the cottage. In the fall, when they sometimes spent a weekend on the Island, Tommy's mother would make their breakfast porridge before she went to bed, leaving it to stay warm on the big iron range where the coals glowed all night, just as her mother had done. Tommy's father put butter and brown sugar on his porridge—he always called it porridge, too; never oatmeal—though his mother said the butter wasn't necessary with the cream so rich it was almost the color of butter. Tommy liked the custom of packing for the Island in the summer, and of draping the furniture with sheets so that the house looked as if it were inhabited by strangely shaped ghosts. At Easter he liked bringing out the china egg that was borne by the hands and feet of a laughing baby on its back, the egg hatching a tiny yellow chick that had once been fluffy but had lost a lot of its down over the years. The china egg had belonged to somebody, too, maybe his grandmother. Tommy liked laying flowers on the graves of people he had never known or scarcely heard of but whose blood he shared, whose history, known to him or not, was part of his history: people who had died years ago of pneumonia, like his father's baby brother, or of tuberculosis like his Uncle Jonathan, who was not buried there but out West where he'd died long before Tommy was born. There were a lot of young people in the cemetery, many of them younger even than Tommy, and their gravestones were old and worn. Next Decoration Day, he realized, they would be taking flowers to his grandmother's grave, and he wondered if she would know it from her still, dark place in the earth. Going to the cemetery on Decoration Day was a custom his father liked to observe, and sometimes Tommy and his father and brothers would go there without his mother, who was never much for going to the cemetery. One reason Tommy liked being with the Steers was that they had so many customs they revered: the Christmas cookies, the candles on the tree, the fruitcakes. Tommy liked the idea of fruitcake as much as he liked the rich dark cake itself. Oh, he loved Mrs. Steer. She loved customs as much as he did. "When you've seen the terror of anarchy," she once said to Tommy as she was baking Christmas cookies, "you learn to appreciate the comforts of form."

"Anarchy? What's that," Tommy had asked her.

"Disorder," she replied, checking her cookies. "Chaos. Nihilism. Nothingness." She looked stern. Tommy didn't pursue the subject. He didn't feel comfortable, and he left.

Mrs. Steer liked their custom of the Thanksgiving hymns, probably more than the hymns themselves, being an atheist, and she sang them along with everybody else. When she was there, she observed the customs of Tommy's house, the carols at Christmas as well as the hymns at Thanksgiving. Customs kept the world in its orbit, the river in its course, and Tommy in his bed in the night, but he wasn't sure their customs were strong enough to sustain all that: the freight was so heavy and the thread so frail. Without customs it seemed to Tommy there would be no family, and without a family he would have to live in the Evelyn MacCracken Children's Home, he supposed, on top of MacCracken Hill, with the other orphans.

At least it would be fun to slide down the fire chute from the second-floor window to the ground, if that were allowed. That would be one good thing about the MacCracken Home, and the thought made him smile. He'd always wanted to slide down that chute. As his father had often said when he was having a good time, "You can't beat fun." He'd heard him say it once that very day, the kind of occasion—full of people and drinks and food and laughter—that he liked to orchestrate. Nonetheless, Tommy preferred to be in his own familiar house, following his mother to the big piano in his own living room where, he knew, she would soon begin to play one of the familiar Thanksgiving hymns as the company gathered around. He couldn't remember which she played first—there were five of them, and the order never varied—and then—oh, yes!—the familiar words and music:

> *Praise God, from whom all blessings flow;*
> *Praise Him, all creatures here below . . .*

The chords of the Doxology thundered from the piano, and the voices—even his father's, who didn't sing very well and usually avoided it in church—rose in a swell, filling the house with sound that mixed with the smell of spices and roasting turkey from the kitchen. If Tommy listened closely he could single out each person's voice, and tell who was not singing, too. He remembered clearly his grandmother's voice, her singing voice more than her speaking voice, and he thought of how she could also whistle, which was something Tommy had not yet been able to master though his brother David said he'd learned to whistle when he was still in his crib. Tommy could distinguish Cousin Maud's shrill, papery tones and Cousin Gertrude's voice on a tune of her own, Mrs. Sedgwick's fluting soprano—she sang as if she were in an opera—and Mr. Hutchins' deep bass, Mr. Sedgwick's monotone something like his father's, Emily's high, nasal voice that seemed to match the expression on her face, as if she were especially pleased with herself and her place in the world, and Mrs. Steer's rich, throaty sound, although she didn't know the words very well. Tommy's mother said that Mrs. Steer had a deep contralto voice; his father said it sounded more like a baritone to him.

Tommy liked those words: contralto, baritone. His father also said that Mrs. Steer's being an atheist was just part of her being against the government—"like you," he said to Tommy. Tommy figured his father meant that because he didn't always want to do what his father wanted him to do, that was being against the government; but it was difficult to know just what his father did want him to do, since he hardly ever told him. One thing his father wanted him to do, which he did, sometimes with a little prompting, was to stand up when his elders entered the room, and another was not to interrupt, but while he tried not to, he often failed at that. Frequently it seemed to Tommy that interrupting meant stating his own case, or coming to his own defense. "Yes, but," Tommy would say, and his father would exclaim in exasperation, "Yes, but! I don't want to hear 'Yes, but' coming from your mouth again!" And Tommy, the response springing automatically to his lips, would blurt out before he knew it, "Yes, but"—and all hell would break loose, as John would say. However, that hadn't happened today. His father was in a good mood and Tommy was trying hard to behave.

The Doxology was followed by *"O beautiful for spacious skies, for amber waves of grain . . ."* Tommy loved to watch his mother play the piano. She often played when she and Tommy were alone in the house. Her hands looked as if they had a special relationship with the keys, as if they belonged there, hands poised and fingers tripping the cascade of sound. Tommy marveled that her fingers could strike so many notes so fast when they had trouble opening the clasp on a new handbag. Sometimes Tommy had to show her how it worked, and how to fasten her jewelry, too, and the lesson often had to be repeated several times. "I'm not very mechanical," she would say. His mother's hands were small, and except on special occasions like today, she wore only one gold ring, her wedding ring, which she never took off. Her knuckles had grown too big and she couldn't get the ring off her finger. It was strange, Tommy thought, that such clumsy hands, hands that could never manage even to put on her own rubber boots—Tommy's father always did it for her, or his brothers; she had tried to teach Tommy to do it, but he wasn't very good at it—that those hands could slam a golf ball a hundred and seventy yards down the fairway, and hit all the notes in "America the Beautiful."

When they were alone, Tommy would sometimes sit under the piano, feeling the boom of the tingling strings, watching his mother's small feet pumping up and down on the pedal, listening as she sang. She often sang as she played. He thought of that now as his mother began playing

> *Now thank we all our God,*
> *With heart, and hands, and voices . . .*
> *Who from our mother's arms*
> *Hath blessed us on our way,*
> *With countless gifts of love,*
> *And still is ours today . . .*

and he was carried back to his mother's comforting, encircling arms pressing him to her soft bosom, a bosom, she said, that had nursed him until he was a year old. The thought made him squirm. He couldn't imagine such a thing, and he didn't understand how it worked. "Mothers produce milk for their children," she had said, as if that explained it, but Tommy didn't know how, though he did know where. He thought of the wolf in the Courthouse Square. The thought not only made him squirm, it was actually embarrassing—miracle, as his mother called it, or no—that his mouth would have been buried there in the flesh and folds of her body that she took pains to conceal. Once in her bedroom when she was dressing to go out in the afternoon, she had drawn the shade of the window that looked toward the Slades' house, and Tommy asked her why. "So Mr. Slade won't see me," she had said, although it seemed unlikely to Tommy that Mr. Slade would have been home at that hour or that he could have seen her across the distance if he'd tried to. "What would happen if Mr. Slade did see you?" Tommy asked, his mind working slyly as his mother emerged in a slip from her closet, which was almost as big as Tommy's bedroom. "Why, I'd be mortified," his mother replied, surprised, as if the answer should be obvious. Tommy didn't know what mortified meant. No, Tommy was glad he couldn't remember his mother's nursing

him, and what did nursing mean, anyway? A woman in a
white cap? Sick people? His grandmother had had a nurse for
a while. The story in his book of heroes about wounded soldiers and Florence Nightingale? If he'd remembered that business, he would have had to do something about it. He would
have had a choice, and his choice would have been to drink
Mr. Matson's dairy's milk from the battered silver cup with
ANDREW THOMAS MACALLISTER and the date of his birth, 9
MARCH 1931, engraved on it, the cup that his teeth had stip-
pled and that was gold inside, the cup that he'd once peed in
and then peed in again, several times in all. He remembered
how his own yellow water had looked against the pale gold
of the cup. He didn't know why he'd done that; he'd just felt
like it. He felt now like being under the piano again, and he
eased along its curvature and nestled in the hollow. He looked
over at his cousins. Charlotte and Julie were standing behind
his mother, singing along, but Steve didn't know the words
yet. He looked down at the great solid rounds of wood, at
the massive black legs of the piano that had been turned like
the spools Mr. Steer made on his lathe and that were ridged
along their length. He liked to run his hands over those
mighty pillars, feeling the bumps and ridges and the cold
black wood; they contrasted so with his mother's own slim
legs, sheathed in auburn silk hose. Pretty as a girl's, Tommy
thought, smiling quietly to himself. "Why, Mother," he wanted
to say, "look at your little legs! They're pretty as a girl's." Of
course, he didn't say it. There were remarks that were better
kept to himself, and this was one of them. His mother didn't
shave her legs. Women don't have hair on their legs, she had
said to Tommy, although there were some hairs on hers, not
black and thick like the hair on his brother John's but hair
nonetheless. Sometimes she took the hair off with a cream
that smelled terrible. He could see the hairs now, through her
stockings, as her foot moved up and down on the pedal and
she began *"We gather together to ask the Lord's blessing."*
He remembered those times when he was little and his mother
had him bathe with her, how he had to sit in front of her in
the steaming bathtub, cramped and uncomfortable but curious, trying to avoid looking at her—he knew he shouldn't,

123

yet how could he not?—while her hands fluttered in vague awkward attempts to hide herself. It was hard to hide if you were in a bathtub together. He didn't think he wanted to be. It wasn't big enough for the two of them, and the water was too hot. He didn't want to wash her back or like her to wash his; he could reach his own well enough. If his father liked her to wash his back, well that was his business, and at least she didn't get into the tub with him. Besides, his father usually took a shower. Tommy wanted to take his bath by himself, and he coaxed his mother to let him, but if she was in a hurry she didn't give him a choice. In those days, before he'd started school, he would have his bath early in the afternoon, before the arrival of Rose and the time for his nap, and then his mother would go out shopping or to the country club for lunch and bridge or golf. That was a long time ago, of course, but he remembered, and he knew that underneath her silken hose his mother's naked legs were white as alabaster, with blue rivulets of veins here and there like lines on a map. He turned away at the thought. Actually, Tommy thought, his mother's legs looked much prettier with stockings. In fact, his mother looked much better with clothes; every old person he had ever seen naked did. Not that he had seen many: his mother, sort of; his father a few times because he never wore the bottoms to his pajamas; his grandmother almost, though she would always slip her nightgown on over her underclothes, and then pull her corset and her long cotton underpants out from underneath. His brothers didn't count; they weren't that old. In his mind's eye Tommy saw Mrs. Aldrich sitting on the dock at the Island. He had looked up her dress. He couldn't help it, the way she was sitting. Maybe he could. He didn't keep from staring anyway, and his eyes kept being drawn back to penetrate the deep blackness between Mrs. Aldrich's legs, until finally she shifted position and he couldn't see anymore. He wondered if she could feel his stare. He was afraid she would, but she never said a thing. He wondered if she was wearing a foundation. Women had to wear foundations because they were women; the garters held up their stockings. His grandmother wore a corset, but it looked the same. Men didn't need them. Although his father always wore garters, he wore them around his legs, just below the knees. It was all very mysteri-

124

ous. With Amy Steer it was different. He had pulled up her dress once, although he didn't really have to. After the first time she was eager enough to pull it up herself as long as he pulled down his pants. It was quite astonishing, that little slit, and the smooth white skin around it. He didn't understand where she peed, but she said it was no problem. When Amy touched him with her cold hand on his funny little sack with the two tiny eggs that hurt if you squeezed them, it gave him goose bumps and his sack wrinkled up tight. Usually it hung down loose. She asked him what it was. Tommy didn't know what it was; nobody'd ever said. He told her that it was his, that's all. Once his mother almost caught them like that, in the back stairway off the kitchen, but they had heard her coming and their clothes were pulled in place by the time she opened the door and asked what they were doing. Tommy said they were looking for an apple. That's where they were stored. He wondered if Amy, standing there next to her mother, was thinking about that now.

Everyone was singing, *"The wicked oppressing now cease from distressing. . . ."* Tommy joined in the hymn. They were getting to the funny line: *"Sing praises to His Name; He forgets not His own."* Well how, Tommy always wondered, could God possibly forget his own name? God was everywhere and knew everything—too much, Tommy thought. Once, when he had talked back to his mother, God made him bang his elbow. That's what his mother said, that God was punishing him for his sauciness. So if he knew all that, and more and worse besides, it was preposterous that he might forget his own name. Tommy certainly never forgot his. He wasn't allowed to. And it wasn't the Andrew or the Thomas that was important; it was MacAllister. MacAllister was his father's name, and he was lucky to have it. It meant something, but it wasn't an easy name to have and to have to live up to.

The hymns were coming almost to an end:

> *Let Thy congregation escape tribulation:*
> *Thy Name be ever praised!*
> *O Lord, make us free!*

Tommy was glad they would soon be sitting down to dinner; the smells were making him hungry. Tommy loved the final hymn, *"Come, ye thankful people, come."* His mother always played it through once unaccompanied while Tommy handed out the words she had printed herself so people could sing all four verses, and Rose—and Ruth, too, who had been borrowed from Mrs. Sedgwick for the occasion—opened the big oaken doors of the dining room. Then his mother rose from the piano, taking Mr. Sedgwick's arm, and led the way to the feast, followed by his father and Mrs. Sedgwick, the other grown-ups and children trooping behind, all singing the rousing lines,

> *Come, ye thankful people, come,*
> *Raise the song of harvest home:*
> *All is safely gathered in*

—by that time they were gathering in the dining room, finding their seats from the name cards that were placed in the slots of the little nut dishes—

> *Ere the winter storms begin.*

The table, long and rounded now only at its ends, was laden with dishes, as was the smaller circular table for the children. The great turkey, glistening in its steaming juices, rested on its accustomed platter, splendid in the moment of glory it had been bred for before its swift dismemberment into wings and thighs and drumsticks and slices of clean white breast at the skilled hands of Tommy's father. He was a master carver, everyone said—his own father had taught him—and the long knives and the sharpening steel with their handles of silver and horn, which lay there next to his mother's biggest platter, had belonged to Tommy's grandfather, the man with the gold watch, and bore his monogram. When Tommy's father had finished cutting the flesh from the bone, and offered the pope's nose on his long fork—there were seldom any takers; it was a joke—Tommy knew that the turkey would be nothing but a great shredded skeleton with a few bits of flesh still clinging to its bones, and that Rose would take the carcass into the kitchen and break it into fragments that would fit into the soup pot and become, in a day or two, the turkey soup that Tommy hated.

Sometimes Tommy thought there were a great many things he hated, despite the fact that hate was a terrible word; it was forbidden, as Mrs. Steer forbade him to use "idiot," though he had heard her say it. He could hear Mrs. Steer's voice now, above the others', singing *"Unto joy or sorrow grown."* A long time ago, when Tommy had screamed in rage and frustration that he hated his brother David, his mother had said absolutely, "Of course you don't hate him, Tommy—he's your brother!" How did she know he didn't hate him? Tommy wondered; right then he had been certain of it. "We don't hate anyone," his mother had said. Well, maybe *she* doesn't, and Tommy thought with amazement: maybe she really doesn't.

"Do you love me?" he had asked. He asked it a lot; he couldn't seem to help it. "Yes, of course I love you," his mother had replied. She was going through the kitchen cupboards, making out the grocery list on the back of one of the old envelopes she saved for that purpose. "You're my baby, and mothers love their babies." Tommy frowned. "Oh," his mother said, "that's right—you're not a baby anymore, you're a child, already in kindergarten, for heaven's sake." Tommy was in kindergarten then. It was two years ago. He still believed she was twenty-two. "But you'll always be my baby, Tommy, even when you're grown up. You'll always be your mother's baby." She moved toward him and hugged him to her. "What a darling child you used to be, and what a sweet disposition you had." It was not the answer Tommy was waiting for.

"Do you love me more than David and John?" he had asked, pursuing the line of questioning even though he was afraid, even though he knew it would soon irritate his mother. "I've never had any favorites. I love all my children the same," she replied, a note of impatience edging her voice. She had returned to the cupboards. "You know," she said, turning to look at him, "Dr. Scanlon told me the day you were born that you'd be a great comfort to me when the other boys were grown up"—the other boys *were* grown up, and Tommy did not feel that he was being a comfort to his mother now— "and now look at you!"

"Do you love Daddy?" Tommy persisted. "Of course I love

Daddy," his mother replied. She was really exasperated now. "He's my husband! He's your father! Now Tommy, stop being a pest." But Tommy, unable to resist, asked, "Who do you love more, me or Daddy?"

"I love you both," his mother said, softening a little. "It's a different kind of love, that's all. When you get older, you'll learn that love is a lot more complicated than it seems, my darling. A lot more complicated. It's not at all simple."

It seemed simple to Tommy. Love was love, he thought, and that was that, the only difference being that you loved some people more than others. How could there be different kinds of love? He loved his mother; he wasn't so sure about his father. He wasn't really sure his father loved him. His father used to love him, though—his mother had said so, how much his father had loved him when he was a baby. Tommy had heard his Aunt Elizabeth say, "Mac adores children until they're old enough to talk—then they talk back." Tommy thought of the photograph of his father holding him in his arms on the dock at the Island. Tommy was a baby then. He still had the blond curls his mother liked so much. Tommy was looking straight into the camera, his hands outstretched, and his father was looking at him with an expression of mild amusement or maybe puzzlement on his face, as if he might be about to correct him, or tell him something. Tommy wondered what his father was thinking in that photograph, and what he was thinking, too.

Tommy loved his brother John, although not so much as his mother, of course. He definitely did not love David, and the feeling was mutual. You were supposed to love your neighbor, and Tommy did love Mrs. Slade—he certainly liked going to her house, anyway—but he didn't think his mother loved her. That, too, was a different kind of love, his mother had explained, when he had once tricked her into agreeing that yes, she did love her neighbor, and therefore forced her to say that she loved Mrs. Slade, though he knew she didn't. Mrs. Slade had never even been in their house.

Tommy wanted to ask his mother if she loved his father more than she had loved her own mother, but he didn't. His mother was being nice now, and he was afraid that if he kept this up she would threaten him with the Ping-Pong paddle that lay all too accessible in the next room. Anyway, he knew, if he asked about his grandmother Bigelow, what she would say: that she was a wonderful woman or a truly fine woman; that there was not another woman like her; or that she was a good mother and sacrificed for her children; or that she had an aristocratic nose, and a whole lot of other things besides, none of them, Tommy thought, very interesting. And none of them would answer the question. But regardless of which of his grandmother Bigelow's virtues she mentioned, his mother would invariably add that she'd treated her mother with respect. His mother always said that. "I never once talked back to her. I wouldn't have dreamed of it. No, I never talked to my mother the way you talk to me." True, sometimes Tommy did not talk very nicely to his mother, and he could torment her with questions. She was a nice mother. Maybe, Tommy thought, he should stop acting like the brat he knew he was being, the brat Madge McGhee referred to when she asked David, "Where can we stow the brat?" There was no doubt Tommy could be really awful, really mean, when he put his mind to it, and usually he didn't have to work very hard at it, either. Sometimes he just wanted to be bad; sometimes he didn't know what he wanted. He wasn't even sure he wanted answers to the questions he kept asking, so much as he was curious to see how his mother would react to them. Maybe his questions were unanswerable. He didn't get answers, in any case. He didn't get the Ping-Pong paddle either, not that day. Tommy's mother gave him a little squeeze around the shoulder instead, and told him, "You're the apple of my eye, the apple of your mother's eye. Oh, you were such a sweet child! What happened to that child?" his mother asked him. She gave him a big hug. "Let's bring him back. I want him back. I want that cunning baby in the sweet dresses I sewed until my fingers bled from the needle. I thought I'd go blind, all those fine stitches! I even put lace on your little slips." She looked into the distance. "My eyes were better then," she added, kissing him and walking him out of the kitchen. "I think you need a nap. You look tired." Tommy thought it was more likely his mother who was tired; he certainly wasn't.

Oh, there were times when Tommy did hate, even though he knew it was a terrible thing, and sometimes he wondered if he didn't hate too much, if he sometimes secretly hated his own mother, and his father, too. But of course he didn't really, and he'd better not, either, or they might hate him, and then where would he be? Sometimes he just wanted to wash his hands of the whole thing. He joined in the end of the hymn:

> *Gather Thou Thy people in,*
> *Free from sorrow, free from sin . . .*
> *Come, with all Thine angels, come,*
> *Raise the glorious harvest-home.*

Mrs. Steer, gazing at the feast, asked of no one in particular, "You'd hardly believe there was a Depression raging outside, would you?" Mrs. Steer mentioned the Depression a lot—it had changed her life—but she said President Roosevelt was getting us out of it, while his father said the President just made it worse. That was a boring argument, and Tommy hoped it wouldn't come up today. There was one good thing about eating at his own small table: he didn't have to listen to the arguments. But Mrs. Steer was right. Looking at that dining room with its oak wainscoting, the plate rail that held his grandmother Bigelow's fancy plates with latticed borders— what was left of the Hopkins china that matched the platters and the tureen—the silver, his grandmother MacAllister's china and the damask cloths gleaming in the pale thin light of the November afternoon, all the food on the table . . . well, you wouldn't know there were poor people outside. They were hoboes, and they lived in Hobo Jungle just beyond the railroad station in shacks hammered together from tarpaper and scraps of wood and metal, and they kept warm over open fires. Sometimes they came to the door, usually to the back door, asking for a meal. Once when Tommy's mother wasn't home his father had brought two of them right in the front door, through the house and into the kitchen where they sat down at the kitchen table while his father made peanut butter sandwiches for them. Tommy really liked peanut butter; so did they. That was the only time Tommy had seen his father make anything in the kitchen, even a sandwich, though he did sometimes cut a piece of cheese that he put on a cracker. When his mother was home, she had the tramps sit on the back porch while she or Rose gave them something to eat. Sometimes they were Rose's friends, Indians, and his mother thought they looked awfully rough. Sometimes they did, too. Bill used to come regularly, to meet Rose and to get something to eat. Bill was all right—he was her husband—but some of the other Indians frightened his mother, and she told Rose that if another man was going to meet her, he should wait for her at the corner and not at the house.

But not all the poor people were strangers. There was his mother's sister Louise, who lived on the farm and didn't even have electricity or running water, and there was his father's brother Archibald, who kept moving from apartment to apartment with Pat, his wife. Tommy supposed that Archie was not so poor now that his grandmother was dead. Not that Tommy's grandmother was rich; "comfortable" was how his mother described her situation. She had been comfortable. Tommy figured that was something like well-to-do but not quite. Nice people didn't talk about money because it might embarrass people who didn't have as much and hurt their feelings. That was why he was punished when he gave a nickel to the street sweeper. It might have embarrassed him, and you were supposed to be nice to poor people but you didn't want to make them feel bad.

Louise and her husband, Arthur, and Archie and Pat weren't coming for Thanksgiving dinner. Tommy's mother told him she didn't think they'd feel comfortable, and probably they wouldn't; they never seemed much at ease when they visited Tommy's house, which wasn't very often. So Tommy and his father had taken a turkey and a carton of Lucky Strikes to Archie and Pat, and some whisky to Louise and Arthur, the weekend before Thanksgiving. They hadn't taken Louise and Arthur a turkey because they raised them on the farm, and chickens and cows, too. Tommy didn't know why they didn't take any whisky to Archie and Pat, but he guessed it was because his father thought they bought enough of it on their own. Tommy had never been in any of Archie's apartments— usually he stayed in the car with his mother while his father went inside—but this time his father insisted he come in with him. "I want you to see how you never want to live," he had said. His father hadn't smiled. Tommy wondered if he were angry; sometimes it was hard to tell. Archie and Pat's apartment was very small—just a kitchen and a living room, both with linoleum on the floors, and a tiny, dark bedroom. The place had a peculiar smell. It wasn't very neat; there were a lot of newspapers stacked around, and dirty dishes in the sink. Tommy knew his father thought that was no way to keep a house. Tommy liked Pat, though, even if she wasn't much of a housekeeper. He could tell she wanted to be friendly. He liked her better than Louise. Louise seemed goofy, and she had a high-pitched nasal voice that grated in his ears. He didn't feel comfortable around Archie, who was fat and didn't talk much. Tommy never knew what to say to him. Tommy's father took Archie into the kitchen, and Tommy saw him pass Archie some bills. He did it quickly, as if he didn't want it to be noticed. Probably he didn't want to embarrass him. Then Archie asked his father if he'd like a drink, but his father said no, it was too early. Tommy's father also gave Arthur some money when he was talking to him in their kitchen, and Arthur let Tommy stand on a stool and work the pump to make water splash into the sink. The pump had to be primed. Tommy's father seemed to like Arthur, probably because Arthur was a farmer and his father liked farms. When they left, Arthur thanked his father for the money and also for the whisky; he didn't seem at all embarrassed. Neither did Archie.

A few days before Thanksgiving, Tommy and his mother had fixed a box for the poor people. His mother called it a basket but it was really a cardboard box. They had filled it to overflowing with sacks of flour and sugar, cans of pumpkin and squash, sweet potatoes, apples and nuts, and some of their old winter clothes that she was getting rid of, and they had left it at the church. They were all good, nourishing things, his mother had said, but their own Thanksgiving dinner looked a lot better to Tommy. The big dining table seemed to hold every candlestick in the house, and every dish, too, filled with acorn squash and potatoes, both mashed and sweet, extra dishes of stuffing, green beans, boats of gravy, glass dishes with green and black and stuffed olives, pickles and celery and carrot sticks, cranberry sauce that his mother had made herself, hot rolls and butter, and of course the turkey on its big platter, flanked by two smaller, matching platters, empty now but that would be used for serving the meat of the great bird and the stuffing from its cavity. In the center, small squashes, a pumpkin, Indian corn, nuts in their shells, apples and grapes and other fruit overflowed and surrounded the china soup tureen with the handles that looked like living squirrels. You lifted the tureen by the squirrels' tails and the lid by an acorn, though Tommy was never allowed to because it was precious. The tureen matched the platters and the dishes on the plate rail. Usually the tureen sat on the sideboard, but the sideboard was filled now too, with plates for salad and for the fragrant pies—mincemeat and pumpkin and apple—that would be served later with the Canadian cheese his father liked so much but that Tommy had never eaten since his Uncle Christian told him it got its flavor from being buried in a manure pile. Tommy didn't know how that cured the cheese, but it instantly cured him from eating it. There was a smaller centerpiece on the children's table, and more candles, although the dinner plates were not the same. There wasn't enough of his grandmother MacAllister's china with the deep red borders edged with gold, so the children got the plain white plates with the gold bands. Tommy's mother called it the wedding-band china. It was Japanese and not so good as his grandmother's. Oh, the whole room sparkled with china and silver and glass and the flames from the candles, and steamed with delicious smells. Yes, Mrs. Steer was right. Tommy wished that she instead of Emily Sedgwick were sitting at the children's table; Emily could be fun but Mrs. Steer was more interesting. His cousin Julie would like her Pi Phi pin, though.

All the guests had found their places now, grace was said, and they were sitting down, beginning to unfold their napkins and put them in their laps. The grown-ups behaved just as Tommy had been taught to do, and none of them put his elbows on the table, either. Tommy's father stood at the head of the table, his back toward the big bay window that looked toward the Slades', and picked up the bigger of the two carving knives, giving it a few sure, swift strokes against the steel. The blade glinted as he sharpened it, and the sound of steel striking steel gave Tommy a chill. Spearing the turkey with a long fork, his father began to carve, deftly, expertly, laying slice after slice on the serving platters that Rose and Ruth began to pass among the guests. From another platter Emily served the children, who all wanted the breast.

Tommy looked beyond his table and the big table with the adults all laughing and talking, and gazed out the bay window onto the tangled, leafless branches of the thornapple and chokecherry thicket that grew between their house and the Slades'. There had been a cold snap, and there was already a dusting of snow lying in thin patches on the dry, frozen ground. There was no life there. The squirrels and chipmunks had already retreated into their snug houses in the trees for the winter; only the squirrels on the tureen, the animal heads on the platters and on the latticed plates on the plate rail still seemed strangely alive, Tommy thought, their porcelain eyes gazing softly out from beneath the glaze. Tommy almost expected them to move or to speak; maybe—he smiled—to cry out with alarm at the slaughter taking place below them. When he ran his hands over them, as he did standing on the sideboard sometimes if no one was looking, he was always surprised that he felt only cold porcelain instead of warm fur. Soon everyone was chewing away at the meat under the mild eyes of the rabbits and the hares, the stags and the does and the wild creatures whose names Tommy did not know, those animals that gazed down at them from their places on the plate rail that bordered the room.

Three

T HAT night, lying in his bed with the sound of Steve's shallow breathing coming from his small solid body in the cot nearby, the words and music of the hymn kept sounding in Tommy's head. *"Ere the winter storms begin."* The winter storms, Tommy thought, had already begun. The leaves had long since fallen, and the northwest winds spattered snow across the river. The days were short and dark; it was barely light in the morning when he went to school. It seemed as if he had been in his winter underwear for a long time. The underwear was flannel, prickly and one-piece. It buttoned down the front and had short sleeves and baggy legs that came halfway down his thighs. It was just barely shorter than his pants. In the winter he had to wear long brown ribbed stockings held up by garters that were suspended from his shoulders. He felt as if he were in harness, and he didn't like it. The farm boys who rode the school bus might have smelled bad, but at least they got to wear long trousers.

Margie Slade's father died the day of the first big snowstorm, just a few days after Thanksgiving. Margie was in her last year of high school, and David had begun to see a lot of her again. That was the day Tommy had gone to school in his snowsuit—the farm boys didn't have to wear snowsuits, either, but boots and mackinaws—and hurriedly pulling off his snow pants in the cloakroom, he accidentally pulled his trousers down with them, to the gleeful shrieks of the other children.

There he stood, in astonished crimson embarrassment, his skinny self revealed in garters and harness and underwear, but he could see the humor in it and he laughed, or pretended to, and quickly pulled up his pants. It wasn't their seeing him in his underwear that bothered him so much as the ridiculous garters and harness. Short pants were all right in the summer, when he could wear short socks, but they were terrible in winter, when he had to wear high shoes, too, instead of the oxfords he liked. That he had to wear garters to hold up the stockings he had to wear because he couldn't do the sensible thing and wear long pants, thus making it necessary to wear a snowsuit, too—well, that was the final humiliation. Who made these rules, Tommy sometimes asked himself, and why? What was the sense? There was no satisfactory answer.

Margie Slade could do anything she felt like. Margie wore her mother's fur coat, if she wanted to, and sometimes her diamond bracelet as well, just as if it were an ordinary piece of jewelry. She even wore them to high school, if she felt like it. Her mother had died a couple of years before, and now they were hers, and if she wanted to wear them, she did. Emily Sedgwick wore a fur coat when she was very dressed up, but she certainly didn't wear a diamond bracelet, and she was in college. Emily might wear her Add-a-Pearl necklace. She was very proud of it. All the pearls were real, and they had all been added. But Margie had a pearl necklace, too. She also had a gold ankle bracelet with her initials on it. "My mother wouldn't allow me to wear an ankle bracelet," Emily once told Tommy's mother, "but I think it does look nice on Margie. She's big enough to wear it." Sometimes Margie even wore two or three on the same leg. Tommy's father acted as if he didn't notice. But Margie didn't have a mother to tell her what she couldn't wear, and her father had loved her so much he let her do anything.

Margie was unpredictable, though. Tommy was never sure what to expect from her. Sometimes she could be nicer and more fun than anybody, treating him like a friend and ally, and sometimes she could be very cold and refer to Tommy as if he weren't there, when he clearly was, and meanly, too, describing him as a brat, as if he had no hearing and no feelings, either. Once, though, she met him after school—she was just standing there waiting for him when Tommy came out of the boys' door—and she invited him to come home with her for a glass of milk and some cake that she had made that afternoon. It was not long after her father had died, and she was feeling very sad. As they were walking she took his hand, and she told Tommy how empty the house was without her father, but that she should stop talking about her troubles, that she knew when you were seven years old you had troubles, too, and they were just as important as older people's troubles, even if older people didn't think so. That brought tears to Tommy's eyes—he hoped she wouldn't stop talking, wouldn't stop holding his hand—and he wanted to tell her that it was all right, but he didn't know what "it" was so he said nothing. He squeezed her hand instead. No one had ever said anything quite like that to him before, treating his own feelings quite so seriously, telling him her own grown-up feelings as if he would understand them. He hoped she wouldn't stop talking, and she didn't.

"All the Slades are mad at me," she said. "They think I'm trying to get their money, but it's *my* money. My father left it to me. He said right in his will, 'To my beloved daughter, Margaret Louise Slade'—he said 'beloved'; Bob Griswold showed me. And now Bob says we might have to sue them. But it was my father's company as much as theirs, and Bob says we'll win if we sue them and they'll have to pay interest on everything, too. If they can hate me, I can hate them right back!"

Tommy didn't know much about money—they weren't supposed to talk about it—and he knew less about wills. The only will he'd ever heard mentioned was his grandmother's. She had left all of them something in her will, but it wasn't any of Tommy's concern now. When the time was right he'd be told about it. He asked his mother when the time would be right, and his mother told him to ask his father, and his father told him the time would be right when he told him so. "And when will that be?" Tommy persisted. "When I tell you," his father said. He didn't like Tommy's asking the question, but then he changed. "When you're twenty-one," he said, "if you behave yourself." Twenty-one! If he behaved himself? He didn't know that he could behave himself for that long. He didn't think he'd behaved himself a lot of the time so far, and he was only seven and a half, eight in the spring.

But Margie wasn't twenty-one, and she knew. She knew that her grandfather had left the dock and the land around it to the city, but he'd left the coal company and the use of the dock to his sons for the rest of their lives. He hadn't thought what would happen when each of his sons died, Margie said, and her father was the first of them to go. Her Uncle Bert, who lived next door to Tommy, didn't want to give her a cent because she was adopted, and her Uncle George was nice when he was sober but he was always drunk so Bob Griswold could never talk to him. Bob told her not to worry, though. There was enough money in the meantime, and there'd be plenty more when the whole thing was over. Her uncles had to give Margie her father's share of what the company earned every year, and he was going to make them give her a lot more besides. "They'll regret it," Margie said. "They'll be sorry they ever treated me like this, and if they want to hate me, I'll give them something to hate me for." She sounded as if she could, too. "And you know, Tommy," she said, "they're the only family I have?"

Margie loved her father very much, more than her mother, who drank gin and hid the bottles in her blue chaise longue. The chaise longue still stood in her bedroom—she didn't sleep in the same room with Margie's father; it must have been a Slade family custom—but Margie hated it and she was giving it to Bob Griswold and his wife. "I took more bottles out of that thing than I can count," she told Tommy. "I flushed a river of gin down that john. Your parents may be hard on you sometimes, Tommy, but you can be glad they don't drink." Well of course they did drink, Tommy thought, but he guessed they didn't drink like that. His mother had never fallen down the stairs at his birthday party, anyway, and he'd never found any whisky bottles hidden in the house. The whisky was always right there in the cabinet, where anyone could find it. His father didn't like people who couldn't hold their liquor.

Unlike Tommy's grandmother, Margie's father hadn't gone

to the funeral home after he'd died, nor had he been buried from the church. He had stayed right in Margie's house where he'd died, and he was buried from it. The undertakers came and got him, and then brought him back in his coffin. He had lain there for three days, Margie told him, and his body was the first thing she saw when she came downstairs in the morning and the last thing she saw going upstairs at night. "You can't imagine what it was like," she said in a hushed voice, "going up to bed, looking down, him lying there, me lying in bed knowing he was there." The undertakers had brought in special lights and they never turned them out, not even in the middle of the night. Sometimes Margie would go downstairs then, all alone, and look at her father's dead body. There was no escaping the crying, and the banks and banks of flowers that filled the house with their thick cold scent, and the body. "I hope I never see another basket of flowers in that house in my whole life," Margie told him. "The smell makes me throw up." They put her father in the city vault on the hill until the cemetery thawed in the spring and he could be buried. That winter every time Tommy went by the granite building with the tiny barred slits for windows, he thought of Margie's father waiting there for his proper burial.

And then Margie was alone. There was the maid, who brought her black coffee every morning before she went to school. Margie was usually trying to lose weight, so she had nothing but black coffee with a cigarette and a small glass of orange juice for breakfast. And there was her guardian, Bob Griswold. Her father had sent him to law school, and now he gave her her allowance. And there were Bob Griswold's parents, who were moving into Margie's house to take care of her, though Tommy's father said it was more likely the other way around. But still, Margie was alone and Tommy didn't think she liked it very much, even though she could do whatever she wanted. Margie loved Bob Griswold. He took care of everything for her and paid all the bills at the stores where she had charge accounts. Margie wouldn't listen to anybody's criticizing him, and people talked about him quite a lot, though not when they thought Tommy was listening.

Bob Griswold was married to a Jewish girl who came from

New York. Her name was Laura. Phil Meyer, who was Jewish although he went to the Episcopal Church, was married to Daisy Addington, whose grandfather, the governor, liked Indians but not Jews. Tommy thought it was interesting that Bob Griswold was married to a Jewish girl—a Jewess, Mrs. Sedgwick called her—and Phil Meyer was married to Daisy. It made things balance somehow. When Tommy said this to his father one day, his father had merely grunted, and, when Tommy insisted, he looked at him and said, "What's so interesting about it?" Tommy didn't say anything. It was just interesting, that's all, and wonderfully strange, like a lot of other things—the way they scored tennis, for instance: love–15, love–30, 15–30, 30 all; fault, double fault; game. David and Nick and Vint Steer, Daisy and Madge and sometimes Laura Griswold had all played tennis the previous summer, the summer before Tommy's grandmother died, the summer David took Madge McGhee in her strapless dresses to the weekly dances at the country club and Margie a couple of times, too. Tommy liked to watch David and Daisy on the court behind the pro shop. Margie didn't play tennis, and David wasn't seeing her then, anyway. Sometimes David played with Madge, but Madge wasn't very good. Daisy was good, though, and Tommy liked to watch her and David volley back and forth, running for the ball, lobbing it, missing it, calling out the score in the mysterious language of tennis. Sometimes they played mixed doubles, and sometimes Phil Meyer and Bob Griswold played, too. But of all the women, Daisy was the best player, the one his brother liked to play with most. "Your brother!" Daisy exclaimed, pretending exasperation, as they all moved laughing toward the clubhouse where Ophelia waited with a root beer float for Tommy and iced tea and real beer for the rest of them. "I serve him love and then he makes me lose the game! He really spins those balls—don't you, David?" She turned abruptly toward him, her voice rippling with laughter. "I'd rather play with him than against him," she said to Tommy, shaking her hair in the sunlight.

Tommy's father didn't like David's playing tennis with Daisy—"she's got one partner," he told David, "and she doesn't need you for a spare"—but then, he didn't like David's spending his birthday, which was in December, with Margie, either. Margie made him a cake and put twenty candles on it and had him to dinner all by himself. It was just a couple of days after Tommy had gone home with Margie after school and become so interested in what she was saying that he had forgotten to call Rose to tell her where he was, and there had been a great hullabaloo and now Tommy had to come straight home after school with no exceptions, not even if he called first.

THAT Christmas, David decorated the house and Tommy thought it had never looked so festive. Outside he tied evergreen boughs to the pillars on the porch and laced them with strings of blue lights. David insisted that the lights be blue; he bought them himself. He tacked more boughs around the front door and tied pinecones on the knocker and put a new wreath on the storm door, not one of the holly wreaths his mother saved from year to year and hung in every window of the house, upstairs and down. David put a small tree on each corner of the porch roof and decorated them with blue lights, too, stringing the wires through Tommy's bedroom window. After his mother had put him to bed and drawn the shades, Tommy would get up and raise them, pressing his nose against the window, watching his breath turn to steam on the cold pane of glass. It was strange how cold the glass could be, and how such cold could burn. When Tommy returned to his bed, leaving the blinds up, he would snuggle down and listen to the sounds of *Kinderszenen*—" 'Scenes from Childhood,' Tommy," and his mother's favorite music— drifting in patches from the piano below. His mother often played in the evenings after dinner when she was home, and usually she played a part of *Kinderszenen*, sometimes all of it. By the time she got to "The Child in Slumberland"—Tommy loved to hear his mother say it in German: *Kind im Einschlummern*—he was supposed to be asleep, and usually he was, lulled by the music and bathed now in the glow from the blue lights twinkling on the dark trees dusted with snow, on the snow that covered the porch roof and the lawn below, reflecting in the crystals of ice on his window and casting its cool radiance against the wall beside his bed. When his mother noticed that the blinds were always raised in the morning, she began to leave them up at night. "So you won't have to get out of bed, Tommy," she said with a laugh. Tommy thought that was nice of her; she was breaking a rule for him. He continued to get out of bed, though, to put his nose against the glass and—very quickly, lest it stick—his tongue. It was sort of an experiment, to see how long he could hold his tongue to the glass without its sticking.

His mother brought the boxes of decorations down from the attic, put the electric candelabrum with its own blue lights in the hall window, and hung the holly wreaths, tying a red bow on each one. The wreaths had faded from a rich true green into a kind of olive—they looked very tired and brittle from their year in a box in the attic—but the ribbons were always freshly ironed. It was David, though, who spread more evergreen boughs across the mantel in the living room and secured them to the archways downstairs, and David who hung the mistletoe from the chandelier in the hall—so he could kiss all the pretty girls who came in, he said. David worked very quickly, smiling, making little jokes. His mood, Tommy thought, was getting a lot better, in contrast to his father's, which had been declining since Thanksgiving. Tommy's father seemed scarcely to notice the decorating that was going on, and when he did it was to observe that the house was beginning to look like a Sicilian's idea of Christmas in Norway, or to ask David if there were any branches left in the woods. Though he laughed when he said it, it still seemed to Tommy that his father never liked Christmas very much, which was strange and sad and not very nice, either. But David was not to be discouraged. Boughs were piled on boughs, and the smell of balsam filled the house. The little crèche figures were placed on the big table in the hall, the six porcelain angels arranged on the mantel, the other choir of angels—the ones who held tiny candles—on the piano. Nothing seemed to deter David in his desire to fill the house with greens, and Tommy was his willing helper. David and Margie even helped Tommy and Jimmy Randolph build a huge snowman in the

144

circle inside the driveway, and Margie made a sign—"HEIGH-HO, MERRY XMAS"—that she attached to a stick and tucked in the crook of its arm. Tommy loved looking forward to Christmas, and this year, going in the doorway of his old familiar house, he felt as if he were passing into a magical, sweet-smelling forest of breathtaking beauty.

The tree itself sat in a bucket of snow on the front porch until the afternoon of Christmas Eve, when David and John, home now for the holidays, brought it in and set it up in the holder in its accustomed place near the piano. They didn't even argue much about how to do it and who was doing it wrong. When the tree was up and the branches had begun to relax in the warmth, David and John and Tommy and his mother began to decorate it. David, because he was the tallest, put the star on top, though even he had to stand on the stepladder to do it. The tree was very tall; its top almost brushed the ceiling. John and his mother arranged the strings of lights with David still on the stepladder, and his mother would step back occasionally to see the effect and to suggest filling in a little here or moving a light from there. When the lights were finally in place, Tommy took the ornaments very carefully from their boxes and laid them out on a table near the tree. He hung his special favorites on the branches he could reach while John and David and his mother decorated the higher branches. His mother even stood on one of the dining-room chairs to do it, which was breaking one of her own rules. Then, when all the ornaments and lights were in place, she straightened out the tattered, crumpled tinsel as usual, pressing it with her hand against the tabletop, and, because no one else would do it, draped it from the branches herself. The sight was touching to Tommy, and he moved to help her. He was filled with a happiness, and a welling sadness, too, there with his mother and her tinsel, his handsome brothers—even David looked handsome to him now—and he wished his father would take part. He made a comment occasionally from his chair, looking up from his business papers and columns of figures from the adding machines at the plant, but mostly he stuck to his work. He wasn't very good at decorating, he said. Well, he couldn't sing very well, either, Tommy thought, but at least he tried sometimes. And then when they were through with the tree, Tommy's mother sat down at the piano to play a couple of carols. They were just singing *"Joy to the world, the Lord is come,"* when there was a knock on the door, John said, "the Lord is come," his mother told him not to be blasphemous, and, the notes still hanging in the air, she opened the door. It was Lucien Wolfe.

"Lucien Wolfe!" Tommy's mother gave a little cry of surprise. "Look at you! Is it really Lucien Wolfe?"

Mr. Wolfe laughed and kissed her on the cheek. "In the flesh," he said. "I mean, in the fur," and indeed he was, in a great hairy coat that seemed to start at his hat brim and end a few inches above his ankles, and cradling in his arm a tall bulky object thickly wrapped in newspaper and green florist's paper.

"When did you get here?" his mother asked. "I'd no idea you'd be in town"—which was funny because Tommy remembered Mr. Hutchins' telling his mother that he'd heard Mr. Wolfe was coming for Christmas. Tommy's father had come to the door, too, and he was pumping Mr. Wolfe's free hand.

"Aren't you going to ask me in?" Tommy's mother was still standing there with her hand on the doorknob. Nobody mentioned the package.

"Well of course we're going to ask you in, Luke! Come in, come in," his father said, "and you're going to stay for supper, too."

"You're just in time," his mother said, collecting herself. "We've just finished decorating the tree and Mac was about to pour us a little holiday drink." Tommy didn't know his father was about to pour them a drink, and he supposed because it was Christmas Eve that he might be able to have one, too, even though his mother said drinks spoiled his appetite. It was odd that drinks spoiled children's appetites but made adults hungry.

"Good timing," Mr. Wolfe said, still laughing. "I'll take that drink, but first, Emma, you take this," and he handed Tommy's mother the package, which she set down on the big table in the hall, tearing away part of the paper to reveal the crimson blooms of a giant poinsettia that to Tommy looked more like a bush than a plant, it was that big. "And just let me reach around the corner here"—Mr. Wolfe's furry back bent over and he came up with a case of whisky in his arms—"and now we can all have a merry Christmas. Happy holidays, everybody," he said.

"A case of Crown Royal!" Tommy's father exclaimed, taking it from him. "Too much, Luke, too much," and he carried it off to the kitchen while his mother finished tearing the paper from the poinsettia, saying she had never seen such a splendid specimen. She moved it to the top of the piano, arranging the little choir of angels before it. "It's lovely, Lucien, truly lovely."

"And for you, Tommy, you can take my coat, but I'll want it back." Mr. Wolfe draped the heavy fur from Tommy's shoulders. "You look like a little king." Tommy sank under its weight. "That's what happens to bad raccoons," he said with another laugh. "We make coats out of them."

Tommy's mother laughed, too. "It's a good thing you're not a raccoon, darling," she said, lifting the coat from his shoulders, admiring it. "Why, look," she said, "they've even put their little tails on the pockets! Lucien, you're the only man I know who could get away with such a thing."

"Ooops. Almost forgot. Open your hand, Tommy," Mr. Wolfe said, "and close your eyes." Tommy did, squeezing his eyes tight shut. He felt Mr. Wolfe drop something large and round and cold in his palm and squeeze his fingers around it, and then he said, "Okay, open up." There in his hand was a silver dollar—a Canadian silver dollar, Tommy saw when he looked at it closely, with the head of the king on it and the year, 1938. "Fresh out of the mint," Mr. Wolfe said, "the last coin of the old year, and made from my own silver, too." Tommy had never had a silver dollar before. "Keep it clean," Mr. Wolfe said with another laugh, and patted Tommy on the shoulder.

"Why, Lucien, isn't that lovely," Tommy's mother said, picking it from his hand. "And made from your own silver! Isn't that nice, Tommy?"

"Yes," Tommy said, "it is. I've never had one before."

"Thank Mr. Wolfe, Tommy," his mother said, reminding him of his manners.

"Thank you, Mr. Wolfe. Thank you very much," and Tommy looked at the dollar again, turning it over in his palm before slipping it into his pocket.

Tommy's father returned from the kitchen with a tray of drinks. Tommy supposed that to be polite he'd had to make them from Mr. Wolfe's whisky, which Tommy knew he didn't like as much as Scotch. Maybe he made his own drink with Scotch; nobody would ever know. He thanked Mr. Wolfe for the whisky. "It's the best," he said, and when Tommy showed it to him, he admired the silver dollar, too. "Hold on to it," he told Tommy. "We might need it."

Because it was Christmas Eve, Tommy's mother gave him an eggnog with nutmeg on top but no whisky in it, even though it was known that eggnogs definitely spoiled your appetite and were more appropriate for dessert. While they were all talking and catching up on Mr. Wolfe's news, David said he was going to see Margie, and John went off to Emily's. The girls were making them go to church at midnight; Tommy's parents weren't going this year because Rose was off and no one would be in the house to stay with Tommy and he wasn't old enough to go with them. Tommy was disappointed that his brothers left, and a little disappointed that Mr. Wolfe had shown up so unexpectedly, too. Tommy had hoped that the family could be together, and that his mother would make popcorn after supper and play the Christmas carols that they would all stand around the piano and sing— even his father, in the monotone he sometimes joked about. "Some men—and Mrs. Steer, of course—are baritones," he told Mrs. Sedgwick. "I'm a monotone." Then his mother would turn out all the lights but those on the tree and bring him close to her on the couch and he would snuggle up in her warmth and softness while she read "The Night Before Christmas." That wouldn't happen now. Probably his brothers were too old for "The Night Before Christmas" anyway, and they wouldn't have stayed home for it. Tommy could feel the silver dollar in his pocket.

They had oyster stew for supper. It was always supper on

Christmas Eve, and always oyster stew, too. That was a custom that his mother's family had brought all the way from New England and that his mother faithfully observed. See, Tommy thought, she did have some customs that she kept. Really she had a lot of customs that she kept, like the tinsel and the holly wreaths.

After Tommy had finished his oyster stew and taken care to leave all the oysters in the bottom of the dish and conceal them as best he could, after he'd hung his stocking by the chimney just like the children in the poem his mother didn't read this year, Tommy left the three of them alone downstairs. "You've had a lot of excitement for one day," his mother said, sending him off much later than usual because it was Christmas Eve. A few minutes later she came up to tuck him in snug, kissing him good night and singing "Silent Night" while he watched her in the shadows. When he reminded her, she raised his blinds so he could look out at the blue lights twinkling in the cold clear night. He didn't want her to leave, but she couldn't read him a story because she had to get the house ready for Santa, and of course she had to be nice to Mr. Wolfe. "Let Daddy talk to Mr. Wolfe," Tommy told her, but no, that wasn't possible, and after another verse of "Silent Night" and a final kiss she left his room to join the two men downstairs. When she had gone, Tommy put the silver dollar on his windowsill. He could see it shining from his bed.

Though it was long past his regular bedtime, Tommy tried to stay awake, hoping to hear his mother bring down the gifts from their hiding places in the attic and in his grandmother's bedroom where she had wrapped them, but she and his father and Mr. Wolfe went on laughing and talking for a very long time. Tommy wondered what was happening at the Steers', where they had their big Christmas dinner and opened their gifts on Christmas Eve, the custom in Denmark. He wondered why Mr. Wolfe didn't go to the Steers' instead; after all, he knew them, too. Mrs. Steer thought Mr. Wolfe was very sophisticated, very dashing, and very dangerous— "a real Lord Byron," she said, and explained when Tommy asked her that Lord Byron was an English poet, one of the great Romantics. "Maid of Athens, ere we part, Give, o, give me back my heart! Or, since that has left my breast, Keep it now and take the rest!" That, she said, is a great Romantic —"and a great rogue, too." Tommy wasn't sure what to make of that, or what Mrs. Steer made of it either. In some ways Mr. Wolfe reminded Tommy of his Uncle Andrew, whom he liked a lot. Mr. Wolfe spent a lot of time in the Canadian woods looking at mining claims which sometimes made him a lot of money and sometimes lost him a lot, too, but he was not a prospector like the grizzled old man who came to the door every few months to see Tommy's father. Not at all. Lucien Wolfe—funny name—was entirely different. Tommy's father didn't give him money, for one thing, and he wasn't grizzled and dirty but looked like everyone else, only better. He was thinner—"Lucien's slim," was how Tommy's mother described him—and he had thick black hair and a mustache like Tommy's Uncle Roger's, and he spent so much time outdoors that even in the winter he was tanned. No one really knew when he might turn up in Grande Rivière. He usually spent some time on the Island, and he kept an apartment in the old McNaughton Mansion that he hardly ever used. Sometimes his business kept him away for a year at a time. It took him all over the North—he had been to Alaska, the Yukon, and the Klondike—and to places like Mexico, too, where he spoke Spanish and took pictures of the Gila monster, which he explained was a poisonous lizard; if it bit you, you were dead. Mr. Wolfe took a lot of pictures of animals, and a lot of the animals were dangerous. He had shown a movie on the Island the summer before, about bears in the North. The bears were funny, they looked like big clumsy toys—like his own ragged Teddy bear that he had put in a shoe box and buried near the Indian cemetery on the Island that summer, only a hundred times larger—but they were ferocious, Mr. Wolfe said. They didn't look it; they looked friendly, as if you could play with them. You'd better not, though. They could rip you apart with their claws, and sometimes they did. Mr. Wolfe said the difference between a grizzly and a brown bear was that the grizzly would climb a tree right after you while the brown bear, who couldn't climb, would shake you out of it. Either way you were in trouble. If you'd been near a salmon, the Kodiak bear would eat you right up because he could smell the salmon on you and salmon was his favorite food. Some of Mr. Wolfe's pictures were so good that they were printed in *National Geographic*, even though he was only an amateur photographer. No, Mr. Wolfe didn't work the way other men worked. He said he couldn't, that he'd rather be broke with the chance of hitting the jackpot once in a while than go to work in an office every day and play golf on the weekends, even in the evenings, as Tommy's father often did. Mr. Wolfe had to be his own man, people said. Tommy figured that was probably why he'd never married, so far as anyone knew. Daisy Meyer knew a lot, and she said that nobody could catch him. "He moves too fast." Maybe that was why Mrs. Steer called him a great Romantic. This Christmas, Mr. Wolfe must have hit the jackpot, Tommy thought, or else he wouldn't have brought a case of whisky to his father and that big plant to his mother. Tommy wondered, if Mr. Wolfe had children, would he have brought them fur coats, like his mother's father? Then they could have sold them when they were poor, too. Margie Slade had had a fur coat when she was little; it was white, and Tommy had seen a picture of her wearing it. He was very glad—very, very glad—that nobody had ever brought him a fur coat and made him wear it. It was all right for his mother, and all right, he supposed, for Mr. Wolfe, too, the only man he'd ever seen in a fur coat. His mother's coat was sealskin, but there weren't any tails on it. Margie's was made of Persian lamb. Probably everyone who had a fur coat was wearing it tonight, it was so cold and clear. The lights catching the crystals of frost in the corner of his bedroom window made it seem even colder. High against the sky he could see the orange glow from the furnaces in his father's plant. The furnaces burned day and night, summer and winter, year in, year out; the fires could never go out. He heard the dull grinding of his own furnace. The new furnace burned oil, and nobody ever had to tend it the way the old coal furnace had to be tended, the way the furnaces in his father's plant could never be left alone. Tommy snuggled farther down in his bed, watching the motes of blue light sparkle from the trees on his roof, in the frost on his

window, in the silver dollar on his sill. He closed his eyes
tight to see the points of light popping against his eyelids like
tiny fireworks, and snapped them open to see the lights still
twinkling on the trees, cold and sharp, and the reflection of
the fires at the plant shimmering in the distant sky. The blue
lights sparkled like the amethyst his mother had once worn
as a pendant until the hook broke and ever since Tommy
could remember had lain in the jumble at the bottom of
her jewelry drawer. Sometimes Tommy put the amethyst to
his eye, trying to make it stick there like a monocle, turning
it and watching the familiar objects of his world break up in
the flashing blades of colored light, displaced but not dis-
torted. Finally, against his wishes and his better judgment,
Tommy drifted into nervous sleep, hearing in his mind his
mother at the piano and thinking not so much about sugar-
plums—whatever they were—but of what he might find under
the tree in the morning. He did not hear his mother carry
the packages down from their secret places.

THE first thing Tommy saw when he rushed around the
bend in the stairway Christmas morning, before anyone else in
the house had awakened, was a desk just his size with a top
that rolled down, two drawers—one of them with a key in its
lock—and a chair that matched. He did not know whether
to laugh or to cry, he was so thrilled, so happy, so full of grati-
tude. He paused there on the landing for a second, gazing at
the desk and at the packages that surrounded it and spilled
out from underneath the tree, spreading to the piano and
beyond. The room in its winter light seemed filled with beautiful boxes of all sizes and shapes, and before it all his desk,
his own most splendid desk. Tommy ran back upstairs shouting "Up! Up! Everybody up! It's Christmas. It's Christmas!
Merry Christmas, everybody," and he threw open his brothers'
doors and shook them, and opened, a little more carefully, his
parents'. His mother, already awake, reached over to hug him
and give him a kiss. "I love it! I love it!" Tommy shouted,
throwing his arms around her. He couldn't stand still, and he
ran around to his father's side of the bed and gave him a hug,
too—"You're awake," Tommy said, surprised, and his father

laughed and said if he weren't he'd have to be deaf, and hugged him back—and Tommy danced around the room and back out the door and down the stairs. His father called after him, "It's just like the desks at the plant, Tommy, just like the desk you like to sit at in my office." Well, it wasn't quite like that but it was close enough, and Tommy shouted back, "Joy to the world, my desk is come!" His very own desk. With a drawer that locked. His very own private place that he would never let David into, except that he might open it just long enough for him to see treasures there but not long enough for him to see what the treasures were before Tommy would slam the drawer shut, lock it, slip the key into his pocket, and move on. Ha, but David would be furious! At least, Tommy hoped David would be furious, and he was eager to try it on him but he'd have to wait for the right moment.

The desk was too big to wrap, of course, but his mother had tied a bow to the back of the chair and put three Christmas balls on top of it with a sprig of balsam—the balsam might have been David's idea, Tommy thought. He sat down in the chair and rolled back the top—it did disappear into the back of the desk just like those at his father's office—and inside were five pigeonholes and still another very small drawer, though this one didn't lock. It took a while for Tommy to begin to notice the pile of gifts that stretched out around him and around his beautiful, almost grown-up desk, now his most prized possession.

His mother, having stopped to admire his desk and the tree and to give Tommy another little hug, was already in the kitchen making coffee, and his father was coming downstairs in his bathrobe. David, who was dressed, started the fire in the fireplace and plugged in the lights on the tree, and John was on the telephone calling Emily to wish her a Merry Christmas.

"Can't that wait for a minute, John?" his father asked. But Tommy didn't care. John could talk to Emily as long as he wanted, if Tommy could play at his desk. Tommy's father took his cup of coffee upstairs and came down a few minutes later, dressed, and made John get off the telephone. Tommy's father didn't like anyone to talk on the telephone for long because he might get an important call from the plant. They had their orange juice and David helped his mother with breakfast, which they took into the living room and ate as they opened their gifts. Tommy ate at his desk, and when he opened a gift he would take the card and put it into the drawer that locked. When he opened a little box with a pair of dice in it from David, he put that in there, too. He wanted to learn to shoot craps with them—maybe David would teach him; he knew how.

Tommy was glad it was just the family here this Christmas so they didn't have to sit at the dining-room table and finish breakfast before any of the gifts were opened, the way they'd done two Christmases ago when they'd visited his Aunt Clara and Uncle Andrew in Chicago. His Aunt Clara had so many rules. One of his mother's rules, which she sometimes allowed Tommy to break, was that gifts were opened one at a time so that each of them could see and admire one another's presents. There were a lot of them—the unwrapping took most of the morning and the floor was soon a jumble of ribbons and wrapping and boxes—not only from his parents and his brothers but also from his aunts and uncles, whose packages had been arriving at the house for the past few weeks and immediately whisked out of sight by his mother, though Tommy knew where she had hidden them: in his grandmother's bedroom closet, under her bed, and in the attic. He had looked at all the cards and poked and shaken each box, so that he knew from the wrapping which was whose, but he'd never found the desk. His mother must have hidden it under the dark eaves in the attic, which was a place Tommy didn't like to explore alone. Everyone in his mother's and father's families gave everyone else gifts. Well, they didn't get anything from his Uncle Archie and Aunt Pat, or from his Aunt Louise and Uncle Arthur, either, but that was different. His mother gave them things, though. Soon the telephone would be ringing and they would be putting in calls to Chicago and Arizona and Grosse Pointe and Minneapolis or wherever his relations were. Sometimes it took a long time to get the calls through, and it was sort of a race to see who got through first, his aunts and uncles or his parents. Tommy was happy, and happy that everyone else seemed happy, too, even his father, who always got fewer gifts than anyone else. That was because he was a man and harder to buy for, his mother explained, though Tommy thought when he was a man he'd be pretty easy to buy for. He loved presents; he loved the wrapping and the unwrapping, and the ribbons and the tissue and the beautiful paper on his aunts' and uncles' gifts, and the boxes with the names of city stores written on them: Marshall Field's, B. Altman, Hudson's, Saks Fifth Avenue.

"Ha, ha, David," Tommy said, "I bet you'd like to know what's in my drawer now."

"Would I ever," David said, suddenly lunging for the desk and tugging at the knob.

"It's locked," Tommy said. The key was in his bathrobe pocket. He thought he'd said it very suavely.

"No need to shriek," his father said, "David's right here in the room."

"Let me see," said David, "you've got a rubber toad, seventeen yards of ribbon, all your gift cards, and two little dice." Except for the rubber toad, which David had just made up, he was almost right. That is, there was a lot of ribbon in the drawer and all his gift cards, and the dice David had given him; but there were some other things, too, and Tommy wasn't telling what.

"Wrong," he shouted, triumphant. "Double wrong! Let's play Fifty-two Pickup. My deal." And he unlocked the drawer to flash before David's eyes the deck of cards John had given him.

"Finish your cereal, Tommy," his mother said. "And David, stop teasing. No Fifty-two Pickup today. We're going to pick up all this paper instead." His mother always saved the prettiest paper and the best ribbons to use again another year, like the tinsel on the tree. The excelsior and the discarded wrappings were burned in the fireplace. The glasses for drinks that his father always got were packed in excelsior. Sometimes they were highball glasses, sometimes old-fashioned glasses, and sometimes cocktail glasses. His father had a lot of glasses.

"Oh, you can find such wonderful things in the city, such beautiful wrapping," his mother said, pressing out with her hands the paper that his Aunt Elizabeth had wrapped her gifts in. You had to be careful of her packages because his aunt pinned the paper to the box instead of taping it, and the bows were always pinned to the paper. Inside, her boxes were full of pins, too, and the sweater she had given Tommy and the blouse she had given his mother were stuck with pins that you couldn't see so you were always getting pricked when you didn't expect it. His mother just used colored tape or ribbons, but his mother wasn't really very good at wrapping presents. "It's the thought that counts," she always said, "not the gift or the wrapping," which was why Tommy got to make his own gifts. "People like them even more if you make them yourself," his mother said. "It's like giving away a part of you." Tommy didn't think of it like that, but this year he gave everybody boxes of matches that he'd decorated with pictures from old Christmas cards. Mrs. Steer had shown him how to do it, and he and Amy had spent two Saturdays before Christmas cutting out pictures from the Steers' old cards and gluing them to matchboxes. Tommy would get a little bundle of six boxes and wrap them together and tie them with a paper ribbon that he tried to make curl, and then he hid them at the bottom of his underwear drawer and gave them to everyone in his family and a package to Mrs. Steer, too. His mother was very surprised, and so were his father and his brothers. His mother said they were almost too pretty to use, but she put them around the house next to the ashtrays for their guests. His mother didn't smoke, but he knew that Mrs. Steer would use hers. She had a double supply, because she had gotten some from Amy, too. Tommy didn't like to admit it, but Amy's matchboxes looked nicer than his. You couldn't see the paste at the edge on Amy's and she was better at cutting out.

"Now, Tommy, let's get some clothes on," his mother said. She was still in her robe, too. "Someone might be dropping in and we wouldn't want them to find us like this. You can play with your things as soon as you're dressed." They went upstairs together while Tommy's brothers finished burning the Christmas wrapping and his father went into the kitchen to see about the eggnog in case anyone should come by.

Neither his father nor his mother liked eggnog—it wasn't a proper drink, they said—but they always served it at Christmastime anyway. It was sort of a tradition, Tommy supposed.

It took Tommy's mother a lot longer to get dressed than it took Tommy, and when she came down the long stairs she was wearing a dress as red as lipstick with the poinsettia pin she had worn every Christmas for longer than Tommy could remember. Its leaves were long and sharp, and they pricked his face if his mother hugged him. She matched Mr. Wolfe's plant, Tommy thought. His father had already fixed himself a drink because it was a special occasion—on ordinary occasions he never took a drink until dinnertime, but, as he said, it was almost noon and it was Christmas Day—and when his mother appeared on the stairway his father raised his glass and said, "Here comes the scarlet woman." His mother looked startled. "Oops," his father said, "I meant, 'Here comes the bride,'" and Tommy began singing, *"Here comes the bride, short, fat, and wide,"* and his brothers laughed, and his mother, who liked her red Christmas dress and her poinsettia pin and also worried about getting fat, said, "Sometimes you boys are too much. What was it Queen Victoria said? Oh, yes. 'We are not amused.'" But his father was, and he gave her a little pat and said, "There's the old sweetheart," and immediately the doorbell was ringing. Sometimes Tommy's mother and father seemed to know what was going to happen; his mother had said someone might be dropping by, and here they were, Nick Kingsfield—he didn't want to be called Farnsworth now—and Margie Slade.

Nick brought flowers for Tommy's mother—"Oh, Nick, you're always so thoughtful," she said, hugging him and catching her pin in his jacket—and for Tommy a little toy car that when you wound it up ran in circles around the room, making a lot of noise and crashing into everything and everybody, and making them jump, which was fun. Tommy saw that his mother didn't think it was that much fun, though, and after she had given him a couple of looks he picked it up and slipped it into his drawer, which he locked. He loved his drawer that locked.

Margie brought a gift for each one of them, except for

David, but she'd already given him his present the night before. David didn't show it to anybody, either, or tell anybody what it was, though Tommy begged him to. Tommy never even saw the package. "I'll bet it was just a kiss," he said to David, who told him he should be so lucky. "Just a measly kiss," Tommy repeated. "Ugh." Once in the car with David and Margie and some of her girl friends, she had said she was going to kiss him, and she tickled him and made him giggle and finally laugh so hard he was afraid he would wet his pants, and she pinned him down so he couldn't get away and finally planted a big kiss on his ear—"a big wet smooch," she called it—and left a lipstick mark, too. Tommy didn't see anything lucky about that, and if that was what she'd given David, and he bet it was, well, David could have it. Probably he stood under the mistletoe so she had to. But what Margie brought Tommy was better than any kiss. It was the finest Monopoly set Tommy had ever seen, and it thrilled him almost as much as the desk. The hotels looked like ivory, not wood like Jimmy Randolph's, and Tommy knew it must have been expensive. Well, maybe she had given David something exciting; he'd have to find out. Next to the desk, he thought the Monopoly set was his favorite gift, and he loved Margie very much. He was sorry he hadn't thought to make any matchboxes for her, but she used a lighter anyway. His mother hadn't gotten anything for her, either, and she was astonished —she said she was astonished—when she unwrapped Margie's package and pulled out a leather handbag. "What a handsome bag," she said to Margie, opening it and examining the things inside. She didn't have any trouble with the clasp. His mother looked up at Margie and repeated, "A very handsome, a very elegant bag. My, won't I look smart?" His mother was being polite. "You shouldn't have done it, Margie, but thank you. I love it and I can always use it." It was curious that women could use so many handbags; his mother had a shelf full of them, some in cloth bags of their own, like his Aunt Clara's suitcases, which were leather and had their own canvas covers that zipped. The covers kept the leather nice, but you couldn't see the leather with the covers on them, so nobody would know if it was nice or not. Tommy thought again how glad he was that they weren't with his aunt this Christmas, though she had sent him a lot of nice gifts. She always sent him more gifts than anyone else, except for his parents. His Uncle Christian sent him a book, as he usually did, and usually Tommy liked it, too. This one was full of strange drawings—in sepia, his mother said—of fish that didn't look like any fish Tommy had ever seen: fish that lit up, fish that looked like horses, fish that looked like balloons, fish that were poisonous, fish that were friendly, like Finger-fins. The book was called *Fingerfins: A Tale of the Sargasso Sea.* Fingerfins lived in the seaweed. He couldn't survive any-place else, and if he fell away from the seaweed he would die. Tommy thought he'd like to go to the Sargasso Sea, an ocean within an ocean, the book said, with a separate life of its own. How could that be? Tommy wondered if Mr. Wolfe had ever been there, and he thought he might ask him about it, and about how there could be a separate sea within the sea, and how you could know the difference since it was all water, and why it had its own life different from the life of the ocean. Tommy had never seen the ocean, but his parents had and so had his Aunt Clara. They had sent him postcards from Bermuda that his brothers had had to read to him be-cause he didn't know how to read then. His Aunt Clara and Uncle Andrew had been there again, with his Uncle Christian, which was where he said he had found the book. He wrote that on the card Tommy put in his drawer. That was a long way from his living room in Grande Rivière, Tommy thought. He couldn't imagine a Christmas without snow, and it didn't snow in Bermuda. There were palm trees in Bermuda, just like the Christmas cards with the wise men at Bethlehem, and Tommy had never seen a palm tree, either. There were a lot of things he would have to see when he was grown.

Tommy's mother was admiring the wool shirt that his father had just unwrapped and that Margie had given him. It had pins in it, too, Tommy noticed, and it came from the best department store downtown. He thanked her, of course, but Tommy's father was funny about gifts. He returned a lot of them, or gave them to the Salvation Army. Those were business gifts that were delivered to the house a week or two before Christmas and came from the companies that did business with Tommy's father, and they were usually something to eat or drink. Tommy's mother didn't think they did any harm—they were delicacies, she said, and expensive—but his father said that it wasn't right. So he wrote the people and explained that he didn't accept gifts. It seemed to Tommy that he spent as much time returning those gifts as he did opening the ones under their tree. Mr. Bonnaro's was the only one he kept. Maybe that was because Mr. Bonnaro brought it to the house himself, or maybe it was because he made it. The gift was always the same: two gallon jugs of wine that his father put in the cellar and never drank but that he thanked Mr. Bonnaro for just the same. Mr. Bonnaro didn't speak very good English because he was an Italian, but he said he knew how to make good wine. He knew how to grow vegetables, too, and in the summer Tommy's mother bought vegetables from his garden. Mr. Bonnaro had worked for Tommy's father for a long time, and his father liked him even if he didn't like Dago Red, which was what he called Mr. Bonnaro's wine. His mother didn't think that was a nice name, but she didn't think Mr. Bonnaro's children were nice, either. Two of them were in Tommy's grade. Carmen was Tommy's age, and Tommy liked him better than Leo, who was older even though they were in the same grade. Tommy's mother thought they were both rough, but Carmen really wasn't. Both of them came to the door with Mr. Bonnaro just after his father had opened Margie's gift, and all of them stood in the front hall while Tommy's father thanked him for the wine and Mr. Bonnaro said, looking into the living room at the piles of gifts, "Lucky family, lucky, lucky family—so much of the things, so much of the love."

"Yes," his mother said, "fortunate. We're all so fortunate, aren't we, Mr. Bonnaro, to be here in this country where there is so much."

"So much, so much," Mr. Bonnaro said, only he pronounced it "much-a." That was his Italian accent.

There was, indeed, a lot, and Tommy felt a little embarrassed at the sight of it all. He got the windup truck that Nick had given him and showed it to Carmen and Leo. He would have shown them the Monopoly set, but he was afraid it looked too fancy.

When the Bonnaros had left—they stayed only a minute because Mr. Bonnaro said they had to leave Mr. MacAllister's family to their Christmas—Tommy's father took the wine down to the cellar, where he put it with the jugs from other Christmases. When he came back up, he went straight to the desk in the hall. The desk had a lot of drawers and all of them locked; nobody but his father and his mother were allowed in it. When he came into the living room he went over to Tommy's mother, who was sitting on the piano bench explaining to Margie and Nick that Mr. Bonnaro brought Mr. MacAllister wine every year—"He makes it himself, you know, from the grapes in his garden"—and he bent over and gave her a kiss, right on the lips. His mother seemed a little surprised, and she pretended to be surprised when his father handed her a check, neatly folded in half. She opened it a tiny bit, peeked at it, and said, "Oh, my, won't I have fun?" She kissed him back. In addition to the usual check, though, Tommy's father gave his mother his grandmother's pearls. They were still wrapped in the tissue the undertaker had put them in. His mother took them out of the paper, letting it fall to the floor, and tried to fasten the pearls around her neck, getting them tangled with her poinsettia pin.

"Oh, Tommy, you help me, will you? I can never manage to figure out these clasps," she said. Tommy knelt behind his mother on the piano bench to fasten the clasp at the back of her neck. It was a beautiful clasp, and precious; there were real sapphires in it. When he had finished, his mother shook the pearls to untangle them from her pin. Tommy's arm reached around his mother's shoulder to help her, his own fingers tangling with hers, with the pearls, and with the pin on her bosom. When the pearls were finally loosed, she stood up, putting one arm around his father's shoulder and kissing him on the cheek. "Thank you, dear," she said, "thank you," and the pearls seemed to glow against the scarlet of her dress, the whiteness of her throat. They looked very beautiful. For a minute Tommy felt sad, and he remembered the vivid sweet smell of his grandmother's currant biscuits floating through the house on Christmas morning, biscuits he would never taste again.

TOMMY wanted to leave. He wanted to see the Steers' Christmas tree and what Amy Steer had gotten for Christmas, and he wanted to show Jimmy Randolph his Monopoly set. He asked if he could go, and since the morning's festivities were dying down his mother said yes, he could, but he shouldn't be gone too long because they were all going to the Sedgwicks' for dinner later that afternoon. His mother made him get into his snow pants, even though he promised to hurry and the Steers lived only at the corner of the next block—he could see their house from his window—and she strung the mittens she had knit him for Christmas through the sleeves of his jacket. She gave him mittens every Christmas, and they were always attached to each other with a knitted cord so he wouldn't lose them. Even so, he sometimes did.

Tommy picked up his Monopoly set, said goodbye to everybody, and went out. The street was empty because it was Christmas, and Tommy walked in the middle of the road. He was happy. The sun was shining and the snow wasn't very deep. He could still see over the snowbanks and see the lighted Christmas tree inside the Randolphs' house. He was eager to see the Steers' tree, and he thought Mrs. Steer might give him a piece of her rum pie, if there was any left over from Christmas Eve. She always made rum pie for Christmas Eve, and she always wore a long dress and invited Mrs. Wentworth and Mrs. Addington, Mr. Treverton, Dr. Rodgers and his wife and their children, who were in Amy's class, and sometimes other people, too. Tommy and Amy would have been in the same grade, but Amy had skipped one and she went to the Catholic school, even though she wasn't a Catholic. Mrs. Steer said you got a better education there, and she must have known, because Mr. Steer used to be on the school board. Everybody was mad at him when he sent Amy to the Catholic school, and he was defeated in the next election. Sure enough, Mrs. Steer had saved him a piece of pie. She thanked him for the matches, too, and she had a little present for him underneath the tree, a package of the Christmas cookies she had been making and storing in coffee tins ever since Thanksgiving. She had arranged the cookies in three overlapping circles in the box, which she had wrapped in red tissue paper and tied with a golden cord. She decorated the box with a Christmas ornament she had made from half a walnut shell. Mrs. Steer was good at making things like that.

Amy showed him the old china doll with porcelain eyes that her mother had given her. She was very proud of it, because now she was old enough to handle it right. The doll was very big and had been her mother's as a child in Denmark. It still wore the same blue velvet dress with the lace collar that it had worn when her mother played with it. Mrs. Steer had also sewn a whole new wardrobe for it, and Mr. Steer had made a cradle for it to sleep in. The doll was very fragile. Amy wouldn't let Tommy pick it up, but that was all right with Tommy. He didn't really like dolls, and he was never envious that girls could play with them and boys couldn't. The thing that interested him most about dolls was that there was never anything underneath; sometimes they had a belly button but that was all. He did like playing dress-up and make-believe, though, and Mrs. Steer had a lot of old clothes that he and Amy would play in. Tommy always had to be the prince or the villain—sometimes the prince was the villain—but either way he got to wear a burgundy velvet cape that had once been a curtain in the Steers' house until Mrs. Steer's mother died and she had done the house over. He liked the cape, and he liked making up the story as it went along. Once they were on an ocean liner and the waiter brought them peas for dinner and they threw the peas over their shoulders on the people at the next table. The plates broke and the waiter had to scramble to pick up the peas, which rolled all over the place because the ship was rocking. The people were very mad, and he and Amy were very haughty to the waiter and told him not to bring them peas anymore, that they hated peas. It was all make-believe, even the plates—even the waiter, because no one would play him. And in the summer, before they all moved to the Island, they would set up card-table-and-blanket tents in Tommy's backyard. His parents had a lot of card tables, so there were a lot of rooms in their playhouse. That was a lot of fun. It should have been cool inside the tents, but instead it was very hot though the light was dim, and they would take off some of their clothes. Jimmy Randolph played, too, and also the two Slade girls next door. Lily and Jenny always wanted them to take off all their clothes and play greeny-and-whitey, which was what they called that game, but since they wouldn't take off all of theirs, though they had promised, nobody ever wanted to play it. It wasn't fair. The tent was like a big cave because you could crawl from one card table to another, and it was fun. They always wanted to spend the night in the cave, but Tommy wasn't allowed. He had to sleep in his own bed. So did Amy. Besides, the card tables had to come inside or the morning dew would ruin them.

"Well, Tommy," Mrs. Steer said, "if you come back later, when it's getting dark, I'll light the candles on the tree."

"And bring your Monopoly set," Amy interjected. She didn't have one. They always played on Jimmy Randolph's.

"You know you're invited. You know you're welcome."

"Thank you, Mrs. Steer," Tommy said. He did feel invited; he did feel welcome. He wanted to come back, too, but he was afraid that by the time they got home from the Sedgwicks' his mother would think it was his bedtime and too late to go to the Steers' even if Mrs. Steer had promised to light the tree, just for him. Maybe his mother would make an exception. Maybe they would leave early, though Tommy didn't have much hope of that; his parents never left early. Tommy loved to watch Mrs. Steer light the tree, candle by candle, holding the silver porringer full of kitchen matches in one hand and striking them against the underside of a table, sometimes the sole of her shoe. Mrs. Steer was tall enough to reach the highest candle without a stepladder, but their tree wasn't as tall as Tommy's. As she lit the candles and they began to burn, the haloes of light seemed slowly to intensify, illumining piece by piece the ornaments on the tree, the silver, the porcelain and the old furniture from Denmark, the pale green walls, the silk curtains, and the whole room would begin to glow, even the walnut furniture giving off its own golden light. It was a very beautiful sight. "I have to go to the Sedgwicks' for dinner," Tommy said. "I wish I didn't have to go." He blurted it out quite by surprise. "But maybe I can come back afterwards?" He said it more as a question; it was his hope.

"Well, if you can't," Mrs. Steer said, "we'll do it tomorrow. You come by tomorrow and you and Amy can play Monopoly. I'll make you some hot chocolate and then we'll light the tree. It'll be just as pretty then."

"Yes," Tommy said. "I'll come by tomorrow—maybe tonight, too," and he put on his jacket and picked up his Monopoly set and his snow pants—he didn't bother to put them on—and ran over to the Randolphs', eager to show Jimmy his elegant new Monopoly set, and to see what Jimmy had gotten for Christmas. He always got a lot.

"Why, hello, there, and Merry Christmas," said Mrs. Randolph when she opened the door. "How's my little friend? And what's that?" She pointed to his Monopoly set. Tommy put it down and showed her before he even got his jacket off.

"That's beautiful, Tommy, just beautiful. What Santa Claus dropped that down your chimney?"

"Margie Slade," Tommy told her. "Mrs. Slade's her aunt."

"Oh," said Mrs. Randolph, "Margie. Well it's very nice." Mrs. Randolph didn't seem too friendly with the Slades, even though she had gone to New Orleans with Mrs. Slade and Dr. Randolph. She'd just packed up and gone on a moment's notice because she wasn't going to be left out of the fun. That happened more than a year ago, but everybody still mentioned it now and then, and Tommy's father said, "Mrs. Randolph's got spunk."

"Jimmy's in the cellar," Mrs. Randolph said. "He's got something to show you, too. I'll get you a Coke and you go on down."

And sure enough, Jimmy did. Jimmy was playing with his favorite Christmas present—even more favorite than the new bicycle that Tommy saw as he passed by their tree, but of course Jimmy couldn't use the bicycle now, with all the snow. Jimmy was on his way up when Tommy got to the cellar stairs, and they went back to the tree to look at the bicycle. It was the fanciest bicycle Tommy had ever seen, maroon with a baked enamel finish—"just like a car," Jimmy said. It even had shock absorbers on the front, right below the handlebars, and a rearview mirror, too. Tommy couldn't have a bicycle yet. Maybe when he was nine, like Jimmy, he could. Bicycles were too dangerous, his mother said, like the candles on the Steers' Christmas tree, although when his mother was a girl they'd had candles on their tree. You couldn't buy Christmas lights then. Everything was very old-fashioned when his mother was young. Tommy used to wonder if she'd worn hoopskirts, but she hadn't. "My goodness, Tommy, I'm not that old," she said. "That was long before my time. We wore hobble skirts, although I don't know how we did it. We suffered for fashion." They called them hobble skirts because they were so tight around the ankles you couldn't walk in them; you had to hobble.

"But wait till you see this," Jimmy said, pushing him toward the cellar. "You've never seen anything like this," and he was right. Tommy had never seen anything like the set for making lead soldiers that Jimmy was playing with. The cellar was hot because there was a fire in the jack—the Randolphs still had a jack for hot water but they didn't use it for that anymore—and on it Jimmy was melting lead in a long-handled pot. It was called a crucible. He showed Tommy how it worked. Jimmy poured the molten lead—he had to be very careful because if it touched you it would give you a terrible burn—from the crucible into a mold. There were four places for soldiers in each mold, and four different molds. The lead hardened, you opened the mold, and you had four lead soldiers. They were still too hot to touch but the lead cooled quickly. Then you had to separate them because some of the lead overflowed the molds and there were little strings of metal between them that you broke off. Jimmy let Tommy try it. They melted an ingot on the fire, watching it slowly soften and lose its form, like chocolate on the stove. They shook the lead in the pot, watching the patterns swirl and dissolve, slippery as silk. The lead had become very shiny now, like silver, and almost as thin as water. If you spilled a drop on the stove it formed a little ball that sputtered and jumped on the hot surface. The cellar was filled with the acrid smell

166

of metal. Jimmy let Tommy pour the shiny molten lead into one of the molds, and when it had cooled it was dull again, like lead, not like silver at all. He and Jimmy made a lot of soldiers. They used up all the lead, so they had to melt the soldiers down and start over. It was more fun to make them than to play with them, Tommy thought, as they lined the soldiers up on the cellar floor.

They heard Dr. Randolph come in. Tommy was glad he was home for Christmas this year. Last year he'd been away by himself. Tommy wanted to go upstairs. Dr. Randolph had been out on his calls, even on Christmas. Jimmy said that probably Mrs. Slade was sick again. She was always sick, he said; that was why his father had had to go to New Orleans with her. Tommy thought that if Mrs. Slade was sick, maybe he'd better go see her, too, but first he had to show Jimmy his Monopoly set. Jimmy looked it over and said, well, it was nice, but not so nice as his bike. But then, it wasn't a bike, it was a Monopoly set, and it was better than Jimmy's and newer. He'd thought Jimmy Randolph would say something like that. Dr. Randolph liked it, though. He said it was pretty fancy. "Better watch your step, Jimmy, Tommy'll beat you." Tommy usually beat him anyway, and then Jimmy would get really mad, especially because Tommy was younger. He wanted to have things his own way, and when he didn't get them he wouldn't play. Usually Tommy did what Jimmy wanted, and if he really didn't want to, well, then, he wouldn't play either; he'd just go home. He liked to read, and he liked playing by himself well enough.

"Say, Tommy, come here," Dr. Randolph said. "You're a red little pecker, aren't you?"

"P.T.!" Mrs. Randolph didn't like him to talk like that. Tommy giggled.

"Let me feel your forehead," and Dr. Randolph put his cool hand on Tommy's forehead, bending his head back uncomfortably. "Open your mouth." Tommy did. Dr. Randolph grasped Tommy's chin and peered down his throat. "Are you feeling all right?"

"Yes," Tommy said, "I'm feeling all right." He wondered if he really was.

"Well, you feel hot to me," Dr. Randolph said. "Not like

Lucille over here. Lucille's cold as a dead nun's tit. Come here, Lucille, I'll heat you up." Dr. Randolph laughed hilariously and slapped his leg. Tommy was shocked—he had heard Dr. Randolph say "tit" before, but he'd never heard him say it to Mrs. Randolph like that—and then he was embarrassed. Mrs. Randolph was disgusted. She went into the kitchen to baste the turkey, giving Dr. Randolph a look. Tommy heard her open the oven door. He could hear the grease crackling, and the smell of the bird filled the room. The Randolphs' dining table was already set with the new china they'd gotten at Gump's in San Francisco. The china had fancy red service plates—it looked something like Tommy's grandmother's china but newer—and demitasses to go with them. Dr. Randolph was very proud of it. "Look at these plates. You don't see china like this every day," Dr. Randolph told him. "It's Lenox," and he picked up a plate and turned it over to show Tommy where it said LENOX. "It's American, and you can't buy any better." Tommy's grandmother's wasn't; it came from Europe. "Lucille," Dr. Randolph called into the kitchen, "who else would give you china like this?"

"P.T.," Mrs. Randolph called back, "I've earned every plate." She was still mad.

Jimmy had started to play with his Erector Set. He ignored most of his father's jokes but he was proud of his father because he made so much money and no other doctor in town could take out an appendix in three minutes.

"Tommy," Dr. Randolph said, feeling his forehead again, "you go home and tell your parents you're not feeling well and that they should keep an eye on you." Tommy put on his jacket and picked up his Monopoly set and his snow pants and went across the street to his house. He decided he shouldn't go to the Slades'.

Margie and Nick had already left. Tommy didn't tell his parents that he wasn't feeling good. It was Christmas, and he thought he felt all right. He certainly felt all right to play with his presents, and he knew his mother would say that if he felt good enough to play with them, he felt good enough to go to the Sedgwicks'. So he didn't say anything, and a little later they went out for dinner. John didn't ride with them.

He took their mother's car because it was his turn for it and he thought he'd be staying later than his parents, so David had to walk. He was spending the rest of the day with Margie. They were eating at Bob Griswold's. Daisy and Phil Meyer were going to be there, too, and Bob's parents. Tommy felt sorry that they wouldn't all be at the Sedgwicks' together.

DINNER at the Sedgwicks' was not much fun. They were all grown-ups. The Hutchins were there, and Emily's college roommate whose name was Molly—she was nice—and Nick Kingsfield, and Lucien Wolfe, too. Emily thought it would be nice if Molly and Nick hit it off. She thought Nick was a good catch. Everybody thought Nick was a good catch, and now that his mother had died they probably thought he was an even better one. Tommy didn't believe his parents thought Margie was a good catch, though her parents were dead, too. It was curious. Everyone looked at the Sedgwicks' Christmas presents, and they all exchanged small gifts. Emily gave John a record that she put on their Victrola, singing along with it: *"I was a good little girl, till I met you; You set my heart in a whirl, when I saw you,"* and everybody smiled but Mr. Wolfe laughed. "That's a good one," he said.

Tommy was glad that he'd taken his book. He read it by himself in the Sedgwicks' sun-room before dinner. When he had a chance he'd have to ask Mr. Wolfe about the Sargasso Sea, but really he wasn't feeling very good. Dr. Randolph was right. He could hardly eat any of his turkey, and he took only one bite of his plum pudding. Ruth brought it to the table. She was working on Christmas. Rose wasn't. Rose was going to come over the next day to stay through New Year's, and she had to have some time off, his mother said, so she didn't work Christmas Eve or Christmas Day, either. Tommy's parents were going to be out so much, and his mother knew that unless Rose stayed in the house where she could keep an eye on her, she'd probably not show up at all, and his mother needed her. Mrs. Sedgwick was in the kitchen a long time before the pudding came out. She'd had a hard time getting it lit, she explained, and then finally she rushed into the dining room and sat down, Mr. Sedgwick turned off the lights, and Ruth brought the pudding to the table. It was supposed to be flaming, but you could hardly see the fire, just a little blue flicker that went out right away. Everybody admired it anyway, and exclaimed over it, and Mrs. Sedgwick looked pleased. Tommy asked to be excused before the others had finished, and he went back to the sun-room where Mr. Sedgwick kept all his weather instruments, including the barometer with the pen that charted every change. The weather was one of Mr. Sedgwick's hobbies. Trains were another, and when Tommy heard the whistle blow in the distance he thought that Mr. Sedgwick would know which train it was and where it was going, but he didn't feel good enough to ask. He didn't even feel good enough to read, and he curled up on the couch and pulled the afghan over him that Mrs. Sedgwick's mother had made. He could hear the laughter from the dining room. He wanted to go home. He was afraid he was going to be sick to his stomach, and he didn't want to be sick to his stomach at the Sedgwicks'. If that were going to happen he wanted to be home, and feel his mother's cool hand on his brow and have her hold his head if he threw up. He didn't want to think about it. He was afraid if he thought about it, that would make it happen. Finally he called her. "Mommy. Mommy." Then louder, "Mommy!" She heard him that time, and came into the sun-room.

"What's the matter, Tommy? Are you all right?" She looked concerned and put her hand on his forehead.

"No," he said, "I'm not all right. I'm sick."

"Oh, Tommy, no," his mother said. "Where do you feel sick?"

"All over," Tommy said. "In my stomach."

His mother took his hand and sat down beside him on the couch. Tommy didn't like the jiggle it made. She put her hand on his forehead again. "I think you're feverish." She seemed surprised.

"Can we go home?"

"Of course, darling. In just a minute. You lie there. I'll be right back." She kissed him and returned to the dining room. Tommy heard her say that he was sick. "Tommy always gets sick on holidays," he heard her say. That wasn't true, Tommy thought. When had he been sick on a holiday? He wasn't sick at Thanksgiving. But he didn't feel good enough to care. He heard Mrs. Sedgwick say, "Well, there's no need for both of you to go and break up the party. Why doesn't one of you take him home?" Tommy bet Mrs. Sedgwick wanted his father to stay, and in a minute the three of them came into the room to see how he was feeling. He felt worse, if anything.

"Tommy, you wouldn't mind if your father stayed for the rest of the party," Mrs. Sedgwick asked.

"No," Tommy said, "that's all right." But it turned out after some more discussion that Tommy's mother was going to stay instead—they worked it out somehow—and Tommy's father said he was taking him home. His brother could take his mother home later. All Tommy wanted was to be in his own bed, and he and his father left. Although it wasn't far from the Sedgwicks' to his house, Tommy fell asleep in the car, under his father's arm, opening his eyes as they drove up to the house, the two trees like sentinels shining on the porch roof, the evergreen doorway sparkling with lights, and snow beginning to fall. Tommy passed through the enchanted doorway into the big hall festooned with boughs. He looked with longing at his desk near the tree in the living room, but he felt too sick to approach it, to let his hand brush across it, and he went straight upstairs. His father got him into his pajamas and into bed, bringing him a glass of ginger ale and crushing the ice because he thought it would be good for his stomach, but Tommy couldn't drink it, though he tried.

He woke up with Dr. Randolph standing beside his bed. "What did I tell you?" he said, but he said it nicely. "You're a sick little boy," and he stuck a thermometer into his mouth and made him keep it under his tongue and not bite it. Tommy wanted to cry, he felt so awful, but he didn't. "You've got a high fever," Dr. Randolph said, looking at the thermometer before he shook it down. He felt Tommy's neck and looked at his throat again and into his eyes. Then he pulled up Tommy's pajamas and looked at his stomach and chest. "I'm going to give you a pill," he said, "and you've got to swallow it." Dr. Randolph reached into his medical bag for a bottle of pills, shook out a few of them, and gave one to

Tommy, who swallowed it with the ginger ale that was still beside his bed. He put the rest into a little envelope. "Here are half a dozen more," he said to Tommy's father. "Give him one every three or four hours if he wakes up. He probably will. Don't wake him, though, unless he still seems feverish. This should take his temperature down, but check on him." Dr. Randolph reached into his bag again. "I'm going to paint your throat, Tommy," he said. "It'll hurt, but you can take it." He dipped a swab into the bitter blue-green medicine that Tommy had had before, made him say "aaah," and pushed the stick against the back of his throat. Tommy gagged. The medicine tasted awful. He was afraid he'd throw up, but he didn't. "I'll stop by tomorrow," Dr. Randolph said, and he and his father left the room and went downstairs. Tommy heard the door shut before he fell asleep.

Later he woke up and heard his mother come home. She wasn't with his brother but with Mr. Wolfe. She came up to check on him, but Tommy was only half awake. She made him take another pill. "Where's John?" Tommy asked. "John and Emily went skating with Nick and Molly," his mother said, "and Mr. Wolfe drove me home."

"I know," Tommy said, and fell asleep again as the sounds of *Kinderszenen* floated up the stairs. He heard the first tune, but he didn't hear the end of the second, "A Curious Story." It had the same name in German.

It was very dark when Tommy woke up again, and the house was silent. Nobody had thought to raise his blinds. Tommy was soaking wet, and his pillow was wet, too. He was very thirsty and had to go to the bathroom. He was shivering. The dim hall light cast blurred shadows on the walls. The heavy blue curtains at the top of the stairway, closed to prevent drafts, moved as he passed. Tommy shuddered. Someone had left a light on in the bathroom at the other end of the hall, the one his brothers shared, and he went there instead of to the bathroom at his end of the hall, between his bedroom and his parents'. He went to the toilet and drank two glasses of water. He heard a noise, which frightened him, and then he heard footsteps coming down the hall, saw a man's huge shadow falling across the floor and up the wall. "What are you doing, Tommy?" It was his father. He was standing at the bathroom door. "Are you all right?" His father was wearing only his pajama top; the rest of him hung out naked. Tommy didn't want to look. He felt dizzy. "Yes, I'm all right," he said, turning out the light. He didn't know if it was scarier with the light out, or not. "I was thirsty." He could see his father and his father's shadow in the dim light of the hall.

"I'll take you back to bed," his father said, putting his arm on Tommy's shoulder. He pulled Tommy toward him and guided him down the hall. "Why did you use the boys' bathroom?"

"The light was on," Tommy said.

"Just a minute." His father went into his room and grabbed the bathrobe that went with his pajamas. They were maroon silk. Tommy's mother had given him the set for Christmas. "Is he all right?" Tommy heard his mother ask. "Yes, he's fine. I think he's a little better," his father replied, and slipped into the robe as he took Tommy back to bed. When his father noticed how wet the pillow was, he got a fresh pillowcase, and put him in clean pajamas, too. That was nice of his father.

"Pull up the shades, Daddy," Tommy said. Mr. Wolfe's coin glinted in the amethyst night. Then his father sat down on Tommy's bed and rubbed his legs because Tommy said they ached. He wrapped them tightly in his blanket, the blanket Tommy had had ever since he could remember, whose satin binding that he loved to touch was frayed beyond repair, and the blanket so worn, too, that his mother had said it would have to go soon. Tommy didn't use it as a blanket; he just took it to bed with him sometimes. He would get rid of it soon; he was too old for baby things. His father gave him another of Dr. Randolph's pills—"just to be on the safe side," he said—and continued rubbing his legs, making them warm, until Tommy stopped shivering and fell asleep. He didn't know when his father left his room.

TOMMY didn't feel so sick the next day, but Dr. Randolph came by in the afternoon and said he'd have to stay in bed for a few days anyway. He had a light case of the measles, Dr. Randolph said, and he'd have to keep his shades drawn and his lights out, and he couldn't have any company except for his family. "You may not feel so bad today, Tommy," he told him, "but measles are a serious business. You mustn't have any lights, and you mustn't try to read."

"Can I play at my desk?"

"I'm sorry," Dr. Randolph said, "you can't play at your desk, either. You've got to stay in bed with the lights out. But don't worry. You've got a mild case and it won't last long. You'll be fit as a fiddle by New Year's."

New Year's! It was practically a whole week away. What would he do? Well, there wasn't much he could do. He just lay in his bed and slept, and when he was awake he thought about his Monopoly set and the desk he'd gotten for Christmas. John carried the desk upstairs and set it up in the hall outside his bedroom, so he could see it when the door was open. He wasn't supposed to play at it, but as the days wore on he sometimes did, if no one was there. For a while he lay on his back with his legs in the air and pumped, pretending he was riding a bicycle. He examined the red spots on his stomach and chest, trying to decide if there were more or less of them, if they were getting bigger or smaller. He listened to the comings and goings of his parents and his brothers and their friends; someone seemed always to be going in or out the door, and he wondered if they thought it was like a magical doorway to an enchanted forest, too. Mrs. Steer came to see him, even though he wasn't supposed to have any visitors but family. "I've had the measles, Tommy," she said. "I'm not afraid. But I can't let Amy come over. No children allowed." She laughed when she said it. Tommy thought about the Steers' Christmas tree, which he hadn't gotten to see with the candles lit, but Mrs. Steer told him that he'd be better by New Year's Day and that he could come over after Mr. Treverton's open house; she would light it for him then. And toward the end of every afternoon his mother, when she came home, would smooth his sheets and fluff his pillow and begin to read to him by the light of a small lamp that she had shaded so the beam of light fell only on the book in her lap. Her face and the rest of the room were in shadow. Tommy loved to have his mother read to him, and he would poke her if she dozed off, as she sometimes did. Then she would open her eyes with a start and pick up where she'd left off.

" 'Many strange creatures live among these weeds wherever they drift,' " she read. " 'One of the strangest is a little fish.' "

"That's Fingerfins," Tommy said. He already knew the story.

His mother continued reading. " 'Some call him the mouse fish because he is small, and always hiding in the weeds, and others call him the Sargasso fish.'

"He sounds like you, Tommy. Sometimes you're like a little mouse fish hiding in the seaweed.

" 'This is to be the tale of a Sargasso fish,' " she went on, " 'who hatched out from one of the many eggs laid in the weeds by his mother.' " Well, of course his mother hadn't hatched him from an egg in the weeds. She'd carried him next to her heart, like everyone else. Tommy had found *that* out. He'd seen a lady who was very fat, and Jimmy Randolph had told him that where she was fat was where the baby slept. Jimmy's mother had told him that ladies carry their babies next to their hearts until they're born. Tommy's mother didn't know that Tommy knew that. " 'He and all the other little creatures who lived in every drifting clump made a sort of floating town, a City of Sargasso Weed.' " Like his very own town, Tommy thought; like his very own island floating in the river. The river was frozen now, and Tommy supposed it never looked much like the Sargasso Sea anyway. " 'This little fish had *hands!*'

"What did I tell you, Tommy?"—his mother looked up from the story—"If you were a little fish you'd be just like this one. 'And that is why we call our hero Fingerfins.' "

Tommy loved the story. He made his mother read it many times. He thought it was his favorite book, and though his mother wouldn't allow him to look at the pictures now, she would describe them, and he could recall each one from before he got sick. He never got tired of hearing about Fingerfins, whose grandfather tried to eat him but Fingerfins got away by puffing up so big his grandfather couldn't get him in his mouth. "His own grandfather tried to *eat* him?" Tommy asked. What kind of a grandfather was that, he wondered, and if Fingerfins' grandfather would eat him, why wouldn't his father, but Fingerfins' father wasn't a character in the story. Well, that wasn't like Tommy. If anybody tried to eat him, he couldn't puff up any bigger than he was, which wasn't very big. All he could do was run. He could run pretty fast. Or maybe he could make them laugh and forget it. It would be fun to be able to puff up big, Tommy thought, and surprise everybody.

And then there was the lantern fish. " 'Daylight hurt their eyes,' " his mother read, " 'and so they could only come to the surface of the sea at night. On their dark bodies many spots glowed in the night. Each had an extra bright cluster of lights just in front of its tail. The ladies of the party wore their lights on the upper side, the gentlemen had theirs underneath.' " Tommy giggled. His mother told him to stop being so silly or she wouldn't read any more, so Tommy didn't giggle but that didn't stop him from thinking it was funny.

When his mother had finished the story—it was a fairly long story—Tommy pleaded with her to start over but his mother said, "No more today, Tommy. My eyes are worn out, and I think I've learned *Fingerfins* by heart. I'll bet you have, too. It's time for your dinner. I'll see if it's ready." She took the book with her; she was afraid he would turn on the lights and read it, otherwise. His mother could be quite smart, Tommy thought, but Fingerfins could be clever, too. Though he had many adventures, some of them terrifying—like when his grandfather was about to swallow him, and when he was caught by the scientists who wanted to label him—he always managed to escape. Nobody ever ate him, and nobody captured him for good. It helped that he was small and hard to see. He was colored very like the world of weeds he lived in, the book said, and had tatters hanging from his skin which looked like torn and ragged weeds. As long as Fingerfins didn't move, he was fairly safe. Tommy practiced being as still as he could. He couldn't go very long without moving.

In a few minutes, Tommy's mother brought his tray. He had all his meals in bed, and she always stayed with him while he ate his dinner. At first she didn't want him to sit up, so she tried to spoon the food into his mouth while he was propped up on two pillows, but she spilled it all over his pajamas and the pillow too, and finally she relented and let him sit up and feed himself, which Tommy was perfectly capable of doing. When he was sick in bed he always got a straw in his glass, but the straw would bend and then he couldn't get anything through it. One day his mother came home with straws that were pleated like an accordion so they bent easily. Tommy liked those straws, but his mother saved them for when he was sick; he couldn't use them at other times.

Every evening before he had to go to sleep, Rose brought him ginger ale and a dish of the custard that Mrs. Steer had made for him. It was better than the custard his mother made. "Perhaps she puts more sugar in it," his mother said. "I think it's sweeter." Maybe she did; it was better, anyway. One good thing about being sick was that he didn't have to eat what he didn't want to, though he wasn't allowed to eat what he wanted to eat, which was fruitcake and orange juice. He could have the orange juice but not the fruitcake. It was too rich, his mother said. Twice Rose let him have some, though. It was easy to get around Rose. She was sleeping in the maid's room now and using the bathroom in the cellar. She wasn't allowed to use their bathrooms because his mother said you never knew where she'd been and you could pick up germs from toilet seats. That was why his Aunt Clara always carried a pair of white cotton gloves when she was traveling, and never sat on the toilet seat, either. She used the gloves only for going to the toilet. That way her hands didn't have to touch the handle on the door or on the toilet either, and she suggested to Tommy's mother that she do the same thing. Aunt Clara was very fastidious, his mother said. Tommy's mother didn't go that far, but she never used the toilet in the cellar, either. None of them did; it was just for the help. Tommy thought probably you could pick up a lot of germs down there. The bathroom was dark and dank, and there was usually a spider-web in the corner. Tommy really hated spiders. He didn't even like daddy long-legs, and they were harmless, not like the black widow, which was poisonous and you died if it bit you. Like Mr. Wolfe's Gila monster, Tommy thought. It didn't have to eat you to kill you, the way the bears did; it just had to bite you. It didn't even want to eat you. What did it want, Tommy wondered; just to be mean? It was interesting that Mr. Wolfe spent so much time around such dangerous animals. When Tommy had asked him why, he laughed and said, "Birds of a feather flock together." Tommy didn't know if he liked Mr. Wolfe or not. He didn't like it that he'd come to the house Christmas Eve, because then they'd had to entertain Mr. Wolfe instead of listening to his mother read "The Night Before Christmas." But he had liked Mr. Wolfe's movies on the Island last summer, and he liked his silver dollar well enough, but not so much as his mother did. She would see it on Tommy's windowsill and say how nice it was of Mr. Wolfe to give it to him. "Isn't Mr. Wolfe a nice man, Tommy?" she would ask. "He's certainly nice to you."

One good thing about having to lie in bed and be sick was that even David was nice to him. Sometimes David would come into Tommy's room and sit on the chair and talk to him very nicely, without teasing him at all. He would even straighten his sheets, and then his bed would feel cool instead of hot and rumpled. But David wasn't home very much. If he wasn't working at the plant, he was out with Margie. They spent a lot of time at Bob and Laura Griswold's with Daisy and Phil Meyer. They were all very good friends—"too good," Tommy's father said. Tommy's father thought Daisy was pretty, but he didn't think she always behaved properly. When you were married, you were supposed to go out with married people—"birds of a feather," Tommy figured—and when you weren't married you went out with people your own age who weren't married either. But not everybody was married. His Uncle Christian wasn't married, and who did he go out with? His Aunt Clara and Uncle Andrew, probably, because he lived with them and worked for Uncle Andrew. Mr. Treverton wasn't married but he had been; his wife was dead, like Mrs. Addington's husband. And Mr. Wolfe wasn't married, and he went out with Tommy's parents. Everybody in Tommy's house went out practically every night, and every afternoon, too. John was probably whispering sweet nothings in Emily's ear; that's what Emily called it when they whispered. "What did he say?" Tommy would ask. "Sweet nothings, just sweet nothings,"

Emily would reply in her high fluting voice, batting her eyes. That was very irritating; Tommy wanted to *know*, and "sweet nothings" gave him scarcely a clue. It was silly besides. Tommy's mother was never silly. She laughed, but she never giggled. She seemed always the same—unlike David, who was more like his father. They could both be in a terrible mood for weeks at a time, and then, unpredictably, something would turn them around. It didn't usually happen at the same time, though, and you never knew what did it. Of course, it was hard to tell what put them in a bad mood in the first place. Sometimes Tommy thought it was each other. His father was certainly in a bad mood when David didn't go back to college, and David wasn't very happy either, because he had to work in the drum factory at the plant and he said the drum factory was the worst part of the whole place, it was so boring. Tommy used to think they made drums there, and it seemed nice that his father made drums, but it turned out they weren't that kind of drums. They were steel barrels, but they called them drums, and when the drums were made they went to the packing room where they were filled with the chemicals that were made in the furnaces, and then they went to the shipping room, where they were put on trains and sent away. Tommy thought the furnace room would be the scariest place to work. It was dangerous, and Tommy's father didn't let David work there. Besides, you had to know what you were doing to work in the furnace room, and Tommy's father thought David didn't know what he was doing a lot of the time. He knew how to play tennis and golf and dance with the girls, his father said. He didn't know how to study or work, but he'd better learn. That's what he was doing at the plant, learning to work. David told Tommy that the men at the plant called his father "Black Mac," but not to his face. No, Tommy thought, they'd better not call him that to his face. He wouldn't like it, and if he didn't like something, you knew it. But his father loved his work, and he worked all the time. "If you don't like your work, quit," he would tell people, and he said it as if he meant it. But David didn't like his work, and his father wouldn't let him quit. It was strange. His father also said, "You can't beat fun," and fun was what his mother said they were having at all the parties they went to while Tommy stayed in bed, in the dark, waiting for New Year's.

New Year's Eve was the biggest party of all. There was a dance at the country club, and at midnight everyone would pop champagne and the corks would fly into the big Indian canoes that were suspended from the ceiling. Mrs. Steer said the canoes were full of corks and God knew what else. This year Mr. Wolfe was taking Tommy's parents and some other people to dinner before the dance. He was going to be in town most of the winter and he wanted to do something nice for his friends, his mother said. Because Mr. Wolfe didn't have a wife to plan it, Tommy's mother had to give him a lot of help. One day after lunch she went to the hotel where he was giving his dinner to look at the menu and wrap the favors. Favors were little presents at each person's place, and they all had to be wrapped. Tommy thought Mr. Wolfe should have asked someone who liked to wrap more than his mother did, and who was better at it, but it was nice of his mother, Tommy thought, to help Mr. Wolfe with his party. She'd spent a lot of time on it. She'd helped him pick out the favors and order the flowers, the sort of things that had to be done when you were giving a party. Sometimes a favor might be a bar of special soap for the ladies or a tiny bottle of perfume, his mother said. For the gentlemen it was going to be a lighter. "Daddy doesn't use a lighter," Tommy said. "He likes safety matches."

"I'm sure he'd love to have a lighter," his mother said. "They're so much cleaner."

It was a lot of work to give a nice party, and Mr. Wolfe's dinner had grown so that it was now quite large. The Sedgwicks had decided to give a cocktail party beforehand, and Tommy's mother persuaded his father to give a big breakfast after the dance. Yes, it certainly was a lot of work, his mother said, and when she came home in the late afternoons she was tired but she would read to him nonetheless, and sometimes she talked about what she might or might not wear New Year's Eve. "Should I wear Grandmother's pearls?" she asked him; but she didn't. Not that night. She'd worn them to the Sedgwicks' on Christmas and several times since, but she decided they didn't look best with her new black chiffon dress. She showed the dress to Tommy. It looked very pretty.

And Dr. Randolph was right. By New Year's Eve Tommy was better. In the morning he played at his desk, and that afternoon he was allowed to go out for a while, and then Jimmy Randolph and Amy Steer came over while his mother was out putting the finishing touches on Mr. Wolfe's party and they played Monopoly on his new set. Tommy beat them both, too.

IT was very cold that day, but warm inside the house. Tommy could hear the furnace running all the time, and the radiators were too hot to touch. Rose set pans of water on them to keep the air from drying out. By nightfall it was storming. Playing at his desk, Tommy could hear the wind howl around the corner of the house. He went to his front window and stood there, watching the snow swirl around the trees on the roof, making them fade into the whiteness, reappear for a moment, and fade again. Sometimes he could not see the dark trees at all, only the glow of their lights, blurred and fuzzy in the snow. He looked down. The snow was so fine it had blown under the edge of his storm window and was piling up in a little drift against his pane. It was a bad night to go out, Tommy thought, but his parents didn't mind. They were used to the weather.

His brothers didn't mind, either. It was John's night for his mother's car, which made David really mad. He said he was taking it at midnight even if John had to walk Emily Sedgwick all the way through the snow from the country club to her house, which was a very long way. John got mad and they had a big fight and shouted at each other and fought over who would use the bathroom first, which David got by locking the door when John was called to the phone in the middle of his shaving. It was Emily, of course. "Tell her to be sure to put on her galoshes," David shouted when John was on the phone. "It's a long walk and there's a lot of snow." When John came back to finish shaving, he banged on the bathroom door and cursed at David—he said "God damn," which they were never supposed to say, and called David a "son of a bitch," which was even worse—but David was in the shower singing at the top of his lungs, and he let on that he couldn't hear John's shouting. David was singing the song that Emily had given John for Christmas, and that made John even madder. John hardly ever got mad, but he was sure mad now. Finally Tommy's father came down the hall and told both of them to cut it out or their mother would take the car herself and they'd both walk. His mother was vexed. That was a new word Tommy had learned from *Fingerfins*, when the professor felt terribly vexed that he'd lost his prize fish; Tommy's mother had explained what it meant. She told the boys when they were dressed—they looked very handsome in their tuxedos, even David—that that was no way to end the old year, and she hoped they'd try to begin the New Year on a better note. Then she told John that his language was terrible. "That's no way to talk when your mother's in the house," she said. David made a face at John when she said it, but his mother didn't see him. Finally they drove off together. They were hardly talking. The young people were all going to Nick Kingsfield's before the dance. They weren't going to Mr. Wolfe's dinner, either, but Daisy and Phil were and so were the Griswolds. Tommy bet Daisy would rather go to Nick's, but she liked Mr. Wolfe, too. She liked people who were lively and attractive, she said, and Mr. Wolfe was both. She didn't like people who were stuffy, and she thought some of the people who went to the country club were very stuffy. But Tommy thought Daisy would liven up the party, if it needed it.

It was quieter in the house when his brothers had left, and his mother drew her bath. When she was going to take a long bath with bath oil, she always drew it; otherwise she just took it. Tommy's father had to use the boys' bathroom for his shower, and he didn't like the mess they'd left it in. He said he was going to speak to them about it. His mother took a very long time in the bath—he could hear her humming there —and the bathroom was warm and fragrant when she left it. His father was almost dressed when she came out. He was waiting for her to help him with the studs and cuff links for his shirt. He had to use studs because the shirt had no buttons. It always took him a long time to get into it. It was stiff as a board, there was so much starch in it, and the front was piqué. That's what they called it. It looked uncomfortable but very fancy. The studs and cuff links had belonged to Tommy's father's father, and someday they would probably belong to John because he was the oldest. Then his mother shooed Tommy out of their room. She had to get dressed, but she would call him back when she was ready.

Tommy loved it when his parents dressed up, and tonight his mother looked more beautiful than he had ever seen her. Her hair was pretty and soft, and she was wearing the black silk dancing shoes that she had gotten especially to wear with her new dress. The shoes had buckles that sparkled. Tommy remembered when his mother had gotten the buckles. They had belonged to Mrs. Henderson, who loved to dance but whose legs had been cut off so she couldn't. The summer before, Tommy and his mother were in town one day from the Island and they had gone to see Mrs. Henderson. They were standing on her porch—she always called it the veranda—and Mrs. Henderson was in her wheelchair. She was older than Tommy's mother but his mother said she still loved to dance, so it was especially sad that she'd lost her legs. She couldn't get used to the artificial ones. Tommy had seen them standing in a corner of the Hendersons' downstairs bathroom—Mrs. Henderson lived downstairs now—and they had shoes on them. He didn't like to look. He wondered what had happened to the legs Mrs. Henderson lost. Tommy was a little afraid of Mrs. Henderson, but he liked to help push her wheelchair, which she would sometimes let him do if he would be gentle. That day on Mrs. Henderson's porch, where the clematis she was so proud of climbed up a trellis from the garden below, she had given Tommy's mother a pair of shoes with the same buckles clipped to them. The buckles were silver and studded with stones. "You're the only woman I know with such tiny feet," Mrs. Henderson said, "and Emma, you do love to dance. I want you to have them," and she handed his mother the shoes, saying, "Here, dear, dance." It gave Tommy a chill. His mother didn't wear the shoes. She put them in a chest in the attic. But she removed the buckles, and tonight she had clipped them to her black silk slippers. When she moved and the dress rippled around her feet, the buckles sparkled.

Tommy loved his mother's black chiffon dress. It was made of silk and had a bare back and a short train with a strap attached so she could hold it up when she danced; otherwise, someone might step on it and tear it. Though it was black, it seemed to pick up the light from the lamps in the room and give off a soft shine of its own. His mother said it didn't shine; it had a sheen, and there is a difference. Tommy watched her as she sat at her dressing table, picking out her jewelry, trying it this way and that. Her neckline was square, and she fastened a jeweled clip at each corner. "No, they're not real diamonds," she said to Tommy, "but for fun let's say they are tonight. It will be our secret." They sparkled like real diamonds, Tommy thought, and his mother sparkled, too. She put her jeweled arrow in her hair—it took her quite a while to fix it in place—and when she had finished she put on her earrings, which were small but had tiny diamonds in them— they were real—and in each one a single sapphire the color of night. When she had finished, she slipped the sapphire ring on her finger, the one Tommy's father had given her a long time ago that had a star in it that Tommy had a hard time seeing. Then she stood up and twirled around for Tommy's and his father's admiration. Tommy could smell her perfume as she moved in the soft glow of the bedroom lamps, and she swept Tommy into her arms and danced him around the room. She was flushed and felt warm. Tommy asked, "Are you feverish?" and his mother looked startled and slightly annoyed. "No, of course I'm not feverish," she said, releasing him.

"Well, you might be getting the measles," Tommy said in order to explain.

His mother laughed. "Only children get the measles," she said. "I'm simply in a glow. It's nicer to say that I'm glowing."

She was, too, from her head to her toes, as she danced gaily around the room, now seizing Tommy's father and making him dance with her as she hummed a tune, occasionally breaking into words. She reached to the bed for her white silk handkerchief shot with silver threads, the one she used when she wore a long dress and went dancing—"so you don't stain your partner's jacket with your warm palm," she explained. The handkerchief floated from her hand as she moved in time to the music. Suddenly she said, "Run along, everybody, I've got to catch my breath," so Tommy went downstairs and his father followed a minute later. Tommy put John's record on the Victrola, even though he wasn't supposed to, but his parents didn't care and his mother sang along with it—"*I was a good little girl, till I met you; You set my heart in a whirl, when I saw you*"—as she slowly descended the stairs, the black chiffon dress floating around her, her hair and dress and shoes and eyes sparkling with lights, and she entered the evergreen bower. Tommy and his father stood at the foot of the staircase and applauded. His mother glided past them into the center of the hall, under the mistletoe, where she paused, looking like a fairy queen in her enchanted wood. "Well," she said, extending her arm, "isn't anyone going to kiss me and break the spell?"

Tommy rushed over and threw his arms around her. "Gently, gently," his mother admonished him.

"We only want to break the spell, not your mother," his father said.

Tommy kissed her very gently, and then his father kissed her and danced her three times around the room before he helped her into her coat and boots. "Even the queen of the night has got to wear her boots," he said, and got into his own coat and left to bring the car to the door. His mother told Tommy no, he absolutely could not stay up until midnight—maybe next year—kissed him goodbye, said good night to Rose, and left the house. As she passed through the lighted doorway her black dress swirled beneath her black fur coat, and she walked hurriedly to the car in the stormy night. Tommy could see the jewels shining from the arrow in her hair.

After they had gone, Rose said, "That's a good one! 'Even the queen of the night has got to wear her boots,' " and she chuckled at the joke. She gave Tommy a piece of fruitcake and some orange juice and talked to him for a while before insisting he go to bed. Though the tables were already set up, she still had a lot of work to do to get ready for the breakfast party. "You'll be sound asleep and dreaming," she told him. And he was.

WHEN he woke up it was dark, dark like thickest night. The storm had subsided. There was just an occasional flake of snow in the air. He heard the door opening and closing, people stamping their feet, coming in, and laughter and voices floating up the stairs. Someone put the Victrola on, playing the same record that Tommy had left there. He was suddenly wide awake, and excited. It was already the New Year. His parents had come home for their breakfast. Tommy loved parties. He loved his mother, she was so beautiful, and he loved his handsome father. He loved his brothers as well. Tonight he loved everybody. He hoped his brothers had stopped fighting and loved each other too, and that David hadn't made Emily walk home through the snow. He didn't think David would really do that, but you never knew with David; he might. Well, John could get a ride with someone else, anyway. He didn't hear his brothers' voices, but he could hear his parents', and the Sedgwicks', and Mr. Wolfe's, and the Steers', and a lot of others. They were all laughing and talking, and the Victrola was playing *"I was a good little girl, till I met you,"* and then other records for dancing the fox-trots and two-steps and tangoes his mother loved—not the classical records she played when she was alone. The music was loud. It would be interesting to be like Fingerfins and never shut your eyes to sleep at night. That way you wouldn't miss a thing, and Tommy thought he missed a lot. There were so many mysteries to the grown-up world. Still, he had to shut his eyes to sleep. Fingerfins couldn't because he had no eyelids. When he was a tiny boy, Tommy had thought that eyeballs were called eyebulbs, like light bulbs. He had a theory that they gave off light and that was how you could see, but when he got a little older and thought about it a little more, he realized how ridiculous that was. But it was an interesting idea. If your eyes gave off light you could penetrate the darkest corners, like a searchlight.

Tommy could see fairly well in his room. He had made

Rose raise his blinds. The night was clear now, and the lights from the roof gave everything a blue glow. Tommy got up to look out the window. He watched the cars pull up the driveway to the house, and heard the sharp, crackling sound of snow crunching beneath tires, car doors slamming like shots, and bursts of talk and laughter. When the ladies got out, he could hear the snow squeak under their feet as they hurried up the walk and the steps, clutching their coats around them. Clusters of people in twos and threes and fives dotted the street, the driveway, and the walk. Their breath came out in little puffs of vapor. His own breath frosted the window. It must have gotten very cold, a bitter night.

Tommy put on his bathrobe and slippers and tiptoed out of his room, although there was so much noise downstairs it was hardly necessary. He parted the curtains at the top of the stairway without opening them—opening them might make too much noise—and he took a few steps down the stairs. He took them one at a time and kept close to the wall. Tommy paused when he got to the landing by the big window and wondered if he ought to turn back. His mother wouldn't like it if she saw him, he knew that. After a minute or two he continued down, more quickly now because he didn't want to be seen, but Mr. Hutchins saw him and called out, "Happy New Year, Tommy." Mr. Hutchins had confetti on his shoulders. Hardly anyone else noticed him, and Tommy pretended that he was invisible in the enchanted forest of his house. He liked being invisible, and he thought of the emperor's new clothes, but he wouldn't like that much. Of course, that was different; it was only the emperor's clothes that were invisible; the emperor was plain enough for everybody to see, and he was stark naked. "Tommy, you belong in bed!" Mrs. Steer had spotted him. "You've just gotten over the measles." But Tommy moved quickly along and Mrs. Steer was talking to Dr. Rodgers anyway and didn't pay attention to him. The house was filling with people now. They were talking in groups here and there. Some of them were dancing in the big hall; others were sitting down at the small tables that had been set up that afternoon in the living room and the library. Tommy saw his father in the library, and he avoided that room. He decided to crawl

under one of the tables in the living room. With the table-
cloths on them, they were just like the tents they made in the
summer, and the light was dim, too. There wasn't much room,
and Tommy realized that there wouldn't be space enough for
him when everyone had sat down, even though the card tables
had been expanded with the special round tops his parents
had. He'd get kicked. He waited there for a few minutes, listening to the voices. Mrs. Sedgwick was telling Mrs. Hutchins
how Daisy had danced a great deal—those were her words, "a
great deal"—with Bob Griswold, and she observed that they
seemed very thick. Her voice sounded thick when she said it.
Mrs. Sedgwick had a way of saying things that made you think
she was saying more than she was. But Mr. Wolfe, Mrs.
Hutchins said, had danced a few times with Daisy too, among
others. Mrs. Sedgwick repeated "among others. My," she said,
"the attractive men just buzz around her like bees to honey.
It reminds me of the days before I married Tom. So many
beaux, such a lot of fun." Tommy heard his father's voice
approaching, and Mrs. Sedgwick said, "Oh, my, I'm being
taken to dance," and her laughter rippled off toward the hall.
Tommy got out from beneath the table when his father had
gone. He thought it might be safer in the kitchen with Rose.
He darted into the dining room, sticking close to the wall,
then the kitchen. Oh, oh! Tommy's mother was in the kitchen.
He moved to the doorway of the maid's room, which was dark.
He stood there against the door, not moving, trying to be still
like Fingerfins. His bathrobe was dark, too, dark and ugly,
Tommy thought, with its frayed cord. But it was almost as if
he were invisible, standing there against the door to the maid's
room while Rose and his mother moved deftly about the
kitchen. At least his mother moved deftly; Rose was too fat
to move very fast. Mr. Wolfe was standing in the kitchen,
too, and Mrs. Sedgwick had come in to help, and also Mrs.
Steer. Tommy could hear Mr. Steer's voice from the living
room. He was telling a story and people were laughing. He
was good at that, just as he was good at getting them all into
a terrible argument. But tonight they were laughing instead
of arguing. That was lucky; his parents didn't like Mr. Steer's
arguments. Mrs. Sedgwick was arranging the bacon and

scrambled eggs on platters—she was good at arranging things nicely—and Rose was carrying the platters to the sideboard in the dining room. Tommy's mother had gone to the stove to pour the boiling water from the teakettle into the coffeepot, and Mr. Wolfe was helping her while Mrs. Steer made toast. There were so many people and so much work to be done that Rose couldn't handle it by herself. Mrs. Sedgwick said she sometimes thought Rose was more decorative than useful, anyway, and tonight she was wearing a black dress and white apron and a little cap. She didn't usually, but tonight was a fancy party and she was supposed to look like a maid. It was funny that Rose and his mother both were wearing black; they certainly didn't look much alike otherwise. Tommy noticed that there was a little tear in his mother's hem. She must have forgotten to hold her strap. Tommy really did feel invisible, there in the darkened doorway. No one was seeing him at all. It made him gleeful, and he loved it. He loved the excitement and watching the people walk in and out, leaving little trails of confetti and carrying noisemakers, and all talking at once. Mr. Sedgwick came in and blew a noisemaker in his mother's ear. It made her jump, and she spilled the water she was pouring. "Tom!" His mother gave a short cry of alarm as the boiling water fell from the teakettle onto her dress. As quick as a flash Mr. Wolfe had grabbed the butter from the kitchen table and his mother was raising her dress to unfasten her garter. She loosed her stocking and peeled it down her leg. Mr. Wolfe made her sit down, crouching before her, raised her leg to his knee, and began to rub her leg with butter. "No, it's all right, Lucien," she said. "Really it is," but his mother's extended shin looked very red to Tommy, and her face looked flushed. Tommy wanted to rush over to her, to see if she was all right—he didn't want his mother to be hurt—but he was frozen; he couldn't move. He heard Mrs. Steer say that butter was the worst thing you could do for burns, that it just made the skin fry, like bacon, and Tommy dashed out of the kitchen. He knew his mother saw him out of the corner of her eye, but there was too much excitement then and she didn't see him dart under the dining-room table. It was the closest, seemed the safest, place to hide. He couldn't run through the hall and up the stairs without running into his father. He shouldn't have come down; he shouldn't be there at all. He was beginning to wish he weren't, but he didn't know what to do. He would surely be in trouble if he were caught going upstairs. He would be in trouble if he were caught underneath the table, too, but he didn't think that was likely. Tommy could make himself very small, and he wedged himself between the halves of the pedestal. When the leaves were out of the table, just one big round pedestal, like a column, supported it, but when the table was expanded with leaves the pedestal split in half. There was plenty of room in the middle for Tommy. He wrapped his arms around his legs, put his head on his knees, and braced his back and his feet against it. He would disappear. He didn't want his mother's skin to fry. He felt like crying, as much for the deep trouble he would be in if he were caught as for his mother's burn. The guests began to serve themselves from the sideboard as Rose passed them plates. He could hear the clatter of china and silver, and people walking about the room. They began to sit down at the tables in the living room and the library. He could hear their chairs scraping across the rug. His father was sitting in the library. Tommy could tell because his voice was far away, and Mrs. Sedgwick was with him, too. That would mean that his mother would sit in the dining room because they wouldn't both sit in the same room when they had so many guests, and his mother would want to be close to the kitchen. Soon people began to find their places at the table. Tommy could hear the plates going down: thump, thump. The people were pulling out the chairs and sitting down. They had to raise the cloth to sit down because it almost touched the floor and they couldn't get their legs under the table otherwise. His mother was in the dining room now. Her voice sounded gay, not hurt. She sat down at the foot of the table, where she always sat, and Mr. Sedgwick sat at the head. He dropped his napkin and had to reach under the table for it, but he didn't look and he didn't see Tommy. Mr. Wolfe brought Tommy's mother a plate, and he sat down next to her. When everyone was sitting, Tommy could look around the circumference of the table and see the folds of the cloth

flowing in motionless waves around it, up for a lap and down
in between, up and down, up and down, all around the table.
There was a real pattern to it, and it was quite pretty. It
looked like the scallop shell his grandmother had brought
back from Florida a long time ago and kept on a table in her
room; it was still there. Tommy could tell who was sitting
where, too, and he counted the people at the table. There were
ten. Mrs. Steer was sitting across the table from Mr. Wolfe,
between Mr. Hutchins and Dr. Rodgers. Mr. Hutchins was
on his mother's left. Mrs. Steer's dress was light gray and fell
like a fluted column, in heavy folds to her feet. Her feet were
big, and because she was tall she never wore very high heels.
Mr. Sedgwick's legs were skinny and Mr. Hutchins' were fat,
but both their stomachs bulged against the table. Mr. Wolfe's
were slim, and his stomach didn't bulge. He'd pulled the legs
of his trousers up when he sat down, and Tommy noticed that
he didn't wear garters; his socks just stayed up. His socks were
black silk like his father's, and there was a black silk stripe
running down his trouser leg, too. Tommy could see the hairs
on Mr. Wolfe's leg between the top of his socks and the
bottom of his trousers. His legs were dark. After his mother
had been sitting down for a while she pushed off her shoe with
her other foot, and it lay there empty on its side. One stocking
hung loosely around her ankle. His mother's poor leg. It was
white now against the blackness of her dress. Her stockings
were black too, but you could see through them, like his
father's and Mr. Wolfe's—like all the men's at the table, in
fact. All the women's stockings were different. Mrs. Steer's
were pale gray like her dress; Mrs. Rodgers' were beige, like
his mother's regular stockings, but her dress was blue velvet
with a long brown sash. Tommy supposed her stockings
matched her sash, but the dress was ugly, not pretty like his
mother's. Mrs. Rodgers' stomach bulged, too, and her legs
were fat. Tommy giggled to himself and hugged his knees
tighter. How funny, he thought, that the unblinking eyes of
the animals on the plate rail were looking down at all these
people and that his own eyes were looking up at them from
his secret place in the dark middle of the table—all those eyes
looking at them as they chewed and he bet they didn't even

know it. Tommy remembered the crazy man outside the church the day the bishop dedicated Mrs. Wentworth's Resurrection Window. "Nothing is hidden from the scouring eye of God," the man had shouted, while everyone looked very annoyed and his father rushed Tommy and his mother to the car, "and His hand shall smite the sinner down!" Tommy shivered at the memory. The man was filthy and he looked crazy. He showed up two more times at the church, but the last time the police took him away and Tommy had never seen him again. Tommy's mother pulled her dress up a ways, over the leg she'd burned. She had one black leg and one white one. The wet spot on the chiffon where the water had spilled was drying out, and her dress fell in soft ripples from her knees. You could hardly see the tear in her hem. Mrs. Steer's dress looked pretty, too, though hers fell like marble, Tommy thought, like a statue. Tommy compared Mr. Wolfe's lég with his mother's. His mother must have taken the hair off hers. Mr. Wolfe's had a lot more hair on it. He ate with one hand in his lap, just the way Tommy had been taught. If you weren't using your hand, it belonged in your lap. Not all the adults had their free hands in their laps, but perhaps they were using them. Mr. Wolfe's hand—it was his left hand, the one next to his mother—reached over and touched his mother's leg, just grazing it with his fingertips. His mother shifted slightly in her chair, moving her leg a little. Mr. Wolfe dropped his napkin. He reached down for it without looking and grasped his mother's ankle, suddenly lifting her leg and his napkin to his lap. He did it so quickly Tommy hardly realized what had happened. It was the leg his mother had hurt. Oh! Mr. Wolfe would hurt it. Oh, oh, oh, his poor mother's leg! She adjusted it in Mr. Wolfe's lap. Her dress shimmered faintly. The conversation continued. His mother hadn't paused. Her voice was the same. She was talking across the table to Dr. Rodgers, who sat on the other side of Mrs. Steer. His stomach didn't bulge, either. Mr. Wolfe was talking to Mrs. Rodgers, on his right. Dr. and Mrs. Rodgers were the only couple at the table. "That shouldn't be," Tommy's mother said with a laugh. "You see each other all the time." He knew his parents liked to separate married couples when they sat down at the table. It was all right if you weren't married—John and Emily always sat next to each other—but not if you were. Tommy could see the buckle on his mother's empty shoe shining in the gloom. He could have reached out and touched it. Her leg was still on Mr. Wolfe's lap, and he was rubbing it gently. Perhaps he was treating the burn. Why hadn't she asked Dr. Rodgers? Tommy thought. Maybe he should tell her: "Mommy, ask Dr. Rodgers to fix your leg." But if he did that he would be caught. Oh, his mother's poor leg. What could he do? Tommy's eye was riveted to it. His eye burned. His whole face burned, and felt hot as his mother's leg must feel. He wondered if her skin were frying right there on Mr. Wolfe's knee, his hand rubbing slowly up and down, up to her knee and back, up around her knee and back, as the silver clattered and the conversation went on above him, all about the party and Mr. Wolfe's grand dinner—Tommy didn't care about Mr. Wolfe's grand dinner—and about what a fine couple John and Emily made, and how David seemed to be smitten—that was the word Mrs. Rodgers used—with Margie, and my, wasn't Daisy Meyer a beautiful dancer, as good a dancer as she was a golfer and a tennis player, and how Mr. Hutchins hoped that Bob Griswold was settling Margie's father's estate in good order—all the usual things they talked about in Tommy's city, his own city of Sargasso weeds. Nothing was different; something was different. Tommy was transfixed. He heard the sounds of chewing. He heard his father's voice from the other room, making all the ladies at his table laugh. "Nobody ever got drunk on Scotch," he said. Tommy looked over toward Mrs. Steer, who picked up Dr. Rodgers' hand which had fastened on her knee and dropped it—actually dropped it—back in his lap. That must be what they meant when they laughed about Dr. Rodgers' roving hands. Tommy smiled. He wasn't supposed to have heard that. It was so hot under the table. Tommy wondered how he'd ever escape, and he wanted to, he wanted to so much. He looked back toward his mother, hoping she might help. Mr. Wolfe's hand was kneading his mother's soft flesh as if it were a lump of dough. The thought made Tommy feel sick. They must be almost finished with their breakfast. Oh, please, let them be finished,

Tommy thought. All he wanted was to be in bed with his eyes closed, sleeping. He saw his mother's hand with the dark star ring reach down and stay Mr. Wolfe, quickly pulling up her stocking and deftly fastening her garter. She was good at that. Tommy always had to use both hands for his, and still he had trouble. Her leg was on the floor now, and she was slipping her foot into her shoe. Tommy heard the front door open, and his mother rose from the table. John and Emily, David and Margie, Vint Steer, the Meyers and the Griswolds, and Nick and Emily's roommate had just come in from the dance. Tommy's mother told Rose to put on more eggs and bacon, and people began leaving the table. Tommy heard something drop from Mrs. Steer. "My earring," she said. Dr. Rodgers said, "I'll get it." Mrs. Steer said, "No, I'll do it," and they both went under the table at once. Their heads bumped— Tommy almost giggled—but Mrs. Steer found the earring herself. She also found Tommy.

"What's this?" she said, pulling on his bathrobe and peering farther under the table. "Tommy! You've been there all this time!" Tommy's father had come into the dining room, and Mrs. Steer said, "Mac, one of your guests is under the table. I don't think he was invited." She laughed and made Tommy come out. He was afraid, but he did, and he stood there in his hideous blue bathrobe with the frayed cord and looked at the carpet.

"Emma," his father said, "I think we've got a visitor here who needs to be put to bed. And he's sober as a judge, too. He must have been drinking Scotch," his father added. Everyone laughed, and Tommy tried to. His mother came into the room and saw him.

"Where have you been?" she asked, astonished.

"He's been hiding under the table," Mrs. Steer said.

"I thought I saw you go to bed," his mother said.

"I didn't," said Tommy. Everyone was making a fuss over him now, his parents' friends and his brothers and their friends, and all of them thought it was hilarious. They were all happy because of the parties and nobody seemed to mind very much what he'd done, but Tommy was very tired and he asked his mother to take him to bed. He asked her how her leg was, and she said it was fine. "But you burned it," Tommy said. "I saw it happen."

"Oh, it doesn't hurt a bit," and his mother extended her leg, clad in its dark stocking, the silk slipper on her foot. "It's just a little burn," she said, patting her leg with her hand. "Nothing to worry about at all. You go ahead upstairs now. I have to speak to Rose, but I'll be with you in a minute." Tommy waited by the stairway. He refused to go up alone. He wished he had never come down.

WHEN his mother finally took him up to bed, Tommy was crying. He was overtired, his mother said. He had had too much excitement. But she was not so annoyed as she might have been. All she did was close his curtains and pull his shades. She insisted that the lights would bother him.

There were tears in her eyes, too, Tommy thought, when she bent to kiss him and tuck the blankets around him so he'd be snug and warm in the frozen middle of the first night of the New Year. The cold heavy clips she wore in the neck of her dress brushed against him as her soft lips touched his own soft cheek. Tommy hugged his mother tightly to him. "Mommy, Mommy," he cried, "why did you burn your leg?"

"There, there," she said. She sat on the edge of his bed and began to sing her familiar lullaby: *"Bye baby bunting, Daddy's gone a-hunting, Gone to get a rabbit skin to wrap my baby bunting in,"* but the lullaby did not assure him. The pale light from the half-open door to the hallway radiated from behind her. It caught in the stones in her ears, in the jeweled arrow in her hair, in the two clips she wore like tiny shields on her dress, and flared in the prism of his tears like a shower of cold, infinitesimal, brilliant darts. He could not see her shadowed face.

His mother kissed him again, and patted his chest. She sat there for a time, her hand resting lightly on him, trying to soothe him as the tears turned into sobs and were now subsiding slowly and without hope into a soft, almost silent crying, impersonal and relentless as the encroaching frost that glazed his bedroom window. Finally his mother said good night. "Sweet dreams, my dearest, my darling boy," and left him, shutting the door tight so he wouldn't be disturbed by the sounds from downstairs, though the dark, to Tommy, seemed more disturbing.

When she had gone, Tommy lay awake for a long time, listening to the voices and laughter float up beneath him, feeling his tears run from the corners of his eyes, wetting his face, his pillow. Tommy didn't know why he was crying; he just felt very sad, as sad as he had ever felt in his entire life. He wasn't sure he'd ever felt true sadness before, but he was sure that this was it. It was a feeling so empty and alone, as though something were lost, lost forever and for all time, never to be regained. The tears welled up within him from an endless spring, and he imagined his tears filling his bed, over-flowing onto the floor, washing down the stairway into the floor below, filling the living rooms, the cellar, the house, the street; and he imagined his house and all its inhabitants float-ing away in the flood of his tears, like Noah and his ark. The thought made him smile a little, as he drifted slowly into sleep, abandoned to his dream, which was not sweet as his mother had ordered.

In the dream a man appeared in white shirt sleeves, his arms near his sides, his face wreathed in a luminous plume of thick white smoke that rose slowly from the cigarette he held in his beckoning hand and curled about his face, ghost-like, before it trailed off into the darkness above his head. The man stood beside Tommy's bed, his dark eyes burning into him as Tommy lay there helpless, unable to move. The man motioned again with his hand. As if in thrall, Tommy passed through the open cellar doorway and down the steep steps, the man directly behind him, shutting the door. The cellar was dark, very dark. Its darkness absorbed like cotton wool the dull light from the bulb that hung above the great scarred block of wood where they sometimes split logs for the fireplace. Flames from the coal fire flared out from the open furnace door. There were other men in the room, shadowy figures, in the background. Tommy could see them silhou-etted on the wall from the light of the flames that flashed and flickered, their shadows suddenly looming and dissolving and looming again, dancing against the blackness. The tools stood beside the furnace, ancient iron rods as tall or taller than Tommy's father: the grappling tongs for the cinders, long pokers hooked at the end and pokers that were straight and pointed, the big axe for the firewood and the iron wedge that split it. Tommy, terror frozen in his throat, lay immobile on the block, the back of his head to the furnace door, arms tight to his chest, hands clenched beside his face, waiting for what terrible thing to happen he did not know, at the hands of a man he sometimes seemed to recognize but could not. He was choked with terror, his eyes trembling, paralyzed with fear and helpless to resist. He was going to die. If he were not to die, he had to kill, and he could not kill. He did not have the power to kill. Oh, God, why did he have to die? What had he done to deserve to die? The man, his shirt sleeves rolled up near his elbows, moved closer. Tommy could feel the light burning from his eyes, the light flashing from the furnace, bursting the shadows that flickered and vanished and appeared again. He moaned—ah, ahh—and struggled to emerge from the dream, too terrified to scream, moaning louder—ahhh, ahhhh—and opened his eyes to the blackness of his room; and then he screamed.

In an instant Tommy's father was standing over him. "Oh, God! Oh, God," Tommy sobbed, his face to the wall, hands clasping his head. "Oh, God, help, help!" And his body heaved with sobs in the black night. Heaved and heaved and heaved. His father put out his hand to touch Tommy and Tommy shrank back. He did not want to be touched; he wanted to be touched. He wanted his father to hold him, to make everything all right, but he was afraid, still caught in his dream, a dream more vivid than his father's shadowy robed presence looming above his bed.

His father sat down on Tommy's bed, rubbed his legs in the blanket, and tucked it tight around him. "There, there," he said. "There, there." His father sat with his hand on Tommy's shoulder for a long time and told Tommy that he'd been dreaming, that it was only a dream, a bad dream but still only a dream. Everybody had bad dreams once in a while, he said. He didn't ask what the dream was, nor could Tommy have told him or anyone else. He didn't know. All he wanted to do was forget it. It was the first time he had dreamed it. Tommy asked his father to raise his blinds, and he did. His father returned to the bed and stroked Tommy's legs and back—Tommy was still facing the wall, not wanting to look his father in the face—until at last and again he dozed off into a fitful sleep, and then sank into a very deep, deep sleep.

When he awoke, the sun was shining through the east window into his room, and shining on the thick snow that coated the pines and the bare branches of the maples, weighed down the thornapple and chokecherry thicket, and transformed the contours of his familiar, visible world. It was New Year's Day.

THAT afternoon Tommy went with his parents to Mr. Treverton's open house. It was held every New Year's Day, and almost everyone Tommy knew—everyone who had been at his parents' breakfast the night before, probably everyone who had gone to the dance as well—was there along with their children. Fires blazed in Mr. Treverton's two fireplaces, the dining-room table was filled with platters of ham and turkey and cheese, the Christmas tree lighted the big hallway, and the children drank hot chocolate and eggnogs. The adults drank hot buttered rum; it was Mr. Treverton's custom. The smell of hot buttered rum made Tommy feel sick, but everything else was delicious.

Mr. Treverton—all the grown-ups called him Trev—had a skating rink next to his house. Many of the adults, wrapped in their furs and overcoats, hats and gloves and scarves— Tommy's mother, for instance, who loved to skate, and Mrs. Steer who loved it even more and was very good at it—glided around the ice in a brisk but stately rhythm, mufflers streaming behind them, under the small white lights that were strung from a pole in the center of the rink to the edges, bordering it and making a kind of pavilion of lights above the ice, against the sky. Mr. Treverton had an old sleigh with a seat, which could be pushed by two handles. The children took turns going around the rink in it, pushed by one or another of the men or by Mrs. Steer, the whole company coalescing in a kind of procession behind the child in the sleigh, the very young children carried by their parents, the children

Tommy's age skating along, ankles wobbling, supported by the hands of one or two adults, his brothers and their friends occasionally darting in and out of the line. It was, Tommy thought, beautiful to watch, as if the procession of all those lives had taken on a single life of its own.

The sun, which had been shining brilliantly earlier in the day, was overcast by the time they got to the Treverton house on the river, and the snow had begun falling again, softly, in big flakes that drifted lazily down from the darkening sky, dusting the rink with patches of snow that the older boys cleared away from time to time with the big scraper. Mrs. Steer loved the snowflakes. She told Tommy and Amy that each was different, that each, if you examined it closely under a magnifying glass, had a pattern, and that no snowflake was exactly like any other snowflake in the entire world, even though they looked much the same to the superficial eye. "Just," she said, "like us. And just like the millions of cells in our bodies. No matter how much they resemble each other, each one is different, and different from anyone else's, too. That," she said after a pause, "is the meaning of unique."

"What about the snowball?" Tommy asked. "Every snow-flake in the snowball is different, too?"

"Yes," she said, "every last one."

"That must be crazy for the snowball," Tommy said, sticking out his tongue to catch a flake.

"No more than it is for us," said Mrs. Steer, laughing and taking off her skates to return to the house for a hot rum toddy. Tommy thought about twins, and wondered if not even twins were alike. They looked alike. He often imagined himself with a twin brother, a mirror image of himself in which he could see himself and his life, his thoughts and feelings, reflected back at him, but differently. He would have liked that, he thought, and someday he must ask Mrs. Steer about twins. But not now. Now he wanted to build a snow-man with Jimmy Randolph, who had come to the party with his parents even though Jimmy's father drank nothing but Coke.

Tommy's brothers, Nick Kingsfield, Vint Steer and their friends, Bob Griswold and Phil Meyer, even Lucien Wolfe, began a pickup hockey game, now that most of the older people had left the rink for the warmth of the house. Phil Meyer had helped Tommy make it around the rink three times without falling. Tommy was a very wobbly skater, and the skates that had been his brother John's and then his brother David's didn't fit him very well. They were still too big. Amy Steer had gotten a new pair of white figure skates for Christmas—CCMs, the best kind. Amy was a better skater than Tommy, and he envied her ability to glide across the ice, almost as if she'd been doing it for years. But at least Tommy could use real skates now, instead of the double runners his parents had started him out with. "Let me tell you a secret, Tommy," Phil Meyer said. "Nobody could learn to skate on double runners. The only way to learn is to get up on those single blades and wobble through." Tommy wondered why, then, had his parents given him double runners to begin with. "Everyone falls at first," Phil Meyer said. "Don't worry about it."

While he skated with Phil, Daisy went around the rink with Tommy's brother David, their arms linked behind them, and then David skated with Margie, and Daisy with Bob Griswold. Alone, Daisy Meyer was a very fancy skater. Everyone admired her skill. She didn't look as if she had ever fallen in her entire life. Indifferent to the hockey game that flashed around her, she now darted onto the ice and leisurely carved a figure-eight, then flew across it, arms and legs extended like a bird, as if the law of gravity that had such a dire effect on Tommy had no effect on her at all. All other movement began to slow and slowly cease, the hockey game, the work on the snowman, as Daisy cut her graceful loops across the brilliant unyielding surface of the ice. And then, lowering her leg slowly to her other shin, Daisy began to turn, slowly at first, then faster and faster, until her body seemed a spinning blur that could go on spinning forever—when suddenly she stopped in a shower of ice and stood there poised for a moment, statuelike under the lights. Tommy could feel the sting of the ice in his nostrils.

The hockey game could not compete with such intensity, and soon the players broke it off, and, except for Mr. Wolfe, who went inside for his hot toddy, they all helped work on the snowman. When it was finished, David and Nick began throwing snowballs, and within seconds everyone, Tommy and Amy and Jimmy included, was laughing and shouting and pelting everyone else with the snow that was now dropping thickly down from the black sky into the twinkling lights, onto the rink, the people around it, onto the winter trees and the frozen river in the distance, and onto the Treverton house, which beckoned them now with its bright windows, its warming fires, and its glowing Christmas tree.

The tree was a fragrant balsam hung with hundreds of ornaments and cookies and chocolate wrapped in shining colored foil that the children were urged to take off the tree and eat, along with all the other good things that burdened Mr. Treverton's table. It was fun, and Tommy ate a lot before his parents gathered him up to leave the party.

"Now you, young man," Mr. Treverton said to Tommy as they stood at the door, "did you have your hot chocolate and your eggnog?"

Tommy said that indeed he had, and thanked him. He wondered who had helped Mr. Treverton with his party, since his wife was dead.

"And you two," Mr. Treverton said to his parents, "did you follow my rule—three hot rum toddies followed by a cold one?"

Tommy's parents allowed that they had, his father having broken his Scotch-whisky rule for the occasion.

"Then now," concluded Mr. Treverton, "you're fixed for the New Year."

"Yes," his father agreed, "very well fixed indeed," and Tommy, his mother, and his father departed. When they got home, Tommy went to the Steers', where Mrs. Steer lighted the candles on the Christmas tree, as she had promised.

Four

LATE that winter afternoon, there was a terrible explosion at the plant and three men were killed. Tommy saw it. He saw it happen. It was a little before five; the four-thirty whistle had blown a while before, signaling the end of the day shift. David was already home—he was always the first one out the gate, his father said—and Tommy had seen the last of the men with their empty lunch pails pass the Steers' corner a few minutes before. He was standing at his bedroom window, the curtains filtering the glow from the furnaces against the sky. It was almost dark. Suddenly the glow from the furnaces intensified, like a surge of heat lightning, then immediately faded from the sky. Tommy parted the curtains with his hand and peered into the darkness. A second or two later there was a sharp, violent crack, followed by a cloud of black and white smoke billowing into the sky, and then the tongues of orange fire.

"David! David! Something terrible's happened. The plant blew up!" Tommy was trying to tie back the curtains. His brother was running down the hall to Tommy's window. He had heard the explosion—the crack like his father's rifle, and then the long thunderous roar—followed by the surging smoke and the flames that filled the air and reflected in the snow on the porch roof and flickered against the bedroom wall behind them. Tommy heard the sound of a siren from the plant—it was the alarm—and soon sirens filled the air.

"It's the fire trucks," said David—"and the ambulance. My God, what happened?" Even Rose had rushed to Tommy's window, and the three of them stood there transfixed, their eyes piercing the glass and the night.

"The plant blew up," said Tommy, his voice hushed. "The plant blew up." Suddenly, "Daddy! What about Daddy?" Tommy raced into his parents' room to call the plant. He had never called the plant before. He was not supposed to call his father at work, but he had heard the number often enough, and he knew it.

"Don't use the phone," said David, grabbing it from his hand. "Dad will be trying to call. And Tommy, the plant didn't blow up. There's just something wrong with the furnaces."

In a few minutes the phone did ring. It was his father's secretary, the one who'd told David that he'd gotten the infection in his elbow from bending it so much on the Northview bar, which wasn't true. Neither Tommy nor his brothers nor his mother liked his father's secretary, but his father did. She was loyal, he said, and she never repeated anything she wasn't supposed to, the way Tommy sometimes did. Tommy seized the telephone, but David snatched it from him.

"Yes," he said. "No, she's playing bridge. . . . At the country club, I guess. What's the matter? . . . Oh," he said. "Oh. . . . Yes. . . . Okay. I'll tell her."

"Tell her what?" Tommy screamed. "Tell her *what*?"

"Dad's all right. He wanted Miss Ernst to call and tell Mother."

"Oh, thank God," said Tommy, who swore that never again would we have an evil thought about his father. "Thank God."

When his mother came home a while later, Tommy was the first to tell her. David was mad. "You know what they do with messengers who bring the bad news, don't you?" he said. "They kill them."

"Mommy," Tommy said, "David said he's going to kill me. You just wanted to be the one to tell her," he said to David.

"Don't be foolish, Tommy," his mother said. "And David, for heaven's sake, stop your teasing."

His mother hadn't seen the explosion because she'd driven

home the back way, and she guessed the country club was too far away for her to hear the noise.

"Noise?" Tommy was incredulous. "It wasn't a noise. It was a big explosion. A huge explosion! You can still see the smoke. Look!" Tommy pulled his mother into his bedroom and toward the clear view from his window, the clearest view in the house. "Look." Across the way the clouds of luminous orange smoke still hung quivering in the air, like a living thing. They were all silent. Even his mother was shaken. "Dear God," she said. "Dear God."

After a moment his mother said, in a voice she was trying to keep from trembling, "That's enough now." She released the ties that held the curtains from the glass. "Everything will be all right. Daddy's all right—we know that—and he'll call us soon. The plant didn't blow up. There was just a problem in the furnace room. Rose," she said, "would you get Tommy his supper—and see that he eats it—while I rest for a few minutes. I'm afraid it'll be a long night."

"But Mother," Tommy said, taking the curtains insistently from her hand, "I want to *see!*" He pushed them back to tie them.

"Oh, Tommy," she said, pleading, "surely you've seen enough. Everything will be all right. There's nothing we can do now, and there's no point in standing here looking at it any longer. It'll just make you upset." The curtains fell in soft gauzy folds over the window, filtering the terrible smoke and flames and making them look quite pretty, like lamplight in a painting, like a sunset. But when his mother and David and Rose had left his room, Tommy tied the curtains back and stayed there watching—it did not look like a painting then— until Rose called him for supper, which he ate with David. His mother would wait to eat with his father. In the meantime, she was resting after her bath. Bridge was tiring. Often Mrs. Steer came home from the club with a migraine and had to go to bed; but she always won, too. She was the club champion.

TOMMY knew about the furnaces. He knew how danger-ous they were, how they looked like a fiery lake. Although he

207

had seen their glow in the sky for as long as he could remember, he had looked on them for the first time close up
the Saturday after New Year's. His father had taken him to
the plant that afternoon, as he sometimes did on Saturdays or
Sundays, to play at the adding machines in the outer office
where a lot of people worked, but not on Saturday afternoon,
and at the rolltop desk in his own office that overlooked the
river. While Tommy played, his father worked at another
desk, a big flat mahogany one whose top was covered with
glass. He almost never used the rolltop anymore, but once
he'd used it every day and he still liked it—it reminded him
of the old times, he told Tommy—so he kept it in his office.
Tommy was glad that he did. It was almost like the desk he
had gotten for Christmas, only a lot bigger, and the top itself
and all the drawers locked with a key. He loved to play there
while his father worked at producing the things that made
the tall brick smokestack—a free-standing chimney, really,
taller than any building in town—give off its fragile plume
of smoke and the furnaces give off their dust and fire. Tommy's
father had big jars in his office filled with chunks of coke and
limestone, samples of the shipments that arrived by boat at
the plant and, when the limestone had been made into lime
in the clanking kilns by the tall chimney, went into the
furnaces to make the chemicals that were then shipped all over
the country by train. But when Tommy's father worked, he
worked at piles of paper, and sometimes with columns of
figures from the adding machines that Tommy liked to play
with. Tommy always brought his tapes home, and sometimes
he showed them to David, who asked him what they meant.
"What do you mean, 'What do they mean?' " Tommy asked
him. "They're just my numbers." But Tommy knew they had
to mean something more than that, and it annoyed him that
he couldn't tell. They were just numbers that Tommy had
punched out on a machine, and as David said, "By themselves they don't mean a damn thing," and as Tommy told
him, "Well, if you're so smart, why aren't you in college like
John?" and David would slam his door and that would be
the end of that. So Tommy would pore over his figures, just as
his father did, and he would make them mean something,
at least to himself. They were his own secret.

Tommy was playing at the rolltop desk in his father's office that Saturday after New Year's when his father's phone rang. "MacAllister talking," he said. He talked for a long time, and then some men from the plant came to see him in their work clothes and Tommy went to the adding machines, where he produced long tapes full of numbers, some of them in red. The men left, and after a while his father came out to get him. He was wearing a white smock and carrying an old shirt of his own that he told Tommy to put on. "We're going out in the plant," he said. "This will keep the dust off you. You must stay right beside me and not touch anything, anything at all. You could get hurt, or hurt someone else. And watch where you're stepping, too. You'll be all right as long as you do what I tell you."

They went out the door of the office, which was clean and bright, and into the plant, where dust covered everything and the light was dim. Tommy wanted to see it all. He had never been in the actual plant before, with its electrical shop and machine shop, the packing room and the shipping room and the drum factory where David worked, and the railroad tracks and the lime kilns and all those things Tommy had heard about but never seen, except from the outside, or, like the furnace room, as a light reflecting in the sky. Some places it was so noisy you could hardly hear, and in others it was quiet and empty. The air smelled the way it did after an electrical storm, and the dust burned. Tommy covered his mouth with his free hand so it was easier to breathe. His father held his other hand, and together they hurried along, Tommy wanting to stop, his father pulling him on, up and down stairs and past a lot of machines, some of them working and some of them quiet, through a lot of rooms and down a lot of corridors, and finally they came to the big doors of the furnace room, solid except for a tiny slit of dark glass too high for Tommy.

His father stopped. "Tommy," he said, "we're going into the furnace room. Put on these goggles." His father reached into a pocket of his smock and handed Tommy a pair of thick dark goggles. When he saw that Tommy had them on securely, he put on his own pair. Tommy was very excited. "When I open the door you mustn't look at the furnaces. Even with goggles you're liable to hurt your eyes. When we get to the control room, you can look through the windows. The glass is smoked, so the light won't hurt you. Keep your goggles on, do absolutely what I say, and don't talk and don't get in the way of the men." His father pushed open the heavy doors. Tommy recoiled from the heat and the blast. Taking Tommy by the hand, his father walked quickly to the control room. Tommy was afraid to open his eyes, but he did.

What he beheld was astonishing: a vast, cavernous room partly open to the sky, and three great squares of molten fire like burning lakes, like something out of the Bible, fire and brimstone. He thought of the crazy man, the one who said, "Nothing is hidden from the scouring eye of God, and His hand shall smite the sinner down, and he will burn forever in the unquenchable fire!" Tommy had forgotten that last part, but he remembered it now. He shuddered. At the same time, he felt very grown up, that he was allowed to be in a place of such danger, and he didn't let on that he was afraid. He hardly noticed when his father introduced him to Mr. Anderson, the foreman. Tommy looked through the smoked glass and saw the three furnaces in a line and the tiny furnace-men who worked them from behind their big asbestos shields, bigger than the men. The shields moved back and forth on wheels, back and forth, as the men stoked the fires with very long rods—so long and so heavy that they were on rollers too—protruding from a slit in the shields that protected them from the heat and the light. Above the slit there was a tiny window of thick glass, like his goggles, and the men wore thick white suits and helmets that completely covered their heads, with the same glass over their eyes. Three men worked each furnace, pushing the shields before them. When one man moved forward, another went back, and the rhythm of the men was like the waves moving back and forth on the water, not in a line but separately. And then when the time was right, the foreman in the control room would pull a lever, and down from the roof would swing a long metal arm with a mouth at the end of it that would open and pour a stream of chemicals into the furnace, causing it to flare up with a white light while the men drew back before they continued their stoking and tending of the fire. Tommy had never imagined anything quite like it. When his father talked of the furnaces, Tommy had thought of something like their old coal furnace, only larger; and these were nothing like that. He thought his whole house could have fallen into just one of them.

The foreman looked at Tommy's father. "Shall I let him?" he asked. "Sure," said his father. "Let him try it."

"Here, Tommy," the foreman said, gesturing toward the panel of levers, "bring your hand over here and give it a try."

"Me?" Tommy didn't believe it. He glanced toward his father and back to the foreman.

"Nobody else," the foreman said. "You can do it. Don't you want to?"

"Yes, I do," said Tommy, facing the panel of levers that controlled the furnaces. There were a lot of levers and knobs and dials.

"Okay. Put your hand on this one—it's for the Number One furnace, the closest one," the foreman said, "and wait until I tell you. When I let you know, you just pull this handle gently toward you, and then when I give you the signal, push it back." Tommy put both his hands on the lever, preparing to summon all his strength. "You don't have to jerk it," the foreman cautioned him, "just go slow and easy, slow and easy like it's a lady." The foreman laughed. "It's a lot easier than you think. You'll get the hang of it right away."

Tommy stood there watching the foreman. His father nodded and the foreman said, "Now! Give it to her quick!" Tommy jerked the handle toward him, and it gave a start. It moved a lot more easily than he had thought. "Slow! Easy," the foreman called out. "Just real smooth, boy, real slow and smooth like I told you." Tommy pulled it slowly toward him. It really was easy. When he pulled the lever toward him, the long crane swung down from the ceiling over the furnace, the men behind the shields all moved back, and when Tommy had pulled it as far as it would go, the foreman said, "Now give it a good hard twist," and Tommy did with all his strength and the mouth opened and poured its white powders into the furnace and the furnace flared with a white light. It was like

211

magic. Right then Tommy decided he would be a chemist when he grew up. "Now turn it back," the foreman said, and as Tommy did the flowing powders trickled to a stop, the mouth closed, and the crane began to bend in half and fold slowly back to its place in the roof. "Can I do it again," Tommy asked.

"Not yet," the foreman said. "We've got to see how this mix works. But if your father says it's okay, you can do it again later, or some other time."

The foreman and Tommy's father started talking. "Why are we getting these surges, Andy?" his father asked. But the foreman didn't know. He had a hunch there was a problem with one of the transformers.

"What in the hell is that furnaceman doing?" Tommy's father suddenly exclaimed. They all looked. The middle furnaceman on Number One had his rod plunged deep into the furnace. Tommy's father ran out onto the floor. He didn't even have a protective suit on. When he opened the door, the heat and the crackling roar of the furnaces, muffled in the control room, blasted them. "That's your father for you," the foreman said. "He don't miss much around this place." Tommy's father ran right over to the furnaceman, grabbed the end of the rod, and began raising it. Tommy could see that it took a lot of strength, and when he got it up, the long tip of the rod glowed whiter than the furnace. His father gestured at the furnaceman. Then he took the furnaceman's gloves and began moving the rod slowly back and forth just under the surface. He stopped, gave the furnaceman's gloves back to him, and made him do it. He talked to him for a few minutes, moving his hands a lot, and then came back to the control room.

"You keep an eye on that one, Andy. He could get us in a lot of trouble doing it like that when the mix has just been added. It's all in the timing. Why, little Tommy here could do better than that."

"He's the new man," Mr. Anderson said. "I'll watch him good. You've got to treat those furnaces like a lady," he repeated, "and even then you never know what Number One will do. She's acting strange."

Tommy's father said he'd talk to Simpkin about the transformer. Mr. Simpkin was the electrical foreman. He'd talked to him already, he said, but he'd do it again. "If we're not careful, somebody'll get hurt around here."

The foreman agreed. "Nothing wrong with the product, though," he said.

"No," said his father, "there's nothing wrong with the product. The product tests all right. But there sure as hell is something wrong with Number One. Ease up on that lever," he told Mr. Anderson, who was operating the control for Number Three. "You don't want to overdo it." He peered through the glass. Tommy peered through the glass, too, but he couldn't tell if there was a problem or not. Since he'd never seen the furnaces before, he didn't know what to look for. They all looked pretty hot to Tommy. So he just watched, and listened to his father and the foreman talk. Even in the control room it was very hot. They were all sweating. It was hard to believe that outside great drifts of snow covered the ground, and the snowbanks were so high along the walks to their house that Tommy couldn't see over them. Snow would never last in here, Tommy thought; it would all turn into boiling water.

"Okay, Tommy," his father said. "Let's get out of here. This place is hot enough to make your blood boil, and we can't have that, young fellow. Call me, Andy, if there's any trouble"

"Come again, Tommy," Mr. Anderson said, "and I'll put you back to work. I could use some good help."

Tommy and his father returned to his father's office, where his father took off his smock and Tommy's shirt and put the goggles away. While they were inside, the men had washed Tommy's father's car. It was waiting for them, black and gleaming, by the door, and they drove out of the plant by the main gate. It was almost dark.

"I want to go see Simpkin for a minute," his father said. "You'll have to come with me, but you wait in the car." They drove over to Mr. Simpkin's house, which was in another part of town but not too far from their own house. It faced a big field and, far away at the other end of the field, the lime dump where the lime the plant couldn't use because it wasn't pure enough was piled up like a range of mountains. Tommy could see it shining whitely in the dusk.

"I think I'll be a chemical engineer when I grow up," Tommy said. He thought his father would like that, but his father didn't say anything. He was thinking.

Tommy looked off toward the lime dump. The lime dump was absolutely, strictly off limits to everyone. Lime could burn, and once a long time ago the daughter of someone Tommy's parents knew had been burned to death playing there. It was a terrible thing. There was a pond right next to the dump, though Tommy had never seen it, and she had rolled down the mountain of lime and straight into the pond, but she hadn't drowned; she'd burned to death. Tommy didn't understand how the lime could burn when it didn't look hot and water put out fires. "It doesn't make sense that lime can burn," he said to his father. "Why wouldn't the water put out the fire?"

"Well," his father said, "you know pepper? It's like pepper. Pepper burns if you get too much of it. Or like iodine. You know how it stings?" Then his father looked at him and said, "If you don't understand that lime is dangerous and burns, then you'd better not be a chemical engineer. I'm not sure you're smart enough. You might blow something up."

His father was cross again. Tommy didn't say anything, but he thought sometime he'd show him that he was smart enough. He was only seven, but he'd be eight in almost two months. He'd grow up and he'd put chemicals together and he'd make them burn and then he'd put out the fire with chemicals of his own. Why, he wondered, did his father have to be cross like that? He could be so nice one minute, and the next thing you knew he'd say something mean, like that. So Tommy retreated into his own thoughts as they drove up to Mr. Simpkin's house.

While his father parked the car, Tommy saw the most extraordinary thing. Through the Simpkins' front window he could see Mrs. Simpkin, sitting in a chair by a round table, bathed in lamplight. Mr. Simpkin was standing behind her silently brushing his wife's long hair. It was not beautiful hair, just a kind of mixed dark gray, and Mr. Simpkin brushed from the top of her head to its ends, which were so long they hung in soft waves over the back of her chair. Her hair would have come to her waist if she were standing, Tommy thought, and it shone dully in the lamplight, like silver that was a little tarnished; like heavy satin. The two of them were facing a corner of the room near the window, so their faces were almost in profile. They were not smiling; neither of them appeared to be speaking, and yet they did not look unhappy—nor happy, either. They were just there in the amber light, like figures in a painting, Mrs. Simpkin sitting back, her left arm resting on the table, Mr. Simpkin brushing with his right hand and lifting the hair a little with his left. Tommy felt as if he shouldn't be looking, it seemed such a private moment, but it was so beautiful he couldn't move his eyes away, and he felt privileged to witness it. As Mr. Simpkin brushed, tiny sparks flew from Mrs. Simpkin's hair, like the static electricity Tommy could make by sliding his feet across the carpet in his living room. Then, if he touched a piece of metal, he would get a tiny shock, not unpleasurable. He wondered if they could feel the sparks that flew between them, the tiny tingling shocks. Tommy's father had gotten out of the car. Tommy wanted to say, "Stop! Don't do it," but his father was already on their porch and knocking at their door. For a moment Mrs. Simpkin looked alarmed, and Mr. Simpkin put the brush on the table. He helped his wife off the chair. She leaned against him as they moved somewhere toward the back of the house, out of sight. Mrs. Simpkin was sick; they called her an invalid, like Mrs. Matson, and Mr. Simpkin had to take care of her a lot. Tommy was sorry his father had disturbed the picture, and he thought that if he were too dumb to be a chemical engineer, then maybe he'd be a painter so he could capture the mellow light, the gesture of the hand, and the pewter hair. He knew, though, that he couldn't draw very well. Mr. Sedgwick's friend Miss Moore, his kindergarten teacher, had told him that. Mr. Simpkin came to the door and he and his father stepped into the hallway, closing the door behind them. They must have stayed in the hall talking, because Tommy didn't see them in the living room, which was

empty now, save for the light, the table, and the chair. His
father stayed for a long time in Mr. Simpkin's hall—at least,
it seemed like a long time to Tommy; he was getting cold—
and when he came out they drove directly home.

So the night the furnaces blew up, Tommy knew all
about them. It happened at the very end of January, only a
few weeks after he'd gone to the furnace room and pulled the
lever and made things move and the furnace flame. He was
proud of that. After supper Tommy went back to his room.
He put out the light and returned to the window. The curtains
were still tied back. For a long time he stared into the billowing smoke and the flames, subsiding now, as if to impress them
forever on his memory. His mother found him standing there
at the window when she came to put him to bed. It was a
school night, she said, unfastening the curtains and drawing
the shade, and already past his bedtime.

Tommy went to bed, but he did not fall asleep. He was
listening for his father to come home, which he finally did,
but not until after the telephone had rung many times.
Margie called, wanting to know what had happened, and
David went off to see her. Many of his parents' friends called:
Mr. Sedgwick and Mr. Hutchins and Mr. Wolfe. They all
wanted to know what had happened, but his mother didn't
know any more than they did. She talked to Mr. Wolfe a
long time from the telephone in her bedroom, and then
Tommy heard her say that she had to get off the phone. "Mac
may be trying to call and he'll wonder who on earth I've been
talking to all this time." She said she'd try to see him tomorrow,
but if she couldn't tomorrow, then soon.

Finally his father did call. He talked to his mother for only
a few minutes. Tommy called her and she came into his room.
"What happened?" he asked her.

"Well," she said, then stopped. Tommy could tell she was
very upset. "Well," she began again, "there was a violent
surge in the Number One furnace and it blew up. Oh,
Tommy," she said, and tears ran down her cheeks, "it was
terrible. Three men were killed." She almost whispered it.

"Killed? You mean three men are dead?" Tommy thought

of the liquid fire he saw the afternoon he went to the furnace room. He knew it was a dangerous place, but he hadn't realized how truly dangerous it was.

"I shouldn't have told you," his mother said, "but I just couldn't help it. Oh, poor Daddy! It's awful for him. And the poor men. . . ."

"Was one of them Mr. Anderson?" Tommy asked.

"Your father didn't mention him," his mother said.

"Was one of them the man Daddy talked to that day I went to the plant with him, the new furnaceman who wasn't doing it right?"

"I don't know," his mother said. "I don't know who they were. Daddy's gone now to see their families. He'll be home very late. I'm going to fix you some warm milk. It'll help you sleep. I'll wait up for Daddy."

His mother left the room and returned a few minutes later with a glass of warm milk. Ordinarily Tommy hated warm milk, but he didn't mind it so much tonight. His mother tucked him in and kissed him good night, and told him she would be nearby if he needed her. She was going to be in her bedroom. When she left, Tommy heard her close her bedroom door. Then he heard her giving the operator a telephone number, but Tommy couldn't hear the number so he didn't know who she called, but she was still talking when Tommy fell asleep, lulled by the soft blurred murmurings of her voice.

Tommy was asleep when his father at last came home, but he woke up when he heard them talking. His father's voice was loud. He was very angry and upset. "God damn it," he said, "God damn it! That transformer was supposed to be fixed. God damn it!" His father was yelling. "And that new furnaceman didn't know what he was doing! He didn't know the power. He didn't know what he was fooling with!"

Oh, no, Tommy thought. Oh, no. Tears came to his eyes. He liked the new furnaceman. He liked the way he looked. He seemed like such a nice man. He just wanted to do it right but he didn't know how.

"He must have hit an electrode," his father said. "Nothing could stand up to the current in that arc. Christ, his rod just melted away, just melted away . . . and he's dead. He and

Jim and Johnny." Everything was silent for a moment. "I'm ruined."

Tommy could hear his mother's quiet murmuring. "For Christ's sake," his father shouted. "I don't mean that *I'm* ruined. *They're* ruined. Ruined! Three men dead. I should have known. I should have seen it coming. I knew that transformer wasn't right. I knew that furnaceman didn't understand the power. He didn't know how to handle it. And I'm left with the wreckage."

His mother murmured again. "No," his father said. "Not the plant. That's easily fixed. Of their *families*! They had families—don't you understand?" Tommy heard his father walk out of their bedroom, and he heard his mother call, "Don't fix yourself another drink. Please, don't fix another drink." She was pleading. "You don't need it. You'll be better without it." But Tommy heard his father come back upstairs a few minutes later and he could hear ice clinking in his glass. "I know when I need a drink or not," he said to Tommy's mother, very coldly. "You let me decide that. You decide what to bid at the country club. You decide the favors for Luke Wolfe's parties, that—"

"Hush," his mother interrupted, "you'll wake Tommy." She sounded awfully sad, but angry too, and Tommy heard her shut their bedroom door. He couldn't hear words anymore, just the sound of voices, and eventually he fell asleep. He didn't mind that his mother had unfastened the curtains and pulled the shade. He didn't need to look at the fire in the sky; he remembered it well enough.

That night he dreamed his terrible dream again, but he didn't call out when it pulled him reluctantly, groggily from his sleep. When he woke up and went to school the next morning, the whole town was covered with a fine gray dust, but the fires were out.

TOMMY's father was right. The plant was easily fixed. The two furnaces that had been shut down when Number One blew up were gradually started up. It was a slow, careful process, but they were working in just a few days, and the familiar glow was back in the sky a week after his parents had

218

gone to the funeral of the three men. There was just one funeral for the three of them. They were all Catholics, and it was held in the Catholic church one morning when Tommy was in school. They prayed for them and their families the next Sunday in his church, too. The Number One furnace took longer to fix, but not so long as Tommy would have thought. It was back in operation in a little over a month, and the glow in the sky was bright as ever.

After the two furnaces were working, Tommy's father went away. He had to talk to some engineers in New York to try to figure out exactly what had happened so that it would never happen again. He was also going to arrange for some help for the families of the men who were killed. You couldn't leave them with nothing, his father said. He wouldn't have that. It seemed as if his father were gone a long time, and except for a few days when Tommy had the croup again, he went to school every day, and played Monopoly with Jimmy Randolph and Amy Steer, and played with Jimmy's lead soldiers, and he could hardly wait for spring, when Jimmy might let him try his new bicycle.

Tommy wasn't much interested in school. His mind wasn't on his work. It never was. For the most part, school was easy and it was also boring. They went over the same things again and again: how to print letters, how to add, how to read. Tommy was already trying to teach himself to write script, like his mother but with a pencil, and he was smart enough to figure out how to add. It was easy, once you got the idea. Often his teacher just let him read by himself, and that was all right. He was getting better at it all the time, and the books he loved were a lot more exciting than school. He would have read all day, if Miss Case had let him, but sometimes she made him pay attention, especially during the arithmetic lesson. Tommy wanted to learn about geography, but that wasn't supposed to happen until fourth grade, when they would go upstairs. Sometimes she got angry with him if he asked too many questions or if he was talking too much while she was trying to teach. She said he was disturbing the class with his chatter, and to some of his questions she said she didn't have answers. "Nobody has *all* the answers," she said. "God does,"

Tommy replied. "Yes," she said, "but nobody else." Still, Miss Case had a lot more answers than he did. She even had a boyfriend; his brother John had seen them at the movies one night before Christmas. Miss Case never pulled his chin, though, the way she did Carl Smith's, who she said was saucy when he talked back to her. Tommy liked Miss Case and he thought she liked him, too, even if he did talk too much and ask too many questions. He couldn't help asking questions, any more than he could keep his nose out of a book—that's what his mother said: "Tommy's always got his nose in a book"—once he'd learned what interesting things happened in them. The day he came home from the library, the library his grandfather had even built, with a book called *Appointment with Death,* his mother called Miss Pratt, the librarian, and told her, right in front of Tommy, not to let him take out books like that. "He's a high-strung child," she told her, "and he's got too much imagination as it is. If he starts reading books like this, his father says none of us will be safe." She laughed when she said that; she didn't want Miss Pratt to feel bad, so she made a joke, but she made Tommy mad and he bet his father had never even said it; he wasn't even home. His mother didn't trust Tommy to return the book; she did it herself. But Tommy had already looked at it and decided it wasn't as interesting as its title. Probably it was too hard for him, he thought, but sometimes he liked things that were hard, and he did like mysteries, even if, as his mother said, they caused his imagination to race too feverishly. It was his imagination, and he liked it. Yes, the interesting things in his life went on in books, Tommy thought, or at home, among the swimmers in his inland sea. They hardly ever happened at school.

His mother was thinking about redecorating the house, but so far all she was doing was thinking about it. Her heart wasn't in it, she said, but she had to get her heart in it soon. The work had to be done before their anniversary party at the end of summer. That seemed a long way off. It wasn't even spring yet. Every once in a while his mother would leaf through the wallpaper books that Mr. St. John had left her, and sometimes she would ask Tommy if he liked this one or that one. She wondered what he'd like for his room, but

Tommy didn't know; he said he liked his old wallpaper, he liked his room just the way it was. Then she'd close the big book and say she'd think about it another time. When Mr. Wolfe came by, as he sometimes did, she'd ask him what he liked, too, and Mr. Wolfe would look at the books with her but neither of them seemed very much interested. His mother said that Mr. Wolfe was helping her with the wallpaper just as she'd helped him with his party favors.

One day when Tommy came home from school, Mr. Wolfe and his mother were sitting at the dining-room table. Lately Mr. Wolfe was there a lot. He had eaten a piece of cake— Tommy could see the crumbs on his plate—and he and his mother were drinking coffee. His cigarette lay in the ashtray, and the smoke drifted slowly in the currents of air and rose toward the animals on the plate rail. *"Smoke gets in your eyes,"* Tommy sang. It was one of his brothers' songs. Mr. Wolfe looked at Tommy. "Smoke will get in their eyes," Tommy said.

"Smoke will get in their eyes?" Mr. Wolfe said it as a question.

"The animals on the plates," Tommy said. "They won't be able to see."

"Oh, Tommy," his mother said, "you have the strangest imagination for a little boy." She laughed. "We were just looking at wallpaper," she said. "Mr. Wolfe was trying to help me." She got up and went into the living room. The books of wallpaper were lying on the floor in front of the comfortable couch. His mother picked up the top one, opened it, and asked, "How would you like this for your room?" She sat on the couch beside Tommy, spreading the book across her lap, and Mr. Wolfe sat down on the brown silk chair that Tommy liked to read in when the weather was warm because the chair was so cool. He thought of it as his chair.

Tommy looked at the wallpaper. It was green like the sea— he liked that—with wavy brown lines in it. "I don't like it," he said. "I don't like the brown lines."

"Tommy," his mother said, "some days you don't like anything." That was true; some days he didn't. "But maybe you'd like a piece of cake," and she went to the kitchen to get him one. Rose hadn't shown up today, she said. When she returned with the cake and a glass of milk, which she put on his own table in the corner of the dining room, Mr. Wolfe said he'd have to be going. His mother walked him to the door. "'Mac will be home next week," she said.

"We'll all have to get together," Mr. Wolfe said. "Maybe I should have a dinner to welcome him back. Emma, call me," he said, and Tommy's mother closed the door and returned to the dining room to sit with him while he ate his cake and drank his milk.

Tommy wondered why his mother liked that paper for his bedroom; it was ugly. He wanted his room painted. Mrs. Steer's house was painted and he liked it, but he knew that his mother didn't like painted walls. She thought paper was nicer, and easier, too. Mr. St. John could put it on right over the old paper. Mrs. Steer said there was a right way to do things, and a wrong way. The wrong way was to paint over wallpaper. When she had painted her house, she had stripped all the wallpaper off, and she'd replastered some of the walls, too. Mr. St. John did the plastering—Mrs. Steer couldn't do everything, she said—but she did the stripping and the painting, and then it looked like new. Tommy told his mother that Mrs. Steer said it was always better to take the old wallpaper off. "Oh, you'll never know the old paper was there," his mother said. Tommy would, though. He knew that he could look at whatever new paper his mother put on the walls and see the old patterns underneath it, at least in his mind's eye, and he knew that the animals on the plate rail could, too.

David went to Chicago later that week. He had to see if Northwestern would let him back in the fall, and he was going to stay with John in their fraternity house. Tommy envied him. He wished he were going. His mother picked him up from school at noon—it was a Thursday—and together they drove David to the station. She had brought sandwiches, and they sat in the car and ate their lunch while they waited for the train. Tommy remembered his own train ride to Chicago, how the porter had shined his shoes, and how much fun he had had in John's fraternity house that had the picture of the naked lady over the bar in the basement. Tommy hated to see

David leave. His house would seem empty without him. Even though David spent most of his time at Margie's, at least he came home to sleep. Tommy and his mother would be all alone. That would be nice, too. Tommy liked being alone with his mother, but still it made Tommy sad when the train arrived and David got on it. David waved at them from the window as the train pulled out, and Tommy kept on waving until the train went around the bend and out of sight. He hated goodbyes.

He still felt sad when his mother dropped him off at school. To cheer him up, she told him that if he were very good for the next two days she might let him spend Saturday night at Jimmy Randolph's. She had never let him do that before. That would be exciting—all the Cokes he wanted and Jimmy's lead soldiers to make. Tommy resolved to be very good and try to be helpful by saying nice things about the wallpaper. He could get interested in the wallpaper, if he wanted to, and he did care what went on his bedroom walls, since something was sure to go on them. After school he told Jimmy that he might be able to stay with him Saturday night, and the next morning he got up when his mother called him instead of staying in his warm bed until she had to call him twice or even three times and finally be cross because his breakfast was getting cold and he would be late for school. He was downstairs before his mother had even finished making his cereal, and when she spooned it into his bowl—the bowl from the broken set his father had had when he was a little boy; it wasn't broken then, though—he ate all of it, though he didn't want to. He was never very hungry in the morning. His mother got him into his snowsuit—it was early March and still winter, she insisted—and he covered her cheek with kisses and gave her a feathery butterfly kiss with his eyelashes on her forehead—that was how butterflies kissed, with their eyelashes, and so softly you hardly felt it but you could tell—and he left by the kitchen door. Before he'd gotten down the steps he turned around and came back for another kiss and a hug. "There are never enough kisses," Tommy's father used to say, "but there are usually enough to go around." Tommy pondered that: not enough, but enough.

He walked to school through the alley—he sometimes did —and his mother waved from the window of the maid's room. Tommy walked backwards, waving and blowing his mother kisses, until finally he passed out of sight of the house and had to run to school or else he'd be late. He would have liked nothing better than to stay home from school that day to be close to her, to watch over her. He loved his mother so much. He loved his mother more than anything, and he longed to be with her now. She would read to him, and make him happy. Maybe he should have said he was sick. Maybe he should go back now, though he was already approaching the schoolyard and the bell was ringing. He could still say that he was sick, that it had come on very suddenly. But no, his mother would never believe him. Maybe he wouldn't go to Jimmy Randolph's Saturday night after all. He would stay home to be with his mother, and she would make popcorn and then they would sit on the couch and she would read to him and they would talk just like old times. Tommy was never happier than when his mother read to him. He would feel warm and snug and safe. And so would his mother. He was the man of the house now. That's what David had said when he got on the train: "Take good care of things, Tommy, and watch over our mother. You're the man of the house now."

After school he stopped first at Jimmy's and told him he couldn't stay Saturday night after all. He had to stay home to take care of his mother.

"Oh, you're going to New Orleans, are you?" Dr. Randolph said to him.

"New Orleans? No," Tommy replied, "I have to stay with my mother. David's gone to Chicago and she's all alone."

"That's what I meant," said Dr. Randolph.

"P.T.," Mrs. Randolph called from the kitchen. "P.T.!"

Jimmy said if Tommy wanted to be a mamma's boy, that was all right with him, but Tommy didn't care what Jimmy said. Right then he wanted nothing more than to be his mother's boy, and he ran across the street to his big old house, eager to see her.

Rose met him in the hall. She gave him a kiss, and said she

had some cookies for him and a glass of milk. "Where's my mother?" he asked.

"She called to say that she'd be late. She was at the country club and she's going out to dinner from there."

"I'm going to call her," said Tommy, and he went to the phone and told the operator "Seven-four-oh." Ophelia said his mother wasn't there.

"She's not?"

"No, sir," Ophelia said. "I don't see her."

"Well, if you do see her, would you ask her to come home. Tell her I'm sick."

"What's the matter, Tommy?" Ophelia asked him.

"I don't know," he said. "I have a headache."

"Would you like a chicken sandwich, honey? I'll fix it the way you like it." Ophelia had such a nice voice. "Mrs. Steer is here. I'll send it home with her. Would that make you feel better?"

"Yes," Tommy said. He thought that would make him feel better.

"I'll do it right now," Ophelia said. "I think a good chicken sandwich will make you feel a lot better."

"Thank you," he said. "Goodbye," and he hung up and took the milk and cookies to his room. After a while Mrs. Steer arrived with the chicken sandwich but she couldn't stay, and later he ate it for dinner, even though he was supposed to have a hot meal with vegetables. Rose didn't mind, though; she ate his dinner and hers too. Later she put him to bed. Tommy woke up when his mother came into his room to see that he was tucked in and to kiss him good night. She almost always came into his room when she got home, no matter how late, to see that he was covered and to give him a kiss.

The next day Tommy told her that he wasn't going to Jimmy Randolph's that night after all, that he was going to stay home and take care of her.

"Oh, Tommy," his mother said. "Oh, how sad. I've got plans for tonight. The Rodgers are giving a dinner at the club. Didn't I tell you?"

"No," Tommy said. "I don't remember it. I don't think you told me. Is Mrs. Steer going?"

"Well I don't know," his mother said. "I doubt it. The Steers aren't so friendly with the Rodgers these days. I suppose they got into an argument."

"Mr. Steer is always getting into arguments," Tommy said. "But why are you going out? Do you have to?"

"Tommy, I'm sorry," his mother said. "Don't be disappointed. Yes, I have to go. I said I would. They're expecting me. They'll have a place for me at the table, and you just can't change your mind about something like that at the last minute. It would ruin their seating, and they'd be annoyed. So would I, if it happened to me."

"But you could be sick," Tommy said.

"Well, yes, of course, if you're really sick you just couldn't go. But I'm not sick. It wouldn't be honest to say I was. Don't be disappointed," she said again, hugging him. "I'll be home all day tomorrow, and tomorrow I won't be going out at all. We can have one of our nice times then."

Sunday seemed like such a long time away. But at least his mother stayed in the house until she had to go out in the evening, and she read to him for a little while in the afternoon and she played the piano, and they had a good time. They played three games of rummy and Tommy won one. She seemed happy, and after Tommy had had his dinner and she had sat with him at his table to make sure that he ate his meat and all his vegetables, she went upstairs to get ready. "I must draw my bath," she said, laughing. "I must draw my bath like a lady." And she went off up the stairs while Tommy helped Rose clean up. His mother had asked her to spend the night because she expected to be quite late and she didn't want to have to drive Rose home at the end of the evening. She didn't like to go into that part of town by herself, and besides, the roads were terrible.

Tommy went into her bedroom while she was finishing dressing. The curtains that Mrs. Matson had made for her a couple of years ago were closed, falling in soft silken folds to the floor, shining with the rosy light from the lamps on his mother's dressing table. The whole room cast a soft pink glow, and in the center of it stood his mother in her slip, her arms raised, pulling her dress over her head, taking care not to disturb her hair. Tommy could not see her face; it was still

226

hidden in her dress. "Will you and Daddy ever go to New Orleans?" Tommy asked.

"We've been there, my funny darling," his mother said, smoothing the dress down over her slip. "Why?"

"I just wondered."

"Well of course we might go again. Would you help me with this zipper? I can't reach it." Her dress zipped up the back. It was a new dress, a deeper shade of pink than the curtains, and she thought it was very stylish. "But it certainly is hard to get into," she said.

Tommy moved away from her dressing table to the big rocker in the corner, the one his mother used to rock him in when he was a baby and sometimes still did. He watched her intent face mirrored between the lamps in the glass while she put on her lipstick in that funny way she did, powdered her nose, and curled her eyelashes with a little implement from her drawer. She almost never curled her eyelashes. She touched a comb to her hair. Tommy thought of Mrs. Simpkin. His mother was much prettier than Mrs. Simpkin. If she were an invalid, Tommy would help her, too. She was examining now the jewelry spread out before her on the dressing table. She picked up the jeweled arrow from the mirrored tray and turned to Tommy. "Do you think it looks better here?"—she held it to the left side of her dress—"or here?"—she moved it across her breast—"or in the middle?"

Tommy came to where she was sitting and stood behind her shoulder, watching in the mirror as she moved the arrow to its various positions. His mother's face was reflected all around him, shining from the big center glass, from the two angled mirrors of her dressing table, in the tray next to her hand. "If I wear it in the middle, should I point the arrow up or down?"

"Point it sideways," Tommy said, but his mother didn't think it looked best that way.

"We'll compromise," she said. "I'll put it here"—she held it to the V of her dress—"and wear it at an angle." She fastened the brooch, but still she wasn't sure that she liked it. "No, I don't like it. It ought to point down," so she unfastened it and fixed it the way she wanted. Then she stood up, dabbed herself with perfume, and said, "There. I'm ready—a little early, even." She turned out the lamps in her room and together they went downstairs. Because she was a little early, she had time to sit on the couch with Tommy and read him part of *Fingerfins*, but she didn't have time to finish it—Tommy knew the story anyway—before the doorbell rang. Mr. Wolfe was picking her up so she wouldn't have to drive alone.

"That's nice of him," Tommy said.

Mr. Wolfe had brought him a book. "I've a present for you, Tommy," he said. "It's about a little boy who lives south of the border in Mexico. I've seen a lot of those little boys. I hope you like it."

"Thanks," said Tommy. He realized he should have said, "Thanks, Mr. Wolfe"—you were always supposed to call people by their names—but it was too late. He opened the book. "It looks interesting."

"Well," said Mr. Wolfe, "you give me a report on it. Tell me the new words you learn. You'll learn some."

Mr. Wolfe helped Tommy's mother into her coat. She bent to kiss Tommy good night. "Go to bed when Rose tells you," she said. When they had gone, Tommy took the book to the brown silk chair in the living room. He looked at it for a while. The book had a lot of pictures and some Spanish words. The boy was very poor. He was called a "muchacho" in Spanish, and he wore a hat that was almost bigger than he was. It was called a "sombrero." There was a picture of him squatting in the dust, wearing his sombrero. The book did look interesting—the family was so poor that the boy, whose name was Pedro, had to help his father in the fields outside of town—but Tommy didn't feel like reading it then. He got up, locked the front door—they almost never locked it, although the windows were always locked, but he did tonight; it made him feel safer, enclosed in his tight house—and he went to his room, where he slipped the book into his bookshelf. That was the second present Mr. Wolfe had given him. The coin still rested on his windowsill, the last coin of the old year, and the new year was already two months old. After a while Rose came up to put him to bed. She always let him stay up later than his mother did, and she let him have his curtains open and his blinds up, too, if he wanted.

Tommy lay there for a long time, looking at the dull orange glow in the northern sky, thinking his own thoughts. He could see lights at the Randolphs'. Maybe he should have stayed at Jimmy Randolph's after all; he would have had company and it would have been a lot of fun, drinking Cokes and playing. He wondered if Jimmy was in bed yet. Probably not. He was sure Amy Steer was, though. He wondered why the Steers weren't going to Dr. Rodgers' party; they'd been friends at New Year's. He wondered what Mrs. Slade was doing. He got out of bed and looked out his east window, the window that faced the Slades'. There were lights in Mrs. Slade's bedroom, too, but she hardly ever went to bed at night; she slept a lot during the day. He hadn't seen Mrs. Slade in a long time. She hadn't been well again. It must have been two years ago that she'd gone to the Mayo Clinic and had her operation. And then she burned herself when he was in first grade. David was at college that year. He'd seen her a lot then, and after she'd gotten back from her trip with the Randolphs, too. He'd seen her when his grandmother died, but he didn't like to go over there if Mrs. Slade didn't want to play with him, and sometimes she didn't. All Lily and Jenny wanted to do was get him to pull down his pants, and they never pulled theirs down—or only once, Lily, the younger, did. Jenny had hair and wouldn't do it. At least, Jimmy said she had hair, but he didn't believe Jimmy'd ever seen it either. When he was a little boy, his parents sometimes brought him into bed with them on weekend mornings, and Tommy would snuggle down in the hollow between them for a while. That was nice. It was warm and cozy, and they had a big comfortable bed. But they never wanted to do anything. They wanted to sleep, and Tommy would get bored after a while, and then he'd start to get restless, and his mother would tell him to settle down and close his eyes and pretend he was falling asleep, which he would for a minute but not for long. It was hard to pretend he was falling asleep when he was wide awake. And then his father would roll over toward him, and he'd feel squashed between them, and he'd have to push their bodies away. It took all his strength. He'd use both his hands, and brace his feet against his mother, and push his father with all his might. And then his mother would wake up and tell him to pretend he was sleeping again, and she would doze off. That really was a long time ago. He didn't think he'd done it since he'd found out his mother wasn't twenty-two years old. That was a joke. Imagine his ever thinking that his mother was twenty-two. She certainly didn't look twenty-two to him now. That was John's age. No, his mother looked old. Well, she didn't look so old as some of the other mothers Tommy had seen, even though she was older than most of them. She didn't look as old as Mrs. Randolph, and Mrs. Randolph must have been pretty old, too. She didn't even look as old as Mrs. Steer, though Mrs. Steer was younger. His mother was smaller, though, and prettier than Mrs. Steer. How old was his mother? He couldn't remember exactly. Forty something. Forty-five? Something like that. It didn't matter. She was his mother no matter how old she was. And he would always be her little boy, that's what she'd told him, only she'd said "baby" and Tommy hadn't liked it. He wasn't a baby. He was a boy, a fine young man his grandmother had said a long time ago when he really was practically a baby. That was nice of her. His grandmother was nice, and he thought of her now, all alone in the frozen earth except for the other people all alone too, and he missed her. He missed her a lot sometimes, even though she was strange before she died and called him by his father's name and got him all mixed up with his brothers and his father and people whose names Tommy didn't recognize. That's what happened when you got really old, you got everything all mixed up. Tommy didn't want to get that old, just older. He was cold. He jumped back into bed, but his bed was cold, too, and he thought maybe he could fall asleep in his mother's bed. Maybe he would get into that big warm comfortable bed, where he'd hidden under the blankets while his parents slept, or tried to, and pretended he was making tents. But it used to be so hot and stuffy and dark, and finally he would have disturbed them so much that either they'd send him back to his room to play, which was what he wanted anyway, or they'd get up. It wouldn't be hot and stuffy and dark now, though; there was no one there. It would be cozy and warm and comfortable; and he got out of his cold bed and went into his mother's room in the dark. He opened all the curtains and raised the shades so there would be a little light, and then he opened one of the windows facing the porch roof and opened the storm window, too, so there would be air. The storm window worked on a hinge, and you could push it out from the bottom. He felt the draft of cold air, and he jumped quickly into his mother's big bed under the downy comforter and between the cool sheets, which soon warmed up, and in a short time he grew very sleepy watching the shadows pass slowly across his mother's mirrors, the gray reflections of the night.

He knew it was very late when his eyes popped open. It had to be very late. He heard a strange noise. It was on the porch roof. A thump, and then another thump. He called out, "Mommy! Mommy!" but then he remembered that his mother wasn't there. She was out, and he was still in her bed. Oh, why wasn't he in his own bed? He heard the thump again. He became very frightened, and he lay very still, listening, watching. Thump. He heard crunching noises—they had to be on the porch roof, they were so close—and suddenly a shadow, a figure across the window of his mother's bedroom! Shadows flickered across the mirror. Tommy froze in terror. This was no dream. Was it? No. This was no dream at all. This was an actual man, and his hand was reaching under the storm window to pull it farther open. It could open very wide, wide enough for someone to slip through and to raise the window behind it. He heard the noise the window made. They were going to be robbed. There might be a murder; he might be killed. *Appointment with Death.* His eyes were frozen wide. Tommy tried to move. He couldn't. Suddenly, gathering all his force of body and will, he hurled himself fiercely from the bed and raced to the opening window, to slam it shut on the man's hand, to break the man's hand and make him howl with pain, and he grabbed the window and tangled with the curtains at the same time and pulled them from the wall, rod and all, and they fell over his head, enveloping him, blinding him, before he could force the window shut. He thrashed furiously against the curtains, striking out with the terrible strength within him. He heard a voice. "Tommy?" It was practically a whisper. "Tommy?" And then the voice spoke in another direction and said, "Tommy's awake."

"Oh, no." It was his mother's voice.

"Tommy," the voice whispered, "it's all right. It's Luke Wolfe." Tommy was pulling the curtains away from him. He had lost his breath and couldn't say a word. "It's Luke Wolfe and everything's all right. You locked your mother out, that's all."

Tommy could feel his heart racing in his chest. His breath was coming in short gasps. He tried to catch it. "I broke the curtains," he said. "I tore them right off the wall." He stepped out of them and stood amidst the rose-colored silk, gray in the dark, as it lay in a crumpled heap on the floor at his feet. "Where's Mother?" He was shaking, trying to keep his teeth from chattering.

"She's standing on the porch, waiting to be let in. We got the ladder from the garage and had to climb up to the roof to find an open window." They never did lock the garage. "She didn't have her key. She didn't expect to find the door locked."

"I locked it," Tommy said. "I forgot." He was still shaking. Mr. Wolfe was still standing outside the window. "May I come in now?" he asked.

"Why didn't you ring the doorbell?"

"We didn't want to wake you. I guess we did, though. I'm sorry if I scared you. Will you let me in? It's cold out here." For the first time Tommy felt the cold air blasting into the room. He stood aside, and Mr. Wolfe hunched over and came in the window, stepping across the sill and onto the curtains. He squeezed Tommy's shoulder and said again that everything was all right, and tiptoed downstairs to open the front door. Tommy guessed they hadn't wanted to waken Rose, either.

Tommy got into his bathrobe and came halfway down to the bend in the big stairway. He could see everything from there. His mother threw her coat on a chair in the hall and rushed toward him. "Oh, darling," she said. "I'm so sorry you were frightened." She repeated it. "I'm so sorry you were frightened. I love you so much. I wouldn't frighten you for the world." She hugged him close to her. Tommy could smell the faint warm traces of her perfume. "What time is it?" he asked. "I don't know," his mother said. "It must be quite late." She hugged him again. "Give us a kiss," she said.

"Where's your arrow? Did you lose it?"

"I took it off," his mother said. "The clasp broke. It's in my purse." She asked Mr. Wolfe if he would go into the kitchen and warm some milk on the stove. "Don't wake Rose," she whispered.

"Nothing could," Mr. Wolf whispered back, laughing.

His mother held Tommy close as she walked him back up the stairs and into his own small room.

Mr. Wolfe brought the glass of warm milk to his bedroom. He told Tommy again that he was sorry he scared him. He seemed really sorry. "I wasn't scared," Tommy said. And Mr. Wolfe told his mother that he'd come back tomorrow and fix the curtain rod. His mother said, "Lucien, would you let yourself out?"

"Yes, of course," he said. "Goodbye, and thank you. Good night, Tommy. Better dreams now."

"It was a lovely evening," his mother said, "and thank you for seeing me home. I'm sorry it was so much trouble." They heard Mr. Wolfe shut the door behind him, and his car start and drive away. Tommy sat in his bed, propped up on his pillows, and drank his warm milk. He stopped shivering after a time, and he told his mother to go down and lock the door.

"There's no need to lock the door, Tommy," she said, "we're all in the house now." But Tommy insisted. "I wish Daddy were home," he said. His mother did lock the door, and then she came back to his room and sat beside him, humming her lullabies, until finally he fell asleep again.

The next morning the curtains still lay crumpled on the floor where they had fallen, rod and all. Tommy could see Mr. Wolfe's footprint on them.

They were all up early. His mother had to drive Rose home after breakfast. "I'll be back soon," she said. "It won't take me long, and then we'll have our day together."

"I'm going over to the Steers'," Tommy said. "Jimmy and Amy and I are going to play. Didn't I tell you?"

"No," his mother said. "You didn't tell me. It's too early to go over to the Steers'. I'm not at all sure that you should."

"Oh," Tommy said, "I thought I told you. Well, if it's too early, Mrs. Steer will tell me and I'll come back home."

In the morning light, Tommy thought it was funny that

he'd locked his mother out of the house. She wasn't even mad at him—she didn't tell him that he *couldn't* go to the Steers'—and the happenings in the middle of the night, now that the sun was shining, that the day was here, struck him as quite funny—their having to get the ladder and climb onto the roof and open the window—and even exciting, like a mystery story; not like *Appointment with Death*; more like one of Jenny Slade's Nancy Drews. He could hardly wait to tell Mrs. Steer about it. He'd make a funny story out of it, and she would laugh.

She did, too, but Tommy guessed she didn't think it was as funny as he did. Amy did, though, and so did Jimmy, who was already there. "I would have pushed the ladder right off the roof," Jimmy said. "I would have jumped out the window and pushed it off the roof with him on it." Well, Jimmy was two years older, and stronger, and he didn't really know Mr. Wolfe, either. Mrs. Steer, who was listening to them, said that would have been an even worse disaster. "All your mother would have needed would be Lucien Wolfe spread-eagled on the ground in the middle of the night with a broken leg—or worse. The whole neighborhood would have been aroused. No"—she chuckled—"I think that would have been the wrong thing to do, Jimmy. Definitely the wrong thing to do."

"Well, my father could have fixed it," Jimmy said.

"If you'd been at the party, Mrs. Steer, you could have taken my mother home," Tommy said. "Then everything would have been all right."

"I'm afraid Dr. Rodgers thinks I'm stuffy," said Mrs. Steer, "and your mother still would have been locked out." Tommy knew that Mrs. Steer could have handled the ladder as well as Mr. Wolfe. She'd carried ladders all around her house when she was painting. "Of course, she could have spent the night here and wakened you in the morning with a phone call. Well, that's enough of that," she said, picking up her book. "You children run along now. Find something to do. I'm going to read."

"What are you reading?" Tommy asked her.

"I'm reading a book called *Anticipating the Eventual Emergence of Form*," she said.

"What a funny title," Tommy said.

"Yes, I suppose it is. But it's what we all hope will happen someday, someday before we die. Run along now, all of you," and Mrs. Steer opened her book and began to read, the ash of the cigarette in her hand growing longer and longer. She wouldn't talk anymore. She didn't even look up, and the three of them went outside to play for a while until Amy decided she wanted to go home and Tommy and Jimmy went over to Jimmy's house.

Dr. Randolph had just gotten back from making his house calls. Even on Sunday he made house calls. They were about to have lunch, and Mrs. Randolph asked if he'd like to stay. "I'll have to call my mother," Tommy said, "but yes, I'd like to." His mother said it would be all right, and the four of them had hamburgers and French-fries. Mrs. Randolph liked to make French-fries. She was the only person Tommy knew who did. They were a lot of trouble to make because you had to cook them in deep fat, and the fat had to be very hot, hot enough to cook the potatoes but not hot enough to catch on fire.

Jimmy told his mother that Tommy should have spent the night. "He got in trouble," Jimmy said.

"No," Tommy said, "I didn't get in trouble. *You* would have gotten in trouble, though. You would have pushed him off the roof and he might have died. People die when they fall off roofs, you know." That's what happened sometimes in the Depression. People jumped off roofs. Timmy Stephenson's father had even shot himself. That was a long time ago, before Tommy had started school, but all the children knew about it because Timmy and his mother moved away right afterwards. Tommy didn't know where they'd gone. It wasn't something the grown-ups liked to talk about in front of the children.

"You did too get in trouble," Jimmy said. "You locked your mother out of the house, and I'll bet she was real mad." Tommy didn't like this. His mother wasn't mad, but Tommy was getting mad at Jimmy.

"What are you two talking about?" Mrs. Randolph asked.

Jimmy told her what had happened, only he tried to make

himself the hero, telling them what he would have done and never saying what Tommy had done, except that he'd gotten scared and pulled the curtains off the wall, which wasn't the way it really happened at all. "Dad would have fixed his leg," Jimmy said.

"Shot him, that's what I would have done. Just like a horse," Dr. Randolph said, pouring ketchup on his hamburger.

"P.T.," Mrs. Randolph said, "would you stop talking like that? You're so funny that some days I can't stand it. If anybody ought to be shot, it's you." She wasn't laughing, and Tommy didn't think she thought Dr. Randolph was being very funny. Tommy couldn't eat much of his hamburger. He wasn't very hungry.

"You're eating like a bird, Tommy," Mrs. Randolph said. "Try to eat some more of your hamburger. If it's too much for you, I'll take it off the bun and you can just eat the meat." She didn't wait for his reply but reached over and took the hamburger out of the bun. Tommy ate a little more, but he couldn't finish it. He thought he ought to go home. This was the day he was supposed to spend with his mother.

"Take care of yourself, my little friend," Mrs. Randolph told him as he was leaving. "Take care, tender heart."

When Tommy got home, Mr. Wolfe had already been there and left. He'd fixed the curtain rod and put the curtains back, and Tommy's mother was trying to take his footprint off the curtain. The room was filled with fumes from the cleaning fluid, and the windows were open wide. It was cold in the room. When she finished, you could hardly tell that the curtains had been stepped on. The fluid dried very rapidly, leaving only the faintest ring around the edges of the print. You had to look very closely to see it. "There," his mother said. "No one will ever notice."

"Only if you knew where to look," Tommy said.

"What was the matter with you Friday?" his mother asked.

"Matter? Nothing was the matter," Tommy said. "What do you mean?"

"Ophelia asked about you last night. She said you'd called the club after school and told her you were sick."

"Oh," Tommy said. "Oh, yes. I forgot. I guess I wasn't feeling good. Ophelia made me a chicken sandwich and Mrs. Steer brought it home. I think I had a headache, that's all. It wasn't anything."

"Then why did you call?"

"Because I wanted you to come home," Tommy said, "but you'd already gone."

That afternoon his mother played the piano for a long time, and Tommy played by himself in his room and at his desk. He was having a good time. He liked playing by himself, and he loved hearing his mother at the piano, the music floating up the stairway, filling the house. After she had played a very long time—she played all of *Kinderszenen* twice and a lot of other pieces Tommy didn't know, and it was beginning to get dark—the music stopped. There was silence downstairs. After a time, he heard his mother's footsteps on the stairway.

She stopped at his desk where he was playing. "Come into my room, Tommy, I want to rock you. Wouldn't that be nice? Just like we used to do, when you were very young, when you were the sweetest, most adorable boy." She took him by the hand. Together they walked into her room. She pulled the shades and the curtains, then sat down in the big rocker. "Wouldn't that be nice?" She opened her arms to him. Tommy snuggled into her lap. It was harder to fit now. His legs were getting longer. "We'll pretend there's a blackboard," his mother said, "we'll pretend the mirror is a blackboard"— Tommy looked at the mirror—"and we'll pretend there's an eraser, and we'll take that eraser and we'll erase every mean- ness, every mean thing, every sad thing, every bad thing, and they will all be gone forever." Tommy looked at the mirror. The room was dim. There were no lamps burning. The light from the hall was the only light, that and the last traces of the day fading at the edges of the curtains, where the curtains met the wall. "Like that," his mother said, holding him in her arms. "Just like that. So simple. See, Tommy, wasn't it simple?"

"Yes," Tommy said, entering into her game and settling deeper into her arms. "Yes, it was simple." His head rested on her shoulder, his face in the soft flesh of her neck. He smelled her warm smell, and he was aware of something else, too, in his nostrils. Oh, yes, it was the faint odor of the cleaning fluid she had used that day. His mother rocked slowly in the chair and Tommy succumbed to the motion, content in his mother's warmth. He thought of something Jimmy Randolph had told him: that babies come into the world covered with blood. That was a strange and ugly notion. Jimmy could have made it up. Still, his father was a doctor and sometimes Jimmy knew things that other children didn't. He'd seen pictures, he said, in the medical books they weren't allowed to look at, and the babies were covered with blood. Why would that be, Tommy wondered drowsily, and why had that thought come into his mind, but his mind, full of love, floated on to other things. "When I grow up," he said, "I'm going to marry you." His mother laughed and hugged him close. "No," she said, "you won't want to do that. You can't do that," she said softly. "Well," Tommy said, "if I can't marry you, I won't marry anyone."

"You'll change your mind," his mother told him. "You'll forget all this." No, Tommy thought, he wouldn't forget; he wouldn't change his mind. "Mr. Wolfe didn't," he said. His mother gave him an odd look. "Tommy," she said, "when you're a fine young man you'll find a girl—a nice girl—and you'll forget all about your mother. You'll fall in love, and you'll want to marry her, and you will. And then someday you'll have a little boy, a lovely little boy of your own, and you'll love him very much."

"Like Daddy," Tommy asked.

"Yes, like Daddy," she said, and began to sing her lullaby: *"Bye baby bunting, Daddy's gone a-hunting, Gone to get a rabbit skin to wrap my baby bunting in."* Tommy wondered if his father loved him that much. "And then you'll settle down in a house of your own and live happily ever after."

"Like you and Daddy?"

"Yes, like me and Daddy."

"But you and Daddy settled down in Grandma's house. It wasn't a house of your own."

"We tried to make it our own," she said. His mother gazed across the room, but there was nothing there. "Someday," she said, "you'll understand above love, and about what it means. You'll know it when it happens, and you won't be able to help it. You won't want to help it. Life is very lonely without it, and cold. She paused for a moment. "I can't really explain it. It's a mystery that I cannot explain."

Tommy heard the wind whistling around the corner of the house. "It's going to be a blustery night," his mother said. "You know what they say about March: it comes in like a lion and goes out like a lamb—and it's acting like a lion tonight." The curtains trembled and parted in the draft from the window. It was almost as if an invisible hand had reached in from outdoors, parting the curtains momentarily, disclosing a glimpse of a vista, before the hand released them and the curtains fell back into their accustomed folds. Tommy watched the curtains. They continued to move, to ripple with the barest perceptible motion, in the currents of air. His mind drifted to the book Mrs. Steer was reading. *Anticipating the Eventual Emergence of Form.* A strange name for a book.

"It'll be a good night for popcorn, don't you think?"

Tommy had hoped his mother would say that. "Yes," he said. "Will you make some and we can have popcorn and milk for supper? That would be fun. We could have a fire."

"We'll have popcorn by the fire," his mother said. She rocked him a little longer, in silence, before they both went downstairs to the kitchen, where Tommy helped his mother make the popcorn. She let him shake the kettle. "Oh, Tommy," she said, "I meant to tell you."

"What?"

"About that silly business last night. It sounds so silly that I would have forgotten my key and that the night I did, that you would have locked the door."

"But, but—"

"Everyone would think I was very foolish if they knew about that, and especially if they thought I had to use a ladder to break into my own house. Don't tell anyone. I'd be embarrassed."

"But Mother," Tommy said. He could feel the flush rising to his cheeks. "But Mother—"

"No 'buts,'" his mother said. "No 'buts,' just a promise."

"Okay," Tommy said. "Okay."

Tommy continued shaking the kettle while his mother went

into the living room to light the fire. By the time the popcorn was finished, and his mother had put it into the big bowl and melted the butter for it and salted it and shaken it up so that everything would be mixed, the fire was blazing in the fireplace. He and his mother sat beside it with their milk and their bowls of popcorn, and they had a nice time before Tommy had to go to bed.

"That was a nice evening, Tommy," his mother said, "a lovely, nice family day and evening, just as we'd planned."

"Yes," Tommy agreed, kissing her good night, "it was."

Tommy's father would be home soon. The damage to the Number One furnace had been repaired and the transformer rebuilt, but they couldn't start it, David said, until his father had inspected everything very closely and was standing by to supervise the slow, difficult process of heating it up. David had returned from Chicago the first of the week and told everyone that he would be going back to college in the fall, which was a great relief to Tommy's mother, and to his father too, when she told him over the telephone. David had brought him a present, a windbreaker jacket from Marshall Field's for his birthday. It was a really good one, as good as David's own. David might have been extravagant, but he could be really nice, too. Tommy's father couldn't get home for his birthday. He was supposed to be home, and he tried, but he'd called two days before to say that he wouldn't make it.

Tommy's birthday was just a small family party, an early supper. Mrs. Steer and Amy were there, and Mrs. Randolph and Jimmy; his brother David, and his mother, too, of course. She had made the angel-food cake and frosted it with lemon frosting and put nine candles on it, the ninth for him to grow on. Because he was so excited, his mother let him open his gifts at the table before they ate. They all sat at the big table in the dining room, Tommy at the head of it, unwrapping his gifts: the windbreaker from David and the beautiful box of crayons, Binney & Smith Crayolas, that his brother John had sent him in the mail from college. There were more colors in the box than Tommy knew existed. How did John know he'd wanted a big box of crayons, not one with only eight colors in it? Jimmy Randolph and his mother gave him an Erector Set like Jimmy's, which Tommy knew would be a lot of fun—he liked putting things together—and Mrs. Randolph gave him a separate card with a message that she'd printed on it: "I.O.U. 6 COKES," and there were six slips of paper in the card with "GOOD FOR 1 COKE, PAYABLE ON DEMAND" on each of them. Tommy was delighted with that. It would be like a game. He would give Mrs. Randolph the piece of paper and she would give him a Coke. Tommy laughed and showed everybody. Mrs. Randolph didn't know that he didn't drink Cokes at home, only Vernor's ginger ale and not very often at that. But his mother smiled at the card and didn't say anything. She was being very nice to Tommy and hardly ever got mad at him these days, no matter what he did. There was just one present from Mrs. Steer and Amy together. It was a small telescope that collapsed into itself but that extended quite a ways when you pulled it out. Tommy opened it and peered through it. He couldn't see anything. "It takes practice," Mrs. Steer said. "It's just a beginner's telescope, Tommy, but it works. You'll be able to see things through it that are hidden from the naked eye. You just have to have some idea of what you're looking for, and then it will bring that thing close so you can see it clearly. Point it out your bedroom window at the sky some night, point it at the Milky Way, and you'll be surprised at what you'll see."

David said, "That kid sees too much already," and everybody laughed. Tommy liked the telescope. He turned it over in his hands, looked at the small gleaming eyepiece and at the larger lens at the other end. It was an interesting gift and unusual, just what Mrs. Steer would pick. She knew he was interested in astronomy.

He saved his mother's gift for the last. It came in a long slender box, about the size of Mrs. Steer's. Tommy could tell that his mother had wrapped it herself, using the paper ribbons that you curled with the back of the scissors. He untied the ribbons and opened the box. It looked just like the telescope Mrs. Steer and Amy had given him, only the telescope was black and this was brightly colored, as if it had been sprinkled with confetti. Tommy picked it up. He didn't know what it was. "Look through it, Tommy," his mother said, "and point it toward the light. Close your other eye." Tommy did. He saw tiny brilliant bits of color, as many colors as there were in John's box of crayons. More. "Now turn it," she said, and as Tommy did the colors began to flow and form new patterns and new shapes, beautiful patterns and shapes in all the colors of the rainbow, and as he turned the cylinder the old pattern dissolved and a new one took its place in an endless succession of combinations. It was fascinating, and it was beautiful. It reminded Tommy of the amethyst at the bottom of his mother's jewelry drawer, and of the many colors he saw there when he put it to his eye. "It's called a kaleidoscope," she said.

"I love it," Tommy said. "Thank you, Mommy." How funny, he thought, that both Mrs. Steer and his mother had given him something to look through, and that his mother's was pretty and Mrs. Steer's was plain. Actually, though, he realized, you didn't look through the gift his mother had given him; you just looked into it and watched it do its magical things. He would have to learn to look through Mrs. Steer's. He passed the kaleidoscope around the table, and while everyone took turns playing with it he turned away from the table and pointed the lens of the telescope out the window toward the thornapple thicket and the Slades' house.

"Everything is still blurred," he said.

"You have to focus it," Mrs. Steer said, and she showed him how to turn it until things were clearer, and they did become clearer—not perfectly clear, but clearer than they had been.

"Isn't it funny that both of you gave me something interesting to look through," Tommy said.

"It's quite a coincidence," Mrs. Steer said.

"What's a coincidence?"

"It's when two things happen by chance at the same time," his mother said. "Let me see if I can think of an example." She thought for a moment. "Well," she said, "if David were thinking of Margie," and she laughed and looked at David, "and Margie suddenly showed up at the door, that would be a coincidence."

"I get it," Tommy said, and Rose began serving their supper. Tommy was just thinking he was hungry, so it was a coincidence.

They were finishing their meal—creamed chicken on toast, which Tommy liked—when the telephone rang. His mother answered and said it was long distance, for him, that the operator was asking for him by name. It was the first time in his life that he'd ever gotten a long-distance call, and he was very excited. He ran to the telephone. "Hello," he said. The operator's voice said, "Is this Andrew Thomas MacAllister?"—she used his whole name—and Tommy said, "Yes, it is," and the operator said, "I have a person-to-person call for you from New York City. Go ahead, please." There was some crackling on the line and then Tommy heard his father's voice. That's a coincidence, Tommy thought. Then he realized his father was trying to sing. *"Happy birthday to you."* It was his father's funny voice. *"Happy birthday to you."* He went through the whole song, *"Happy birthday, dear Tommy, happy birthday to you."* Tommy liked hearing his father's voice; he knew how much he hated to sing.

"I got a whole lot of presents," Tommy said. "I got a telescope and an Erector Set and a kaleidoscope. And David gave me a windbreaker, and Daddy, John sent me a huge box of crayons from college! Daddy," he said, "it's the biggest box of crayons I've ever seen. There are forty-eight colors in it!"

"That will give you a lot of choices," his father said. "What will you do with forty-eight crayons?"

"I'm going to lock them up in my desk drawer," Tommy said.

His father laughed. "I guess you want to make sure that nobody steals them," he said. "It sounds as if they'll be pretty safe, if you hold on to the key." Then he asked if David was behaving himself. That was a joke, because he knew that David was always teasing him. "Are you taking good care of your mother?" he asked him.

"Oh, yes," Tommy said, "I'm trying to. But Daddy," he said, "I'm only just eight."

"It's never too early to start," his father said, and then he asked him if he'd blown out all the candles on his cake.

"We haven't had the cake yet," Tommy said. "We're just finishing dinner."

"Don't forget to make a wish," his father said, and then he said goodbye. "I love you," he said. "Goodbye." He didn't even ask to talk to anyone else; the call was just for him.

When Tommy returned to the table, Rose and his mother had already cleared it and they were in the kitchen with the door shut. When it opened, his mother came in bearing the cake with its candles burning, the flames pale in the slanting afternoon light. She was singing "Happy birthday" and everyone joined in, even Rose, and then Tommy blew out the candles and took them off the cake and cut the first slice. His mother cut the rest. He couldn't do it too neatly, and it was hard to get the cake onto the plate without spilling. Rose passed the plates as his mother filled them, and everyone had a piece, Rose too, who stood eating by the sideboard, the plate in her hand. "That's a good cake," she said, and everyone agreed. Tommy loved it. He and Jimmy and Amy and Rose had another piece, and then Jimmy and his mother went home. Jimmy had homework to do.

They were still sitting at the table when the doorbell rang a few minutes later. It was Mr. Wolfe. He'd come over for his piece of cake. He had a present, too, and he handed Tommy a small box wrapped in white tissue paper and tied with a green ribbon. Tommy wondered who had wrapped it. "I wrapped it myself," Mr. Wolfe said. Well, Mr. Wolfe was a pretty good wrapper, Tommy thought; it looked perfectly fine. He opened the box and inside was a stack of silver, eight silver dollars—Tommy counted them—one for each year of his life.

"'Look at the dates, Tommy," Mr. Wolfe said. He picked the one from the bottom and showed him the year, 1931.

"That's the year I was born," Tommy said. He looked at the others and saw that each was different, that they were stacked in order from the year of his birth and they went up to 1939, skipping 1938 because Mr. Wolfe had already given him a 1938 dollar for Christmas. Tommy laid each one out before him. They were Canadian, just like the other one, and like that other one, they'd been struck from Mr. Wolfe's own silver. That's what he said. Tommy had never had so much money in his life. Eight whole dollars; nine, counting the one upstairs. What would he do with them? How would he spend them?

"Have fun with them, Tommy," Mr. Wolfe said. "There'll always be more."

"Ah, the sweet solipsism of youth," Mrs. Steer said. "They think that no matter what they spend, their resources are never depleted." That was Mrs. Steer, all right. Tommy didn't know what "solipsism" meant, and he bet no one else did either, not even his mother. He'd have to ask Mrs. Steer when they were alone.

Tommy piled up the coins again, in order from 1931. They made a neat little stack. "Maybe your mother will take you to Canada soon," Mr. Wolfe said, "and you can spend them there."

"Wouldn't that be fun?" his mother said.

"I don't know," Tommy said. "I think I may keep them. I like them. Thanks, Mr. Wolfe. Thank you very much."

Everyone left a little while later, and a while after that Tommy carried his presents upstairs. He put his telescope and the kaleidoscope on top of his dresser, next to his front window. He slipped the crayons into his desk drawer and locked it, and he put the stack of silver dollars on his windowsill, next to the one Mr. Wolfe had given him for Christmas.

"Aren't you going to keep them in your desk?" his mother asked when she was tucking him in for the night.

"No," Tommy said. "I like to look at them. "They shine in the dark." Like the lights on the fish in *Fingerfins*, he suddenly thought, only the fish were living things.

"I'm going to the club a little later," his mother said. "Mr. Wolfe is going away tomorrow, back to Canada, and a few of us are having a farewell drink with him. Rose will be here."

"Okay," Tommy said. "Good night," and he gave his mother a kiss. "I had a nice birthday," he said. "I'm glad Daddy called. I hope he comes home soon."

"He will," his mother said. "He'll be home soon."

When his father did come home, three days later, he brought him a beautiful black fountain pen, a grown-up pen in its own case, a lot like his own. Tommy had never used a fountain pen. He'd never used any kind of pen. They hadn't started script yet in school, but when they did, next year in third grade, they used wooden pens with steel points, and you dipped the point in the inkwell. They had desks in third grade, too, not like the big tables that everyone sat at in second grade, and each desk had its own inkwell. Tommy was eager to learn.

"I got this in New York, Tommy. It's for your birthday," his father said. "I'm really sorry I missed it, but I'll bet you ate a lot of cake." He gave him a big hug. "Did you blow out all the candles?"

"Yes." Tommy giggled.

"Did you make a wish?"

"Yes, I made a wish."

"Well, don't tell it," his father said, "or it won't come true." Tommy wouldn't tell it. The truth was, he didn't know it; he couldn't remember his wish.

"I've never used a fountain pen," he said. "I've never had one."

"You'll learn," his father said. "You'll learn to use it."

Tommy was almost afraid to try. He looked at it for a long time that day, turning it over in his hand, feeling it, admiring it, taking the cap on and off and touching the gold point, looking at the little window that told you there was ink in it. He hadn't filled it yet; he didn't have any ink of his own. He could use his parents', of course, but he didn't. Finally he put the pen in his drawer. He'd use it when he felt old enough. In the meantime, he was happy just to admire it, and he was filled with love for his father for giving it to him.

The Number One furnace started without incident a few days later, and the terrible accident became a memory. It was comforting to see the glow back in the sky as bright as ever, to have his father home, and to return to the smooth regularity of their places and their days.

IT was very smooth, his life: the house, the Island, the country club, his school, the people on his street, the swimmers in his sea. It was a smooth and regular life, with only an occasional interruption like the redecorating of their house, which his mother hadn't seemed to be able to interest herself in very much when his father was away but which she now threw herself into with a vengeance. That was his father's word. The books of wallpaper multiplied; samples were spread on tables, on chairs. The floors were too dark; they ought to be redone. It would be more modern if they were light. Perhaps she should do something with the kitchen; with the boys' bathroom, which was such a wreck. Of course, if David would just learn to hang up his towel instead of dropping it on the floor, it might not look such a wreck, his mother said. There were any number of possibilities. She could redecorate her bedroom—a new rug, new curtains, get rid of the rocker, slipcover her boudoir chair—that's what she called it: her boudoir chair—a pretty new bedspread. Mrs. Sedgwick was consulted frequently because she was known for her taste. His father and his brother David were enlisted in the project; even Tommy was asked his opinion, and together they looked at the various wallpapers as his mother turned the pages of the book and then another book and another. There was enough wallpaper to cover every room in every house in the entire world, Tommy thought. When his brother John came home for Easter vacation, he too got into it. Nobody escaped, but it was his mother who really cared. Everyone else liked the house just the way it was, especially Tommy, who couldn't remember it any other way. Nor did he particularly want to see it any other way. But he didn't have a choice in that. It was going to look different, like it or not.

It turned out that Margie had a flair for decoration, too. The first time she came to dinner in their house, when John was home for Easter and Emily was there too—everybody was on Easter vacation, except his parents and David—they were all sitting in the living room having their drinks before dinner. Margie didn't have one, though; she didn't drink. "That's because of her parents," Emily whispered to John when they went together to freshen their own. Tommy had just gotten back from Mrs. Slade's. It had been an exciting afternoon and he wanted to tell about it, but his mother was talking about her favorite project and Tommy couldn't interrupt. Margie got quite interested in it. She thought the pale gray wallpaper with the white plumes and the fine yellow stripe would look wonderful in the living room, and then they could put the gray and yellow and white-striped paper in the hallway and up the stairs, and perhaps in the upstairs hallway, too, though she hadn't seen that, of course. "Of course not," Emily said. "Off limits to us girls," and she laughed in that way she had. It was sort of a silly way, Tommy thought.

"It would look wonderful with yellow curtains," Margie said. Tommy could tell she was trying to be helpful, but she also seemed truly interested.

His mother was quite surprised. "Why, yes," she agreed, "wouldn't it?"

"Let's do it," his father said. Tommy thought he was tired of looking at wallpaper.

"It would pick up the yellow in the rug," his mother said. The rug was mostly red and blue, but there was a yellow something-or-other here and there. In fact, there was almost every color you could think of in the rug. It was a complicated rug, and hard to figure out the pattern in it.

"I was at Mrs. Slade's today," Tommy said, but nobody paid any attention.

"And you could cover this couch"—Margie was sitting on the big comfortable couch—"with blue. The color of iris," she said; "and throw some pale gray pillows on it." Margie was getting as excited about the whole thing as his mother. "I love irises," she said, "and I love the gray in this wallpaper. It catches the light."

"Mrs. Slade's nice," Tommy said.

"Why, yes, of course she is, Tommy," Emily said. "You know she's Margie's aunt." Tommy knew that.

"That settles it," his father said. "That settles the wallpaper."

"Well, almost," his mother said. "We still have to think about the bedrooms."

"But not now," he said. "It must be time for dinner." Tommy could tell his father was getting impatient. His mother went into the kitchen to see what remained to be done, and when she returned she announced that the soup was on the table. They all trooped into the dining room and began to eat. It was mushroom soup, Tommy's second-favorite, next to tomato. Margie helped Rose clear the soup plates, and then his father carved the roast and served the mashed potatoes and carrots. Tommy could hear Rose washing up in the kitchen. He was trying to eat, but the soup had filled him up. He ate some of his meat, though, and he was looking at the carrots, wondering how he could avoid them, when Margie asked him what he'd been up to that day. Margie was trying to be nice to him, Tommy could tell. And he started to tell his story about Mrs. Slade and her needle, and everybody froze and his mother stuffed carrots into his mouth and started talking about what she'd read in the paper that day and Emily started talking at the same time about college and where did Margie think she'd like to go, and Tommy was excused from the table and went outside to play for a while. It was still light. Tommy was mad at all of them, except Margie, who was only trying to be nice. He didn't even get to finish his story.

When he came back he said good night to everybody and went up to his room. John came upstairs a few minutes later. "What are you doing?" Tommy asked him.

"I'm getting a sweater for Emily," he said. "She's cold. Listen, Tommy, you don't have to tell everything you know. Don't tell it all."

"I don't know anything," Tommy said, but whatever he knew, he was afraid he'd already told it. It was then that John explained to him about Mrs. Slade's shots, and after he had told him Tommy pulled his shades and went to bed. The next morning his mother told him he wasn't to play at the Slades', so Tommy didn't go over there that day, though he wanted to. He waited until the next day when his mother was playing bridge and Mr. St. John was there and he was supposed to stay out of the house as much as possible.

Mrs. Slade was in her bedroom, her hair up, trying on hats. They looked sort of funny with her negligée, Tommy thought. "My mother's got a new hat," Tommy told her. "It has a veil. She got it for Easter."

"Well, I'll bet she looks real fancy," Mrs. Slade said. "How do you like this one?" she asked Tommy. "Don't answer," she said. "I don't like it," and she tossed it to the floor. "You didn't like it either, did you? We'll try another," and she reached into one of the boxes that surrounded her and pulled a hat out of the tissue. "What the hell do I want a hat for?" she asked herself, looking at the hat in her hand. "I never wear one. Well, hardly ever." But that didn't stop her from putting it on. She sat there in front of the mirror in her negligée, with the hat on, looking.

"Where's Luke?" she asked him.

"Luke?"

"Luke Wolfe," she said, "wicked Luke Wolfe, everybody's sweetie."

"He's away," Tommy said.

"Yeah, I know he's away," Mrs. Slade said. "Where did he go?"

"I don't know. I think he had to go up North to look at his mines," Tommy said. "He's not everybody's sweetie."

"No, of course he's not, Tommy," Mrs. Slade said. "Just mine. I wish." She laughed. "Every girl needs a sweetie. You be mine." She hugged him, knocking her hat askew. "I'm sick of hats." She threw it to the floor with the others and loosened her blond hair so that it streamed down her back.

"He might go to Mexico, too," Tommy said. "That's what he said. He might end up in Mexico, you never know."

"He likes it where it's hot," she said, "not in this iceberg. He'll go there, if he's not there already. Yes," she said, "every girl needs a little love, and Tommy, right now you're all I've got. Think you can handle it?" She laughed, and winked at him. "Do you have enough love for me, Tommy?"

"It's a mystery," Tommy said.

"What's a mystery?" she asked.

"Love," Tommy said. "That's what my mother said. That you know it when it happens, but you can't explain it. You just can't help it."

"Help it? Who'd want to help it? Not this one," Mrs. Slade said. "It's no mystery, honey, I can tell you it ain't no mystery. It just makes you feel real good. Real good. That's all there is to it. Simple. But it can be a son-of-a-bitch." Tommy giggled, fascinated, puzzled. And then he was sad.

"Mrs. Slade," he said, looking at the reflection of her back in the mirrored wall.

250

"Yes?" she replied.

"Mrs. Slade, umh, I've got to stay home more. I, I probably won't be over for a while."

"Why, that's all right, honey." She hugged him to her again. "That's all right. You'll still be my sweetie, and I'll miss you. But you come back when you can."

"Mrs. Slade?"

"What?"

"Mrs. Slade, may I ask you a question?"

"Fire away."

"Mrs. Slade, why do you use those needles?" He could see one of them now, the glass tube and the steel shaft with the point, lying on her dressing table.

"My needles?" She brightened. "Why, they make me feel good. They make me feel real good"—but her face seemed strange. A frown passed over it, and suddenly she looked very sad. She struggled up from the dressing table, kicking a hatbox out of her way. "I'll tell you why I use the needles," she said. "For the pain. You understand that? For the pain!" Tommy didn't know Mrs. Slade was in pain.

"Don't you think this hurts?" she said, throwing open her negligée. "Don't you think it hurts when they cut off your tits? Any woman knows that, even if she's got 'em. Ask your mother, if you don't think it hurts. She'd tell you. She'd tell you that it hurt likes hell." Tommy looked at her bare scarred chest. He looked at her reflection in the mirrored wall, and saw his own small self there, too. He looked back to her chest. He'd seen it before, but he was shocked. He was truly shocked. "And that's not the only thing that hurts," she said, "that's not the only thing. . . ."

Tommy wanted to throw his arms around her, to hug her and make her feel better. He didn't want her to hurt, and in his own pain and confusion his eyes filled. He couldn't stop it. He was afraid to speak. He didn't think he would be able to. He couldn't move. He just stared speechless at her, her blurred face, her white negligée streaming to the floor, her yellow hair and white panties, and the mirrored wall swirling around him.

"There, there," Mrs. Slade said, moving toward him, "there,

there." She drew her negligée around her and pulled him toward her. "It's all right. Everything will be all right, Tommy," she said, brushing his hair back from his face, holding him lightly. "You run along home now, but remember your pal Maxine. Remember your pal Maxine."

Tommy left the house. Lily and Jenny were at the dock with their father. Tommy was glad of that. He didn't want to see them. He didn't want to see anybody. And he walked slowly through Mrs. Slade's yard toward the greening thorn-apple thicket and the fence between them, and he climbed it and sat for a while in the sunlight on top of the tall stone pillar in the corner, between his house and the Slades'. Mr. St. John and his men had started to sand the floors in his house that day, and Tommy wasn't supposed to go in if he could help it. From his perch he could hear the roar of the sanding machines.

WHILE they were sanding the floors there was dust everywhere, and a kind of hot smell that was a mixture of the sanding machines and sawdust, and then that smell was replaced by the smell of varnish, which took a long time to dry and while it was being put on and drying they had to go in and out through the kitchen door, and go upstairs by the back stairway. They couldn't go into the living room, the library, or the dining room at all. When they did the upstairs floors, everything was in an even worse mess and everybody slept in different rooms on different nights, and they did half the upstairs hallway one day and half on another day so that they'd have someplace to walk. But finally the sanding and the varnishing were finished—it was true, the dark floors came out light—the smell of sawdust and varnish faded, and the smell of wallpaper paste took over.

All the wallpaper had been decided on and a lot of it was up, including the new paper for Tommy's room, which had a green design on it. His mother, though, insisted it was blue. Sometimes Tommy had a hard time telling the difference between blues and greens. It looked green to him but probably it was blue, if his mother said so. They put the paper Margie liked in the living room and the other paper she liked

in the big hallway and up the stairway and all over the upstairs hall, and Mrs. Matson was making new yellow curtains
for the living room. The house began to look fresh and new
and sparkling clean. About the only thing that didn't change
was his parents' bedroom. Tommy's father refused to have
new wallpaper; he liked the old, so Mrs. Munter came with
her cans of wallpaper cleaner and cleaned it. Tommy loved
to watch Mrs. Munter clean wallpaper. She took a handful of
the pink dough from the can and kneaded it into a ball, and
then she wiped it across the wallpaper in broad downward
strokes, starting from the top, kneading the ball again and
again as it grew darker and darker until finally it turned almost black and she threw it away and took a bright new piece
from the can. As she stroked the wall, the soil magically disappeared, and Tommy could see by the line of her stroke that
the paper, which had never looked dirty to him before, really
was. After the wallpaper had been cleaned, the curtains,
freshly aired, were rehung. The curtains were the same too,
but his mother did get a new rug that was lighter than the old
rug and Mrs. Matson made a slipcover for the chair and his
mother ordered a new bedspread from Marshall Field's, but
it hadn't arrived yet. His grandmother or his great-
grandmother, one of them, had made the old white spread
all by hand. It was too good to throw out; maybe his Aunt
Martha would like it, his mother said. In the meantime, she
put it on the bed in the room they called the big guest room
now to distinguish it from the other guest room, and she
moved the telephone table her father had made, which used
to stand beside her boudoir chair, there too. Her father hadn't
made it for a telephone, because they didn't have any then.
Her father was very good at making things, and the table was
elaborately inlaid with many different kinds of wood. His
mother put a plant on it, and she found another table for her
telephone.

Tommy didn't like Mr. St. John very much, and he could
hardly wait for him to be finished. He might have been the
best painter and wallpaperer in town, but he liked to tease, too,
and not in a very funny way. The day Tommy took some of
David's Vaseline hair tonic and put it on his hair—something

neither of his parents liked him to do, or David either, for that matter—Mr. St. John swiped him with a sheet of the wallpaper he was putting on the stairway, and his hair left a greasy mark on it. Mr. St. John put it on the wall anyway, and Tommy could still see the mark. Tommy asked Mrs. Munter if she'd try to get it out, but she was no more successful than his mother had been when she tried to remove Mr. Wolfe's footprint from her curtain. Both stains were so faint, though, that nobody else ever noticed either of them.

Not too long after that, Tommy's parents went away. His father was tired from all the work at the plant after the explosion in the furnace, and he couldn't stand the mess in the house. So after the furnaces had been operating normally for some time and when the house was almost finished, he decided to take his mother on a little trip, a second honeymoon, he called it. Mrs. Moran came to stay with him and David. Rose was all right for a night or two, his mother said, but she wasn't responsible enough for more than that, and she couldn't cook very well, either. Tommy liked it when Mrs. Moran came to stay. Her powdery smell reminded him of his grandmother.

The most exciting thing that happened while his parents were away was that David got engaged to Margie, and Tommy was the first to know. He thought he had never been so happy in his entire life, and David and Margie took him down to the hamburger stand by the river, and they ate hamburgers with mustard and raw onions, and they had French-fries and Tommy drank a Coke, too. His brother didn't care, and Margie loved Coke. She was on a diet, but this was a celebration. Tommy didn't mind at all when they dropped him off at the house after dinner and they went on to Margie's; he was eager to tell Mrs. Moran all about it.

Mrs. Moran thought it was good news too. "Oh, it's a very nice thing to be young and in love," she told Tommy, "a very nice thing." Tommy hadn't thought of Mrs. Moran as ever being young, let alone in love. She'd been married once, and she was married a long time until her husband died. But that was long ago. Tommy had a hard time imagining any of the older people as being young or in love. As his mother said, it was a mystery.

254

After he'd told Mrs. Moran about David's engagement—how he'd found them sitting on the big couch in the living room when he came home from school, and how David had tricked him into going over to Mrs. Randolph's for a plant—he suddenly remembered that the plant was for her, and he found it in the kitchen where he'd put it. He handed it to her. "Why would Mrs. Randolph give me a plant?" Mrs. Moran said. "Isn't that nice of her?"

"She said it would flower in the winter," Tommy said. "She called it a Christmas cactus. Mrs. Moran, will I be related to Mrs. Slade when Margie and David get married?"

"I don't think so," Mrs. Moran said.

"Not at all?"

"Oh, maybe you'd be some kind of in-law, but you wouldn't really be related."

"That's too bad," Tommy said. Then he went to his room. He was thinking about the strange letter that had arrived that day, and he wanted to read about Mexico. He found the book Mr. Wolfe had given him, but that didn't really tell him what he wanted to know. The story took place in Mexico, but it didn't tell much about it. It was warm there and the people were very poor, that was all, so poor that the children had to work. *Lands and Peoples* would tell him more, he thought. So he looked through the volumes until he found the one about Central and South America. There was a map, and Tommy examined it. Mexico was next to the United States, just like Canada, but at the other end. He could see Canada from his window, beyond the glow in the sky from his father's furnaces. There were jungles in Mexico, and ancient ruins; there were no jungles in Canada, only miles and miles of forests that started just a little ways across the river and went on almost forever, until the ice of the Arctic. Tommy had seen some of the forest when he'd gone on picnics to the Montreal River. That was the end of the road. He took Mrs. Steer's telescope from his dresser top and pointed it out the window toward Canada. Through the lens the light from his father's furnaces shot toward him, brighter than ever, the currents of fire flowing in the air like the waters in the canal, but red and glowing. He moved the telescope and tried to focus it on

Canada, but he couldn't see anything, only darkness, and then back to the wildly swirling fire. It looked very hot and fierce through the telescope; the telescope did bring the fire up close. From his bedroom window, with his naked eye, it looked more like heat lightning or the northern lights of late summer, ebbing and flowing in the distant sky. He did like Mrs. Steer's telescope, and he was learning how to use it. She was right: it took a little practice and you had to have some idea of what you were looking for, where to point it. He put the telescope back in its place on the dresser and returned to his book, to the pictures of Mexico with its beautiful green jungles, its great ruined temples and strange gods. He recognized one of the figures. It was called Quetzalcóatl. Tommy wondered how you'd ever pronounce such a name. It had huge teeth, and a funny kind of feathers on its head, and it was called a plumed serpent. It was a god. The same figure was on one of the stamps on the envelope downstairs. He decided to go look at it again, and he picked it out of the pile and brought it upstairs to his desk. He handled the letter carefully, because he thought it might be valuable. The stamps were large and brilliantly colored, certainly like none he'd ever seen before, and he laid the envelope next to the book he was reading so that he could look from one to the other. A plumed serpent, Tommy thought. Think of that. There were some very strange things in the world, especially in ancient Mexico. There was another animal, a jaguar, that the ancient Mexicans called the beast of darkness because they thought it swallowed the sun every night. He didn't see the jaguar on the stamps, but there was a picture of a great stone head with blank eyes. The head was gray and the background was orange and green. The third stamp on the envelope showed a smoking volcano against a bright blue-and-yellow sky. Tommy looked for the mountain in the book, and he did find pictures of two volcanoes but he couldn't tell if either of them was the one on the stamp. The ancient Mexicans knew a lot about astronomy, too, though they didn't have telescopes; they just studied the sky night after night from the tops of their pyramids. They called them pyramids but they didn't look like the pyramids in Egypt. The Aztecs were a very cruel people. They sacrificed humans

256

by cutting out their hearts. Tommy could hardly believe it, but it said so, right in *Lands and Peoples*. They cut out their hearts! Mr. Wolfe's book certainly didn't say anything about that. Every year they cut out the heart of the bravest young warrior and placed it in a special vessel and offered it to their gods and the rest of the warrior to the people. It was sickening, the most sickening thing Tommy had ever heard of. Tommy thought none of the warriors would have wanted to be very brave. Why would you want to be brave if they were going to cut out your heart and offer it to the gods? They must have been the cruelest gods in the world, to demand such a terrible sacrifice. Sometimes they wanted more than one, too. But of course they weren't real gods; they weren't *God*. The Aztecs and those other people had just made them up. The real God was good. The stamps on the envelope that had at first looked so strange and beautiful began to look scary to Tommy now, and he decided to move it out of sight. He put the letter in his special drawer and locked it. Because it might be valuable, he didn't want it to be lost; he didn't want to have to see it, either.

Tommy remembered the envelope when he got home from school the next day. It was another beautiful day, and on his way home he noticed that Mrs. Steer's garden seemed to have grown more flowers overnight, soft and beautifully colored flowers, not like the colors on those stamps. Tommy went right to his desk and got the key from its hiding place and unlocked the drawer. The envelope was still there. He didn't want anyone to find it in his desk; he didn't want to be caught with it. He didn't want to see it, or even know that it existed. He wondered what was in the envelope, but of course he couldn't open it. Mail was private, even if the envelope had already been opened. Even postcards were private. His mother had really punished him when she'd caught him reading David's letters from Margie. She didn't like that one bit, and it didn't make a shred of difference, she had said, that the envelopes were already opened: "You don't read anyone else's mail without their permission," she said. "Ever." And then she'd spanked him, so she'd really meant it. It was almost worth the spanking, though, the letters were so funny and it made David so mad when he started reciting them that night at dinner. Tommy wondered who this letter was from. There was no return address, and he didn't know the handwriting. There was only his mother's name and their address, and then there were the stamps. He looked at them and began to get scared all over again. He got up from his desk and walked to the far end of the hall. He stood in front of the attic door. He looked at the door for a minute. The door was always bolted, just like the cellar door, to keep out drafts. He unbolted the door and walked quickly up the winding attic stairs and directly to his secret place, the floorboard that nobody knew was loose and could be lifted. He'd sometimes put strange things in it before he'd gotten his desk. He'd dropped three marbles in it and they'd rolled out of sight. Once a long time ago he'd even gone to the bathroom in it, a real bowel movement—a small one, but still. He lifted the floorboard. The movement was still there, but all shriveled and harmless-looking. Tommy shoved it back with a stick. And there he put his mother's letter with its foreign stamps, replaced the floorboard, and left the attic as fast as he could. When he got to the hall he slammed the door and bolted it. He leaned against it while he caught his breath. No one would find the letter there, and someday, when his mother was home, he'd have to remember to give it to her. After all, he hadn't opened it; he was just keeping it safe. He'd have to wait for the right time so he could explain to his mother why he'd been protecting it.

Why did his house have so many scary places, he wondered: the cellar with the big old furnace they didn't use anymore now that they burned oil; the coal bin, black as a piece of coal; the fruit room, with Mr. Bonnaro's jugs of wine and its unchanging rows of jars on shelves, jars that everyone was afraid to open because the food was probably spoiled but that no one ever threw out, either; and the attic, sometimes the scariest attic in the world but on nice days in the spring and in the fall an interesting place to play. On those days the sun came through the windows, warming the air and catching the motes of dust, and the attic smelled dry and warm and old. In the winter it was too cold to play in the attic, and in the summer it was too hot and besides, they were usually on the Island in the summer. There was a broken sewing machine that he sometimes played at, with a wooden box full of bobbins of colored thread. There were old books and toys, the rocker in the shape of a swan that he'd had as a baby, his crib, a playpen, discarded lamps and pieces of furniture and boxes that had belonged to his grandmother—all coated with a thin film of dust. There were his father's fishing boots, hip boots, stuffed with newspaper and hanging from hooks on the wall, like somebody's legs. There was the old chest of drawers where his mother had put the shoes that Mrs. Henderson had given her. And at the windows there were usually spiders, and sometimes a wasp, and almost always flies that got caught in the spiders' webs. The attic was full of strange things, and a long time ago, in exploring these things, Tommy had discovered the floorboard that came up, and the secret place beneath it.

When his parents did get home from their trip, and Tommy had told them all about David's engagement and how he'd gone out to dinner that night with David and Margie and how he thought it was the most exciting day of his life, he suddenly remembered the letter, up there in its hiding place. What reminded him was when his mother was telling David that Hot Pink was wondering why he never replied to her letters. His mother called her Madge, not Hot Pink, of course; that was just John's name for her, but Tommy liked it. That didn't seem like the right time to tell his mother about her letter, though.

LATER that month, Paul Malotte made his First Communion. He was only Tommy's age, just eight, but Catholics made their First Communion then, when they were in second grade and seven or eight years old, old enough to know the difference between right and wrong. Paul was very proud that day. His family had saved a lot of money—it was hard, because they were so poor now that his father was dead, and he'd been dead at least a year, Tommy thought, maybe two— and they bought Paul a white suit and white shoes, and he wore a white shirt and a white tie and white socks and a white belt, too. Except for his face and his hair, which were dark

like the French, Paul was white all over the day he went to
the Catholic church to make his First Communion. They
even got his nose to stop running for a while. Afterwards
Paul's mother had a little party. The cake was white, too.
The party was just for Catholics. Tommy and Jimmy and
Amy couldn't go, even though Paul lived right at the end of
their street and kitty-corner from Amy's house. But Paul
hadn't been at Tommy's birthday party, either. He would
have felt he had to take a present, and he couldn't afford a
present and he might have felt bad.

When he got home from church, Paul came out in his yard
to show off his new clothes. You have to wear white, he said.
It means purity, and you have to be pure to receive Communion, you have to try to be as pure as the Baby Jesus. That
was impossible because the Baby Jesus was God and the purest
thing that ever lived, but you had to come as close to it as you
could. You couldn't show disrespect to your parents or the
nuns—sometimes he called them the sisters—or the priest;
you couldn't be disobedient; you couldn't use bad language—
Paul did, though; Tommy'd heard him—and you couldn't
have bad thoughts.

"What are bad thoughts?" Tommy asked him.

"Bad thoughts," Paul said. "You know, bad thoughts. What
the Ten Commandments tell you you can't do. You can't
kill anybody. You can't swear. You can't covet thy neighbor's
wife, or commit adultery, or steal. You can't do any of those
things or you'll go to hell."

"What about if you take something and hide it?" Tommy
asked him. "Can you hide something from somebody?"

"That's the same as stealing," Paul said. "If you take it
and it's not yours, then you stole it."

"Well," Tommy said, "what about when you stole the bub-
ble gum from Mr. Lavelle, from Mr. Lavelle's store? I saw
you."

"You did not!"

"I did too. I saw you take it."

"I put it back."

"You did not. You put it in your mouth, that's where you
put it! I saw."

"I'll beat you up," Paul said. "If you say that again, I'll beat you up, you dirty bastard, and I can, too. You take it back."

"You can't beat me up," Tommy said. "You'll get your suit dirty and your mother'll be mad."

Paul grabbed him by the shirt and Tommy thought maybe Paul would beat him up, right there in the dust of his yard, white suit or not. "Okay," Tommy said, "I take it back."

"Take it back again," Paul said. He hadn't let go of his shirt, and now he was twisting it.

"I take it back again," Tommy said. He was humiliated. Why was he such a coward? His father would be ashamed of him.

"Besides," Paul said, "I put a penny on Mr. Lavelle's counter one day when he wasn't looking. So I paid him back. That was the same as giving it back to him." Then Paul's mother stuck her head out the kitchen door and yelled at Paul. "You come in here right this minute! It's time for the cake." Paul went in to join his family for the celebration that the rest of them couldn't go to because they weren't Catholics. Probably there wasn't enough cake for anybody else, Tommy thought.

CARMEN Bonnaro died that same month, right after he'd made his First Communion with Paul Malotte. He drowned in the pond by the lime dump, the pond where nobody was ever supposed to swim and there were signs that said "No TRESPASSING," and if you violated them it was against the law. Carmen thought he could swim, but he couldn't do it very well, and he got a cramp and drowned. He went under three times, and the third time he stayed there in the murky water and never came up again. His brother Leo saw it happen. They had to drag for his body, and because the water was so cloudy and deep it took a long time to find it. A lot of the older boys went down to watch the dragging. When they finally pulled Carmen's body from the water, it was covered with weeds and they said it had turned blue and was bloated from being under the water so long. They buried him in his white suit, the one he'd worn to his First Communion.

"Did he look blue?" Tommy asked Paul Malotte, who'd seen him.

"Sort of," Paul said. "He didn't look like Carmen at all. He had lipstick on. He looked terrible." Paul had gone to the funeral home when Carmen died. He said the undertaker had tried to fix him up, but it was hard to fix up drowned people. Everyone in Paul's grade went to the funeral home to say a rosary for Carmen, and they were all crying, the nuns too, and Carmen's mother had to be held up by some of her friends, and she moaned and screamed. Even Carmen's father was crying. "Everybody was crying," Paul said. "It was the saddest thing that ever happened," and when he looked at Carmen in his white suit, lying at the end of the room in his white casket with big candles all around it, and holding a rosary in his hands, Paul cried too. It almost made Tommy cry, just hearing about it. Somebody he knew and had played with, somebody who'd been in his class and even at his house for a minute on Christmas Day and Tommy had shown him the windup truck he'd gotten instead of the Monopoly set— and now he was dead. It seemed like one of those terrible stories, one of those fairy stories that there ought to be a happy ending to but there wasn't.

Paul said Carmen had gone to heaven, though. "He went straight to heaven. The priest said so. He'd already gone to confession and made his First Communion, and Jesus loved him so much he wanted Carmen to be with Him and the angels in heaven."

Well, Tommy thought, Carmen used to get in a lot of trouble in school, before he'd transferred in the middle of the year to the Catholic school, but he'd always been kind to Tommy. He'd defended him when Tommy refused to fight Lois Marks. Tommy wouldn't fight with a girl. Carl Smith called him a sissy, but Carmen said he wasn't a sissy, that boys who had fights with girls were the sissies. Then Tommy had to fight Carl in the space between the turn-over bars and the swings. Tommy was scared. He didn't like to fight. He didn't want to hurt anybody else any more than he wanted to be hurt himself, and he was afraid that if he got really mad he would hurt somebody terribly. So Carl beat him up, which still made Tommy mad. He knew he could have beaten up Carl Smith if he'd tried, and next year, if Carl picked a fight with him, he would.

Carmen was a good fighter, and Carmen stood up for Tommy. Carmen even liked him, though they hardly ever played together, just on the playground. Carmen had a nice smile, but Leo didn't. They were both good at sports, but Leo played mean. When Carmen transferred, Tommy wished it were Leo who had gone, and now it was Carmen who was gone for good and the priest had said it was because Jesus loved him. Tommy hoped that Jesus didn't love him that much. He was happy enough with his mother and father, although Tommy thought that maybe he didn't always honor his mother and father enough, the way the Commandments told you to, the Ten Commandments that Paul had had to memorize and could recite by number without stopping. Tommy's mother had said more than once that she'd never talked back to her mother the way he sometimes did to her, but Tommy wasn't as good as his mother. He'd told some lies, and his mother didn't, only white lies and they didn't count. And he did, he knew, sometimes have bad thoughts.

Tommy's father had gone to Carmen Bonnaro's funeral. He always went to funerals in families of the men at the plant, but this one was different from the others, and his father was very upset. "My God," he said, "what next?"

TOMMY didn't know what next. One thing that happened, though, was that they started to build a big chain-link fence around the lime dump and the pond next to it. The fence was very high and there was barbed wire on top of it so that no one could climb over it and drown in the pond or burn in the lime, and the gates were always locked. Mr. Steer said that it was about time the plant did something to protect innocent people from that menace. And another thing that happened was that everyone in school, Miss Case and all the pupils, tried to be especially kind to Leo, who seemed nicer now than he used to be. The third thing that happened was that Tommy got an ingrown toenail on the big toe of his left foot, and it got infected and Dr. Randolph had to remove the toenail. He froze it when he did it, and the operation didn't hurt much. Tommy was determined to be brave, and he didn't cry once. His father said he was proud of him, and his mother said she was too. His father cut the end out of a tennis shoe and Tommy had to wear it to school until the bandage came off, and he couldn't play on the playground for a few days. He didn't mind that; he got to read instead, and his mother drove him to school every morning because she didn't want him to get his bandage dirty.

One morning, a beautiful morning in early June—school was almost over—his mother dropped him off and came back again just a little while later. Tommy was surprised to see her walk into the classroom and whisper to Miss Case. His mother almost never came into the school; she didn't believe in interfering with the teacher. Miss Case called him up to her desk and told him he was being excused that day. In fact, she told him he didn't have to come back at all, that she was passing him into third grade in the fall, and there were only two more days of school anyway. "It's been a pleasure having you, Tommy," Miss Case said, "and we'd love you to come back for the picnic on Friday." Tommy was glad that he'd passed, although his mother didn't seem to think there'd been any question about it, and he wanted to come back for the picnic.

In the car, his mother explained that Rose hadn't shown up again—"Sometimes I could just kill that Rose," she said—and she had a golf date with Dr. Rodgers' wife and a couple of other ladies and she would be gone all day and no one would be home when he came home from school, so she was taking him to the country club with her. Tommy didn't mind. It was such a fresh morning—the dew was still on the grass—and he liked playing at the country club. "Ophelia will keep an eye on you," his mother said, "and you'll find something to do." Together the two of them drove past his father's plant and down the River Road to the country club.

"Can I have a root beer float and a toasted cheese sandwich for lunch?" Tommy asked her.

"*May* I," his mother corrected him. "Yes, you may."

Five

Dᴀɪsʏ Meyer was already on the golf course when Tommy and his mother arrived at the country club that June morning. His mother was in a hurry and she rushed past the few ladies sitting on the porch, greeting them quickly, explaining that she was late for her foursome. She went into the ladies' locker room, where Tommy wasn't allowed, though he'd seen it once a long time ago when he was very young. He was much too old to go in it now. His mother had to change into her golf shoes and pick up her clubs, and when she came out she went directly to the first tee, where the rest of her foursome and her caddy were waiting. Tommy walked to the end of the porch by the driveway and watched his mother greet the women, who were sitting on the bench talking, clubs at hand. She apologized for being late. Tommy couldn't hear her but he could tell what she was saying. She gestured across the driveway toward Tommy as she slipped her ball into the slot in the little white ball washer on the post next to the tee and pushed the paddle vigorously up and down. She always liked to wash her golf balls herself, rather than letting the caddy do it. She said it brought her luck. Tommy figured his mother was telling the women that Rose hadn't shown up again, and she'd had to pick Tommy up from school, and so on and so on. The ladies didn't seem to mind the wait; they'd been enjoying the morning sun and the fresh air. His mother took a practice swing. Tommy didn't stay to watch them tee off. He walked back the length of the porch, past Mrs. Appleton and the other women who were sitting there rocking and talking, and then came back and sat down near them on the broad steps facing the fairways and, far across the fairways and the River Road that wound by the country club, the river itself, glinting in the sunlight, the river that flowed by the Island where they would all soon be going. He could see the green trees of the islands, too, quiet in the distance.

A white figure replaced the flag in the fifth hole near the road. The woman picked up her golf bag where she'd dropped it next to the green and walked toward him and the sixth tee. As she approached, Tommy could see that the woman was Daisy Meyer. He didn't think he'd seen her since New Year's. She must have gotten an early start, if she'd already finished the fifth hole, which was a long one. You had to drive your ball across the country club driveway, and the cars paused as they turned in from the River Road to make sure that a ball wasn't flying through the air. Once in a while—not very often, but it had happened—a car got hit, and then everyone apologized all around. Tommy's father said it was really the driver's fault. The driver was supposed to stop and look, as the player couldn't see the oncoming car because of the trees. Daisy was playing by herself. It was hard, when you were good, to find people to play with. A poor golfer could hold back your game, and that made it boring. People liked to play with golfers who were better than they; they didn't like to play with those who were worse. Of course, everybody had to now and then; you just tried to avoid it as politely as possible.

Tommy looked to his left, across the driveway to the first tee. His mother's foursome had already teed off. Tommy could see the tiny figures marching down the fairway between the woods and the rough. His mother didn't drive her ball as far as some people did, but she drove it straight as an arrow. Her long game might not have been powerful, but it was a pleasure to watch just because it was so straight. Everyone said so. She always knew where her ball was going to go, and that was where it went, too. That made David mad when he played with her. David could drive a ball more than two hundred and fifty yards, but some of the time it hooked into the woods or sliced into the rough, and then he would swear. That wasn't being a good sport, his mother said, and once when David took his club and broke it right over his knee after he'd made a particularly bad shot, his mother got furious and said she wouldn't play with him until he'd learned to control his temper. She was really mad. Tommy thought David wouldn't have been so mad if his mother hadn't hit her ball smack down the middle of the fairway. She always did, and in two or three strokes she got it straight to the green, and she really knew how to play the greens. Her short game was as good as anybody's. Sometimes it took David two or three strokes just to get his ball out of the woods or the rough, and if David missed his ball, as he sometimes did, his mother always counted it as a stroke. Sometimes David even got a penalty. His mother played by the rules, and she didn't make exceptions just because David had a bad temper. Temper was no excuse, she said, writing down his score. You controlled your temper. His mother never lost hers. She was the only one in the family who didn't, though John didn't do it very often. Still, David always beat her in the end.

Tommy watched Daisy move toward the tee. Her white dress shimmered in the sunlight. It was a brilliant morning, and when she passed under the shade of the elms she continued to shine against the thick green of the grass, still, under the trees, glistening with dew. She leaned her clubs against the rack, selected an iron for the sixth hole, and took her practice swing. She didn't look toward the porch where the women rocked and Tommy sat on the steps, his toe sticking out of his tennis shoe. She approached the ball and shot it off with a solid thwack. The sound hit his ears. The ball rose slowly in the air, making a perfect, graceful arc, and seemed to hover there for a moment before it dropped to the green. There was a scattering of brittle applause from some of the women on the porch, breaking the hush as Daisy made her drive. She acknowledged the clapping with a short nod. She saw Tommy and waved at him, laughter brightening her face, then walked off toward the green, where she sank her putt. She always sank her putt. "A birdie," one of the women said. Mrs. Appleton smiled. She didn't play golf. Her sport was gossip, Mrs. Steer said. The women resumed their conversation. "Remember the pitchers," Mrs. Appleton said. Tommy didn't like her. She was always smirking, and Tommy felt there was something mean about her. One of the mean things about her was that she hated cats—a regular phobia, his mother said—and there were always a lot of cats around the clubhouse. They didn't belong to anybody, they were just stalking the field mice, prowling the porch, ignoring the people and going about their business.

Tommy got up and went inside. He thought he'd find a magazine in the lounge. The members brought their old magazines there for others to read. No one was playing the slot machines; no one was there. Tommy was leafing through the magazines, trying to find one that looked interesting—he'd seen most of them at home—when Ophelia came out to the bar. She looked at his foot.

"What happened to you?" she asked him, and Tommy told her about his operation and how Dr. Randolph had frozen his toe so that it didn't hurt. "Let me look at it," she said, coming out from behind the bar. "That's a mighty big toe."

Tommy laughed. "It's almost better," he said. "Dr. Randolph is going to take the bandage off in a day or two."

"Well, you just take care of it," Ophelia said, "and don't go running around too much today. You stick near me. Come on into the kitchen. I'll fix you a treat." She opened the gate to the back of the bar and led him behind it and through the swinging door into the kitchen. Tommy had never been in the kitchen before. He wasn't supposed to go there. Ophelia and the others slept above the kitchen, but the kitchen was sort of like their living room, too. There were a couple of old couches in it and a floor lamp. "Here's a hot biscuit," she said, putting one on a plate for him with some of the conserves that she made. "It'll fix your toe right up." She laughed. Tommy was excited to be invited into the kitchen. Nobody ever was.

"When will Buck be here?" he asked her.

"Buck will be up next week, as soon as school is out, with Katherine and Junior and George," she said. Buck was a few years older than Tommy. He was Ophelia's nephew. Junior was related to George, but Tommy didn't know exactly how. Katherine was Ophelia's daughter, he knew that, and George was her husband. Katherine and George were teachers, but they came to the country club in the summer because the weather was so nice—it was cooler than Kentucky—and there was a lot of work to be done, especially in the summer. They were all part of Ophelia's family. It was a big family and they were all related in one way or another, only Ophelia knew exactly how, and in the summer a lot of them were there.

"I hope Buck gets here soon," Tommy said. Sometimes it was boring to be at the country club by himself, and Buck was always full of strange lore. Amy Steer came once in a while but not very often, and Jimmy Randolph hardly ever came. Paul Malotte didn't come at all, but his family didn't belong and you had to be a member or they wouldn't let you in. Tommy finished his biscuit and Ophelia told him to run along, she had work to do. "Just ring the bell if you need anything," she said. There was a little bell on the bar that Ophelia could hear in the kitchen. Tommy liked to ring it. Sometimes he rang it just because he wanted her to come out and talk to him, but he wasn't supposed to do that. "You come back when you're ready for lunch and I'll fix you something you'll like," she said.

Tommy went back to the magazines. He thought he'd seen them all, or, if he hadn't, he didn't care if he did see them. He wished he had a nickel to put in the slot machine. He wandered into the lobby and looked at the canoes hanging there and wondered how many corks had popped into them on New Year's Eve. He liked to imagine the scene that Mrs. Steer had described to him, the men opening the champagne bottles at midnight and trying to make the corks fly into the canoes. It must have been fun, Tommy thought, as he sat down on the bench near the doors, and he wondered if he would ever get to do it, if he would ever be old enough to put on a tuxedo and go to the country club on New Year's Eve and pop champagne corks. Maybe when he was old enough he wouldn't even want to, he thought; maybe he'd be somewhere else. He heard the voices of the women on the porch. Mrs. Appleton laughed. "He's a regular night climber," she said, "but he picked the wrong window that time. I wish I could have seen the look on his face. Can you imagine what that child thought? And that poor darling man—he couldn't have any idea. Our *other* friend has a very good idea, I'm sure of that. Those Jews are shrewd."

Tommy hated Mrs. Appleton. "Jews are shrewd." What did she mean by that? Of course, he'd heard his father say the same thing more than once, but he didn't say it with that nasty tone in his voice, that tone that suggested she meant more than she was saying. Tommy's father just said it. It was a fact. He sort of admired it. Maybe he even envied it. Jews are shrewd. That's why Mr. Meyer had so much money. He gave a lot of it to the Episcopal Church, too. That was funny, Tommy thought. He liked that. With some of the money Mr. Meyer had given them they bought a new red carpet for the chancel and the sanctuary and the main aisle and the entrance, where the baptismal font was. Everybody said it cost a lot.

Tommy went out to the porch, and the conversation stopped. "My, my," one of the ladies said, "such a lovely day," and they resumed talking again, now about the weather. He was certainly good at getting them to change the subject. "When will you be moving to the Island, Tommy?" Mrs. Appleton asked him. She always wanted to know everything.

"Pretty soon," Tommy said. Actually he didn't know if they would be moving to the Island this summer, the way they usually did. His mother said she thought they ought to keep the house open because it would be so much trouble to close it when they had all these guests coming for their anniversary dance and there would be so many preparations and she'd have to be uptown a lot. But Tommy wasn't going to tell Mrs. Appleton that.

"Why don't you ask Ophelia to bring us a lemonade?" she said. "Yes, wouldn't that be nice, girls? Tommy, go ask Ophelia. You'd like to do that, wouldn't you?"

He went in and rang the bell. "The ladies on the porch want some lemonade," he said.

"They just want you out of the way," Ophelia said, but

Tommy didn't care if they did. He walked around to the side of the clubhouse. He could see the tiny figure of Daisy at the far end of the course. At least he supposed it was Daisy. She was on the seventh green, which was the farthest from that end. There were five holes on this side of the driveway; the first four were on the other side. The cats were playing beside the porch. He thought he might drop one of them in Mrs. Appleton's lap, just to see what would happen. He wasn't ever supposed to bring a cat near her, and he wondered what would happen if he did. She couldn't really hate cats; they were nice and furry and soft, and they liked to play. They didn't like to be picked up, though, and the one Tommy had picked, a black one with white feet, struggled in his arms. He carried it to the corner. He could hear the ladies all talking on the front porch. He brought the cat around, held it up in front of Mrs. Appleton, who jumped back in her chair, and dropped it in her lap. She screamed. She didn't give just a little scream; she really screamed, and she started out of her chair, knocking it over behind her, still screaming, and Ophelia ran out the front door—she was carrying a tray of lemonade and set it on the floor. Two of the women rushed to Mrs. Appleton's side, one of them saying very sternly to Tommy, "You'll give this poor woman a heart attack. Don't you know she hates cats?" And the three of them, one on each side supporting Mrs. Appleton, followed by Ophelia, half-walked, half-carried her into the clubhouse and the ladies' room, where there was a couch. He supposed they laid her on it. Well, now he knew. Mrs. Appleton really didn't like cats. He'd never seen anybody react like that to a simple cat. What could a cat do to you? It was harmless. The cat had disappeared. Probably Mrs. Appleton had scared the cat more than the cat scared her. Ophelia came out, picked up the tray, and set it on a table in front of where the women had been sitting. She took him by the shoulder and marched him into the clubhouse. "Tommy, you know better than that," she said. "My Lord, that lady could drop dead. You'd better keep out of sight—your mother will have a fit." But that was all she said to him. He bet Ophelia didn't like Mrs. Appleton, either.

Tommy decided he'd avoid the front porch for a while, so

he went around the corner again to the side porch where hardly anyone ever sat, and stood there watching Daisy approach the ninth hole, sink her putt, and walk toward the clubhouse.

"Let's have lunch," she said to him when she came up the steps. "Will you have lunch with me, Tommy?"

That would be fun. "Yes," he said, "I'd really like to. Thanks."

"Let me go into the locker room and wash up. I'll be with you in a minute."

Tommy was sitting at a table in the lounge when she came out. "What ever did you do to Mrs. Appleton?" she asked him. "She's having apoplexy in there."

"I dropped a cat in her lap," Tommy said. "What's apoplexy?"

"It's a fit," Daisy said, "a first-class, grade-A genuine fit," and she burst into laughter. "It serves the old bag right," she said. She looked at Tommy. "I'll bet that's why you did it."

"No," Tommy said, "I just wanted to see what she would do."

"Well, you certainly saw. You certainly did see. But don't worry about it. She'll survive, stronger and nosier than ever."

Tommy laughed. He really liked Daisy. He liked the way she joked with him. No one else joked with him like that. Maybe his brothers sometimes, but no one else, not even Mrs. Steer. Mrs. Steer said things once in a while—like Mr. Sedgwick's an idiot—but she said them differently.

"What would you like for lunch?" Daisy asked him.

"I'd like a toasted cheese sandwich and a root beer float," Tommy said. "Can I ring the bell?"

"Sure," Daisy said. "Ring the bell. I think I'll have the very same thing."

Ophelia came out when she heard the bell and put the sandwiches on the grill and started making the floats. "Mrs. Appleton still alive?" she asked Daisy.

"The last time I saw her she was," Daisy said. "Unless she's had a relapse."

While they were eating, Bob Griswold came into the clubhouse and came over and joined them. "Did you hear what

Tommy did?" Daisy asked him. "He dropped one of those mangy old cats in Mrs. Appleton's lap and she had a stroke! She's still in the ladies' room with her harpies fluttering over her. Isn't that rich?"

"God is just," Bob Griswold said, and he clapped Tommy on the back. "Do you think she'll survive?" he asked Daisy. "We could maybe help her along. Slip a cat in the ladies'-room door."

Tommy was very excited. They thought what he'd done was funny. Tommy loved it. He loved being funny. He loved making them laugh. He thought he'd drop another cat in Mrs. Appleton's lap sometime, but Daisy said no. "Really, no. Don't overdo it," she told him. "Once was enough."

"Once is never enough," Bob Griswold said.

Daisy gave him a look. "In this case, once is quite enough," she said. "Not more than enough, not less than enough, but quite enough."

They had finished their lunch by that time, and Daisy was going to play another nine holes in the afternoon. But before she did, Daisy and Bob left in Bob's car. They sped out of the driveway without pausing, and headed not in the direction of town but the other way, out along the river.

Tommy's mother finished her foursome a little while later. Tommy could hear her voice and the voices of the other ladies as they came into the clubhouse. When his mother came out of the locker room, she called his name. "Tommy? Tommy?" He thought he'd better answer. "I'm in here," he called from the cardroom off the lounge. His mother came in. "I'm surprised at you," she said. "I could hardly believe what I just heard. I've never seen Mrs. Appleton so upset. She's getting ready to come out. When she does, you're going to apologize to her."

"I won't," Tommy said.

"You won't? What do you mean, you won't?"

"I mean I won't," Tommy said. "I won't apologize to her. I hate her."

His mother's golfing partners came into the lounge just then. "Emma, we're ordering lunch," Mrs. Rodgers called out. "We're starving. Don't make us wait." So his mother had to go into the lounge and have her lunch with the ladies, and Tommy went back out to the side porch where the cats were playing again. He stayed on the side porch until he heard Mrs. Appleton get into a car with one of her friends and drive off.

His mother gave him a stern lecture on the way home that afternoon. "You're never to do such a thing again," she said, "and you will apologize to Mrs. Appleton the next time you see her."

The next time he saw her, Tommy did. "I'm sorry I dropped the cat on your lap, Mrs. Appleton," he said, but he wasn't. It was a lie. He wasn't sorry at all. And Mrs. Appleton was still mad, too, Tommy could tell, though she said she accepted his apology. "What else can I do?" she sighed to no one in particular. Later Tommy heard her tell one of her friends, "I've never had such a fright as that boy gave me. She just lets him run wild, just run wild." She was talking about him, but Tommy didn't care. Mrs. Appleton talked about everybody, and she never had anything nice to say about any of them, either.

TOMMY hadn't gone to the cemetery on Decoration Day, when his father went down with the geraniums to plant on Tommy's grandmother's grave. His father took David with him to help. Tommy couldn't go because he was still supposed to stay off his foot as much as possible. He'd just had the operation a couple of days before. His mother stayed home too, to watch him. He didn't go to Chicago the weekend after he'd dropped the cat on Mrs. Appleton's lap, either, when his parents went down for John's graduation. David stayed home with him that time, and David thought it was hilarious that Tommy had dumped the cat on Mrs. Appleton. Tommy hoped even his mother might think it was a little bit funny, but she never let on at all. But Tommy did go to the picnic the last day of school. Dr. Randolph came over to his house that morning and took the bandage off his foot and told Tommy he was fine, that his toe had healed just fine and he didn't have to think about it anymore. The picnic was fun. Everybody brought a sandwich, and Miss Case had made

Kool-Aid and a cake, and Leo was still being nice and didn't try to pick a fight with anybody.

On his way home, Tommy saw Paul Malotte playing by himself in his yard. The Catholic school always ended earlier than the public school. Paul was shooting marbles under the big tree where there was no grass and the dirt was packed. It was a good place to shoot marbles. Paul's yard wasn't grassy and green all over, like Tommy's. A lot of it was dusty, and they had their big vegetable patch in the back. Tommy walked over to talk to him. Paul was still trying to be very good because of his First Communion. He'd been to Communion every Sunday since, and every Saturday he went to confession, too. There'd been only about three Sundays since, though. Tommy didn't have a First Communion. In Tommy's church you didn't take Communion until you'd been confirmed, and that didn't happen until sixth grade, when you were twelve, and had learned your catechism. You had to learn it by heart, just as Paul did, and then you were confirmed and then you could take Communion, just like the grown-ups, and drink the wine from the cup. It was real wine, too, but it wasn't something for children.

"What happens when you make your First Communion?" Tommy asked him.

"You stick your tongue out," Paul said, "and the priest puts Jesus on it and you let it melt and swallow it. You're not supposed to chew it."

"Come on," Tommy said. He didn't believe a word of it. Jesus on your tongue!

"No, it *is* Jesus," Paul said. "He lives in a little house on the altar, and the nuns take care of it but only the priest can touch it. Nobody else can touch it at all."

"Why not?"

"Because it's the sacred Host," Paul said. "It would be a sacrilege to touch it. It's the body and blood of our Lord. It really is. The Church says so."

"It is not," Tommy said. "It's bread and wine." He didn't care if the Church did say so, even if, as Paul said, the Church was the one true church, not like Tommy's. He didn't believe that, either.

"No," Paul said, louder. "It just looks like bread and wine, but it really isn't. It's really the body and blood of Jesus. I learned all about it. It's not what it looks like," he said, wiping his nose with his hand.

"What does it taste like?" Tommy asked him.

"It doesn't taste like anything," Paul said. "It tastes sort of like paper."

"Then it can't be the body and blood of Jesus," Tommy said. "That's just a story."

"Yes it can too!" Paul cried. His nose was running. He was getting mad. "It's not just a story. It's a mystery, and you have to take it on faith."

A mystery, Tommy thought. He knew about mysteries. He knew Paul was starting to feel bad, too, and even though he didn't play with Paul very much, or think of him as a real friend, he didn't want him to feel bad, either. Paul had enough things to feel bad about, Tommy thought, with his father dead and his family so poor. He'd better stop teasing him. There were nice things about Paul. He was good at marbles and had a lot of them that he kept in a pouch, and he could throw his jackknife in the dirt and make it stick there, too. Sometimes Paul let Tommy try it, and Tommy got so that he could do it almost as well as Paul. That was fun. "Let's play," Tommy said. "Do you want to play?" And he and Paul played a game with Paul's jackknife that they called "Piece of Pie" because you drew a circle in the dirt and that's what it looked like, a pie. Then you threw the jackknife and drew a line from the center of the pie to where the knife stuck and you put the other guy's marble in it. That was the piece of pie. When Paul threw the jackknife, he put one of Tommy's marbles in his slice. The game went on like that. The idea was to make the wedges as thin as possible so that you got more of the other guy's marbles. Usually Paul won, and he would slip Tommy's marbles into his pouch. But he didn't always win. Tommy won sometimes, and Jimmy Randolph won a lot. He was older, though.

Amy saw them playing from her front yard and came over to watch, and then Jimmy Randolph rode by on his new bike. He rode back and forth several times, just showing off, Tommy thought. Finally Jimmy stopped because he wanted to get in the game and win some marbles. Tommy was sorry that Jimmy and Amy had come over because he'd just gotten the conversation back to Paul's First Communion and confession. They were delicate subjects that Tommy was interested in, and it was easy to hurt Paul's feelings and then he wouldn't talk about it. So Tommy was being very sympathetic. Paul had told him that before you made your First Communion you had to go to confession to tell God your sins. The first time he'd done it he was real scared. Then the priest told him to say some prayers and he was forgiven. The prayers were penance. They didn't have that in Tommy's church. You told God your sins all by yourself and He forgave you, and you didn't have to do anything for it, just be sorry. In fact, Tommy had never even done it; he'd never told Him. In Paul's church you told the priest, but Paul said you pretended you were talking to Jesus. You knelt down and it was dark and you couldn't see the priest, just his shadow. He couldn't see you either, but Paul said he thought the priest knew who you were anyway. It was almost like talking to Jesus, though, because the priest would never tell what you'd said, not even on pain of death. It was the sacred vow that he'd made.

"How do you know what to confess?" Tommy asked him.

"They tell you," Paul said. "The nuns tell you what you've probably done wrong, and then you tell it to the priest."

"Well, like what do you say?" Tommy asked him.

"Oh," Paul said, "you have to tell him if you've stolen anything"—Tommy knew about that, and he knew that Paul had done it, too, but he didn't mention it this time—"if you've disobeyed your mother or the teachers, if you've had any impure thoughts."

Impure thoughts. That was a new one. "What does that mean?" Tommy asked. Jimmy Randolph and Amy were there now.

"It's like bad thoughts," Paul said, "sort of like committing adultery. You can't spend a lot of time washing yourself in the bathtub, or spying on your sister when she's getting dressed." Paul giggled. He had a dirty giggle, as if he'd been spying on his sister. He probably had.

"Then Lily Slade has impure thoughts all the time," Jimmy said. "She always wants to get me to take my pants down, but I won't do it. Tommy did, though." Jimmy pointed his finger at him, laughing.

"That's a lie," Tommy said. It was a lie, too. Jimmy took his pants down first, and he said he'd seen Jenny do it too and she had hair. That was more than Tommy had ever done. He had taken his pants down with Amy Steer, though. Amy did too, but Jimmy didn't know that and Tommy wasn't about to tell him. Anyway, it had been a long time since he'd done it. Amy was leaning against the tree. She didn't say a word.

"Ha, ha," Paul said. "You'll go to hell. You took your pants down in front of Lily Slade and you lied about it, too. *Hell, hell, double hell,*" he sang. "You'd better tell the priest you're sorry."

"*Hell, hell, double hell,*" Jimmy Randolph chanted after him, pointing his finger at Tommy. "*Hell, hell, double hell.*"

"I'm going home," Tommy said. Amy had already left. She didn't like the conversation.

It really was a mystery, Tommy thought, as he walked toward his house, the chant still ringing in his ears, but it must be nice, to have somebody tell you that the bad things you'd done were forgiven and that no one but you and God and the priest would ever know that you'd done them, and the priest could never tell, not even if you'd murdered somebody, not even if you'd stolen something from somebody. Tommy thought he would like the Catholic school. Amy went there, but she wasn't a Catholic and didn't have to take religion with everybody else. Mr. Steer saw to that. It was just like Mr. Steer—contrary. He wouldn't let Amy go to the public school, but he wouldn't let her take religion in the Catholic school. He wouldn't let Amy be baptized, either. Tommy had been baptized when he was a baby. He'd seen his christening dress. It was the same one his brothers had worn, and it was real long. Tommy didn't like it.

When Tommy told Mrs. Steer about the mysteries that Paul had told him, Mrs. Steer said that it was all a lot of superstition and she didn't like their talking about it. Mrs. Steer didn't like religion, either, and she didn't like it when Tommy had tried to get Amy to go to Sunday school with him. Mrs. Steer was nice about it, though, and Tommy didn't care if Amy belonged to the Church or not. He just wanted company, and he thought Amy would like the stories from the Bible, the stories about David and Goliath, Samson and Delilah, Absalom, the wise King Solomon, John the Baptist, and the rest. But both Mr. and Mrs. Steer thought the stories were too bloody. They weren't all bloody, Tommy thought, and some of them were really interesting when the teacher told them to you. Sunday school was over for the year, anyway. It always ended at the same time as regular school.

TOMMY and his family moved to the Island a few days after Tommy's parents came back from John's graduation. John was getting the summer off—"for good behavior," his father said—but David had to keep on working, at least until August, when maybe he could have some time off too. Because David was going to work every morning—he had to be at work a lot earlier than his father—and would be sleeping most nights in town, and because his mother would be spending a lot of time there because of all the details connected with her anniversary party, they weren't packing up and closing the house the way they usually did, with sheets draped over all the furniture. Moving was a simple matter this time, with none of the bustle of earlier years. They just packed up a few clothes and went. And the week after that, one of the Indians started rowing Tommy back over to the shore two mornings a week for his golf lesson from Emil, the pro. The lessons were as bad as Tommy had feared, but at least Emil was nice and didn't make fun of him. Tommy wished that he were old enough to be trusted in a boat by himself, but he wasn't; the current was too swift, and the eddies dangerous. At least he got to walk to the country club by himself, though, up from the dock and across the road and cutting across the fairway to the clubhouse and the pro shop, where he met Emil, if Emil wasn't already waiting for him by the practice tee. Sometimes John and Emily rowed him over—they played golf a lot—and sometimes his mother went with him if she was playing or going uptown on some errands, and sometimes Daisy rowed him over. She and Phil had the Addington cottage now, since Mrs. Addington had moved in with her mother last summer, but they weren't always there. And once in a while, after Mr. Wolfe arrived, he would row him over.

Although Tommy didn't enjoy the lesson, he did like washing the balls and setting them up on the little colored tees, and he did finally learn to hit the ball with the mashie so that it would go up in the air—usually, anyway—and land somewhere out there in the general direction of the hole. Emil said he was doing great, but Tommy knew better. He was doing about as great as Mrs. Appleton, who seemed to spend every single summer day rocking on the porch with her friends, who were all like Mrs. Appleton but not quite so bad, maybe. At least they weren't afraid of cats. He could see the women watching him as he practiced his lesson. He wished they wouldn't look; it made him feel silly. He didn't mind so much if Buck watched him. Buck never sat on the porch— he couldn't because the Negroes weren't allowed to—but he used to sit on the grass sometimes near the practice tee, watching Tommy learn. Buck said he'd never learn, but he knew plenty of other things that were more interesting than golf. Tommy was glad that Buck had arrived for the summer. Tommy showed him the kaleidoscope his mother had given him for his birthday. "Pretty," Buck said, holding it up to his eye. "Real pretty. What's it do?"

"That's what it does," Tommy said. "It makes pretty patterns. Turn it and everything starts to move. All the colors whirl around and you never get the same picture twice."

"Doesn't look like a picture to me," Buck said, "no picture I ever saw. Just a lot of colors."

"Well, that's what it is," Tommy said, "but aren't they pretty?"

"Guess so," Buck said.

"Next time I'll show you my telescope. I'll bet you've never seen a telescope. I bet you don't even know what a telescope is."

"I know plenty," Buck said.

"Yeah," Tommy said, "but you've never seen a telescope. You can see things through a telescope. If I pointed it way down the golf course, I could see who that person is. It would bring her up close."

282

"It would?"

"Yes, it would," Tommy said. "The next time I come over I'll show you how it works." Sometimes at home at night, before they moved to the Island, Tommy would open his window and take off the screen and step out on the porch roof. He would point his telescope at the sky, at the Milky Way, and it really would bring it close. Nobody knew he was doing it. Sometimes then it made him feel as if he were floating, floating right off the roof and into the sky, and that he was part of it, part of the whole vast sky, with his town, his river, and the great big earth there below him. "It's wonderful," Tommy said, "it really is. It's magical."

"No shit," Buck said. Buck could use words like that. Tommy could tell he was impressed.

"No shit," Tommy replied. He couldn't believe he'd said that. He thought someone would run out of the clubhouse and wash his mouth out with soap, the way his brother John did once when he'd said a bad word and he didn't even know what he'd said, either. He didn't know what it meant—he couldn't even remember the word—and John wouldn't tell him. Tommy looked back at the clubhouse, but nothing was happening. The women were still rocking on the porch, and the figure at the farthest end of the course, beyond the driveway, was a little closer. But no one was running toward him. No one even knew he'd said it. Tommy smiled. He laughed. He felt proud. "No shit," he repeated. "Really, no shit."

"Where'd you get it?" Buck asked.

"Mrs. Steer gave it to me," Tommy said.

"Will you let me look through it?"

"Sure," Tommy said. "I'll bring it over the next time I come. Then you'll see."

Ophelia was calling. "Buck? Buck? Get in here, Buck. I've got some things for you to do." So Buck went off and Tommy sat alone in the tall grass on the slope between the sixth hole and the River Road, thinking about the things that had changed, watching the figure of the golfer draw nearer. He could see now that it was Daisy Meyer, and one of the things that had changed was that Daisy and Phil weren't spending as much time on the Island, even though they had the Addington cottage to themselves. In fact, Phil was hardly ever there.

SOME things really were different. The Farnsworth cottage was closed, for one thing, and Nick was gone. Tommy missed Nick, who was always nice to him, but he bet his brothers missed him more because they always went to the parties in his cottage, the parties for the younger people that sometimes went on real late and real loud, loud enough and late enough that Mrs. Wentworth had to speak to Nick the next day. "He's plucked all the daisies," Tommy heard Mrs. Appleton say one day, "and he's gone to find another garden to play in." Tommy wanted to throw another cat in her lap. Buck thought that was real funny. Ophelia had told him. "She swore that apple lady was going to rise up and shake hands with her Maker right there on the couch in the ladies' locker room," Buck had said, and Tommy replied, "Well, she didn't."

Another thing that was different was that the Aldriches hadn't shown up at all and weren't expected until late in the summer because Mr. Aldrich was now stationed in Spain, and it was hard to get to the Island from Spain. Tommy's mother said that Michael was learning to speak Spanish. The McGhees and Madge and Phelps might come, no one knew for sure. Mr. Wolfe wasn't there yet, either, but the Indians were opening his house so he'd be there soon. On the whole, it was lonelier on the Island this summer. He had only Amy to play with, and he missed Jimmy Randolph and even Paul Malotte.

But some things were the same. The bridges had to be repaired again. Mrs. Steer went swimming every morning, back and forth between her dock and Boomer Island in her steady, measured crawl. The Sedgwicks worried about the erosion. Mr. Steer got into the same old arguments with Mrs. Sedgwick and Mrs. Steer got annoyed with him and Amy got embarrassed. Mrs. Wentworth still invited the children in for milk and cookies sometimes in the afternoons—"my little tea parties," she said, "for my little friends." The forget-me-nots bloomed by the paths and the lady slippers in the woods, and the cattails appeared in the marshy place on the Sedgwicks' island. And as usual, there were parties in the evenings at one or another cottage on the Island or at the country club on the shore. It was good that the club was so convenient. Some people, like Mr. and Mrs. Hutchins, had summer places farther away and it was harder for them to get there, but they did sometimes, especially if there was a big party. Sometimes they spent the night on the Island, too, usually in the Sedgwicks' guesthouse, which Tommy loved to sleep in because it was like being on a ship with the waves lapping. The Hutchins and a lot of other people were there the night of the Fourth of July when everyone gathered on the Sedgwicks' shrinking but still spacious front lawn and waved sparklers and watched the fireworks that the Indians set off. It was his mother's birthday party, too. She was forty-six. Her birthday was really on the third, but they always celebrated it on the fourth, with fireworks—"the way a birthday ought to be celebrated," his father said: "with a bang." It wasn't a big fireworks show—there were only a few of them—but it was very pretty, and it was fun to see the explosions bursting in the sky, the showers of colored sparks, the faces of the people in the dark suddenly illumined with a kind of pale flickering glow, like fireflies.

Mr. Wolfe had gotten there by the Fourth. Tommy liked watching the Indians prepare Mr. Wolfe's cottage, starting the pump, throwing open all the windows to drive out the smell of mildew, shaking the rugs and the curtains, brushing off the furniture, sweeping out the winter's debris. Mr. Wolfe had a lot of interesting things in his cottage, a lot of things he'd picked up from the Indians in Canada and from the ruins in Mexico: oddly shaped baskets, wampum belts, arrows, feathered headdresses, and strange masks. Mrs. Appleton asked Tommy one day at the country club if Mr. Wolfe was back yet. "I don't know," he said, although he knew perfectly well that he wasn't but that he would be soon because his cottage was all ready for him. "I thought you would," Mrs. Appleton said, "you know so much." Why, Tommy wondered, was she so interested, and why did she dislike him so much? Well of course, she didn't like him because of the cat, and Tommy didn't like her either. He was sorry that he'd ever apologized to her, but he hadn't really had a choice. His mother had made him.

When Mr. Wolfe did arrive, he came with a whole shipment of things, strange and wonderful things that he'd sent home from his travels—he'd been gone since March—and that the Indians had to spend a whole day loading into rowboats on the shore and unloading at Mr. Wolfe's dock and carrying the heavy crates up to the porch, where Mr. Wolfe unpacked them. He opened the crates himself because he wanted to inspect each one for damage, and because the things were valuable and rare. Most of them were very old, and some of them were stone. They made Mrs. Sedgwick's Guatemalan pottery look pretty ordinary, and Tommy thought she was sort of envious when she saw all the things Mr. Wolfe was putting on his walls.

"What are these?" Tommy asked him as he was unpacking one of the crates. They looked like wooden faces, but not like any living face. They were flat, without expression, almost sinister.

"They're old ceremonial masks," Mr. Wolfe said. "The Indians in Mexico used to wear them for their sacred dances. They still carve them, but the new ones aren't quite the same."

"Are they valuable?" Tommy asked him.

"Some of them are," Mr. Wolfe said as he continued his unpacking. "Some of them are. They're my South of the Border plunder." He laughed.

"Were you in Mexico?" Tommy asked him.

"Most of the time," he said. "I had to go to Canada for a little while, but it was too cold. You think it's cold here in the winter, Tommy? You should try it farther north. It'd freeze the balls off a maggot." Tommy didn't say anything. "So I went South. To Mexico." Mr. Wolfe was engrossed in his unpacking. "Oaxaca. Guadalajara. San Miguel de Allende. Teotihuacán. The Yucatán. All over. Then it got too hot."

"Do they still sacrifice warriors?" Tommy asked him.

"Sacrifice warriors?"

"Yes. They used to choose the bravest young warrior and sacrifice him. They cut out his heart," Tommy said. The thought still made him shudder.

"How do you know that?" Mr. Wolfe asked him. "No, they don't do that anymore. The Aztecs used to, but there aren't any real Aztecs left nowadays. You can still see the look of the Aztecs, though, and the Maya, too. Some of the Mexicans today look just like the figures on the temples so you know they're descended from them. But there's hardly any pure blood left there anymore. Most of them are all mixed up with the Spanish and other Indians, and the civilization's been lost. Just a vestige here and there. Nothing like what it was." He looked toward him. "How do you know about the Aztecs, Tommy?"

"I read about them in a book," Tommy said. "Not the book you gave me. One of my other books."

"Did you read the book I gave you?" Mr. Wolfe continued his unpacking.

"Oh, yes," Tommy said. "It was interesting."

"Oh, Bill," Mr. Wolfe called, "come over here and help me with this." Rose's husband came over to the crate Mr. Wolfe had opened. He was struggling with something at the bottom of it, but it was too big and too heavy for him to handle alone. Together the two of them tore the sides off the crate and pulled the packing away from the object within. They both took hold of it and lifted it out to the porch.

"That's a plumed serpent!" Tommy was astounded. Mr. Wolfe and Bill got it over next to the steps to the porch, where he'd decided it should go. "How do you pronounce it?" Tommy asked.

"Quetzalcóatl? Is that what you mean?"

"Yes," Tommy said, "that's what I mean. I didn't know how you said it, though."

"How did you know what it was? Was that in one of your books, too?"

"Yes," Tommy said. "I think that's where I saw it. In one of my books."

"Well, I've got another one, too, in one of these crates. I'll put it on the other side of the steps. They'll guard the house. I think they'd scare anyone away, don't you?"

Mr. Wolfe had almost finished opening his crates. "I think I've got something for you," he said. His hands were rummaging in one of the boxes. "Here." He picked up a mask. "This looks about your size. Try it on."

Tommy held it to his face. The mask was long and narrow. He couldn't see anything because the slits they'd carved for the eyes weren't big enough. "I can't see through it," Tommy said. "Did they use this one in their sacred dances? I don't see how they could dance if they couldn't see."

"Good question," Mr. Wolfe said. "Maybe they peeked." He laughed.

It was an interesting mask, though. Tommy liked it, but no matter how he held it to his face, he couldn't see a thing through the tiny slits in the eyes. After a while he hung it on the wall in his bedroom on the Island, so different from his bedroom at home. The window, the only window, looked into the trees, and at night Tommy could hear the animals out there, creeping through the woods. Mr. Wolfe had given him a lot of presents. Tommy thought he'd have to find something for Mr. Wolfe one of these days.

AFTER Mr. Wolfe had unpacked all his things and arranged the masks and the sculptures, he gave a party. He called it "my plunder party," and all the Islanders and some others came to it, passing by the two plumed serpents as they moved onto Mr. Wolfe's porch and into his house. Mrs. Sedgwick was horrified. "Couldn't you find anything pretty down there, Lucien? Snakes! My word! Do they bite?" She didn't think the masks on the walls looked very pretty either, though she didn't say anything; she just looked. Mrs. Steer did, though. She said, "It looks as if we're preparing for the sacrifice. When do we begin the dance?" Everyone laughed at that.

"Why, the dance is the last day of August," Tommy's mother said. "Thursday night. We'll all be there—but without masks, I hope," and everyone laughed some more. The dance was a long time away, more than a month.

"Perhaps," Mrs. Steer said, "we should keep them on," but in the general conversation nobody paid any attention.

Mr. Wolfe didn't show any movies that evening, no movies like the animal movies he'd shown last summer. He hadn't shot much film this past year, he said. Tommy was sorry about that. He liked the movies. It was raining that evening, so the party couldn't spread out onto the lawn. When they had eaten, Emily and John walked Amy and Tommy to their cottages, Amy first because hers was farther away. Tommy could hear the sounds of Mr. Wolfe's party far into the night. Sounds carried over water.

His parents were arguing when they got home. They hardly ever argued, and they made a lot of clatter when they came in, waking Tommy up, although at first he thought he hadn't even fallen asleep. But he must have. The walls in the cottage were thin, and you could hear anything that happened anywhere in the house. He heard his mother say, "You might care less about those filthy smokestacks and more about this party we're supposed to be giving. I'm sick of doing all the work myself." And his father said, "Those filthy smokestacks are paying for it! How do you think we're paying for it? You think someone else is going to do it? You're good at giving parties. You wanted it, you do it."

"I'm paying too," his mother said. "All this work doesn't come free, no matter what you think!"

"Neither do you," his father said. "I hope no one thinks you do. You're a very expensive lady and you don't come free at all. I'm paying through the nose. Look, leave me alone. I've got to go to work in the morning. I have to tend to the filthy smokestacks. I want some sleep."

"I wish you wouldn't drink," his mother said. "It doesn't make you very attractive."

"You wish *I* wouldn't drink? What do you think that stuff *you're* drinking is? Tea?"

"We've been to a nice party," his mother said. "Why do you always have to start a fight when we leave?"

"I'm going into the bathroom, and then I'm going to bed. Good night." Tommy heard his father slam the bathroom door, and his mother went into their bedroom and slammed that door, too. When his father came out of the bathroom, he said, "What was so nice about it?" And his mother said, "Oh, be quiet. Leave me alone. I want to sleep." Tommy wanted to sleep, too. Why did they have to do that? They weren't the only ones in the house. He lived there, too.

Tommy had a golf lesson the next morning. He had golf lessons on Mondays and Thursdays. That morning his father rowed him across the river, on his way to the plant. "Did you have a good time at the party?" Tommy asked him.

"Oh, yes," his father said, "I had a fine time."

"What do you think of Mr. Wolfe's masks?"

"Interesting," his father answered, dipping the oars into the water. He was concentrating on his rowing. There was a good way to get to the shore and a bad way. Experienced rowers like his father knew how to do it. The good way looked harder, and it was at first, but it was really easier. You left the dock and rowed upriver for a little ways, against the current, and then you turned and the current helped carry you toward the landing on the shore. His father was still rowing hard against the current. He wasn't paying much attention to the conversation, Tommy thought.

"Did you like the plumed serpents?" Tommy asked.

"The plumed serpents? Oh, you mean those figures by the porch." They were turning now in the current and began to glide swiftly toward the shore, carried along by the river and his father's pulling. The oars made little whirlpools in the water as he rowed, dissolving behind them as they pushed ahead. There was a regular rhythm to it. "Well," his father said, "I guess I've never much cared for snakes but you'd hardly know they were snakes, would you? I wouldn't have known if Mr. Wolfe hadn't shown us."

"Mr. Wolfe showed you?"

"He told us what they were. There's a temple down there with hundreds of them on it. They're supposed to help fertilize the earth. I'd stick to horse manure, myself." They had arrived at the dock. Tommy got out of the boat while his father held it for him, and then he tied it up with a double half-hitch. That was the knot they always used.

His father drove away, and Tommy ran across the River Road and climbed through the tall grass and cut across the fairways to the practice tee. You had to circle around the green because you were supposed to walk on it only if you were playing it. The grass was easily damaged. Emil wasn't waiting at the tee that morning, so Tommy went into the pro shop. "I'll be with you in a minute, Tommy," Emil said. He was showing a new putter to a couple of the ladies. Tommy looked at the tennis racquets and the golf clubs that were displayed on the wall, and at the new leather golf bags. Leather ones were the best. He liked their smell. He looked through the glass counter at the funny gloves with little holes in them that some people used when they played, and at the different-colored tees and the gleaming white balls. There were a lot of different kinds of golf balls, but Acushnet Titleist were the best. Everyone said so. Emil had a little machine in the pro shop that stamped your name on your golf balls. That way, if you lost it and if someone found it, he could return it to you. Sometimes people did lose their golf balls. The woods were thick, and even in the rough they were hard to find. People drove them into the creek, too. There were three creeks. One was at the very end of the golf course. It was called Mission Creek because many, many years ago there'd been an Indian mission up there someplace. You had to hit your ball right over the green and off the course to land it in that one, and then it was lost forever. People had drowned in Mission Creek. The main creek was right near the fourth tee. It didn't have a name. You had to drive over it to reach the green. It was supposed to be an easy shot, but a lot of people didn't make it. Every once in a while the caddies would jump in the creek in their underpants, if no one was looking, and dive for balls. They would return them to the owner, but it was really like selling them back because they always got paid for them, though his father called it a tip. Sometimes, Tommy supposed, they probably used them themselves; the caddies could use the course early in the morning before anyone started to play.

"Let me show you something, Tommy," Emil said. He had finished showing the putter to the two women, and they had left. He put a golf ball into the stamper, pressed the handle, took it out, and handed it to Tommy. "See?"

Tommy looked. There on a fresh new ball was his name, "THOMAS MACALLISTER," black against the whiteness of the ball. "Gee," Tommy said. "Gee, Emil, thanks. Thanks a lot." He smiled. He held the ball in his hand, looking at it. He rubbed it against his shirt. He looked again. The name hadn't rubbed off. "Hey, my own golf ball," he said. "I love it." He admired it again. "Thanks, Emil. Thanks," and he slipped the ball into his pocket.

"Not in your pocket, Tommy. You're going to use it. Let's head for the tee."

"Can I use it?"

"You have to use it. Now let's take a few practice swings," Emil said when they got to the tee. "Remember, keep your head down and your left arm straight. Don't bend it at all. Keep your left arm straight, and your right leg. Only the right arm and the left leg bend." Tommy tried it. "That's better," Emil said. "Do it again, and remember to follow through." So Tommy practiced several times, holding the mashie, trying to keep his eye on the imaginary ball, trying to remember which arm and which leg to keep straight, which to bend. He knew, but it was harder to do than to know. "That's a lot better," Emil said, "a lot better. It's all in the form. Now take that ball back out of your pocket and slam it."

"Do I have to use my new ball?" Tommy asked.

"Use the new one," Emil said. "You've got to use it sometime and you might as well start now." Emil set it up on a yellow tee. That would make it easier, he said.

Tommy bent his head, staring at the ball without blinking. He was afraid it might disappear if he blinked. And he swung the club back and smacked the ball—right up into the air! Up, up it went, in a smooth arc through the air, and then it began to drop to the fairway. Tommy was astonished. So was Emil. He whooped. "That was great! That was just great! Tommy, you keep that up and you'll be a golfer in no time. You'll be as good as your brothers someday. Now let's try it again." Tommy did it a few more times, but none of his shots was as good as the first. Some of them were pretty bad, just like always. But at least he was learning, he thought. He'd done it once. For the first time he thought he might actually learn to hit the ball where it was supposed to go, and he was very pleased.

When his lesson was over he told Emil, "That was fun." It had never been fun before. Emil was fun, but not the lesson. This time the lesson was fun, too, and when it was over he

292

went into the clubhouse and rang the bell and asked Ophelia if he could have a Coke.

"You look at me, Tommy," Ophelia said. "You supposed to have Cokes?"

"Oh, yes," Tommy said, "it's all right."

"Don't seem all right to me," Ophelia said. "You know how your mamma feels about Cokes. You can't fool old Ophelia. But maybe we can find a root beer. Maybe we can even find some ice cream," and Ophelia made him a root beer float. That was fine; really he liked that better than a Coke. After he drank it he went out to the side porch—he wanted to avoid Mrs. Appleton—and in a few minutes Buck came ambling around the corner from the back of the clubhouse. They had their own porch back there, off the kitchen, but Tommy had never been on it. It was just for the help and their friends.

"When you going to show me that telescope?" Buck asked him.

"Shit," Tommy said, "I keep forgetting it." He'd said it again. He could hardly believe his ears, but he liked what he heard. "Shit. I'll get it the next time I go uptown and then I'll bring it over. I'm sorry." Tommy wanted to tell Buck about his golf lesson, but since Buck wasn't allowed to play he decided not to. He told him about Mr. Wolfe's masks from Mexico instead, and about the two stone snakes. He made a good story out of it.

"They poisonous?" Buck asked.

"Oh, yes," Tommy said. "One bite and you're dead."

"Deader than if a moccasin bit you?"

"Yeah," Tommy said. "A lot deader." Tommy had never seen a water moccasin, but there were moccasins in Kentucky and Buck had seen lots of them. He'd even picked one up, but it didn't bite him. He knew how to do it. You had to grab them quick behind the ears.

"Well, you take care around them snakes," Buck said. "Snakes is *bad*."

"Buck," Tommy asked him, "have you ever done anything bad?"

"Ain't never done nothin' good," Buck said.

"I mean really bad."

"Don't know that I'd tell you if I did. Why? You done somethin' bad?"

"I think so," Tommy said. He felt funny in his stomach.

"What?"

"Well, one night I hid under the dining-room table," Tommy said, "when my parents were having a party. I hid under the table." Tommy felt terrible. He felt as if something might happen, he didn't know what. Buck was looking at him as if he were crazy.

"You white as a ghost," he said. "That all?"

"And one day I took a letter and hid it."

"Shit," Buck said. "That don't sound so bad to me. That ain't bad like bad be bad."

"It was though," Tommy said. "It was. I have to go now," and Tommy ran across the golf course and down the slope through the tall grass and across the River Road and down the hill to the river, where he sat on the dock and waited. He knew that eventually someone would come over in a boat, one of the Indians or one of the Islanders, and row him back to the Island. He hoped it wouldn't be anyone he didn't want to see, and there was hardly anyone he did want to see right then.

After a while Mr. Sedgwick came out of his channel in his launch, and he gave Tommy a ride back. Tommy liked riding in Mr. Sedgwick's launch. It went fast and made a lot of noise, so you couldn't talk. Tommy sat in the back and watched the waves Mr. Sedgwick made with his boat. When he got to the Island he sat on the Farnsworth porch for a while, leaning against the shuttered door and watching the river flowing.

TOMMY's father went to work most days, rowing himself across the river and driving to the plant. David spent a lot of time uptown. He slept there most nights, and if his father had to work late, as he often did, he would sleep there, too. John spent as much time as he could with Emily, at the Sedgwicks' or playing golf. Sometimes they went into town to the movies or dancing at the country club. His mother spent a lot of time doing the things she did, and some of them involved going uptown, too. There were a lot of things to be done for her party, and most of them had to be done uptown. "Sometimes I hate living in two houses," she told Tommy. "It's difficult. Whatever you want is always in the other house. Always."

Tommy went up with her the day after his first good golf lesson. He wanted to get the telescope, and she let him stay there alone in the house while she ran her errands and did the many things she had to do. The house was different in the summer, cool and silent. It hardly ever happened that Tommy was there all by himself, and he liked it. He got the telescope first thing from his dresser top and put it on the table near the door so he wouldn't forget it. He sat in the brown silk chair in the living room for a while, the chair that felt so cool to his touch and that his mother kept intending to move, and looked at a magazine. Then he went back upstairs to his desk. He rolled back the top and looked at his things. He took the key from its hiding place and opened his locked drawer. Nothing had changed. There was the big box of crayons; there was the case with the fountain pen his father had given him. He opened the case. The pen lay there, held in its place by the two tiny elastics. Tommy touched it. He took it from his drawer and slipped it out of its case. He held the pen in his hand, looking at it, examining it. He took off the cap and touched the point and looked through the window that showed if there was ink in it. The pen still looked as new as it did the day his father had given it to him. Tommy had never filled it. He'd never actually tried to use it; he'd just held it in his hand sometimes and pretended. There was ink downstairs. He went to find it. There were several bottles. One said royal blue, one said blue-black, and one was simply black. Tommy looked at the bottles of ink, trying to decide. The blue was pretty. It was a very bright blue. He opened the blue-black, but he didn't like that so much. He looked at the bottle of black ink. His pen was black. That would be right for his pen. It was a serious pen. He took the bottle upstairs, set it on his desk, and filled his pen. It was messy, filling a pen, and harder than it looked. He got ink on the barrel, and he went into the bathroom to find some paper to wipe it off. He thought he'd better put the top back on the bottle of ink before he knocked it over and spilled it. He was always spilling things. It said permanent. Maybe you could never get it out. He looked through the little window. You couldn't see through it now; all you saw was the black ink. He liked the way it smelled. He took a piece of paper from his desk and tested the pen. He made a stroke, and there was the stroke, black on the paper. He made another stroke, and another black line appeared. It worked. He was making marks with his pen. He decided to practice writing. They hadn't had script yet in school, but he'd watched the older people doing it often enough and he began to try. He would write his name in ink. It took him a long time, and he dropped some blobs of ink on the paper. He got it on his fingers, too, but he wrote out *"Tommy MacAllister."* It didn't look very good. It didn't look like grown-ups' handwriting. He tried it again. This time he decided to write out his whole name, and finally he got it all down on the page: *"Andrew Thomas MacAllister."* There it was. His name. It still didn't look like much, but he'd practice, and he'd get better at it. He'd learn. Writing with a pen couldn't be harder than golf. Tommy was excited. It was the first time he'd ever written out his full name in grown-up script in ink. It didn't look very grown-up, actually. He looked at it, studying it for a while, and then he put his pen and the paper with his name written on it back into his locked drawer. He would look at it the next time he was in town. He didn't want to take the pen to the Island because he was afraid that he'd lose it, and he did not want to lose it. The telescope was too big to lose.

When his mother came home she had a lot of packages, and she asked Tommy to help her carry them in from the car. "I want to show you my new shoes," she said. Then she looked at him. "What have you got all over your hands? Tommy, what have you been into?"

"It's ink," Tommy said. "I filled my pen."

"Well let's wash that off right this minute. Don't touch anything." She took him to the sink in the kitchen and scrubbed at his fingers with a brush. The ink was hard to get off, and even after she'd scrubbed a long time you could see the dark smudges on his fingers. "Why did your father ever give you a fountain pen?" she asked. "You're much too young for it." After she'd gotten off as much of the ink as she could, enough so that it wouldn't stain anything, she and Tommy went to the car to carry in the packages. His brother John showed up then, and his mother remembered this time to ask John to carry the brown silk chair up to the big guest room. Then the three of them went into his mother's bedroom to see her new shoes.

She opened one of the boxes and pulled a pair of shoes from the tissue paper. She held them up. "What do you think of them?" she asked. They were red, and they had high heels and a lot of little straps and no backs.

John laughed.

"What's so funny?"

"What color are they?" John asked her.

"They're fuchsia," his mother said. "Fuchsia. I think it's a beautiful color."

"I think it looks like Madge McGhee," John said. "They look like something Madge McGhee would wear." Yes, Tommy thought, they did look like Miss Pink—shoes for Hot Pink. They were the color of her ink.

"Let me try them on," his mother said. "You can't really tell until I get them on." She took a while getting into the shoes. She had to slip her foot just so into the straps, otherwise they got tangled, and the buckles were tiny and hard to fasten. When she had gotten them on, she stood up, walked in a little circle in front of her dressing table, and said, "Well now, what do you think of them now?"

"Really?" John asked.

"Of course, really," his mother replied.

"I think they're lousy."

"Lousy!" His mother didn't like that at all. " 'Lousy' is not a word you use to your mother. I'm ashamed of you, John."

"Well, you asked," John said.

"You don't have to like them," his mother said. "I don't demand that you like them. But they are not lousy and I won't have you speaking to me like that. I don't care if you are twenty-two years old. Don't you dare talk to your mother

297

like that." She was really mad, and she was more than mad; she was disappointed. She liked her new shoes.

"I don't think they're so bad, Mommy," Tommy said. "I think they're pretty. But they sure have high heels."

"They'll make me taller," his mother said. She always wanted to be taller. It was hard to find the right clothes when you were short.

Tommy walked over to his mother and put his arm around her waist. She really was taller with the shoes on. "I like your shoes, Mommy," he said.

"Well, I'll think about them," his mother said. "If I decide they're too much, I'll return them."

"What's that?" Tommy pointed to a long package that had been sent from Saks Fifth Avenue in Chicago.

"It's a dress. I'm not showing it to either of you."

"I'll bet it matches your shoes," Tommy said, but his mother still refused to show them the dress or what was in the other packages, either.

While she was putting away her things in her room, Tommy asked John, "What's the matter with 'lousy'? What's it mean?"

"Mother's just being sensitive," John said. "She has been lately. You know how the kids in school sometimes have lice? Not you. The dirty kids. If they have lice, they're lousy."

"Well," Tommy said, "Mother certainly doesn't have lice. It's not as if you said 'shit.' "

"Boy," John said, "you're getting a filthy mouth. If Mother heard you say that, she'd drop dead."

"You're the one with the filthy mouth," Tommy said. "You told her her shoes were lousy, I didn't. And I've heard you say 'shit,' too."

"Scram," John said. "Just scram before I wash your mouth out with soap. I did it before and I can do it again."

"I'm learning," Tommy said. "I'm learning real fast," and he ran downstairs and got his telescope and waited for his mother to drive him back down to the shore.

John was usually so nice. Why was everyone so cross, he wondered. Why was everyone getting so mean? His mother hardly said a word in the car, and when they got to the dock there was no one there to row them over. His mother didn't like to row herself. "You'd think one of the Indians would be around," she said, growing more annoyed. Finally she said, "You wait here. I'm going up to the country club to phone for a boat. I'll be right back." She drove off to the club, but she was back in just a few minutes. As she was driving down the hill to the dock, Tommy could see a figure by the boathouse on the Island. He put the telescope to his eye and looked. Mr. Wolfe was coming to get them.

"We've had a little excitement here," he said to Tommy's mother while he held the boat against the dock so they could step into it. "In fact, we've had a lot of excitement. I'll tell you about it later." He gave Tommy's mother a look. That meant Tommy wasn't old enough to hear it.

"What happened?" he asked.

"Oh, just a little trouble among the Indians," Mr. Wolfe said. "They got in a fight. Nothing out of the ordinary. Nothing they haven't fought about before."

When they got to the Island, Tommy's mother told him to run along home, she had to talk to Mr. Wolfe, and the two of them walked slowly along the path in the dappled light toward Mr. Wolfe's cottage. Tommy could hear his mother's exclaiming, and her gay laughter. He couldn't hear what they were saying, but he'd find out. And he did, too. It didn't take long at all. He found out about it that very night when everyone was having a drink before dinner at Mr. Treverton's to discuss what ought to be done and, as usual, they thought the children weren't listening. Besides, there weren't any Indians around.

Rose had gotten into a terrible fight. She'd caught her husband in one of the Indians' houses with Lena, and she'd taken a knife and grabbed Bill by the hair and tried to scalp him. She would have scalped Lena, too, but Lena jumped up and ran into the woods and she could run faster than Rose because Rose was so fat. As far as anyone knew, Lena was still out there, hiding in the woods, and no one had seen hide nor hair of Rose.

"She's probably sleeping it off," Mr. Sedgwick said. "You pay them and they just buy whisky, and then they do this."

Bill had run out of the house and over to Mr. Steer's. It

299

was the closest place. He was wearing just a pair of pants. "He must have grabbed them in a hurry," Mr. Steer said. He was snorting with laughter. He was laughing so hard he was spilling his drink. "Blood was pouring out of his head and running down his face," Mr. Steer said. It didn't sound so funny to Tommy. "I never saw anything like it." Mr. Steer put Bill right in his boat, the outboard, and took him to shore and sped to the hospital. "I made him hold his head out the window," he said. "He bled all over the car. I had to hose it off. He's at the hospital now. Dr. Randolph said, 'Jesus Christ! The Indians are rising! This is the first scalping I've ever seen.' He told Bill, 'Your wife must be some wild Indian.' " Everyone laughed. "Bill's going to be all right, though. It looked worse than it was," Mr. Steer said. "He'll be out of the hospital tomorrow and back in trouble the day after next. He won't need a haircut for a while, though." There was a lot of laughter, and then they all began talking at once, wondering what to do about it.

"Lock up the liquor," Mrs. Addington said. "That's one thing we could do about it. I swear someone's been into mine," and they all talked about that for a while and agreed that it would be a good thing to do.

Tommy heard Mrs. Sedgwick's silvery voice: "Oh, what's a little adultery among friends?" That was what Tommy had asked Phil Meyer about that night on the country-club porch. He'd told Tommy he didn't need to worry about it.

Phil was at the party, too. "I'll pay for the hospital," he said.

"No," Tommy's father said, "let me." Mr. Treverton said he wanted to pay for it. Finally they decided they would split it among the Islanders.

"That's the Indians for you," Tommy's father said.

"All the wild Indians," Mrs. Steer said. "Regular Aztecs." Everyone laughed some more. There was a lot of laughter that night.

Tommy looked at Rose in a different light after that. Mild, sweet Rose who liked to eat ice cream, who worked in his house and often stayed with him at night, and she'd taken a knife to her husband and practically cut off his head. It was a mystery. The Islanders talked about it for a few days. It wasn't as shocking as Governor Wentworth's marrying his adopted daughter had been, but it was still pretty exciting and kept the conversation going for a while until everything settled back into its normal course. Rose seemed the same when she finally showed up again. Lena was the same. Bill had a bandage on his head for a while. Jim was the same. Harry, too. Really nothing had changed, among the Indians or the Islanders. Nothing at all.

TOMMY called Mrs. Slade the next day. He hadn't seen her in a long time and he'd never called her on the phone, but this was a pretty good story. She'd like it.

"Mrs. Slade, guess what happened," Tommy said.

"It's your pal, Maxine, remember? Call me Maxine. Well, what happened?"

"Rose scalped Bill, the Indian. She really did. Bill's in the hospital. Nobody's seen Rose yet."

"Holy shit," Mrs. Slade said. "I'd better keep an eye on old Bert." Bert was Mr. Slade. "I sure don't want to be scalped, and I don't need any more bandages, either. I've had enough."

"Mr. Slade's not an Indian."

"True, he's not," Mrs. Slade said. "He used to be pretty wild, though."

"And Mrs. Sedgwick said, 'What's a little adultery among friends?' and made everybody laugh."

"I guess they would," Mrs. Slade said. She was laughing, too. "I guess they would. What else is new?"

"Mr. Wolfe is back."

"I know."

"With a lot of masks and things from Mexico."

"I told you he'd go there. He likes it hot—but not too hot. What things?"

"He brought me a mask. It's made from wood."

"Take some advice from old Maxine. Wear it."

"I can't see through it. The eyes are too small. He brought some statues, too. Plumed serpents. Snakes. He put them beside his steps."

"That figures. He bring any movies?"

"No."

"Nothing he can show to the fancy folks, anyway. Maybe he can show them to the Indians."

"He didn't bring any. And everybody's going to lock up their liquor. Mrs. Addington said so. Someone's been drinking hers."

"Drinking Daisy's too, I'll bet. Tommy, that Island of yours is a wild place. You'd better come up here and see me. It's safer."

"I will," Tommy said. "As soon as I can. The next time I'm uptown I'll come over."

"You're a sweetheart, Tommy," Mrs. Slade said. "A real sweetheart. Thanks for calling. And you have any trouble, you just tell Maxine. I'll take care of it."

"You're a sweetheart, too, Mrs. Slade. Goodbye."

"Goodbye. And it's 'Maxine,' remember? And remember what I said. Remember!" That was her last word. Sometimes Tommy thought Mrs. Slade was just about the nicest person he knew, even if she was a dope fiend. She was always nice to him.

THE day after that, Tommy had another golf lesson and he remembered to take his telescope. After his lesson, he showed Buck how it worked.

"Wow," said Buck, after he'd gotten the hang of it. "Ain't that somethin'!" He handed it carefully back to Tommy. "You could do somethin' bad with this telescope, boy, somethin' *baddd.* Gimme that 'scope again." He pointed it toward the side porch, where Daisy was sitting talking to Bob Griswold. "You could spy right up that Daisy lady's skirt! See that Daisy lady's daisy! Now, that be *bad.* That be real bad. Your mamma, she spank you good for that."

"Don't," Tommy said.

"That man seen it, though. He see it regular. Bet your brother seen it, too. And that Nick man. I *know* he seen it."

"Don't do that," Tommy said, trying to move the telescope away from the porch. "That's not nice."

"Shit," Buck said. " 'Course it's not nice. It be bad, but it be fun," and he pointed the telescope back toward the porch, toward Bob and Daisy. "Shoot this 'scope right up that white skirt and see that white pussy! Wow! You better not look. One look at that pussy make that little pecker of yours stand up and sing Dixie. Gonna make mine spit like a snake in about half a minute!"

"What's pussy?" Tommy asked.

"Boy," Buck said, "don't you know nothin'? Come here. We're goin' down by the little creek and I'm going to tell you some things, some things it's time you be knowin'." Buck handed the telescope back to Tommy—he handled it like something precious—and together they walked along the creek that divided the seventh from the eighth fairway, and when they found a good spot they climbed down the bank and sat at the edge of the stream, out of sight. It was then that Buck told him about the things that men and women did together, the things that Junior and Bebe did all the time.

Just a couple of days ago, Buck said, Junior had taken him and Bebe fishing when Junior decided he wanted some of that lady. "Junior's only nineteen, but Bebe, she like 'em young," Buck said. "She say I'm too young, though. Maybe soon. Maybe next year." They handed Buck their fishing lines. Bebe sat on the stern seat, legs spread wide, dress pulled up around her shoulders, and Junior dropped his pants and said, "Boy, watch this!"

"It be somethin' to watch," Buck said. "That rod of his snapped up like a snake about to strike, and that rod Junior's got, it's one big rod, and Junior, he get down on his knees and he shove it to her. She like that. She like that as much as Junior like that."

Tommy sat rigid on the bank of the creek, listening to Buck describe the scene in minute, precise, and glistening detail: how Bebe was all hairy and wet and slick as grease between her legs; how Junior stuck this enormous thing right in her and how Bebe swung her legs around his shoulders; how they banged away and jumped around so much they almost swamped the boat, and made so much racket they scared all the fish; how Junior pulled it out and stood up and finished off right there on top of her. "His stuff, it just pumped out of that big prick and shot all over those tits. Lucky she didn't get it in the eye. Would've blinded her. She try to catch it, too. She like it in her mouth. Junior's prick, maybe it be black in the morning, but I swear right then it was red as a whore's cunt!" Buck told him how stuff had oozed out of Bebe's cunt —"you know, pussy, 'cause it's furry like a cat, and man does it purr when you tickle it"—and how she'd dipped her finger into it, held it up to the wind, and said, "Boy, sniff this! Ain't nothing so sweet as fresh jism in a hot woman!"

Tommy had never heard some of Buck's words before, but he more or less managed to understand. At last, after he'd made him repeat the story again, Tommy said, "I have to go eat my sandwich," and he walked back up the fairway alone to the clubhouse. He didn't want to hear any more. Maybe only the Negroes do it, Tommy thought, maybe only the Negroes. He looked for Buck after he'd eaten some of his lunch, but he was busy.

The next morning Tommy told his mother he wanted to play at the country club again.

"Why?" she asked him.

"I want to practice my golf," he said.

"That's good. You go practice. John will row you over. Call when you're ready to come back and I'll send someone for you." So Tommy went back to the country club. He found Buck in back of the clubhouse.

"Only Negroes do that," he told him.

"Do what?" Buck asked.

"Do those things you were telling me about yesterday."

"Shit, boy, you didn't learn your lesson," Buck said. "You be *real* dumb. I told you. I told you *everybody* do it. The whole wide world do it. Those Indians of yours, those Indians over there on your island, they do it. Always gettin' in trouble over it, too. That Daisy lady, she do it. She *love* to do it. Yeah, you be surprised who do it. Even that apple lady, she done it, but she forgot how. She need Junior to show her. He'd show her real good. Everybody do it, Tommy. You'll do it, too, when that little pecker of yours gets big enough. When you get big like Buck here"—he grabbed himself between his legs and stretched up tall—"you'll do it. You'll learn, unless you be a whole lot dumber than you look, a whole lot dumber. I told you the truth, boy. You remember that. You remember that old black Buck, the nigger boy, you remember he told you the truth."

Tommy didn't stay at the club for lunch. He didn't call his mother, either. He thought he'd sit on the dock and wait. He'd take his shoes and socks off and dangle his feet in the water and watch the minnows swim around them, trying to nibble at his legs and toes. Someone would come along sooner or later. He was thinking about his mother's big party. He and Amy were going to cut down a lot of cattails the day before the party, and then the Indians were going to soak them in kerosene and tie them on poles that they'd stick in the ground. When it got dark and people were ready to go home, they would light the cattails and the long driveway would be lined with torches, all the way out to the River Road. It would be beautiful. He hoped he'd get to see it. His mother was really working on her plans now. The invitations had to go out next week, and the list was growing longer and longer. It was hard to leave people out, when you were having a really big party. Tommy wondered if Mrs. Slade would be invited. She might be. She was Margie's aunt, so they were practically related. After a while Jim showed up and rowed Tommy over to the Island. He didn't say a word. There wasn't anything to say unless he talked about the trouble with Bill and Rose and Lena, and he certainly couldn't do that. Tommy told Jim he could drop him at the Aldriches', it was closer, so Jim rowed him to the Aldrich dock, in silence, and then rowed silently off. The Indians could be awfully quiet.

There was a snake sunning itself on one of the flat stones near the Aldrich dock. It was a garter snake. Garter snakes were harmless. Mrs. Steer said they ate bugs, and she was happy when she saw one in her garden. There were a lot of them on the Island. This one was medium-sized. Tommy had seen a lot bigger ones, but he'd seen smaller ones, too. He stood very still, his eye on the snake. He didn't want to scare it away. The snake looked very sleepy, stretched out there in the sun. It wasn't even curled up. Sometimes snakes were. Tommy had an idea. He crept closer to the snake. Suddenly he grabbed it

305

right behind the ears, and he ran with it, the snake wriggling all the way, from the Aldriches' to his house and behind his cottage, where he found a box and dropped the snake into it and snapped the lid on quick. The snake didn't like it. Tommy put a stone on top of the box, and went off to pull some grass and leaves and a couple of buttercups. He opened the box a crack and dropped them in. The snake was still wriggling. Tommy wondered if he had enough air. Maybe not. He found the ice pick and punched some holes in the lid. He didn't want to scare the snake. He wanted to make sure he would have air, and some soft grass to lie on. And then he went into his house. It was a comfortable house, he thought, an interesting house. Even with the dusty animal heads and horns, he still liked it.

Tommy frowned. Mr. Wolfe was sitting in his living room, on one of the couches beside the big stone fireplace. "Hello," Tommy said. His mother came downstairs. "Why aren't you sitting outside?" Tommy asked. "It's a nice day. It's dark in here."

"Give us a kiss," his mother said. "I want a kiss. I haven't seen you all morning and here it is, almost half-past three, and I need a kiss." She walked over to the fireplace where Tommy was standing underneath the moose head and bent over him, offering her cheek. Tommy gave her a little kiss. His mouth was dry.

"A real kiss," his mother said. She was being very bright and cheerful. "I want a real kiss and a hug." Tommy gave her another kiss on her cheek.

"Why didn't you call for a boat?" she asked.

"I forgot," Tommy said. "I was happy waiting on the shore. Jim rowed me to the Aldriches'. Are you going to invite Mrs. Slade to your party?"

"I don't think so, dear."

"Why not? She's Margie's aunt."

"Well, we're not really friends of Mrs. Slade's. I don't think she'd be comfortable, really. She has her own friends."

"Well, she's a friend of Mr. Wolfe's," Tommy said. "Don't you want her there, Mr. Wolfe? Don't you think she'd be comfortable? You could make her comfortable."

306

"Tommy," his mother said, "this is a family matter." She was no longer smiling. "I don't want to talk about it now."

"Well, if Mrs. Slade can't come, I won't come either!"

"Tommy! This is no way to talk. We have a guest!"

"Who?"

"What do you mean, who? Mr. Wolfe, of course."

"Mr. Wolfe's not a guest. He's around here all the time. Aren't you, Mr. Wolfe?"

"I think I'd better be going," Mr. Wolfe said. "I've got a lot of things to do back at the house."

"Wait," Tommy said. He suddenly had an idea. "I have a present for you. You're always giving me presents. I have one for you. You'll like it. Come on out. It's on the back porch."

"Why, Tommy," his mother said, happier now, "what can it be?"

"You'll see. Mr. Wolfe will like it. It's something he likes."

They all walked out to the back porch. Tommy picked up his box—it was quiet inside—put the stone in his pocket, and lifted the lid. "Here," he said. "Look." They both looked into the box.

"Tommy!" His mother screamed at him. "That's horrid! That's disgusting!" She recoiled.

"What's disgusting about it? It's a snake, that's all. A harmless garter snake, and he's pretty, besides. Mr. Wolfe likes snakes. Ask him." His mother was speechless. "You like snakes, don't you, Mr. Wolfe? Remember that picture of the poisonous lizard you showed us last summer, and the plumed serpents? I thought you'd like it." The snake was starting to move. Tommy put the lid back on the box. "I don't want it to get away," he explained. "If you don't want to keep it in the box, you can let it go in your garden. It'll eat the bugs."

His mother was still standing by the screened door, her mouth tight, her face drained of color. She hadn't said another word. Mr. Wolfe was walking down the path beside the house. "Wait," Tommy called after him. "You forgot your present."

"That's all right," Mr. Wolfe called back, "I'll pick it up another time."

"No," Tommy said. "Take it now. I want you to have it,"

and he ran down the path after Mr. Wolfe and thrust the box into his hands.

His mother had scarcely moved. Her hands were clenched at her sides. "You are a tyrannical child," she said. She was white with rage. "A tyrannical child! I am *very* angry with you."

"You're a lying mother!"

"When have I ever lied to you?" She shouted the question.

"About your age."

"About my age?" She didn't know what he was talking about.

"Yes. About your age. You told me you were twenty-two. Remember?" She raised her fists to her head. The knuckles were white. Her eyes were shut. "I remember it," Tommy said. "I remember it. I remember things. And that's not all."

His mother opened her eyes. "Not all? What do you mean, not all?" She whispered it. "What else?" Her voice was hoarse.

"I don't know," Tommy said, and he repeated it softly, looking off toward the distance: "I don't know."

"You'll be punished for this," his mother said.

"Are you going to tell Daddy on me?"

"Go to your room," she said.

"No," Tommy said. He said it very calmly, though he could feel his heart beating in his chest. "I'm going outside," and he walked off the porch and through the path in the woods, across the bridge to Boomer Island and across the other bridge to the island the Steers and Daisy and Phil lived on, and followed the path that went behind the Steers' house and into the woods until he came to the clearing at the old Indian cemetery, where he sat on the field grass, in the sunlight, leaning against one of the little houses, weathered and bleached over the years, that the Indians built over their graves. He sat there a long time, feeling the warmth of the sun, listening to the bees in the wild flowers. It was peaceful there. It occurred to him that he'd never had lunch, but he wasn't hungry. He *was* a tyrannical child, he thought, and he had lied to her, too. Tommy had never seen his mother so full of wrath, nor had he known himself to be so hateful. It was not good. He stayed there a long time, his back against the decrepit shelter. The shadows of the trees were slanting over the cemetery now, and when the shadows grew longer and crept up and covered him, he began to feel chilly. He shivered. He would have to go home, he knew that. He dreaded it, but he knew it. He got up, picked a bunch of wild flowers and put them on the grave, and left the cemetery, returning to his house by the same paths and bridges.

When he got home he went into the living room and stood before the big stone fireplace. The bull moose glared balefully down on him. It was moth-eaten. He wished someone would throw it out. He wished there were a fire in the fireplace, but there were only the ashes from the last fire. He heard his mother stirring in her room, and in a few minutes she came downstairs. She looked different now. She looked quite different. "I've been lying down," she said. She had changed her dress, too. "Tommy, come sit here beside me." She patted the couch on the other side of the fireplace. "Please. Sit down next to me." Tommy sat on the couch. "Tommy, when I told you I was twenty-two"—there were tears in his mother's eyes—"that was such a long time ago, so long ago. It was just a story that I thought would amuse you. You always liked funny stories. You know that." Yes, he knew that. "It wasn't a real lie, just an innocent little fib. A silly story I made up, a white lie." There was a tear on his mother's cheek now. "I wouldn't want to hurt you. I wouldn't want to hurt you for the world. You're the most precious thing I have." She sat there in the corner of the couch, her eyes glistening, her hands open on her lap. "The most precious thing I have." Tommy looked across the rug to the other couch where Mr. Wolfe had been sitting. He didn't know what to say. "I don't want to hurt you," she said again. "Please don't hurt me, either. There's too much hurt in the world, Tommy, too much hurt."

Tommy did not want his mother to hurt. "I don't want you to hurt me, either," he said.

"I wish we had the piano here," she said. "You could sit beside me and I could play the song we love so much. It would make us both feel better." Tommy could hear in his mind the lovely notes of *Kinderszenen*, floating in from far, far away.

"Yes," he said. "Yes, that would be nice." It would be nice to be under the piano again, feeling the tingling of the strings. His mother put some kindling in the fireplace, and a couple of logs, poured some kerosene over them, and lit the fire.

"Daddy will probably be home soon," she said, "and then we'll have dinner."

But his father didn't come home soon. He called and said he'd been having a business meeting and it was running late, and he was going to take the men to the country club for dinner. He'd probably be home afterwards. Mrs. Addington called a few minutes later. She asked his mother if she'd like to join her and Mrs. Wentworth for drinks and a simple supper. "Mac's not home," his mother said, "and I'm here with Tommy." Mrs. Aldrich said something. "Thank you," his mother said, "but really I'm not feeling very well. I have a headache, and I think I'll stay here with Tommy tonight. He's tired out, too. We're both tired." His mother made tomato soup, and they had toast, and then he went to bed. His mother went to bed shortly after, and when his father came home the house was asleep.

Tommy had a strange dream that night. It was like the terrible dream he'd had twice before, the one he called his furnace dream, but different. There was a man in it, and there was the flickering light, and there was a mask in it, too, like the one on his wall but worse, and maybe some Indians and some of the people from the Island, maybe the furnacemen from the plant. He thought Mrs. Steer was in it, and Mrs. Slade. There were a lot of people in it. He could see faces in the light. There was the chopping block, but it was like stone, maybe like some of those Mexican things. It was definitely a bad dream, but not so frightening as the first one, and it was hard to remember. It was the last time he dreamt it.

THEY had a quiet weekend. His mother spent a lot of time addressing the invitations to the dance. His father mailed them on Monday. There were many, many of them, and the Islanders were growing more excited about the party, talking about what they might wear, what sort of gift they might send. The gifts were all being delivered to the house in town, which slowly began to fill with silver. That was nice. His mother liked silver, and some of it was very pretty indeed. There were many arrangements to be made—who was coming from out of town, who would stay where—many plans. The house had to be made ready, and the offers of hospitality for the out-of-town guests accepted. Tommy's mother thought that the family might stay in town that night; some of the people from away could have the cottage. They'd enjoy it. The orchestra had to be confirmed, the menu planned, the champagne ordered. His father insisted on the champagne. A silver wedding anniversary didn't happen every day, and this was going to be very special. It was going to be a party such as hadn't been seen around Grande Rivière in a long time. That's what they all said.

ONE morning a few days later Tommy was standing on the bridge to Boomer Island, watching Mrs. Steer swim back and forth, back and forth, down fast with the current and back more slowly against it. She saw Tommy, too, and he walked over to her dock when she had finished and was wrapping herself in a big towel. The sun was bright, but it was still early, and as it rose slowly higher in the sky its rays grew warmer and Mrs. Steer threw off her towel and dried in the sun. Amy had been invited to breakfast at Mrs. Wentworth's, she said. Mrs. Wentworth did that sometimes. She liked children.

"I've been noticing you lately, Tommy," Mrs. Steer said. "You used to seem so happy, such an open, bright, happy boy. What's wrong?"

"I don't know," Tommy said. "Nothing special, I guess." Then he said, "I've had a funny dream," and he told Mrs. Steer what he could remember about his dream. "You were in it, too," he said.

"When I was a little girl," she said, "and already a fairly good swimmer, I used to have a dream. It was a recurring dream. I was swimming in a sea of leather, and, though trying as hard as I could, I made no progress at all. Sometimes I remember that dream. I remember the feeling of utter frustration. We all have strange dreams, Tommy, from time to time. It's part of life."

They sat there for a while on the dock, in silence. It was

nice to warm themselves in the sun, and Tommy felt very close to Mrs. Steer. She'd never given him one of her dreams before. "I'm going to tell you a little poem," she said. "Listen:

> *You must turn your mournful ditty*
> *To a merry measure;*
> *I will never come for pity,*
> *I will come for pleasure.*

"I don't understand it," Tommy said.

"You will," Mrs. Steer said. "You will. I think I'll write it out for you. Wait here." She picked up her towel and walked up the steps to her cottage. She came out a few minutes later, dressed, and walked back down to the dock. She handed Tommy the poem, written on her own letter paper in the handwriting that was so different from anyone else's. His mother said it was European, that Mrs. Steer spoke perfect English but wrote with a European accent. "Sometimes we all have bad feelings," she said, "like bad dreams. Sometimes we can't help our feelings, but always we can help what we do about them. You'll be a happy child again, Tommy," she told him. "You really will. I promise."

Tommy folded the paper carefully in half, and then he folded it again. "I'll save it," he told Mrs. Steer.

"You don't have to save it," she said, "just remember it." She put her arm around his shoulder and together they moved up to the porch, where Mrs. Steer poured herself a cup of coffee and gave Tommy a glass of milk and some crackers with her own mayonnaise on them. The next time Tommy went to town, he took Mrs. Steer's paper with him and put it in his locked drawer.

THE Aldriches returned to the Island later in the month, but they didn't bring Michael with them. Mr. Aldrich had been called home because of the international situation, which was bad, especially the Bolsheviks, who were being treacherous again, and the distance was too great and the trip too expensive to bring the whole family for such a short time. It was hardly worth opening the cottage, Mrs. Aldrich said, but summer wouldn't be summer without at least a visit to the Island, and she didn't want to miss the party, either. Tommy was sorry that he wouldn't see Michael; Michael would have been interested in the scalping. Bill had a scar on his head but his hair was growing back, and he and Rose were the same as ever. "Just a happy married couple," Mrs. Sedgwick said in that way she had. Lena didn't seem any different, either.

Mrs. Aldrich brought a tablecloth from Spain that she was going to lend Tommy's mother for the party. She called it a banquet cloth because it was so big. It would go on the head table. The tablecloth had been made all by hand, of the finest lace, and was so precious that it wasn't ever washed. Before Tommy saw it, he expected it would be crusted with milk from old spills, spotted with gravy stains, and look very old and soiled. But when he saw it, he was surprised: it didn't look dirty at all. Mrs. Aldrich said that whenever anyone spilled anything, she just cleaned up the spot at once. It was a lot easier for her to treat the spots as they occurred. That way it never showed the dirt. Oh, of course sometime it might have to be washed, she said, but it would probably never look as good again. She'd leave that job for her children or her grandchildren. "You'll have to mind your manners at your parents' party, Tommy," she told him. "I don't want any spills."

"I'll try," Tommy said.

The McGhees arrived for their visit with the Aldriches. Madge and Phelps came with them. Nick Kingsfield came home, but he didn't open the Farnsworth cottage. He didn't know what he'd do with the place, he said, and he stayed with Tommy's brother David uptown. Mrs. Farnsworth's house had already been sold. The out-of-town guests were starting to arrive, and the extra bedrooms on the Island and in town began to fill up. Tommy's Aunt Clara and Uncle Andrew were going to stay in town, because his Aunt Clara didn't like the Island very much—probably because she was so fastidious, Tommy thought, and there was only one bathroom in the cottage. His father's sister, Tommy's Aunt Martha, was staying up there, too, with his Uncle Charles, but they weren't bringing Tommy's cousins. The party was just for grown-ups, and they could stay only a very short time. Aunt Elizabeth and Uncle Roger were going to stay on the Island with Tommy and John, and his parents would divide their time between the places. Tommy's parents didn't have room for everybody, so his Uncle Christian was staying in the Sedgwicks' guesthouse. He loved the guesthouse as much as Tommy did. The population of the Island seemed to double overnight. Mrs. Wentworth and Mrs. Addington took two couples, the Aldriches another, and other friends put some of them up at their houses in town.

As the guests arrived, so did the silver. Tommy had never seen so much silver in his life. Even Mrs. Sedgwick, whose silver was old and came from Philadelphia and had been in the family since the Revolutionary War, was impressed. His Aunt Clara and Uncle Andrew arrived with a set of silver goblets that came from the finest jewelry store in Chicago, and his Aunt Elizabeth and Uncle Roger brought two candelabra from Detroit. His Uncle Christian brought four small silver salt dishes with tiny spoons and blue glass liners. They stood on tiny clawed feet, and they'd been made in England a long time ago. Tommy liked to rub his thumb across them, feeling the design that had been hammered there. His Uncle Christian called the work repoussé, and his mother admired the salt dishes very much. She said Christian had very good taste. Tommy thought the clawed feet would go very well with the other animals in the dining room—the plates on the rail, the platters and the soup tureen, all those china faces with the mild eyes that he knew so well. Tommy wondered if his Uncle Christian thought of things like that. His father's Canadian cousins were too old to come to the party, but they sent a piece of their mother's plate. Mrs. Slade sent a statue from Marshall Field's of an antlered silver elk. It stood about eight inches high, and Tommy told his mother that it belonged in the dining room, too. His father said the dining room was getting to be a regular zoo. Reilly delivered the package himself with a note from Mrs. Slade regretting that she and Mr. Slade wouldn't be able to attend the dance, though they were grateful for the invitation. Mrs. Sedgwick sent a tray that she'd gotten somewhere, and his Aunt Martha brought another when she and Uncle Charles arrived. Mrs. Steer sent something she'd already had, but it was beautiful. It had belonged to her mother, and Mrs. Steer said she could remember it from her childhood, when it had sat in the middle of the desk in the library of her house in Denmark. It was an inkwell. It was made mostly of glass, but it had a silver top with someone's monogram on it. Tommy hoped he might get to use it, but they never did put any ink in it. Tommy wondered if Mr. Wolfe would give his parents twenty-five silver coins, but he didn't. He sent a cocktail shaker, instead. Tommy couldn't keep track of all the gifts, there were so many.

The day before the dance, Tommy and Amy cut down the cattails with Bill and Harry and Jim, the Indians, and they all took them over to the country club, where they cut some more that grew along the banks of the main creek. They wanted to be sure to have enough. Buck helped them, too. "What you doin' that for?" he asked, and when Tommy told him that they were going to soak them in kerosene and light the driveway, Buck said, "Shit, boy, your mamma's gonna set this place on fire."

"No," Tommy said, "she's just going to light it and make it pretty." And she did.

His mother spent most of the next day at the club, making sure everything was in order and that the Indians and the extra help they'd had to get from the hotel knew what they were supposed to do. That morning she had laid out his white pants and his blue jacket, a white shirt, and a tie. Yes, he hardly ever had to wear a tie, but he had to wear one tonight. He was old enough. Not old enough for long pants, his mother said, but old enough for a tie. His mother and father were dressing in town, so his brother John and his Aunt Elizabeth made sure he got dressed right, and John tied his tie for him. Then they left their cottage and walked over the bridge to the Sedgwicks', where they waited for Mrs. Sedgwick and Emily to finish dressing. John was wearing a white dinner jacket, and he looked very handsome. Mr. Sedgwick and Tommy's Uncle Roger and Uncle Christian were wearing the same thing. When the ladies appeared, everyone exclaimed at how pretty they looked, and they did, too, in their pale flowered dresses that rippled when they moved. All three of them, his Aunt Elizabeth included, were wearing flowered dresses. "We're the flowers in the summer garden," Mrs. Sedgwick said. She was very gay; she loved parties. So did his Aunt Elizabeth. She looked very elegant. Tommy, John and Emily, Uncle Christian, and the Sedgwicks were going over together in the Sedgwick launch. An Indian had been mustered up to row Tommy's Aunt Elizabeth and Uncle Roger, because his aunt was afraid of motorboats and his uncle, who certainly could row a boat, didn't know the river very well and it could be hazardous, especially at night.

"Now, Tom," Mrs. Sedgwick said as they were getting into the launch, "go slow. We don't want a lot of water splashing through the air. We're dressed for a party, not for a swim. Besides, I think it would be nice if we could hear something besides the noise of that engine. I think it would be nice if we all sang a hymn." Mrs. Sedgwick liked hymns, and as the launch pulled slowly away from the dock and headed down the little channel toward the twinkling lights on the bridge to Boomer Island and the river beyond it, Mrs. Sedgwick began to sing, *"O God, our help in ages past,"* and Tommy's Aunt Elizabeth and Uncle Roger joined in from their boat a distance back. Tommy could see the Steers with Amy getting into their boat, from their dock, and they began singing, too:

> *Our shelter from the stormy blast,*
> *And our eternal home.*

Tommy loved the hymn, and he loved it that they in the launch—Emily and John, Uncle Christian, and even Mr. Sedgwick—and his aunt and uncle in their boat, the Steers in theirs, all heading in a broken line toward the Boomer Island bridge, were joining in, Mrs. Steer too, and led by Mrs. Sedgwick, they began to go through the verses, one by one, even the verses Tommy didn't know, and when the singers faltered, not knowing the words, Mrs. Sedgwick's soprano voice floated above the water:

> *Under the shadow of Thy throne*
> *Thy saints have dwelt secure;*
> *Sufficient is Thine arm alone,*
> *And our defense is sure.*

The launch purred slowly on, its motor at the lowest speed. As they passed under the bridge and into the broad river, Tommy could see other boats coming from their docks on the other island toward the shore: the Aldriches and the McGhees and their guests, Mr. Wolfe and an Indian rowing old Mrs. Wentworth and Mrs. Addington and theirs in two boats, Mr. Treverton rowing alone. And as each of them heard the hymn from their places on the river, they all began to sing:

A thousand ages in Thy sight
Are like an evening gone;
Short as the watch that ends the night
Before the rising sun.
Time, like an ever-rolling stream,
Bears all its sons away;
They fly, forgotten, as a dream
Dies at the opening day.

How beautiful, Tommy thought, how truly beautiful, there at dusk on the river, the river like an ever-rolling stream, that they should all be singing this particular hymn, their liquid voices carrying over the water, and that all these specks in the current, these swimmers in his sea, should be singing the same song as they floated across the river from their different places to the same big dock at the landing on the shore, to the same club whose purple and amber lanterns beckoned them now, at nightfall on the river, and that their voices should be echoing across the water in the twilight as they all boomed out the last chorus:

O God, our help in ages past,
Our hope for years to come . . .

When they arrived, boat by boat, at the landing, they got into their various cars and drove the short distance to the country club, up the driveway to the long sweeping porch where the paper lanterns glowed in the twilight, lighting the way to the door.

• •

AND there, in the foyer, standing in the soft light, was his mother, who leaned over to kiss him as he came in and approached her from the wide screened doors.

"Happy anniversary," he said. "You look beautiful." She did look beautiful, but not like a flower in a summer garden. Her dress was the color of smoke, like a color Tommy had never seen before, on a dress. Was it blue? Was it brown? Was it white? It was all of them but none of them exactly, and it flowed from her shoulders to her waist to the floor in a haze of smoky chiffon. She was wearing her pearls, his grandmother's long pearls, and the ring with the star in it on her finger, and the little sapphires in her ears, surrounded by tiny diamonds. "You're not wearing your arrow," Tommy said.

"She doesn't want to pierce any hearts tonight," said his Uncle Roger from behind him, and his mother smiled, and his father, who was standing there beside her in his black tuxedo—he was almost the only man there who wasn't wearing a white jacket—said, "Move along, young fellow, you're holding up the line," but he said it nicely and gave him a little hug as he passed. Tommy moved out of the line, but he didn't leave the foyer. He wanted to look at his parents, who truly were a handsome couple as Mrs. Wentworth said; he wanted to watch his mother extending her hand, exchanging kisses with the ladies and the gentlemen, his father shaking hands with all the men and kissing the ladies on the cheek. He watched the guests passing through the door: Mr. and Mrs. Steer, Mrs. Wentworth and Mrs. Addington and their houseguests, Mr. Wolfe, his Uncle Christian, the Hutchins and the Rodgers, crazy Mrs. Barger with her glass eye and her red dress—"looking like a fire truck," John whispered to him—Mrs. Meyer and Mr. Meyer, who gave his mother a big smack and clapped his father on the back, his Aunt Martha and Uncle Charles, Bob Griswold and his wife, Mr. Treverton, and now Margie and David, Dr. and Mrs. Randolph, Daisy and Phil, his Aunt Clara and Uncle Andrew—everyone Tommy knew and some he scarcely knew at all, and they all wore their best clothes, even Mrs. Appleton, who tried to look as good as she could but was as mean as ever. Tommy saw her looking at Mrs. Hutchins, who was wearing a lot of jewelry. She always did. "All her mother's diamonds," Mrs. Appleton said to one of the ladies, "every single one of them, and some more from the dime store, too, I'll bet." Tommy could smell the whisky on Mr. Hutchins' breath when he shook his hand, and he followed Mrs. Hutchins into the lounge, where they were serving Mrs. Barlow's punch from bowls in a corner. In a few minutes Mrs. Hutchins began to sip at her glass of bourbon, her hand and face twitching as always. "Daisy looks just like a bride," she told Daisy's mother, Mrs. Addington, and Mr. Sedgwick boomed out. "You're only a bride once!" Tommy saw that Mrs. Steer was looking at him. He knew she thought Mr. Sedgwick was being an idiot again, but she didn't say anything, and Tommy walked over to her at the same time Mrs. Appleton did. "Yes," Mrs. Appleton said to Mrs. Steer, "and it doesn't always happen at the church. White! Really!" Mrs. Steer said that Amy was in the cardroom—it was his responsibility to see that Amy had a good time, his mother had told him—and he went off to find her, to play with her for a while before she had to leave. She couldn't stay for the dinner, but she got to see the beginning of the party because she'd helped pick the cattails. Mrs. Steer walked away from Mrs. Appleton too, to join Mrs. Wentworth and Mrs. Barlow. Even Mrs. Barlow had made it. She couldn't make it to the Island anymore, but she did make it up the three steps to the country-club porch. She had to sample her punch, she said. If Mrs. Barger looked like a fire truck, Tommy thought, Mrs. Barlow looked like a mountain.

Tommy and Amy walked across the foyer and into the ballroom. There was a huge iron candelabrum on either side of the French doors. They were taller than a man, taller than his brother David, even, and he counted the candles. There were nine in each of them, two ascending circles of four and a single candle at the top. They hadn't been lit yet, but when they were, Tommy thought they'd be really something. He'd never seen them before, and he wondered where his mother ever found them. Not in his house, he knew that. The orchestra was playing softly, but no one was dancing yet—everyone was still in the lounge or the foyer, on the porch or

319

in the cardroom—and above the orchestra was a round mirrored ball, bigger than David's basketball and covered with small chips of glass. It looked like a giant golf ball, if golf balls were made of glass. It revolved as the orchestra played, sprinkling the big room with light. There were tables set up around the edges, all of them with candles and flowers and silver and china, white like the candles, but except for the orchestra the room was empty.

They walked through the big archway, where there were two more of the iron candlesticks, into the dining room. There were small tables there too, but the long table with Mrs. Aldrich's precious cloth and the two silver candelabra from his Aunt Elizabeth stood at the end, the smaller tables extending out from it on either side. Tommy wanted to show Amy the tablecloth. He told Amy that Mrs. Aldrich never washed it, and they both looked it over closely before they finally discovered a stain or two. Tommy found his place card, next to his brother John's at the far end of the table. David's was at the other end, next to Emily's. Tommy bet David wouldn't be too happy about that. They looked at all the cards on the head table and they all went man, woman, man, woman, man, woman, then John and Tommy. There were six women and eight men and they were all family, except for Emily and Margie, who everybody knew would be family sooner or later, and his parents were in the middle, side by side.

The two of them looked for Amy's parents' places. They found Mr. Steer's at one of the tables in the dining room, but they had a harder time finding Mrs. Steer's. Finally they found her card in the ballroom, to the right of Dr. Rodgers'. "My mother won't like that," Amy said. "She doesn't like him anymore." But Mr. Treverton was on her other side, and that was good. Tommy could have told his mother that Mrs. Steer wouldn't have wanted to sit next to Dr. Rodgers, if she'd asked him. His mother had told him once that they weren't so friendly anymore, that the Steers had gotten into an argument with him, but she must have forgotten. Mrs. Steer was friendly with Mrs. Rodgers, though. She was always nice to her. Tommy and Amy looked at all the place cards,

or as many as they could, before Mrs. Steer came looking for
Amy. "We'll be sitting down to dinner soon," she said.
"They're beginning to light the candles," and sure enough,
they were: Ophelia and Katherine and Katherine's husband,
George; Junior and Buck, too; Rose and Ruth and Lena and
the people from the hotel—all moving quickly about the room
to light the candles. "Vint is waiting to take you home," Mrs.
Steer said to Amy, and her brother came up behind her with
Madge McGhee on his arm. Tommy thought that Mrs. Steer
hoped they'd get married. He didn't think she really liked
Madge all that much—she might have been glamorous, but she
wasn't very interesting—but Mrs. Steer had said once that
Vint could do a whole lot worse, and he very well might. She
worried about that sort of thing. Mr. Steer said that was the
Great Dane in her, and Tommy remembered that she'd said
a long time ago that parents in Denmark arranged their children's marriages and they worked out better in the long run.
Her parents couldn't have arranged her marriage, though.
They didn't even know Mr. Steer. That was the odd side of
Mrs. Steer. Tommy walked out to the long porch with them,
and he watched Vint take Amy off to the shore. Amy waved
as she left. Tommy was glad that she'd been there, even if
only for a while. It was an exciting thing to see. Neither of
them had ever seen anything like it before.

Tommy returned to the clubhouse and found his mother
standing with his father in the foyer, near the French doors,
which were now closed. All his aunts and uncles and his
brothers and Emily and Margie were gathered around them.
"Oh, there you are," his mother said. "I'd just asked Buck to
find you. We're ready to begin." His father opened the wide
glass doors. Tommy looked in wonder. The view, now that
the room was lit, was breathtaking. The huge iron candelabra
flamed like torches beside the doorway, and all the shaded
candles on the tables and the mirrored ball turning slowly
above the orchestra filled the room with sparkling light. "Let's
go," his father said, and his mother took his father's arm, the
orchestra struck a chord and went into a sort of march, and
they filed through the doors and into the ballroom, walking
quickly in time to the music, past all the small tables, through

the archway into the dining room, and took their places at the long table, their guests following behind them in clusters of twos and fours and sixes, all chattering away, some still carrying their drinks, and looking for their places at the party.

Well, Tommy thought, all his mother's planning had produced a beautiful sight, and all the people had dressed for their parts in it too, to make it even more beautiful, and now the gaiety was about to begin. It was exciting to sit at the head table, and John was being very nice to him. He said he had to sit at the very end so Tommy wouldn't fall off. His Aunt Elizabeth was on Tommy's other side and his Uncle Christian was next to her, and they all had a lot of fun because his uncle liked to tease his aunt. They were almost the same age. He told her he had known that with all these flowered dresses in the room she would find one that was different. It was, too. It was as if there were a pretty garden growing around her hem, but the rest of the dress was white except for a single flower that started at one hip and ran across to the top of her dress and opened on her opposite shoulder, like a real flower in bloom. His aunt was like that; she wanted to be very stylish, and she was. Tommy could certainly never imagine her in anybody's hand-me-downs. That made him think of his Aunt Louise. Louise and Arthur weren't there, and neither were his Uncle Archie and his Aunt Pat. He hadn't expected they would be.

It was exciting to be at the head table, looking out over the dining room and into the ballroom beyond, the rooms filled with smiles and laughter, but after a while it wasn't so exciting anymore. The dinner was long, and all the grown-ups talked about the things they always talked about, though more brightly and more gaily than usual. The party made them festive. His mother had said that when you were a guest at a party, it was your duty to help make it work, and all the people seemed to be doing their duty tonight. But still, the dinner was long. Tommy couldn't have any wine, though he would be allowed a small glass of champagne so that he could join in the toasts. Finally, with the dessert, the champagne arrived, but they still had to eat their dessert, and nobody seemed to be in any hurry, either. Tommy had thought the dessert would be like a wedding cake, but it wasn't. It was like a custard. It tasted of peaches, and there were small sections of peach in each dish.

"I thought there'd be a wedding cake," Tommy said to John.

"That's for weddings," John said, "and the wedding was twenty-five years ago."

"The cake would be awfully stale by now," said his Uncle Christian, who'd been listening to their conversation.

"What a thing to say," said his Aunt Elizabeth, laughing. "Can't you be just a bit romantic?"

"You're the romantic in the family," Christian said. "You're the romantic little girl waiting for the man on the horse. Does Roger ride?"

"Roger doesn't ride," his aunt said, her brown eyes wide. "You know that."

"He bought you a fur coat, though," his uncle said.

"Are you teasing me?" asked his aunt.

"Now, Elizabeth," his uncle said, "would I tease you?"

"Probably," she said. "You probably would and I wouldn't even know it."

"I wouldn't tease you, Elizabeth," Christian said. "It wouldn't be worth it. It would all be lost. I'll bet it wouldn't be lost on Tommy, though."

Tommy laughed. The party was getting to be fun again, and he liked the champagne. He'd never felt so grown up. There he was, sitting at the head table at a fancy party as big as New Year's Eve's, drinking champagne and listening to the laughter, and keeping his elbows off the table, too, at least most of the time. No one would even know he was wearing short pants; the cloth hid his legs. He had to remember not to spill anything on it. He looked, but he couldn't see any spots, just a couple of crumbs.

The waiters were coming around again, filling glasses. He saw Rose and Ruth and Lena out there working. Ophelia was standing by the doors from the kitchen, her arms folded, supervising things, gazing at the spectacle. Tommy waved at her, and she waved back, smiling. "You drank all your champagne," John said. "You weren't supposed to do that. You were supposed to wait for the toasts."

"Can I have some more?"

"*May* I," his aunt said. "You should say 'May I.' What do you think, John? Should he have some more? We don't want to make him woozy. Emma wouldn't like that. Are you feeling woozy, Tommy?"

"Oh, no," Tommy said. "I feel fine." They'd only poured a little bit in his glass anyway. He was glad his Aunt Clara wasn't sitting where Elizabeth was. She would have said he couldn't have any more, that he was too young. She probably would have made him drink orange juice. But John said he thought it would be all right—he ought to have something in his glass for the toasts—and the waiter poured a little bit more in the bottom of the glass. It couldn't be more than one swallow, Tommy thought. He'd hardly get woozy on that. And then his Uncle Andrew, who was sitting at his mother's right, stood up and tapped his glass with a spoon. It rang like a bell. The tables grew slowly quiet, and everyone looked toward the head table in anticipation.

"To the happy couple!" His Uncle Andrew raised his glass and everyone rose, glass in hand, turning toward his parents and repeating the words "To the happy couple!" John nudged Tommy from his chair. He stood up with his glass and said the words "To the happy couple." The happy couple smiled. His mother caught his eye. She glanced at his glass and back to his eye, giving him a short warning look that said, "That's enough, now," but his glass was already empty.

His Uncle Roger raised his glass. "Twenty-five more years!" Everyone cheered and took another drink, and the waiters scurried around the tables with their bottles, and his parents sat in their places, smiling toward their friends in the crowd.

There were a lot more toasts. "To the bride," Bob Griswold said. Tommy was surprised that Bob Griswold made a toast; he was younger than Tommy's parents, maybe about his Uncle Roger's age, but he wasn't family. He wasn't even a very good friend, but his parents had to invite him. It was such a big party that it would have been rude to leave him out. "You're only a bride once!" Mr. Sedgwick shouted again, and everyone laughed. Mr. Wolfe rose to his feet. "To the lady of the evening," he said, bowing toward Tommy's mother; "to the queen of the revels—and the king!" He nodded toward

Tommy's father, and all the grown-ups raised their glasses to their lips and cheered some more. His mother acknowledged the cheers with a nod and a smile, and fingered the pearls at her throat. Tommy remembered his father's saying on New Year's Eve, "Even the queen of the night has got to wear her boots." Rose had laughed at that. Tommy would have to notice what shoes his mother was wearing tonight. Tommy saw Mrs. Appleton at a table in the ballroom lean across Mr. Hutchins and say something behind her hand to Mrs. Randolph, who didn't respond.

Mr. Treverton, who was quite an old man, rose slowly to his feet. "I want to remind everyone, everyone at this beautiful party, that my New Year's Day rule worked: 'Three hot rum toddies followed by a cold one, and then you're fixed for the New Year.' Everyone here must have followed the rule. We hope Tommy didn't, but I fixed it so it works with the children's eggnog, too." Everyone laughed, and Tommy turned red with embarrassment and pleasure. Suddenly everyone was looking at him. "Yes," Mr. Treverton continued, "everyone here must have followed my rule, because it's working very well tonight, at this beautiful, beautiful party." The men called out. "Hear! Hear!" and Tommy's Aunt Elizabeth leaned toward him and John and said, "Isn't that sweet? Isn't he a darling man?"

And then Mr. Hutchins rang his glass. "To the victor," he sang out. "To the victor belong the spoils," and there was more laughter and a scattering of applause and scraping of chairs, and the glasses were raised to Tommy's father.

"What did he mean by that?" Tommy asked John.

"He used to be a suitor of your mother's," his Aunt Elizabeth said before John could reply. "He was one of her many handsome beaux. She had lots of beaux. Your mother was very glamorous, you know, but she only had eyes for your father. I'll never forget the blue velour hat with the long sweeping feather she wore when they left on their wedding trip. So stylish. I wasn't much older than you, Tommy, maybe the same age, but I was *impressed*."

Mr. Hutchins must have changed, Tommy thought. He sure wasn't handsome now. "Well, I'm glad he didn't win,"

Tommy said. He couldn't imagine Mr. Hutchins as his father. "But what are the spoils?"

"That's what the victor gets after the battle," his Uncle Christian said. "It's the plunder he takes home with him. It's just an old expression."

"Oh," Tommy said.

His father stood up. "Thank you," he said, "thank you. And here's to each and every one of you." He raised his glass to his guests and drank from it, and then touched his glass to his mother's—"And to you, Emma"—and they each took a sip as the crowd broke into applause. "And now let's have fun— and for anyone who'd like it, a real drink! Or more of Sally Barlow's famous punch. Just remember that it packs one, too." Tommy knew his father didn't think champagne was a real drink; it was just something you had to have for celebrations, like Mrs. Barlow's punch.

The band started playing again, and his father took his mother's hand and led her from the table, the rest of them following after. He walked her through the dining room into the ballroom, where he put his arm around her waist and they began to dance as the waiters cleared the tables of everything but the glasses and the buckets with the ice in them for the champagne. Others joined, and soon the room was filled with swirling, dancing, happy couples. His mother, Tommy noticed, was wearing shoes of palest pearly gray, made of silk, not the fuchsia shoes with the straps that she'd shown him and John. Maybe she'd returned them. But she had put her buckles on them, and her feet sparkled as she moved. His mother was a very good dancer.

His father didn't dance very long. He didn't enjoy dancing—he said he danced the way he sang—but it was a man's duty and he did it, and he danced with a lot of the other ladies too, not very long with any of them but long enough to be polite. Tommy knew that he would have to leave soon. He was being allowed to watch the dancing for a little while, but then, when all the tables had been cleared and he had seen enough, Rose was going to take him back to the Island. He could never see enough, he thought. He stood in a corner, watching. His mother was dancing with Nick Kingsfield now.

326

She liked dancing with him a lot more than with Mr. Sedgwick, who stepped on everyone's feet and if he didn't crush your toes he ruined your slippers. The band was playing "South of the Border (Down Mexico Way)," and Nick and his mother were really doing a fancy dance, swooping back and forth and around the floor. Nick was very good. His mother ought to be dancing with Mr. Wolfe to that one, Tommy thought, and in a minute she was but the song had changed. The band was playing "Smoke Gets in Your Eyes," and he could see his mother singing the words to the music.

"That's a pisser," Dr. Randolph said from behind him. Tommy hadn't realized he was there. He was drinking a Coke, but from a glass.

"What?" Tommy asked.

"It's a pisser," Dr. Randolph said again. "This party of your mother's is a real pisser."

Tommy laughed. Dr. Randolph always made him laugh when he talked like that. He walked into the foyer and through the screened doors onto the porch. It was nice on the porch. The air was fresh, and the lanterns were beautiful. His mother was lucky that it was such a fine night. It could have been cold, at the end of August, or it could have been raining, but it was neither cold nor wet: a perfect summer night. He walked the length of the long porch, looking through the windows into the ballroom, hearing the music. All the windows were open because it was so pleasant. The candles were burning still, and the mirrored ball shot beams of light into the farthest corners of the room, spattering it like sunlight through the leaves when the leaves fluttered in the breeze. It was like the kaleidoscope his mother had given him, all beautiful colors and swirling forms, but with music. Phil Meyer was dancing with his wife. Daisy did look like a bride. She liked white. Bob Griswold and Margie Slade were dancing together. Margie was wearing her mother's diamond bracelet. Tommy bet that Emily had noticed that. They'd sat pretty close to each other at the table. Her bracelet looked as fancy as any of Mrs. Hutchins', Tommy thought. Tommy saw David standing at the edge of the dance floor, watching Margie. He was waiting to cut in, and in a minute he did.

327

David really didn't want Margie to dance with anyone else, but sometimes she did. So did David; it wouldn't be polite, otherwise. Nick was dancing with Madge McGhee now— David had said he could have her—and Vint Steer was dancing with his mother. Tommy's mother always said that was a nice thing to do, dance with your mother, but Vint didn't look as if he were enjoying it much. Phelps was dancing with Emily, and then he danced with Daisy. Everybody was dancing. Well, not everybody. A few couples were strolling on the porch, taking the air, and Tommy could see through the doorway that there were people in the lounge, too. He could see Ophelia behind the bar, and he decided to go in and see if she could talk to him. Maybe Buck was free now and they could play Hide-and-Seek around the clubhouse. But when he got near the bar, he could see there was trouble. Mr. Hutchins was having an argument with Ophelia. He'd never seen Ophelia have an argument. Ophelia never argued with anybody, and everybody was always very nice to her. "Are you sure you want another drink?" Ophelia asked him. "Wouldn't you like a hot cup of coffee?"

"Nigger bitch!" Mr. Hutchins shouted. He was snarling, and he was drunk. Tommy knew he was really drunk. "Kiss my white ass!" Tommy couldn't believe his ears, and neither could Mrs. Steer and Mr. Aldrich, who had come into the room together. Mrs. Hutchins sat alone at the table, rings trembling as she put down her bourbon. "Oh, no," she said, "oh, no. He'll ruin this lovely party." She said it softly and stared off, not at Mr. Hutchins but into the distance. Mr. Aldrich ran to the bar, put his hand on Mr. Hutchins' arm, and said, "I'm taking you home," and Mrs. Steer saw Tommy and immediately rushed him into the cardroom and out the side door onto the porch.

"Some people don't know how to behave when they drink," she said. "You'll have to learn that, but I'm sorry you had to learn it now." Tommy already knew that, but he'd never seen anybody act like Mr. Hutchins. "Some people are despicable when they drink," Mrs. Steer said, "and you've just seen someone be utterly despicable. He's contemptible. I'm sorry." Mrs. Steer put her arm around his neck and patted his chest. "I am sorry, Tommy." She stood with him on the porch, holding his hand, and in a minute Mr. Aldrich and Mr. McGhee came out the side door with Mr. Hutchins between them. Mrs. Steer pulled him aside. She didn't even look at Mr. Hutchins. He was too contemptible. The two men walked him off the porch and around the back of the clubhouse. Tommy heard a car door slam, and then another and another, and the car started and drove off. "I don't think anyone noticed," Mrs. Steer said, letting go of his hand, "except for us. I hope not."

"Mrs. Appleton was playing the slot machines," Tommy said. "She probably noticed."

"Well, let's not talk about it. At least your parents didn't see it, and he's gone now."

"Mrs. Hutchins is still here," Tommy said.

"I'd better go talk to her and see if she's all right," Mrs. Steer said, "and apologize to Ophelia." She gave Tommy another friendly pat. "It must be time for you to leave. It's getting late. Isn't Rose supposed to take you home?"

"Yes," Tommy said, "she is. After I've seen some of the dancing."

"You've seen plenty of dancing." She laughed. "I'll find Rose and send her out. Wait here," and she bent and kissed him on the cheek. Mrs. Steer hardly ever kissed him. "I really must try to say something to Ophelia—and to Mrs. Hutchins, too. It's not her fault."

No, it wasn't her fault, Tommy thought, and it wasn't Ophelia's fault, either. He certainly liked Ophelia a lot more than he liked Mr. Hutchins. Right then Tommy loved Ophelia. He wanted to go in and say something nice to her, too, something to comfort her, but he didn't. He wished he could give her something nice so she wouldn't feel bad. If it had happened to him, she would have made him a chicken sandwich. Tommy wasn't in any hurry for Rose to find him, though, so he didn't go back inside, or stay on the porch either, but walked down the steps and onto the grass, listening to the music float out of the clubhouse and across the fairways, and watching the lanterns twinkling from the porch. He noticed that from the golf course you could see the fires from his father's furnaces glowing faintly far off in the sky toward town, and, in the sky, he could see the shimmering of the northern lights. That meant it would be cold tomorrow.

After a while he saw a car turn off the River Road and into the country-club drive. He thought it must be Mr. Aldrich coming back. He walked across the grass to the porch to see what was happening. It wasn't Mr. Aldrich. It was Mrs. Slade's Packard with Reilly at the wheel! He didn't look like much of a chauffeur, but Mrs. Slade wouldn't care. He made a swooping turn and stopped the car at the steps. Mrs. Slade was alone in the back seat. Tommy ran down the steps by the driveway and opened her door. "Mrs. Slade!" He hugged her. "I thought you weren't coming!" She stepped from the car and rose to her full height. Her dress was solid black, and in front it was slashed all the way down to where her breasts used to be when she had all of them, though you couldn't tell anything was missing. But when she moved up the steps the skirt flared out from her hips, and it wasn't solid black at all but had panels of scarlet. She looked incredible. She was clutching a long white fur, and around her neck her ruby necklace glinted in the night, and there were rubies in her ears as well. "Wow! You'll knock them out," Tommy exclaimed. "What happened? I thought you weren't coming."

"I changed my mind, Tommy. Suddenly I wanted to hear music. I wanted to go to a party. I wanted to dance, to see the world of brightness. I wanted a slice of the old life, the grand life. My, this sure as hell does look grand," she said, taking in the lights and the music. She called to Reilly. "Keep the car running, Bucko. I may have to make a quick getaway. But don't worry, honey," she said to Tommy, "I'll behave. Mrs. Rich Bitch knows how to behave when she wants to. Let's have a little dance." The music filled the porch.

"I don't know how," Tommy said. "I can't dance."

"It's easy," Mrs. Slade said. "You put your arm around my waist and we'll take a little turn around the porch. Just follow me and the music. Listen! They're playing 'Lady Be Good.' What could be more appropriate?" She draped the fur around her shoulders, placed Tommy's arm around her waist, and took his other hand in hers, and the two of them twirled around the porch, her black dress flashing scarlet, her rubies twinkling in the lantern light, her white fur flying. Tommy stumbled to keep up with her. "That's wonderful," she said. "All you need is practice, my little beau, and you'll be a wonderful dancer. You'll learn, and you'll love it. So will the ladies. One more whirl!"

Tommy heard the screened doors swing open. Mr. Wolfe had come out during their last whirl and was watching them. "Well, Luke the Wolfe!" Mrs. Slade exclaimed when they stopped. "Doing the cucaracha?" She extended her hand toward him and waited expectantly. "What are you waiting for?" she said. "Kiss it." Mr. Wolfe bent over her hand and touched it with his lips. "It's a habit he picked up in Mexico," Mrs. Slade said to Tommy. "I hope that's all you picked up." Mr. Wolfe hadn't said a word. "I'm going to be very grand tonight," she said. "Mrs. Rich Bitch knows how to be *very* grand." She took the fur from her shoulders and handed it to Mr. Wolfe. "Thank you, Lucien," she said, "that will be all," and she swept toward the door, very grandly, too, and entered the clubhouse. Mr. Wolfe dropped the fur on a chair and walked around to the other side of the porch, off the cardroom.

Tommy watched Mrs. Slade through the screened doors. "Hello, Randy"—that's what she called Dr. Randolph, who was standing in the foyer—"how's the reformed doctor?" Tommy bet Dr. Randolph thought that was a pisser. She strode right by him, though, and over to Margie, who was standing by the French doors holding hands with David, and kissed them both on the cheek. They spoke for a second and Margie pointed toward the ballroom and Mrs. Slade walked purposefully in, tall and straight as an arrow. Tommy ran to the windows and saw her go directly to his mother, who was standing next to one of them, close enough so he could hear.

His mother was surprised. She was very surprised, but she hesitated only a moment. "Well, Mrs. Slade," she said, "how nice you could come after all." She extended her hand. "And thank you for the gift."

Mrs. Slade kissed his mother on her cheek. "Emma, I suddenly realized I couldn't possibly miss this scene. Thank you for asking me. I'm glad you like the animal. I wanted to send you some kind of creature, something appropriate, something silver." She smiled. Then she laughed. His mother didn't speak. "And now that I'm here, I can see that I wouldn't have

331

missed it for the world. I've had one dance already, on the porch, and it's time for another. Where's the bridegroom? The bridegroom must have his dance." The company parted before her as she walked off to find Tommy's father. She was knocking them out, all right. She was certainly knocking them out.

The orchestra was playing John's song now, *"I was a good little girl, till I met you,"* and John and Emily were dancing to it, and in a minute Tommy saw his father and Mrs. Slade swing by the windows.

"What are you looking at?" It was Phil Meyer, putting his arm on Tommy's shoulder. He was startled.

"Oh, just the party," Tommy said. "I'm looking at the party. I've never seen anything like it." It certainly wasn't like Thanksgiving, or any of the other parties Tommy had seen at his house or on the Island.

"Neither have I," Phil said, "and I've been to a lot of parties. Let's sit down." Phil led him toward a chair, one of the chairs the ladies rocked in. "Well, what's on your mind, my friend?" That was Phil's question; he always asked Tommy that.

"Nothing," Tommy said. He wished he could talk to Phil about what was on his mind. He really did like him. "School starts next week. I'll be in third grade."

"How did the golf lessons go?"

"Fine. I learned to hit the ball. The lessons are over now."

"Did you like them?" Phil asked.

"They were okay," Tommy said. He wished they could talk about something else.

"Well, Mac," Phil said, "I told you, you learn to keep your eye on the ball and the rest of the game comes naturally."

"I'm learning," Tommy said. Phil *had* told him. "I learned to see through a telescope, too. That was interesting."

"Well, I'm going off for a little stroll, a breath of air," Phil said. "I'll see you later."

"Goodbye," Tommy said. He wished Phil had stayed. Maybe they could have talked. He watched him fade into the darkness of the golf course. In a few minutes Tommy went back to the windows. Mrs. Slade had finished her dance with Tommy's father. She was standing in front of Dr. Randolph now. He looked as if he wished he were somewhere else. Yes, a real pisser, Tommy thought. It made him smile. She took Dr. Randolph's hand and led him to the floor. The band was playing "Thanks for the Memory," and Mrs. Slade was laughing and looking into Dr. Randolph's eyes. Tommy couldn't hear her, but he could tell she was saying something and that she thought it was funny, too. Mrs. Slade looked beautiful when she danced.

"Do you suppose Mrs. Proper thinks we don't all know?" It was Mrs. Appleton's voice. He heard her voice before he heard the footsteps clumping slowly and heavily down the porch. "It's scandalous, that's what it is. Simply scandalous."

"Balls of brass." That was Mrs. Barlow.

"Sally!" Mrs. Appleton sounded shocked. "Upon my word!"

"Oh, Frances," Mrs. Barlow said, "when you look like a mountain, the way I do, and feel like one, too, you can't help but envy it a little. Now that it's only a memory."

"It's still outrageous. And I'm surprised at you!" The two of them stopped at one of the windows and looked in, listening. They stared in silence for a moment.

"Look at her," Mrs. Appleton said. "Just look at her! She's nothing but a common tramp. What ever made Emma invite her?"

"Blackmail, probably," Mrs. Barlow said.

"I'll bet that woman planned this all along. I'll bet she had that dress made just for this. She picked the right color, too. Scarlet. Well, the dress is nothing compared to what she's made for, of course." Both Mrs. Barlow and Mrs. Appleton laughed.

"That comes later," Mrs. Barlow said. "Maybe. With luck."

"You've got to admit it, she's got more nerve than a barrel of monkeys. They both do."

"No," Mrs. Barlow said, "that's fun."

"What are you talking about?"

"The expression is," Mrs. Barlow said, "more *fun* than a barrel of monkeys. Nerve is something else. Nerve is brass. Like brass balls." Mrs. Barlow laughed loudly.

"I wish you wouldn't talk that way, Sally. It sounds so vulgar."

"I'll try to behave, Frances."

"Well, whatever," Mrs. Appleton said, "she's apparently more fun than a barrel of monkeys, too. Maybe I should have said rabbits."

Tommy walked down to them. He looked through the window at Mrs. Slade. She was dancing with Mr. Wolfe now. "Those are real rubies," Tommy said.

"So are my teeth," Mrs. Barlow said.

"Where did *you* come from?" Mrs. Appleton asked.

"From the porch," Tommy said, and Mrs. Barlow began to sing the song the band was playing. *"You may not be an angel,"* she sang, *"but I'm sure you'll do."* For somebody so fat she could hardly huff her way up the three steps to the porch and couldn't even get into a rowboat to go to the Island anymore, she had a surprisingly nice voice.

"Run along, now," Mrs. Appleton said. "We're talking ladies' talk. It's not for little boys' ears."

"I've heard it all," Tommy said. He knew that was rude of him, but he said it anyway. He didn't care. He couldn't stand Mrs. Appleton, and he walked the length of the porch and around the corner to get away from them. He didn't want to be anywhere near them. He wanted to be alone, but he wasn't. Bob Griswold was running across the grass, his tie undone and his shirt open, his jacket flying in his hand. He ran to the porch, leapt up the steps, and hurried in the cardroom door and directly into the men's locker room. He glanced at Tommy but seemed scarcely to have seen him. Tommy stood there for a while, then walked slowly off. He wasn't in any hurry.

He walked toward the ninth hole. The flag hung limp above the green. There was no breeze. In the dark you could hardly tell that the flag was red. He passed over the green. The grass felt very soft, like velvet beneath his feet. For a time he sat on the little mound near the green. It was so still, and almost sultry. He got up and continued on. He walked over to the pro shop. It was dark now. He looked in the windows. He could just barely see the faint reflections of the glass from the counter, and the steel shafts of the golf clubs glinting on the wall. Emil would be going away soon, Tommy thought. He always left around Labor Day to spend the winter at a golf course farther south where people could play all year. Tommy

334

walked around the pro shop toward the tennis courts behind it. The music was very distant now. It floated in thin patches in the air. It was very dark. The only light came from the stars in the sky, and the wavering glow of the northern lights. He could make out a figure on the tennis court, a figure all in white. Then he saw another, in a white jacket. They were standing near one of the benches. It must be Daisy, he thought, with Phil. It must be Daisy and Phil, Daisy in her white dress and Phil in his white jacket. The perfect couple, he liked to think, he used to think, he still wanted to think. They looked so good together. Maybe he could talk to them now. Maybe he could really talk to them. He'd like that.

He drew closer, close enough to see that Daisy's dress was smudged, and strands of her hair, her lovely yellow hair, were falling over her face. They didn't look so good now. Something was wrong.

"Don't touch me," she screamed. "I can't bear to have you touch me!"

"Why not?" Phil shot back. "Everyone else does." He was reaching toward her.

"You prick," she said. "You filthy bastard prick!" She said it with a hiss. She swung her arm and slapped him. She slapped him hard. Her hair was flying. Phil raised his hand to his face. He didn't move. Daisy's arm was frozen in midair, her hair caught in the motion. Phil's hand didn't move. Nothing moved. The night lay perfectly still.

"Oh, no," Tommy moaned, "oh, no." He didn't want to see any more. He didn't want to hear any more. He raised his hands to his head, covering his head with his arms. They turned toward him. He ran back, around the pro shop, through the parking lot, across the gravel to the lawn and the broad steps looking toward the tee and the river flowing darkly in the distance, and he sat down. He sat there, on the steps, his head in his arms, trying to catch his breath. The music and voices still floated out from the clubhouse; the lanterns continued to glow with their purple and amber light; the leaves of the elms trembled slightly in the air. He caught his breath, and watched the silver reflections on the river. He heard the doors swing open behind him, and the sound of steps going hurriedly toward the drive. He turned when they had passed. It was Mrs. Slade. "Gun it, Reilly," she said, getting into her car, "the queen of the night has got to make her getaway." Tommy smiled. He couldn't help it. Mrs. Slade saw him sitting there on the steps as she sped down the drive, and she blew him a kiss. Tommy watched her make the turn onto the River Road. He noticed that her fur was still on the chair where Mr. Wolfe had dropped it. Tommy went over and picked it up. The fur felt very thick and soft. It was a beautiful fur, really. He held it for a while, and then put it back on the chair. He returned to the steps and sat there waiting. Eventually Rose would find him and take him home.

After a time the doors opened again. Mr. and Mrs. Steer came out with Mrs. Hutchins. Mrs. Steer was surprised to see him, but not too surprised. "I *thought* you'd avoid Rose," she told him. "You'd much rather witness the dance"—she patted his shoulder—"the great dance of life." The three of them moved toward the driveway. "We're taking Mrs. Hutchins home," she said. "Good night."

"You'll miss the torches," Tommy said, "the lighting of the torches." They didn't hear him; they were already out of earshot.

Tommy's mother came out a few minutes later, her dress swirling around her legs. Her stockings were pearly white, and the buckles of her shoes gleamed dully in the night. "I thought you'd left hours ago," she said. "I thought Rose took you home."

"No," Tommy said, "she didn't."

"It's been a long night," his mother said. "It feels twenty-five years long." She laughed, but her face was drawn. "I'm exhausted." She looked it. "You must be dead. I'll get John to take you home." She returned to the clubhouse and came out in a moment with John and Emily. "Did you enjoy the party," she asked him, "your first grown-up party?"

"Oh, yes," Tommy said. "It was a very nice party."

Then Tommy and his brother and Emily went to the car. Buck and Junior were beginning to light the torches as they drove out to the River Road and down to the landing on the water. Tommy could see the torches burning, and the purple and amber glow of the lanterns, as his brother dipped the oars into the current and rowed him across the river. On the river the night was luminous and radiant, and all Tommy could hear was the sound of the oars in the oarlocks and the water moving. Then Emily began to sing. She sang the hymn they'd sung on the way to the party, many hours ago. She sang it quietly, by herself, and John dipped his oars in time to the music.

Six

It was colder the next day, and it was quiet on the Island; everyone was resting from the party. Tommy had to wear the windbreaker that David had given him for his birthday. A northwest wind was blowing, making whitecaps on the river. That afternoon Tommy got Jim to row him to the shore. Jim had to row hard against the wind and the strengthened current. Next summer, when he'd be nine, he'd have to learn to row himself. He didn't like always having to find someone to take him, or to wait on the dock for someone to show up. He was old enough to do it himself.

Tommy wanted to say goodbye to Buck, who was leaving that weekend for Kentucky and school, with Katherine and George. Tommy wouldn't see him again until next summer. He wanted to say goodbye to Emil, too, and he had a present to give Ophelia. He had thought of a nice present for her that day. There were a few golfers on the course, but not many. Tommy went directly to the pro shop, where he thanked Emil for the lessons.

"I told you you'd learn to hit the ball, Tommy," Emil said. "You'll do a lot better next summer."

"I still have the ball with my name on it," Tommy said. "Thanks for giving it to me."

"We'll start out with it next June," Emil said.

When Tommy got to the clubhouse, they were just finishing cleaning up from the party. Buck and Junior were folding up the last of the tables and putting them away in the store-room. Mrs. Aldrich's cloth was gone, the head table had been dismantled, the bandstand wasn't there, and the mirrored ball had been taken down. Buck said his mother had already been there and left, to take her things back to the house. In a few minutes everything looked as it always had. A stranger walking in the door would never have known that there'd been anything unusual the night before, no big party.

"That was some smart party your mamma had," Buck said. "Some smart party. But a lot of work for us folks. What's that?" Buck pointed to the package in Tommy's hand. Tommy had wrapped it himself. He couldn't find a box for it, but he did find some tissue paper and some ribbon and he had tried to make it look as good as he could. He wasn't very good at wrapping yet.

"It's something for Ophelia," Tommy said, and he went off to the lounge to find her. The lounge was empty. He rang the little bell and Ophelia came out, just as always.

"Why, Tommy," she said. "I'm surprised to see you today. I thought you'd be home. I thought your mother would make you rest."

"She's uptown," Tommy said. "I haven't seen her all day."

"Did you have fun last night?" Ophelia asked him. "I hear you got a little more champagne than you were supposed to."

"Who told you that?"

"George. He was pouring it."

"That's right, he was," Tommy said. "I was probably too excited to notice. He didn't give me very much."

Ophelia laughed. "He wasn't supposed to," she said. "He was under orders."

"Yeah, I know," Tommy said. "I have something for you." He was embarrassed. Maybe it wasn't the right thing to do, to give Ophelia a present. Maybe it would make her feel funny.

"You have something for me? Well, isn't that nice!"

Tommy put the package on the bar. "You wrapped it your-self!" Ophelia looked surprised and pleased. "What can it be?"

"Open it," Tommy said.

Ophelia untied the ribbon and the paper fell away. "Tommy," she said. "You shouldn't do this. It's beautiful."

She picked up the kaleidoscope, brightly colored as if it had been sprinkled with confetti. "It's beautiful."

"Look through it," Tommy said. "Point it toward the light and look through it." Ophelia did. "Now turn it," he said. "See? Don't you see things?"

Ophelia turned the cylinder and looked. She kept turning it, peering into the tube and turning it. She looked for a long time. When she took it from her eye, she set it on the counter and looked at Tommy. "You mustn't give me this, Tommy." She reached for his hand. "You mustn't give this to old Ophelia."

"Yes," Tommy said. "It's for you. I want you to have it. Doesn't it make pretty colors? Don't you like the way the patterns all swirl around and change? You never get the same picture twice."

"It's like your mother's party," Ophelia said. "It's as pretty as your mother's party."

"It's called a kaleidoscope. Please take it."

Ophelia leaned over the bar and pulled him toward her. She put both her arms around him and gave him a big hug and a kiss on his cheek. "Of course I'll take it, Tommy. I love my kaleidoscope. I'll always love it. Thank you."

"I'm glad," he said. "I'm glad you like it."

"I think I'll make you a root beer float," she said, "or would you rather have a Coke? I'd make you a chicken sandwich but I'm afraid it would spoil your dinner."

"I think I'd rather have a Coke," Tommy said. "I don't need a glass."

"Well, at least take a straw," Ophelia said, putting two straws in the bottle. "And Tommy, thank you."

"You're welcome," he said.

"Did you see your name in the newspaper?" Ophelia asked him.

"No," Tommy said. "Why was my name in the newspaper?"

"Here," Ophelia said, handing him the afternoon paper. "Read all about it." The paper was folded open, and Ophelia pointed to an article at the top of the page. "MacAllisters Celebrate Silver Wedding," it said. "Tommy, I have to go back to the kitchen now. We're still washing dishes."

343

"Don't forget your kaleidoscope."

"I won't," she said. "I'm not forgetting it." She picked it up and carried it into the kitchen with her.

Tommy took the paper to a table in the lounge and read the article as he sipped his Coke. It was an account of the party. It listed all the out-of-town guests and who had sat at the head table. His name was there. "Master Andrew Thomas MacAllister," it said. He had never seen his name in the paper. It was the first time his name had ever been in the paper, except maybe when he'd been born. Tommy read the article again. It told a lot about the party, but it didn't tell what happened.

Tommy put the paper down and went looking for Buck. He found him on the porch, standing on a chair taking down the paper lanterns. They were swinging in the wind, and as he took each one from its hook it collapsed flat as a plate. He had a little pile of them on a chair. "Buck," Tommy said, "I've come to say goodbye. I probably won't see you again until next summer."

"You'll be a lot smarter next summer," Buck told him, "a whole lot smarter."

Tommy laughed. "Yes," he said. "I'll be smarter. Goodbye, Buck. I'm glad you were here."

"Bye," Buck said, and returned to the lanterns he was collapsing and adding to his pile.

ON Sunday afternoon Mrs. Wentworth gave her annual party for the closing of the season. Everyone was there, all the usual people and those out-of-town guests who hadn't yet left. It was still chilly; the wind was blowing, and the river was full of whitecaps. "Fall is in the air," Mrs. Sedgwick observed; "you can feel it." You could, too. In just two days Tommy would be going back to school. He said he didn't like the idea, but really he wouldn't mind. He would be glad to see the summer end.

Mr. Steer, who liked to take pictures, said that there'd been a terrible oversight: no one had taken an anniversary photograph. He went to his cottage to get his camera, and Tommy's parents posed together, arm in arm, on Mrs. Wentworth's steps. The wind whipped his mother's dress. Then Mr. Steer said, "We've got to get a family photograph," so Tommy and his brothers went up to the steps and stood there, his brothers on either side of his parents and Tommy before them, in the middle, his father's hand on one shoulder, his mother's on the other, and they all smiled into the jeweled eye of the camera. Tommy thought of the photograph taken all those years before, of himself as a baby in his father's arms on their dock on the Island, and he imagined this picture's taking its place with that and the others in the family album, or on the wall in the cottage. Mr. Steer took a lot more pictures of all Tommy's family and their relatives and friends in various combinations: his parents with Emily and Margie and his brothers, his brothers together, his brothers with their girls, Emily and Margie alone, Tommy and Amy together, the Sedgwicks, Madge and Phelps and Vint, Daisy and her mother and grandmother, the McGhees and the Aldriches, Mr. Wolfe and Mrs. Wentworth, Mr. Treverton and Mrs. Wentworth. He took all sorts of pictures before everyone got tired of the whole business and Mrs. Sedgwick said, "Oh, Dick, why don't you put that thing away?" Tommy's mother never liked to be photographed, but she had to put up with it. It seemed as if the only picture Mr. Steer didn't take was one of him with Mrs. Steer. Tommy would have liked that.

The people at Mrs. Wentworth's party were all talking about the dance—every one of them had been there—and about the war. The news was very bad. Germany had invaded Poland the day after his parents' silver anniversary, and everyone was very concerned. Once in a while one of them would go inside to listen for news on the radio. They expected England and France to declare war, but it was something we wouldn't get into, his father said. Almost everyone agreed that this time we wouldn't be drawn into it. Let the Europeans fight their own battles; it wasn't our concern. People were pleased that David would be going back to college soon, and this time his father said he'd better have something to show for it. No date had been set for David and Margie's wedding. His parents wanted them to wait, and so far they were. "We're still trying to recover from one party," his father said. John was talking about going to Chicago to find a job, and when he found one everyone expected that he and Emily would be engaged—she would like wearing his grandmother's diamond —and eventually marry.

Tommy wandered into Mrs. Wentworth's small sitting room. Mrs. Steer was there, trying to find some news on the radio but she wasn't having any luck. The radio was just playing church music. "Damn it," she said. She looked at him. She was not smiling. "The world is blowing up, Tommy." She looked very grim. "The whole world is blowing up. It will make that explosion at your father's plant seem like a firecracker. Nothing will ever be the same again"—and she snapped off the radio and left the room.

THE next day was Labor Day. The rest of the out-of-town guests had left that morning, everyone waving them off to the shore. The family stayed to pack things up on the Island, but there really wasn't much to do. They hadn't moved that much down from town this summer, and they'd probably be back for an occasional weekend as long as the weather was pleasant. Later the cottage would be closed for the winter, but the Indians did most of that work anyway—shutting down the pump, draining the pipes, turning off the power, laying up the boats. Tommy packed up his few things and helped his father and John load the boat. Then the three of them went uptown with the first load while Rose helped his mother finish up on the Island. John and his father were talking about the war. Poland was in bad shape. England and France had declared war on Germany. It was really serious, and his father said that he hoped we could avoid getting into it. "It could be a terrible thing," he said. He remembered the last war.

Tommy was glad to be home. His father went over to the plant for a few minutes, and John returned to the Island to pick up another load. David had already gone on a picnic with Margie. Tommy stayed in the house, looking at all the familiar things and at the changes, too. All his mother's redecoration had made the house look nice. He was sure that the people who had stayed there during the party had liked it. He looked at all the new silver. He found the silver elk Mrs. Slade had given his parents, and he put it in the middle of the dining-room table, where it belonged, with the little clawed feet on his Uncle Christian's salt dishes and the animals on the plate rail. He found Mrs. Steer's inkwell, too, and he put it on top of the desk in the hall. Then he went upstairs to unpack his bag and put his clothes away. He took the telescope Mrs. Steer had given him and laid it back on top of his dresser, in its old place, but then he changed his mind and decided to put it in his top drawer, where it would be safe. He looked at his bookshelf. There was *Fingerfins*. He smiled. He did like that story. He remembered how his mother had read it to him when he had the measles. Sometime he would have to go to the Sargasso Sea. He looked out the window over the porch. His father's stacks were smoking away. He opened the window—he wanted some air in the room—and he noticed Mr. Wolfe's coins sitting there on the sill, the 1938 dollar he had given him for Christmas and the stack of eight he had given him for his birthday. They had gotten tarnished over the summer, and he picked them up and put them in one of his dresser drawers. His room looked good. He went to his desk and rolled back the top. Everything looked the same. He took the key from its hiding place and opened the locked drawer. It was all there: the box of crayons, his fountain pen in its case, the paper Mrs. Steer had given him, the other paper with his name written on it. He looked at Mrs. Steer's poem. It was hard to read her writing. He looked at the paper with his name. He looked at where he'd written it: "*Tommy MacAllister*," and then, beneath it, "*Andrew Thomas MacAllister.*" He took the pen from its case and looked through the little window. There was still ink in it. He drew a line partway across the page, below where he'd written the names. The pen worked, and he wrote out his name again, his full name. It looked better this time. He heard a couple of cars drive into the driveway, so he put his papers away, and his pen, and locked the drawer. He went downstairs to help his parents and John unload the car.

That night after supper his mother laid out his school clothes for the next morning. She made him go to bed early. As she was tucking him in, Tommy said, "I'm going to change my name."

His mother laughed. "Well, you can't change your name,"

she said. "You can't change your name any more than I can change mine, or Daddy his. You're Tommy MacAllister, and you're stuck with it."

"Why can't I?" Tommy asked. "Andrew's my name, too. My first name." His mother pulled the shades, closed his curtains, and kissed him good night. "I prefer Tommy," she said. In a while, not a very long while, either, Tommy was asleep.

HE left for school the next morning. His mother wanted him to wear his blue beret—"It looks so nice," she said; "you look so nice in it"—but he didn't. He didn't want to wear a foolish beret to the first day of school. It was exciting to be in third grade. He knew he wouldn't be eight forever. He passed Mrs. Steer's garden; it was prettier in the spring. In the spring he would be nine. That was a long time away, but he would grow. He would learn. He'd learned to hit a golf ball. He'd learned a lot of things. And when he was grown, he could change his name. He would be called Andrew. Yes, he would. He straightened his shoulders and walked briskly up the street to school, into the currents of time.